Endlewood

A TRAGIC TALE OF LOVE, LOSS, AND HOPE

NOVELS BY ALISSA J. ZAVALIANOS

The Earth-Treader
The Wishing Seed

FEATURED ANTHOLOGIES

The Depths We'll Go To
Aphotic Love

Praise for Alissa J. Zavalianos

"From the author of *The Earth-Treader* and *The Wishing Seed* comes a tale that weaves the themes of family, belonging, and identity in a whimsical young adult fantasy. Zavalianos handles the tough obstacles of growing up, loneliness, and atoning for the past with a soft touch reminiscent of a children's story. Like all of Zavalianos' work, this book breathes an aesthetic, this one of warm summer sun beneath forest eaves amid a culture inspired by medieval and folklore traditions. Looking for your next cozy high fantasy read? This one is it!"

— Cheyenne van Langevelde,
author of *Between Two Worlds*

"*Endlewood* gives such a message of hope and beauty... If you enjoy mysterious magic, renewed identity, and love–this story is the perfect read for you."

— Tara Koch, *Goodreads Review*

"Enthralling, fascinating, and heart-felt... *Endlewood* will keep you reading into all hours of the night."

— Kayla Jones, *Goodreads Review*

"*The Earth-Treader* was an incredibly captivating, deeply imaginative, coming-of-age young adult fantasy novel that depicted the triumph of good over evil. There were so many unexpected twists and turns that I kept turning the pages. Alissa Zavalianos successfully created an original world and lovable protagonists. This novel is worth the read for anyone who loves a good adventure story!"

— Jordan Taylor Nilan, *Goodreads Review*

"This novel made me nostalgic for the fiction I grew up on written by Gail Carson Levine, Jean Ferris, Shannon Hale, and others. While *The Earth-Treader* reads like a love-letter to the works of J.R.R. Tolkien, Zavalianos has entered into the arena of young-adult fantasy authors who inspire young girls to answer the call to adventure."

— Caelah-Beth Butler, *Goodreads Review*

Endlewood

A TRAGIC TALE OF LOVE, LOSS, AND HOPE

ALISSA J. ZAVALIANOS

Printed in the United States of America

Cover by Germancreative
Map by Chaim Holtjer
Edited by Renae Powers
Proofreading by Micaiah Keough

ISBN 978-1-7361371-7-8 (paperback)
ISBN 978-1-7361371-6-1 (hardcover)
ISBN 978-1-7361371-8-5 (ebook)

For my parents—
Thank you for always reminding me of who I am
and Whose I am,
and for never making me question
where I call home.

· GRISKOL ·

TABLE OF CONTENTS

PROLOGUE
From "The Tale of Endlewood"

*T*he sound of sand grating against wood jostles me awake. The scent of salt tickles my nose, and I crack open my eyelids only to shield my sight from the glare of the brilliant sun. After weeks of traveling, the boat has run aground.

No more running.

At least, for now.

Stiff and weary, I stretch my sunburnt limbs and step from the hollow craft; grains of coarse sand gather between my bare toes. The ebbing tide comes and goes, hitting against the hull and biting my ankles, stealing some of my warmth with its every touch.

I survey the land before me.

Tall, dense trees stretch for miles along the shoreline. Their leaves are green and full, with little dips and curves along the ridges. A promising shelter.

Will they find me here? Is it safe?

I trudge up the sandy bank and step beneath the shadow of an oak, my muscles groaning with each footfall. I run my smooth hand against the knotted bark.

What lives in these woods?

A tingling spreads up my arm and lands just below my left ear. The tree acknowledges my presence—welcomes me. I can feel it.

A waft of glimmering copper flits past my vision, dancing through the trees like the sun does the clouds. I peer into the forest and gasp.

A large stag, with its antlers splayed in regal arches, takes a step forward, his movements akin to gliding over air. His breath escapes his nostrils as he paws the ground. And it's when he bends his head that I notice his glossy coat sports a silver crescent in the space just above his eyes.

As if on instinct, I take a step closer, but all too soon, the creature vanishes. The wind takes him away just as swiftly as he had come.

I stand in awe, missing the stag's presence as if I had bid a friend goodbye, even though we're mere strangers. At least I'm resigned to one conclusion: in these woods is life and life aplenty. And where there's life—there's magic.

I tug my hood closer and push deeper into the shadows; a world of darkness encapsulates me as I scan my surroundings.

It's almost too perfect, untouched, and yet...

I take a few more strides forward, marveling at the towering trees, the twittering birds, and the lapping shoreline behind me.

It's as if there are three worlds in one. Shadow and tree, tide and sea, sky and lark...

A calm settles in my core. I am both confident and hesitant to call this place home. It looks safe. But it will be made safer still.

Of the horrors I left behind, I only have this future now. To create a new space here, to flee the title forced upon me.

I've come to it at last.

And my tale begins anew.

CHAPTER ONE
Holland

An impatient poke jabbed Holland's shoulder. "Miss, are you finished yet?"

"Almost, just a few more stitches." She maneuvered her needle through the remaining fabric. "There we go. As good as new!" She cut the excess thread and adjusted the pink bow on the side.

With wide eyes, the girl bounced on her toes, wiggling her fingers in anticipation. As soon as the bonnet was in her hands, she placed it on her head and smiled so brightly she could have been the sun itself. "Thank you, Miss Holland! I finally have something pretty to wear again!" The girl scampered out the front door, the shop bell jingling as she joined her parents on the road.

Holland smiled and leaned forward on her elbows, watching through the window. Being a seamstress in a small village had its benefits, and this was definitely one of them. If only she could make everyone happy.

"Holland!"

She jolted upright at the sound of her name. She turned to see her employer, Beatrand Kershaw, with arms crossed and gray hair shaking in agitation. Holland knew that look; a list of demands would be following it.

"Quit your dilly-dallying. These hems won't fix themselves!" She gestured to the frocks hanging by the door. "And when you're done, check on the chickens; they've been squawking like there's no tomorrow, and it's driving me up the wall." Mrs. Kershaw huffed and began to walk away.

And then there are some drawbacks, too, that offset the benefits.

"Oh, I almost forgot." Mrs. Kershaw turned once more and leveled Holland with her gaze. "I'm having company tonight, so do stay out of sight and out of mind. We wouldn't want your presence to create any unnecessary…disturbances," she said, eyeing Holland skeptically. "Figure out how to be inconspicuous."

And with that came the quick departure of an oversized shadow and a slammed door behind her. The door continued to jostle on its hinges, the only sign that Mrs. Kershaw had left her mark.

The state of Holland's irritation were signs of that too, though after thirteen years of working under her employ, Holland had gotten used to the demands. They were nothing new.

Her parents had passed away when she was a baby, and after a few weeks in the village orphanage, she was adopted by Rossand Annbert. But those years of bliss were short-lived. Mrs. Annbert was old and widowed with no one to love or care for her in return; adopting Holland had seemed like the perfect fix. But then the same sickness that took her parents finished off Mrs. Annbert, and Holland was left alone once again.

At five, Holland was brought to Benneforth Row, a string of rundown townhomes in the southwest part of the village. It was there where she was adopted by Mr. and Mrs. Kershaw, a middle-aged couple who owned all of the Row and let it to needy tenants. Upon her arrival, Holland had been treated well, but soon after Mr. Kershaw's death, tenants began leaving the Row and resources grew even scarcer. Holland was then forced to bring in darics of her own. She was taught how to sew and was given a small workspace in the front parlor of one of the vacant townhomes. A sign reading "Benneforth Row's Seamstress" was plastered above the doorway, and since the age of seven, that had been her job. It seemed death and thread were her constant companions.

Holland retrieved one of the dresses hanging on the wall behind her and then reclaimed her seat. She laid the brown frock flat on the table and pulled at the material to get to the hem. The child to whom this belonged was growing like a weed; already Holland had let out the hem three times. Pretty soon, there'd be no more fabric left to give.

She broke apart the old stitching and couldn't help glancing outside once more.

The family was still there. Content in their dearth, mother and father each grabbed one of the girl's hands and walked toward the denser part of town. Dust clouds trailed behind them.

To be young and carefree. To have a proper childhood. Holland stifled a sigh.

It's not that she minded sewing; it was nice for her hands to have something to do. In fact, sometimes sewing felt like weaving together an intricate story. As each stitch brought material together in a permanent hold, so were her hands spinning a tale. It was like a touch of magic, though she would never say as much.

Magic was feared and outlawed in Griskol. Much like the Forbidden Wood.

Still, part of her wished for something more. She was always someone's property to be handed over and cast aside should time or sickness interfere. For once, she wanted to make her own choices.

Holland groaned, pushing off from her seat. Self-pity was *not* going to fix anything. She was twenty now. That habit should have died long ago. Besides, she had a decent enough life. She had a place to sleep and ate at least two meals a day; it shouldn't matter that her room was drafty or that there was no hot water to be found within a square mile. She should be thankful.

The faint sounds of squawking reached her ears, interrupting her thoughts.

Oh, the chickens! She couldn't forget her feathered friends. Not only would they go hungry, but Mrs. Kershaw wouldn't let her forget it either.

Before Holland left, she closed down the shop, locking the front door and drawing the curtains. It was nearly five o'clock, but she was only supposed to work until half past five anyway. Mrs. Kershaw couldn't fault Holland for the lost half hour if it was used to feed the chickens that were driving her "up the wall."

No, she would be just fine. And to prove that, Holland slid her stool aside and pried up a loose floorboard. She grabbed the book nestled between the wooden beams and stuck it in her pinafore with hopes of finding time to open it later. She'd snuck outside countless times in the past to read, so today shouldn't be any different.

She returned everything to its place and left the shop behind, entering the door which led further into her townhome. She passed the stairwell and a few empty rooms, then walked through the kitchen to the back door. She paused before opening it.

By the time Holland had turned fifteen, Benneforth Row's Seamstress wasn't just her place of work, it was her home. For a small fee each month, this townhome became a refuge away from her employer. She needed it; too often was the connected door to Mrs. Kershaw's frequented—bringing meals, cleaning, and giving her monthly payment. Not to mention, she gave any additional earnings to Mrs. Kershaw as well. That left barely anything to Holland's name.

The thought curdled her stomach.

Holland turned the brass knob and descended the stone steps leading to a large clearing of overgrown meadowland. The sight always took her breath away. The field was boundless, stretching for miles; scattered trees dotted the landscape, and a wide lake sat nearby. The land ended abruptly with a wall of mountains looming to the right of a dense, dark forest.

The Forbidden Wood.

It was a formidable barrier into the country of Eskal, and it was so wide and vast that it took up over half of Andaimon.

No one would ever dream to venture inside it, not even out of simple curiosity. It was rumored that strange things occurred there.

Once you went in, there was no guaranteeing a safe return, nor the hope of being the same person as the one which first entered. It was also said to be the cause of all things that went wrong in Griskol: from sickness, to blight, to poverty. The townsfolk were all in agreement on that issue.

"It's because of those damnable woods, I tell yah."

"Our misfortunes come from within its depths, I'd bet my life on it."

"The wood's haunted by strange folk. Black magic, I'd wager."

"May Tokal help us all!"

Holland didn't know what to believe, but she couldn't ignore their remarks either. The forest was a mystery. And since no one understood its secrets, it was the perfect place to lay blame for one's problems.

The forest was regarded with disdain and fear, and most tried to forget its existence at all. So much so that it received the moniker of the Forbidden Wood. No one dared say more. And due to its proximity, Andaimon was avoided in turn, nearly as cast off as the forest itself.

Though small in size, the region of Andaimon was home to many shops and trade, always bustling with activity—anything for the poor to make a living. And if one squinted really hard, they just might imagine the pinnacles of a castle in the distance. That was Pembroke Fally—the gated region—home to the infamous King Randor Famar II and Queen Rosin Famar who ruled in the palace of Famar, their namesake. It was about a two-day journey to the palace from Benneforth Row if one galloped on horseback, and a little over five if one traveled by foot.

But to Holland, it might as well be another world.

When Mr. Kershaw was alive, he'd had high hopes of building up the Row, pouring his stroke of good fortune into anything and everything to keep it running. He always liked a challenge, wanting to turn poverty around. But not everything went as planned, and in Andaimon, that was usually the case. Thus, his dreams died along with him, and Mrs. Kershaw and Holland were left to pick up the pieces.

Because of Mr. Kershaw's lofty pursuits in his youth, not to mention Mrs. Kershaw's insatiable greed, Holland could have been sleeping with the pigs. She was now part of the reason why Andaimon 'thrived,' though she rather imagined thriving would feel a lot different than this.

She tried to remember a time when the royals reigned with compassion, but within the past five years, things had only grown worse. It didn't bother King Randor and Queen Rosin that there were poor people suffering in the lower regions of their country. And because of their neglect, everyone forgot what it was like to live freely.

Holland sighed. At least being outside eased the burden a touch.

She walked on the patchy grass, her slippered feet kicking up dirt. The sky was clear and the air felt warm despite the recent chill the past few nights. It was a beautiful evening, and it would be made even better after she talked to the chickens. They always looked at her like she belonged.

Holland reached the pen and bent over the bin of feed. She

was about to scoop out a heaping mound of pellets when she noticed a familiar person inside the coop.

"Hello, Markus!" Holland poked her head inside, smiling.

Markus startled, his broad shoulders filling the small enclosure within. He rose and winced when his head hit the low-hanging roof, disturbing his already unruly mop of brown hair.

"Hi, Holland!" He massaged the spot, but not before the chicken in his arm nipped him and flew to the ground. "I know this looks ridiculous." He chuckled, his blue eyes meeting hers. "I just need…"

"Some ice?" Holland tilted her head to the side, laughing. "You know the cool cellar is full this time of year."

Markus smirked like he had a wicked plan up his sleeve. "No. What I need is that bird! It's chicken on the menu tonight."

She rolled her eyes and ignored him. "Speaking of the menu, what did you bring me today?" She replaced the scoop and peered into the burlap sack leaning against the coop. She opened it up and felt her grin spread to her ears. "Parsnips! But I thought they weren't in season!" She grabbed one out of the bag, humming as she nibbled on the raw veggie.

"A farmer never reveals his secrets." Markus winked.

Holland's cheeks warmed. She loved vegetables, and Markus always seemed to remember which ones were her favorites.

"And in exchange for this, you came here to eat Henrietta?" Holland chewed, pointing her half-eaten parsnip at the unfortunate hen.

"Yes, it is a sad thing when one's life must be sacrificed on behalf of another." Markus tsked, shaking his head. "But this little lady had it coming. And besides, I'm ravenous."

Holland feigned an offended look, trying not to smile. She knew Markus was only kidding. "How could you say such a thing? The poor creature did nothing to you! And besides, don't you have enough chickens of your own to feed all of Kirkus?"

"Yes, but I'd rather have yours. And Henrietta here delayed my supper. That's as rightful a cause as any to put this act to justice." Markus returned the attempt at being serious and bent to recapture Henrietta who had wandered back over to him.

He picked her up, stroking her feathered body and listening to her gentle coos. "See? She's happy."

"You're delusional." Holland rolled her eyes.

"Not delusional. A realist. She told me so herself." He stroked the bird's head and placed his hands about her neck before turning around.

Suddenly, Holland heard a horrible, snapping noise.

"No! Markus, how could you? I thought you were only joking!" Stinging pricked the corners of her eyes. Something like bile rose in her throat; she was going to be sick.

Markus straightened, revealing a broken stick in his left hand and a very much alive Henrietta in his right. "I was." He had the audacity to laugh with that infamous two-dimpled grin, the one that made Holland's stomach flutter every time she saw it.

Now she couldn't stand the sight of it.

"Sorry, I couldn't resist!" He wiped his eyes.

"You monster!" Holland charged. She screwed up her face in an attempt not to smile.

Markus dropped the chicken and bolted out of the coop before

Holland could sock him in the arm. He ran a few paces and turned around, running backward up the hill so she could see the goofy expression on his face. His laughter danced on the breeze the farther away he moved.

Holland couldn't help it. Markus' laugh was contagious. Despite her lingering frustration, she found herself laughing wildly as she chased him. *How can someone be equal parts obnoxious and thrilling?* Honestly, how could she expect anything less from her childhood friend?

She eventually caught up to him, her need to punch him gone. She tumbled to the ground to lay beside Markus who was now gazing at the darkening sky above.

She tried to catch her breath and heard Markus doing the same, their chests rising and falling in unison as if in some strange sort of dance.

She followed his gaze, captivated by a stretch of deep blue and the slow arrival of stars winking at the earth.

CHAPTER TWO
Markus

It was nearing six o'clock, and in early autumn, that meant night came quickly. Little spots of light peered through the sky's darkened canopy, and Markus felt the cool breeze off the nearby lake drift and land on his skin and ruffle the sleeves of his coat.

He loved the night sky, and this field was his favorite place to view it. Sure, the farm fields in Kirkus suited just fine, but they lacked company.

Holland. She laid beside him, her gaze directed toward the heavens. In truth, he was shocked she hadn't hit him in the arm yet. After the stunt he'd just pulled, he was sure she would have. And he would have welcomed it.

They were atop a hill, grass splayed all around them like a blanket. Markus also loved the grass; in Kirkus there was plenty of it, stretching in wide swaths as far as the eye could see. There was also a lot of dirt. He was used to handling soil because his sheep, Impa and Irma, tried eating anything and everything green, creating bare patches everywhere. They also wandered far too often from their pens and had a way of stepping on his lettuce that rendered the crop useless. Not to mention Bathilda, the cull cow who didn't listen to anyone. And then there was Hamish...

"It's one of those nights again, isn't it?"

Holland startled Markus from his thoughts.

"The kind where the stars seem to tell their stories." She stared at the expanse above, pointing to the different constellations. "It's magical, don't you think?"

Markus had his hands crossed behind his head, but instead of looking at the sky, he turned to study Holland's profile—the way he often did when she wasn't looking. He didn't miss the way the soft breeze pulled at her raven hair or how the moonlight made her green eyes sparkle a deeper shade. Her small nose had the slightest lift, making her look rather endearing, and her full lips were pulled into a wide grin.

But there was something more; it was the heart beating beneath it all that left him breathless.

"It..." He swallowed past the sudden lump in his throat, not taking his eyes off her. "It's beautiful."

Holland, still marveling at the sky, sighed in awe. "Yes, beautiful indeed."

Markus suppressed a grin, his heart twisting into something he often felt around her. Something he didn't quite know how to put into words.

"Do you ever long to be something other than you are?" she asked.

He blinked. Holland had a way of asking the strangest things. *Did* he ever want to be somebody other than he was? Not really. He'd grown up a farmer's son and inherited the land when his father passed. It was his birthright, after all. He was one of the few who enjoyed his job. He liked working hard and, on most days, was content remaining as he'd always been. If not for himself, then for his family. And at twenty-three, he wouldn't trade that willingly.

Markus didn't know how to respond, but Holland didn't seem to notice.

"Lately—no, more than lately, I've been wondering what it would be like to be...you know...different. To have a different life. To tell my own stories like the stars. To be something special." Holland said the last part in a whisper as if she was too afraid to speak it aloud.

A different life? A weight like an anvil pressed on his chest.

Markus cleared his throat. "You are special. You shouldn't doubt that." Her friendship meant the world to him; she was one of the few who really let him grieve his father's death, who matched him wit for wit and didn't back down from a challenge. She wasn't just special; she was nearly perfect. "Why do you want to be different?"

Holland sat up and reached into her dress pocket. When she pulled out her hand, a weathered book laid in her palm. She held it out for him.

"I've been rereading this story," Holland said.

Markus sat up and grabbed the book, studying its cover. The feeling of icicles trailed up his spine and landed near his ear. He winced, his hand flying to his neck.

"Markus?" Holland's brow creased in concern.

He hesitated. "Just one of those biting midges," he lied,

rubbing the affected spot. It wasn't a stupid insect; he knew that much.

His mind spun. It'd been years since…

He glanced at Holland. She looked like she didn't believe him. Like she wanted to ask a million questions…

He needed to change the subject.

"So, *The Tale of Endlewood*…" He handed her the novel before lying back down on the grass. He knew better than to open it. "You're reading it again?"

She nodded. "Do you remember the story? It's a dark, tragic tale of love and loss—"

"And horribly outlawed. Leave it to you to tote around a banned book," Markus interrupted, laughing away the lingering pain in his back. He was feeling better already.

Holland leaned over and wacked him on the arm, her nose scrunched up in mock irritation.

Ah, there it is. Markus couldn't conceal his satisfied grin. She'd hit him after all.

"Only because of the *magic*. But it's more than that. The story's depressing, yes, but I can't help but feel drawn to it. It somehow makes me feel better about my own life. Which isn't saying much." Holland snorted, twisting a lock of hair between her fingers. "But it's also about belonging. About freedom. I can't help thinking…" Holland paused, biting her lip.

"You can't help thinking, what?" Markus asked, unease filling his stomach. He propped himself up on his elbows to get a better look at her. Holland's fascination with this book made his nerves twitch.

"That there's so much more to be experienced than just working here for the rest of my life." Holland grew somber and looked toward the direction of town. Her eyes seemed fixed somewhere far off in the distance.

Botheration. Markus would rather have a punch to his gut. What was she planning?

From the moment he'd met Holland, he was impressed by her determination, convinced that she could do anything she set her mind to. But even more so, it was the raw innocence and sincerity of heart which captivated him. And sometime during their first encounter, he had silently vowed to be there for her. Always. No matter what.

But how could he do that if she left him?

"So, what are you planning on doing about it?" he asked, plucking blades of grass and twisting them between his fingers. "Find employment in Pembroke Fally?" He said it like a joke. But maybe she'd actually consider going to Kirkus and living with his family... The law would never allow it, but no one had to know.

Holland remained silent, once again biting her lip like she couldn't deny what he just said.

"You are, aren't you?" Markus sat up straighter. She wanted to go that far away? It would take days to get there, not to mention all the visitation laws... "How do you expect to find employment there when Famar wants nothing to do with the filth of the lower-class? You're not thinking of being a Runner, are you?" He couldn't help the sneer in his voice. He hated the hierarchy and imbalance of power more than anyone. Why would Holland want to subject herself to it?

"Are you calling me filth now?" Holland raised her brows and crossed her arms.

Dash it. That came out wrong. He ran a hand over his face. "You know what I mean."

"Calm down, Markus. It's not like I'm actually leaving. I just...want to." Holland shrugged and resumed looking at the horizon.

"Is it Mrs. Kershaw? Has she hurt you again?" Markus clenched his fists and fought the urge to slam them into the ground. The idea of Holland running from trouble made his stomach cramp. He already knew her employer to be heavy-handed at times. It was enough to drive him mad.

"No, it's not that." Holland shook her head, staring him in the eyes. "I just don't want to end up like the characters in this book, lost in perpetual darkness." She held up the offending tome. "I want to know where I belong..."

You belong. Here. With me.

"...maybe even give Andaimon a chance at freedom, too. It's like a cage here; there's no hope of escaping." She sighed, dropping her voice to just above a whisper. "Do you know how hard it is not knowing where you come from, Markus?"

He swallowed the lump in his throat. *No.* He'd never considered it before. Yes, his father had died at a young age, but he still had his mother; he'd always known who his parents were. Holland on the other hand, hadn't. Markus had learned all about her family history, or lack thereof, throughout the years. It was something he often forgot played a crucial role in how she viewed her life.

He shook his head. What words could he say to her?

"I don't expect you to. You're one of the lucky ones." Holland reached over and squeezed his arm reassuringly.

The contact took him by surprise, sending pleasant shoots of heat through his skin.

He placed his hand over her own like he'd done numerous times before. But why did it now feel different? He met her gaze and found he couldn't look away.

"I'm sorry, Holland." Without hesitation, he began stroking her hand in small circles with his thumb. It was the least he could do to comfort her, and if he was honest with himself, a part of him wanted to hold her close so she couldn't leave. Maybe it would even be enough to make her stay.

The longer he looked at her, his gaze found her mouth. The sudden desire to kiss her overwhelmed him. If he did, would she punch him again? Or...?

He didn't have time to find out.

Holland suddenly leaned away, breaking their contact. She cleared her throat. "I-I should get going. I need to feed the chickens before they invoke the ire of Mrs. Kershaw." She stood and brushed her dress repetitively, though there was hardly any grass left on her skirts. By the way she kept her head down, he could tell she was blushing.

Markus groaned inwardly, rubbing a hand along his neck. Why did his dashed instincts have to make things so awkward? He stood to join her, disappointment warring in his gut. He didn't know what to do with his hands, so he stuffed them in his pockets.

He'd come over to bring Holland vegetables, but his visit was proving more confusing than diverting. They were friends, after all. But why did that word suddenly feel so complicated? And was it so wrong that he didn't want Holland to leave Andaimon?

She turned to go, but before heading down the hill, Holland stopped in her tracks and snapped back around. "What? Did you say something?"

"No." Markus frowned. He hadn't said a word. No one had.

He thought she was looking at him, but her gaze seemed to go through him and toward the direction of the Forbidden Wood.

"Is something wrong?" he asked, glancing over his shoulder.

She squinted as if trying to make something out in the distance. "I thought I heard…" Holland bit her bottom lip and continued to study the wall of trees.

Markus followed her gaze and squinched his eyes to see what she was looking at.

The Forbidden Wood appeared as it always had—foreboding and forbidden. It was dark and eerie as if it housed a lifetime of nightmares. Markus was glad Holland at least hadn't shown interest in going inside it… He'd never see her again if she did.

The longer he stared at the formidable forest, familiar pinpricks of ice flared along his spine.

He stifled a groan. *Not again. Not now.*

He massaged the skin and felt cold beneath his fingertips, but thankfully, the pain subsided even quicker than before.

He rolled his shoulders back and stretched his neck from side to side before focusing his attention once more on Holland.

Her brows were scrunched together. "Never mind. It must have been the wind." She shrugged and gave Markus one of her reassuring smiles that told him she was fine. "I'll see you later!" She turned and jogged back to the chicken coop, her skirts billowing behind her.

He watched her retreating figure, the pain in his back lessening while an unsettled feeling grew in his chest. He wanted to shrug it off, but there were two things that bothered him.

One, Holland didn't like living in Andaimon. And two, the wind wasn't more than a gentle breeze tonight; it wasn't even loud enough to make any noise. In fact, there hadn't been any noise at all. Not even a snapping twig.

What had Holland heard? And why did she think it came from within the Forbidden Wood?

A sudden chill crept into his bones, and it wasn't just from the cold. His spine still stung. He hadn't felt this familiar pain in years, and now he'd felt it twice in one day.

He tugged his overcoat closer to his neck out of habit, though his shirt was always covering it. Some marks were harder to hide than others. But as far as he knew, no one had seen this one. Not even Holland.

He glanced in her direction, her petite figure now a small dot in the distance. She was all things vibrant and youthful in his dirt-colored world. And he worried their moments were growing few.

Holland wanted to leave Andaimon, and therefore, she wanted to leave *him*.

Markus' stomach cramped even more.

He tried holding on to her retreating words like a promise, that he *would* see her later and that she wasn't planning on leaving. But that still didn't change anything. Someday, he had a feeling she would. It was only a matter of time.

He wished he was wrong.

CHAPTER THREE
From "The Tale of Endlewood"

*I*t doesn't take long for the other survivors to find me. A few months or so. Maybe less.

Nothing quells their honor. Their submission. They are stalwart in their commitment to the Crown—a life I can never outrun no matter how hard I try.

We are all outcasts here. Searching for a place to belong in this new haven. We may be few in number, but we're growing. Young ones traverse these woods, and newborns only know this wooded land as their first home. They know nothing of what once was, of the land we all fled. Of the ruined garden across the seas, distant and forgotten, ravaged by something fierce and unpredictable.

It's for the best. Any memories belong to nightmares.

Here, the air is sweet and the land fertile; I'm convinced I've made the right decision in coming. And it will remain protected.

"Sir Vesstan."

I nearly trip when hearing my given name. I turn and see the man who addressed me; it's one of the newcomers. He is lanky with shoulder-length, blonde strands on his head. A bag is slung over his shoulder, and a sharp pike is in his right hand.

I can forgive his insolence; in truth, I am only too glad for it. He has yet to learn the customs here. Customs I unwittingly agreed to. "Almar, is it?"

"The same, sir. I just came from the northwest border. I wanted to talk about our kingdom. It might not be safe—"

"Our kingdom?" *I'm stunned at how quickly he claims this place as his own. It's a welcome thought—this notion that I'm looked to as their leader. But this kingdom, in part, belongs to me. Almar has a lot to learn, especially if he waggles his loose tongue around Nindrol.*

"Your Majesty."

Speaking of which. The very man approaches, his graying hair falling across his forehead as he bows.

He uses my proper title almost too religiously.

"What is it, Nindrol?" *I don't have time to go over plans today. The castle is still in its beginning stages, but I trust its progress. I'd grown accustomed to walking barefoot my whole life, of escaping the palace walls back home. A stone floor and painted tiles can wait.*

"I've come to report on some recent activity."

"Activity?" *I look at Almar, who nods his head like he had just been trying to say as much.* "Where?"

Images of fire and hunger flash before my eyes. I've seen enough suffering to last a lifetime. But I've made a vow. This land will be safer than what once was. This land will be protected from any who wish it harm—I've made sure of it. It will be a place of refuge to any who abide here in peace. And a place of terror for any who wish it otherwise.

"The northwest border, your Majesty," Nindrol says.

"That's what I was trying to tell you, Sir Vesstan," Almar interrupts.

Nindrol snaps his head in Almar's direction, his eyes like daggers. "I suggest you address the king correctly if you don't wish your tongue to be on the end of that pike!" He growls at the newcomer, gesturing to the spear in his hand.

Almar flinches, the blood rushing to his face.

Embarrassment is good. It keeps the entitled humble. *These words resound somewhere in the back of my head. Words my father used to say. According to Nindrol, Almar's insolence has stretched far enough. It was only a matter of time.*

I clear my throat. "See to it that you read the scroll in your tent. It might save your tongue. That will be all." I dismiss the fool and return my focus to my advisor.

He scowls at Almar's retreating form, his gaze as fierce as shards of ice. But that's Nindrol; his loyalty knows no bounds. Though I do wish he'd ease his resolve. It was by his council I'd claimed my title at all, penned the words in the scroll, made Lamia a thing of history—all in the name of moving on from what was broken.

A past filled with ashes does little for morale, only burdening the memory.

Nindrol shakes his head. "The nerve. It's fiends like him who'd be better off in the Swamp Wispsnare rather than making this place unfit for company... Dangerous even."

"*Speaking of danger, there's activity in the northwest, you say?*" *I run a hand along my chin and wait for Nindrol to meet my gaze. Unease grows in my middle.* "*Have they... Are they close?*"

"*What does it matter? Do you think the Overseer will prove weak?*" *Nindrol creases his brow, the way he often does whenever I question his authority. Which I do often.* "*Your Majesty?*"

"*No. It's just...*" *My stomach churns again. How do I tell him the sight of blood sends bile to my throat? He probably already knows. Nindrol thinks that watching death unfold is a natural part of life and an assurance that my kingdom still stands in safety.*

I've yet to agree with the breadth of his staunch conviction.

"*Come. I'll show you again just how strong the Overseer is. You can trust it, your Majesty.*"

Trusting it isn't the problem. I am the one who put it in place. I know how it works.

And yet...

I follow after Nindrol, dread weighing my every step.

If the trespassers are in luck, they'll leave the forest with life still coursing through their bodies.

CHAPTER FOUR
Holland

Sunlight streamed through the curtained windows of Holland's bedroom. It was a drafty box of a room, but it served its purpose nonetheless. Furnished with a worn four-poster bed, side-table, and wash basin, the small room still felt empty.

She yawned and stretched beneath her covers, appreciating the warmth they offered. Pushing herself up, the blankets fell from her shoulders, inviting the chill of the morning to nip at her bare skin. She forced herself out of bed and grabbed her shawl, tugging the thin fabric over her shoulders. She shuffled her tired feet toward the fireplace.

Last night had been amusing, though all the running left her muscles aching this morning. Still, as she thought back to chasing Markus and lying next to him on the hill, a familiar blush crept up her neck. Had he almost kissed her? The memory stirred longing inside her chest. For a moment, she had felt wanted, seen. Would it be too ridiculous to think Markus actually cared for her?

Holland stifled a laugh as she kneeled and thrust the poker into the grate, stirring up the ashes. She lit a match and placed the flame near some kindling, waiting for it to catch. The flame took hold, slowly creeping up the wood, but it soon dissipated into a waft of smoke.

She sighed. Yes, it would be ridiculous. They were just friends after all.

Pushing forward onto the balls of her feet, she gave up on the fire and stood before walking toward the window. It was a foggy morning with drops of dew clinging to the glass frame. Her breath fogged up the glass even more. Still, the Forbidden Wood could be seen in the distance, peering out from behind the mist. If the forest wasn't so eerie, she might consider it beautiful.

Had she actually heard something last night? At first, she'd thought it was Markus, but he'd looked as perplexed as she had been. Maybe too many hours in the shop were making her hear whispers in the dark. She needed to get out more if that was the case. Just another reason to leave… Only she couldn't.

Stop it, Holland. You're being ungrateful again.

It was better to be content than to wish for things that could never be.

Markus had guessed her aim last night. She *did* want to be a Runner—someone who traveled all of Griskol by foot to bring food and supplies back to the people of Andaimon. They were usually teenage boys, though—youth and stamina were their armor. Never in Griskol's history had a woman ever attempted such a feat.

But instead of returning, she'd want to keep going, maybe even making it to Pembroke Fally. What would it be like to meet the king and queen? If she told them about Andaimon's poverty, would it be enough to soften their hearts? It felt too big of a task, and yet...maybe it wasn't impossible.

This new idea fit comfortably next to her growing desire to leave. She wanted, no—*needed* freedom and somewhere to start afresh—to explore Griskol at its fullest and find where she belonged. And in the process, maybe she could set Andaimon free as well.

She could dream.

Griskol stretched for miles. It bordered the neighboring countries of Eskal and Irthlen in the west, and Rankol and the Crendian Sea claimed its border in the east. And just off the coast was a small island called Onklo. It was rumored that mythical creatures haunted the land—fin-maidens such as mermaids and sirens, nymphs and dryads—and much like the Forbidden Wood, no one dared travel there.

Holland had always been curious about such things. She had determined she wanted to meet a mermaid one day. Maybe the fin-maiden would be able to tell Holland tales of her past or where her parents lay buried at sea.

It was another one of her silly ideas.

Too silly for the harshness of reality.

In her country, each region belonged to an order of hierarchy, stacked atop one another like bricks. The southernmost and poorest was Andaimon, Holland's homeland. It comprised the poor working class and those who struggled to make a living. Just to the north was Kirkus—a place known for its weaponry, farmland, and street vending. This region was home to the middle-class workers and her dearest friend, Markus. North of Kirkus was

Tiri, home of the upper-class—Snoots, they were called, though not to their faces. They specialized in delicious food, political affairs, and foreign trade. Their fishing ports were some of the busiest in the land, booming with merchant ships and the like coming from countries beyond the Crendian Sea. And lastly, the fourth and northernmost region was Pembroke Fally, home to King Randor and Queen Rosin of the palace of Famar. Only those with exceptional skills, not to mention a lot of darics, were lucky enough to live within the protective walls surrounding this region. And it was an even more unlikely feat if any commoner was privileged enough to step foot inside their palace.

Not to mention there was the dreaded *Name-branding*—the *curse* of Griskol. At least, that's what Holland called it. In a world riddled with fear, spelling meant everything. Boys' names in Andaimon were branded with the ending "mon" while girls' were branded with the ending "and," taking letters from the beginning of their district while boys took them from the end. Thus, Holland's name gave away her station and birthplace.

It was similar for those living in Kirkus; however, both girls' and boys' names were branded with the ending "us." Tiri had it even easier; all endings of names were branded with a single "i." Pembroke Fally didn't reside under this curse, however. All the residents in that region simply added "Fally" after their first name to signify a title of authority.

Originally, *Name-branding* had been a positive way for people to claim pride in their home-regions. All of Griskol had been equal at one point, but when King Randor and Queen Rosin came to power, things turned sour. *Name-branding* was now a way for

Famar to keep everyone in check. To make sure that people stayed where they belonged. And although visitation amongst all the regions was not illegal, it was not exactly encouraged. In fact, it was frowned upon.

This made it virtually impossible for Holland to leave home, to be anything other than she was. Even visiting Markus in Kirkus was difficult. She'd need a whole new identity, and those weren't cheap to come by. Nor were they worth the risk.

She had heard the stories, heard of the public hangings. Any form of trickery reeked of the occult—a deceitful magic. If someone couldn't own up to their self-imposed scandals, they were forced to pay the price in Tiri's public square. Yet another atrocity the king and queen of Famar implemented. They, along with the Snoots, enjoyed the spectacle—a reminder to keep everyone in place, shaming anyone for their lack of integrity.

The hypocrisy of the ruling class to talk about integrity! How could they implement justice when they didn't know what the word meant?

The poor were to remain as lowly as ever without any hope of progress.

A new identity could cost someone their life. And in many cases, it had.

These thoughts filled Holland's stomach with dread. She tried to steer her mind toward more pleasant things but found she couldn't.

Andaimon was deemed the filth of Griskol. Those who lived there were looked down upon and viewed with disdain. No one wanted to visit and thus, no one did.

Only palace wagons braved the long trek from Pembroke Fally, but it was always to take, never to give. They came to Andaimon empty and left filled to the brim, hardly leaving enough darics to people's names or enough produce for them to sustain themselves. And these same wagons would redistribute Andaimon's wares to the upper regions accordingly.

Hence the need for Runners.

Holland pushed off from the window and walked toward her wash basin. Rinsing her face in the cold water, she shuddered and stepped into a worn, mahogany dress hanging limp over a chair. She fastened the fabric around her waist and bust, slipping over an apron to complete the look.

She grabbed a brush and ran it through her thick, dark locks, defeating the knots the wind had tangled in them the night before. Pulling her hair back into a single plait, she coiled the braid into a bun and pinned it in place at the base of her neck.

She left her room and paused at the banister. The stairs looked very unappealing all of a sudden.

Holland swung her leg over the railing and straddled it like a horse, gripping it with both hands as she laid her stomach flat against the wood.

This was another perk of living alone. She could slide down the banisters as much as she wished without ever getting caught.

With her back toward the landing, Holland loosened her grip, the smooth fabric of her dress allowing her to slip down the banister like a drop of water. But it was almost too fast. She lost her balance and by the time Holland reached the bottom, she fell off and landed with a thud against the wall.

Since when did the wall move?

Holland glanced behind her and groaned.

"What on earth do you think you're doing?" Mrs. Kershaw backed away, smoothing down her skirts from where Holland had just landed on them. "You nearly killed me!" Her scowl made her look like an enraged bear.

"I didn't think anyone would be here," said Holland as she stood. The ride had been exhilarating. Too bad it was Mrs. Kershaw who'd broken her fall.

"'Didn't think' is right." Mrs. Kershaw's hands went to her hips.

"It won't happen again—"

Mrs. Kershaw smacked Holland across the cheek.

She recoiled, her eyes stinging with unshed tears.

Mrs. Kershaw pointed her finger at her. "I've heard it all before. What if you broke your hand and risked good business? You foolish, foolish girl!"

Holland tried opening her mouth to speak, but nothing came out.

Mrs. Kershaw straightened. "Your foolishness made me do it. If you'd just do as you're told, we wouldn't be here. Am I clear?"

Holland nodded, though all she could see was red. Anger and mortification burned in her chest, and she was already planning on more ways she could increase her foolishness when Mrs. Kershaw left. If only her employer knew half the thoughts already swimming through her mind—of her dreams to leave Griskol.

"Perfectly." Holland didn't smile, but ground out the words through gritted teeth.

"I'll believe it when I see it." Mrs. Kershaw pursed her lips and proceeded like nothing had happened. "As to business matters, I came here to tell you that two ladies who frequent Abermann's Tea House in town are in need of new gloves. I told them last night you'd finish them before noon today."

Noon? So soon? Mrs. Kershaw was pushing her luck in spades. Holland glanced behind her and looked out the shop window. By the looks of the morning light, she guessed she had less than four hours to get the job done.

Holland was an early riser, but Mrs. Kershaw wasn't. The fact that her employer had come over this morning must mean the gloves were of grave importance. Perhaps to win over new tenants? From what Holland knew, there were still three vacant townhomes in need of renters, and Mrs. Kershaw wasn't adverse for more darics.

"I'm only too glad I came over here when I did, or who knows how long it would have taken you to begin work this morning. Or in what state I'd find you in if I waited any longer." Mrs. Kershaw tsked, shaking her head. "Now get moving! You've delayed long enough! Precious daric is on the line." She walked the short distance to the kitchen and entered the connected door to her townhome, her footsteps fading with her retreat.

Holland rubbed her burning cheek. She really needed to invest in a good lock; too bad her employer wouldn't allow it. Mrs. Kershaw was taking liberties with coming over more often, not to mention violent liberties too, and the fact that she could surprise Holland at any moment was alarming.

Holland suppressed a shudder and walked into her shop. The

morning light already illuminated the small workspace as it filtered in through the thin fabric of the curtains. She pushed aside the material and switched the sign on the door to say it was open before sitting down to begin the day's work.

Two pairs of gloves for the sake of new tenants. Holland would have to either finish them in time or resign herself to the wrath of Mrs. Kershaw.

Her dreams of leaving Griskol would have to be put on hold for another day.

CHAPTER FIVE
Markus

Sunlight danced in a haze of soft pink beneath his lidded eyes. It was dark, and yet, it wasn't. Was it morning already? Too tired to care, Markus wanted to keep sleeping. And he would have, had something slimy not suddenly been plastered on his face.

He opened his eyes to see a giant snout pushed up against his cheek, a tongue licking him furiously.

Blasted mongrel.

"Hamish…" Markus grunted in warning and turned over so his back was toward the dog. He wasn't ready to wake up just yet.

The dog had other plans, though. Plans that involved impaling Markus's gut with his paws. The dog jumped and pounced on Markus until he had no choice but to be fully awake.

"Fine, you win! I'm up. Happy?" Markus groaned. He turned over once again and scratched behind the dog's ears.

Hamish had been a small pup, a runt of the litter when Markus had rescued him. But now? He was the biggest bloodhound he'd ever seen. And he was currently putting all his weight on Markus.

"Get off, will you? I told you I'm awake!" Markus said,

feeling something sharp poking him in the back as he sat up. He reached behind him and pulled a piece of straw from his shirt.

He finally registered where he was.

Markus had fallen asleep in the barn again. If the smell alone wasn't enough to prove it, the countless bales of hay towering around him were.

He was up in the loft, close to the wooden beams of the ceiling and the morning rays filtering in through the east-facing window. He squinted out to the horizon and saw fog dissipating beneath the brilliant sunshine. When had he fallen asleep up here? Sometime shortly after he lugged in the hay bales, he guessed.

After that unsettling conversation with Holland the night before, he hadn't been able to ease his racing thoughts and had decided to work them until they couldn't run anymore.

He may have pushed himself a little too hard this time. His pulse still throbbed beneath his temples, and he hadn't even had a drop of brandy.

On second thought, maybe that's what he needed.

Such was his plight. He cared too deeply. And he always overworked his body so he wouldn't feel any of it. A fault? Maybe. But at least it seemed to do the trick.

Hamish still nudged him, pressing his wet nose against Markus's face and whimpering. He hadn't left Markus's side since waking him up.

What time was it? Had he slept as late as it felt?

"You'll get your breakfast as soon as I find it in me to stand." Markus reached to rub behind Hamish's ears again, but the dog pulled back, craning his neck toward the stairs.

Odd. Hamish was a glutton for attention.

"What's gotten into you?" Markus asked, looking Hamish over in curiosity. Was there something stuck in his paw?

Hamish continued to whimper and headed toward the stairs, looking back to see if Markus was following.

"You want to show me something?" Markus' senses were slowly clearing.

Hamish was a lug, but he could be quick when necessary. What was bothering him?

The dog barked, pacing at the top of the stairs. He pawed at the loose strands of hay, his tail flicking frantically.

"Okay, I think I get the idea." Markus stood and remembered to duck before hitting his head on a low beam. His movements felt stiff, his back sore from lying on his makeshift bed.

At the sight of his owner moving, Hamish barked again before running down the stairs.

Markus followed, slowly. Now he remembered. Last night, he'd made sure Altus and Rizus were in bed before eight, giving his mother some blessed relief; the ten-year-old twins liked when he read them stories. And then Drusus, his sixteen-year-old brother, had wanted to show him something...

Dru had been spending most of his days, when he wasn't doing chores, sketching some sort of diamond-shaped design into the castaway dirt piles next to the shed. He'd found thick timber logs and knotted some old cloth together in the shape of a ball. He'd been wanting to try the new game out, and Markus obliged him a few rounds.

That could also explain the tightness in his muscles.

After all his siblings went to bed, Markus had continued to work until well past four in the morning. And by the looks of the climbing sun, that meant he'd only gotten about three hours of sleep.

He'd done worse before.

He trailed after Hamish and exited the barn, rubbing a hand over his face as the blazing sun stung his eyes. Despite the chill that accompanied fall, he could tell it would be a warm day.

Hamish was running now, his nose close to the ground as if in hot pursuit. He occasionally glanced behind him to make sure Markus still followed.

Markus matched Hamish's speed. There was definitely something the bloodhound wanted to show him, but what?

Hamish took him across the farmland, past the cottage, and into a small copse to the left of his property. They were beneath the trees now; beautiful copper beeches and hemlocks rushed past him as he ran on. They were nearing the river, and that's when Markus heard the cries.

They sounded like a woman's, and they were growing louder.

Hamish stopped running when he met the water's edge. Markus drew up next to him, his hands on his knees as he caught his breath. He scanned the water line.

This wasn't any ordinary river; it was salt water and led to the Crendian Sea. The fact that something this powerful ran through a copse on his property would never cease to amaze him. He'd spent enough time catching fish in these waters with his late father that one would think the novelty should have worn off by now. Not to mention that the river, once filtered properly, helped irrigate his land.

He looked at Hamish.

The dog's snout was pointing in the direction from whence the sound was coming, and Markus followed his line of sight.

There! In the midst of the river was an island. A towering willow near the water's shelf hovered over the location, shielding the maiden from view with its leafy tendrils. All Markus could see were strands of something auburn showing signs of struggle from within the river's current.

"Hold on! I'm coming to help," Markus shouted, hoping to bring assurance of safety. If only he'd thought to bring his wading pants and rubber shoes. Or better yet, a boat.

The woman cried again.

There was nothing for it. Markus waded into the water, the ground quickly sloping downward. He was only halfway to the island and the water was already up to his chest. A few more steps proved to send him under entirely as his foot unexpectedly left the last stretch of ground.

Blast this river. It was deeper than he remembered.

He came up sputtering, wiping the remaining water from his eyes as he swam to the island. Thankfully the earth began to slope upward once more and Markus found his footing. But the lip of the island only went to his waist. That meant he'd have to pull himself up.

And none too soon; the woman was crying something fierce now.

"Please, help me!" she cried through her tears, her pain palpable in her inflection.

In her distress, Markus thought he heard a foreign accent.

"Almost there!" He gritted his teeth and hoisted his body onto land. His muscles were feeling the strain this morning after a grueling night's work. But that didn't matter.

He pushed aside the willow reeds and climbed farther onto the small island. A flash of red caught his eye. He saw the maiden, her upper-half bobbing in the river's current while her lower-half remained submerged.

Is she caught in something?

Markus crawled to her side to assess the situation.

When the maiden looked up at him, he was taken by surprise. Her eyes were a brilliant green; large and round and filled with fear. Her hair was like a flaming arrow, and her skin was as white as porcelain.

"You're not Thallon." The lady frowned.

No, he wasn't. He didn't even know if that was a name.

Markus continued to stare at her. The orange scales along the sides of her face were alarming. This was the most curious girl he'd ever seen.

"Well, are you just going to stare, or are you going to help me?" Her tone wasn't one of annoyance but rather of genuine curiosity.

Her comment unfroze him. Yes, he could definitely hear her accent now. It sounded unlike anything he'd heard in Griskol or the surrounding regions. She must be from across the Crendian Sea somewhere. But how did she end up here?

Again, the maiden cried out in pain, grimacing as she tried to reach below the water.

"Are you stuck?"

"Yes, I think it's a fishing line or something." She motioned to somewhere beneath the water's surface.

Markus reached toward his boot and breathed a sigh of relief when he felt his pen knife. He hadn't forgotten to put it back last night. The knife had been a gift from his father, one of the last tokens left to remember him by, and it continued to prove itself useful time and time again.

He pulled it out and laid himself flat so his torso hung off the edge of the island. He reached down, prepared to feel the tangling of skirts and the kicking of legs.

"I should warn you..." the maiden interrupted his progress.

He jerked his arm out of the water and stared at the racing current. *What was that?* He felt something scaly scrape across his hand.

"Warn me that there's a giant fish right below you?" Markus quirked a brow.

"Something like that," the maiden said, her cries resuming once again. "Please, just set me free."

Markus swallowed hard and bent once more. He tried not to think about the scales and reached to find the fishing line instead. He felt it caught on the rock and steadily pulled the line upward so he could find the point where it was attached to the girl.

"Not so fast." The maiden grimaced.

Markus proceeded slowly, raising the line at a much gentler pace. Was her frock or leg caught at the end of it? It must be digging in pretty hard if she was in this much pain.

"I think I'm almost there." Markus bit down on his tongue,

45

cutting the frayed line that seemed to come out in all directions. But he still needed to get to the main problem. He reached down even farther and was tempted to pull his hand back.

There were the scales again! But they didn't move as if they belonged to a fish trying to get away. No, the scales were stationary, only moving with the river's current.

What is this? Markus focused on the task and cut the remaining line away from the scales. Once she was free, he replaced his knife in his boot and turned to ask how the maiden fared, but she had disappeared. Had the current taken her under?

Markus stood and scoured the water's surface for any sign of struggle. Instead, he was met with laughter and a splash of water at his backside.

He turned and frowned when he saw nothing.

Again, more laughter and another wave of water hit his back.

He turned to see nothing there, either. *What's the meaning of this?* He was beginning to think he was going insane.

Suddenly, something gripped his wrist and pulled him backward. He didn't have time to gain his balance as the water rushed up and enveloped his plummeting body.

Blue and green swam in his vision, and cold nipped his bones. Something orange and scaly whooshed past him as he tried kicking toward the surface. But the scaly creature kept dragging him farther down.

Markus gripped his constricting throat, his oxygen growing thin. Air. He needed air. Black mingled with the crystalline blue of the waters until there was nothing more than darkness and sleep.

CHAPTER SIX
Markus

Something soft pressed against Markus' lips and his lungs filled with what tasted like morning air.

"Breathe, farm boy. Breathe."

He gulped and coughed, but everything sounded muffled. His eyelids fluttered open, and two green eyes peered back at him from within a tangle of fiery hair, only inches from his face.

The maiden? He looked behind her and saw a striking tail of red and orange scales where her feet should have been. Not a maiden then—*a mermaid?* Impossible. They weren't real. As forbidden as magic.

Then again, he was breathing underwater.

Was he dead?

Markus' mind flooded with thoughts of Holland. Of the night on the hill. Of her dreams to travel and see the world. Of the mysterious noise she'd heard. Of his burning back. Did he really know all that much about Griskol after all? Of magic? If he did, he would have known mermaids lived in his backyard.

The fish-girl took hold of Markus' hand and brought him to

the surface. Once his head broke free of the water, his blessed lungs rejoiced. The air had never tasted so sweet.

Now uninhibited, he climbed his way onto the island and laid on his back, breathing heavily. He needed to regain his energy, and if he were honest with himself, garner the restraint not to chide the woman who'd just tried to drown him.

"You're not Thallon," the mermaid said again. Her head rested on top of her arms as she leaned on the island, completely unphased by what had just happened. The rest of her was still submerged in the water. She studied him.

"Do you usually go about trying to drown people who aren't named Thallon?" Markus couldn't keep the frustration from his voice as he sat up.

"I wasn't trying to drown you," she said innocently. "I was rescuing you." Her eyes peered up at him, like he should understand.

"But you dragged me into the water…"

"Yes, so I could rescue you." She smiled.

"That's the most ridiculous thing I've ever heard. You pulled me under just so you could rescue me?" Markus ran a hand through his thoroughly drenched hair.

"Yes! In my clan, it's never wise to remain indebted to another. I couldn't very well let you rescue me without having done something in return." The mermaid had a way of stating things matter-of-factly that made even the most ridiculous of notions seem less crazy.

"All the legends say mermaids are sirens of the sea, luring people to their deaths. I could have sworn that was happening to

48

me." The more Markus thought about it, the more he wasn't sure he could trust this fish-girl.

"Mermaids aren't sirens, though we can be just as cunning. You can't trust every story you hear. Though my parents would say otherwise. Because of them, I'm bound by a fate I can't escape... At least here, you are safe." She flicked her tail out of the water.

What did she mean by that? "What's your name?" Markus asked. He should at least have something to refer to her by.

"Adra. Adra Oshiera Kelbi. I come from a long line of Kelbis. What's your name?"

"Markus." He nodded. Short and simple.

"It's nice to meet you, Markus." Adra sighed. "I only wish Thallon... *He* should have been here."

"Who's this Thallon you keep speaking of? Does he know how lucky he is to have his name?" Markus mock-laughed. He couldn't help thinking that if he were that man, he probably wouldn't have been thoroughly drowned and so ridiculously rescued because of it.

"He's my...swain," the mermaid said hesitantly. "Though as of now, I'm not so sure. He was supposed to meet me here last night, but he never came."

"Why meet here?"

"My family resides off the coast of Onklo. This is the closest river that enters the mainland of Griskol. It's where Thallon and I like to meet." Her large, green eyes grew wider, and she tilted her head to the side. "I thought he'd be the one to rescue me..."

Markus stared at Adra; her gaze was distant as she scanned the water's edge as if willing Thallon to appear. Markus wanted to ask her more questions; it wasn't everyday one met a mermaid. In truth, he felt he needed to ask a million questions because he knew Holland would be hounding him for more information. The thought pulled a smile from the corner of his mouth.

But he feared Adra would keep turning the conversation back to the man who wasn't here. Maybe Markus should just ask about him instead.

"So, this Thallon of yours. How long have you known each other?" It was worth a shot.

"Oh!" Adra glanced at Markus. She had a whimsical smile as she seemed to ponder her next words. "Forever and yet, not long at all. You see, for us fae-kind, the years continue ever onward. They don't progress at the same rate as mere humans. I pity them because of it, I'm afraid."

Had he heard her correctly? *Us fae-kind?*

Markus propped his knee up and draped his arm over it. What exactly had she said? "Are you insinuating that Thallon…is he a mermaid? Or…?"

Was it too hard to believe that more existed? He was talking to a mermaid, after all.

"A fae." She smiled.

"But, that's—"

"Impossible?" Adra laughed. "Humans perplex me. You spend your limited years neglecting to see the world around you for what it is. There are things right under your noses that have yet to be explored. Maybe if you did, you wouldn't question the truth of them or be as shocked when you found out what you didn't know before."

Was that her answer, then? Something twisted in Markus' gut, telling him that she was right. But he didn't want to admit that. It wasn't the answer he was hoping to receive.

"It's time I headed back. I'm duty-bound, and I've already lingered for far too long. I can't have my clan worry." Adra plunged under the water.

"Wait! Will you be back?" Markus called out to her. He still had questions.

Adra's head broke through the surface, her smile mischievous. "Missing me already, farm boy?" Her laugh sounded like pearls dropping on water. "I'll return soon, and with Thallon in tow. He wants to tell me something important—"

"Important? About what?" Markus asked.

"I don't know. Something about Griskol or Endlewood. I can't recall which." Adra shrugged.

"Endlewood?" Markus' ears perked up just as much as his stomach dropped. He thought back to Holland's book. Surely the word was merely a coincidence.

"Do you know what I speak of?" Adra's eyes grew wide. Was it fear or surprise?

"As much as I know what is fiction," Markus said.

"Fiction? You mean make-believe?" Adra looked mortified.

"Yes, they're one in the same."

"I fear you are mistaken." Adra's eyes grew even wider. "Until you learn to open *your* eyes, Markus, you'll remain closed off to the wonders of your country. Tales hold more truth than you think. But never be too hasty to delve into them either. One must exercise caution as much as wonder, but not one more or less than the other."

Markus was taken aback by Adra's speech. He could feel the crease in his brown dipping lower. What did she mean? Maybe she was more of a siren than she thought. He opened his mouth, about to ask another question, but Adra waved him off.

"Listen to me blabbing away! I've worried you." She suddenly blushed. "I suggest you forget about Endlewood entirely. It's of little consequence and doesn't concern you. I shouldn't have said a word. You're only a mortal." Adra drew back in the water.

Markus got to his feet. "I don't understand—"

"Thank you for rescuing me!" Adra interrupted him. "Even if you weren't Thallon." She smiled and waved before plunging deeper into the river.

"Wait!" Markus wanted to ask her more questions, to understand her sudden hesitation to talk, to find out about Endlewood or Thallon's message. But he was left grasping at the willow branches hanging before his face. Adra had already left.

Dash it. His curiosity would be the end of him.

Markus ran a hand through his hair and made for the opposite side of the island. When he pushed through the willow reeds, he could see Hamish on his stomach by the water—waiting.

He was a loyal dog. Possibly loyal to a fault, or else Markus never would have ended up here in the first place.

Markus plunged into the water and swam for the adjacent shore. It didn't take long before he felt solid ground beneath his feet again.

On land, Hamish greeted him thoroughly.

"Did you know you sent me to rescue a mermaid?" Markus squatted and ruffled Hamish's ears, laughing.

Hamish barked, staring at Markus with those warm, brown eyes and looking completely innocuous.

"You're not as innocent as you look, I'm sure of it." He stood, and Hamish followed.

Markus had a feeling another long day of work was ahead of him. Anything to diffuse the new ammunition Adra had just fed his already troubled mind.

Maybe he'd visit Holland later. She was usually good at distracting him. Though after last night, he wasn't so sure.

He'd probably end up telling her all about the mermaid and mention something about *Endlewood*...and he'd be right back to where he started.

On second thought, maybe he should see if Calsius was home. The man was like another brother; they'd been through a lot together, and sometimes, sitting in his presence was all he needed.

The more Markus thought about the fin-maiden, the more Adra's words left him unsettled.

If *Endlewood* was real, he had a feeling Holland would somehow find it.

CHAPTER SEVEN
From "The Tale of Endlewood"

I follow Nindrol through the trees, and our heavy breathing mingles together under the dense canopy. The farther we head from the shore, the more humid the forest feels. The air is thick, but not wholly unpleasant.

When my wooden craft first brought me to this place, it had taken a full week to scout the entire lay of the land. It was untouched by human hands, as if it had simply been waiting to be discovered.

Now, it's been about a year since I first danced under the trees and called them all by name; I've committed everything to memory. I know every timber, every babbling brook, every notch in the bark, every trampled leaf... I know all the animals who live here, too, and they've come to recognize me as one of their own.

Their leader—second to the copper stag.

That realization still rocks me. I escaped leadership only to run into it headlong.

The heart of this forest is my home. It's where my palace is being built—upon Nindrol's orders. It's only a matter of time until *it's finished. Already, the castle is surrounded by servant quarters, soldier barracks, and family homes—some on the ground in tents, others in the trees as high and scattered as the boughs, with gilded staircases and bridges ascending and connecting it all together. It's a sight to behold. Beautiful.*

A new Lamia.

I never would have found this land if I hadn't fled Lamia in the first place. If I'd never sought safety and to seek my destiny elsewhere. Though my destiny now looks much different than what I had hoped for. One can never outrun a title, what they were fated to be...

I walk a few more steps and stop in my tracks. There, just ahead, a wall of golden light arches and dances in an array of lines—crossing, intersecting, slicing.

The Overseer.

"Let's move closer," Nindrol calls behind him, motioning me nearer.

"I'd rather not." I swallow the lump in my throat. I should be used to it by now. My kingdom's safety comes at a cost, though; one that looks an awful lot like Lamia's demise.

Nindrol looks at me and frowns. "For being its creator, you don't seem to remember the Overseer's function. You needn't be afraid."

He's mistaken my hesitancy for ignorance.

I scowl, biting my tongue; there's no use in wasting words on him. Nindrol's my superior by many years and has been advisor to the Crown for ages. He is stubborn as much as he is loyal, and in most cases, he's wise enough to respect me. This isn't one of those times.

"Pray enlighten me, oh wise one. What am I forgetting?" Mockery coats my words.

Nindrol smirks. "If you recall, the Overseer is at work. One can only pass through the magic field if they have fae-blood...magicked blood; otherwise, they die. We need not fear intrusion along the perimeter from mere humans, your Majesty."

"I don't require a lecture, Nindrol. I know how the Overseer works." I roll my eyes. His belittlement grates on my nerves.

"And yet, you cower but a yard from its border. You wanted protection, so you made the Overseer. You came up with this method, so you must agree to its repercussions. Death will trample on your doorstep for the sake of keeping these woods free whether you like it or not."

I grimace, balling my hands into fists. "I'm not cowering. And I don't require your gall to spur my ire." I've had enough of this conversation, all traces of mockery gone.

"I only do as I'm told, your Majesty. I report on activity within the forest walls and along its perimeter, and I also see to the building of your palace. Death is but a mere fact of life amidst it all. I don't need your ingratitude because of it."

I bite my tongue yet again. How has Nindrol been around all these years? He's debased every ounce of my power by condensing it to something trite. He's as much a nuisance as he is helpful. Others might try to question my leadership, but Nindrol keeps them in line. Though of his methods I'm none too sure... He questions me more than anyone.

If he wasn't such an asset to the Crown, I'd discharge him

57

promptly. Send him back to Lamia to boss around the creatures that stole that land from us. They'd probably listen to him. He survived them once before.

I grind my teeth, breathing deeply. I need to let my fury burn off. He's not worth it.

Maybe each of us is needed to keep the other sane.

I hold my hands up in mock surrender. "Fine. You win." Like always.

Nindrol nods and presses on, his face unreadable. "The activity I mentioned is a little beyond the barrier. If we cross it, we might scare the trespassers away. But if we approach cautiously, we might have a show."

"You mean a bloodbath?" I swallow the bile in my throat.

Safety for my kingdom comes with a cost. Already there have been lifeless bodies scattered about the perimeter—the bodies of the curious who wandered too far.

"It's what you created, your Majesty. The utmost protection."

He didn't need to remind me again. It's true. Protection is most important. I can't have what happened to Lamia happen here…

That once protected land had been ravaged and turned to dust. First came the darting shadows and gales, and then came the fire. Scorching breath burned our homes, and we all fled in fear.

A winged snake, its hide a sickly green and its size at least ten times that of a grown man's, alighted upon the earth. Its eyes burned orange, and its teeth were stained with blood. "Prepare to die!" it roared, grabbing the fae-king around his middle.

"Save the women and children, Vesstan! Sathail ilath… Save

them!" *I can still hear the late fae-king screaming as giant claws gripped his body and ripped him in two. My father was no more.*

The image haunts me even now.

Lamia will know no peace as long as the land is terrorized by those winged demons—the Dyvrat dragons.

They are the deadliest and most cunning of all flying beasts. Known for swallowing their catch piece by piece, limb by limb—a slow and painful death wrought upon any and all. Their aim is lifeblood, and they're attracted to magic, surviving off our very life source.

Hence, they came in droves. They sniffed out our power, coming from who-knows-where to destroy us all.

Most of us were devoured—mercilessly killed on the spot. Others of us were forced into indentured servitude, and even fewer of us had gotten away by sheer luck.

I was one of the few. I nominate fear for my hasty retreat and my neglect to follow my father's dying wish. I had thought only to escape the dragons and my title, but I'd lost so much more. Many women and children suffered because of it. Including my own mother.

When your home is burning, and all you've ever known disintegrates before you... You pay little heed to rational thinking. Shock has a way of weaseling its way into the nerves, the mind.

So, I had sought a boat—alone. I can't recall much beyond that, save for the scorching sun and the lapping waves.

The memories are slowly returning now. Memories long suppressed that I'm not sure I want to recall...memories that are forbidden to be remembered according to the scroll.

The Dyvrats have ruined much.

I've been told not all dragons are barbaric savages, that some are actually peaceable. But not these. These only seek to kill and conquer. The Dyvrats are too powerful for fae magic, and we have no means of fighting back.

It can't be cowardice to have fled my way to freedom, even if I fled alone. I am convinced the twenty others who found me would say the same. Nindrol included.

We all have our stories—every one of them marked by fire. And each either begins or ends with, "Take heed, beware the fell Dyvrat."

CHAPTER EIGHT
Holland

The air inside Benneforth Row's Seamstress was dense like the morning fog, the windows magnifying the steady stream of light from outside. Though it was nearing the colder seasons, that made little difference to a small, stuffy room.

Holland leaned over her table to open the front window even wider, but the lever was rusted in place. She inhaled what little breeze the casement allowed in as beads of sweat trickled down her neck.

This infernal thing.

Giving up, she leaned back in her seat and set herself to focus on her sewing. She had to keep going.

Already she had worked away the majority of the morning, slaving over finding the right material. She hadn't had any white cotton or silk fabric left and had to run to the local shop to get some. That had taken up at least half of the time she was allotted to get the gloves ready for the two ladies. And they still weren't quite finished.

Holland glanced outside and guessed it was nearing noontime.

If only she could afford one of those fancy clocks or pocket watches the wealthy seemed to have. She'd heard they were in Tiri; the luxury of being able to tell one's own time was precious.

She did a few more stitches before her eyes wandered to the street once again. An elderly woman was pushing a wheelbarrow full of beets. They jostled with each stone or pothole the wheels rolled over, but that's not what captured Holland's attention.

Two kids, a boy and a girl, ducked behind a tree near the road. Were they up to something? Sure enough, the little girl, her dress not much more than a torn pillowcase with stains, stumbled onto the street and pretended to fall in front of the old woman, acting like she had just been injured. That's when the boy came around the other side and grabbed a few beets from the cart, stuffing them under the wispy folds of his threadbare shirt.

Should Holland stop them? By the looks of the children, they could use a good meal. And some new clothes. Maybe she should sew them some.

In that moment, Holland was taken back to a memory she hadn't thought about in years. These children weren't the only ones who'd suffered hunger.

It was a cool morning in the region of Andaimon. The sun hid behind a veil of clouds, and the basket on Holland's arm was growing heavier with each new purchase she had made. Mrs. Kershaw had given her a set of darics to complete the errands; nothing more, nothing less.

"An eight-year-old should learn how to make such transactions," Mrs. Kershaw had said.

So Holland was doing just that. And every spare daric was to be given back to her employer afterward.

Holland just needed to purchase one more thing. She spotted the ribbon tent beneath a clothesline draped with rugs. Mrs. Kershaw had made it clear to get purple ribbon, not too dark, but not too light either. It was a very specific shade that Holland wasn't sure even existed.

She carefully picked her way along the dusty street in the direction of the stand, being careful not to trip over stray stones or turn an ankle in a ditch. But something drew her eye. A white hare, with something that looked like a net tangled around its neck, bounded around a bush and disappeared further into town.

The sight stirred her heart. Poor thing. Holland couldn't stand to see an animal looking so helpless. She determined it needed to be rescued, and she was going to find the sorry creature and set it free.

She tugged her basket closer and ran after the animal, getting glimpses of it every now and then.

The hare darted around the corner of a cottage and then through an alleyway. Then it was back on the street, darting under carts and beneath people's legs. It kept running and eventually dashed into a thicket of trees.

Holland tried to keep up, her worn shoes threatening to fall apart if she ran any further. But she didn't dare stop. For some reason, she felt that this hare needed her, that its skittishness was but a defense against the world—a defense she knew keenly. By setting the hare free, she'd be giving it a chance to experience a life it otherwise wouldn't know.

They spent a few more minutes like this, the hare running through town and Holland chasing after it. Eventually, the hare entered a wooded glen, and Holland followed, both of them dodging and bounding through Andaimon. Tall, spindly trees rushed past her, and ground thistles crunched beneath her every footfall. The way the sun danced through the green leaves made her want to stop and spin around, soaking in the beauty of it all. But she kept running.

Eventually she made it out of the trees and paused when she caught sight of a long, wooden fence, stretching for miles to her left and right. Sure enough, the hare was caught on one of the beams, the net circling its neck snagged on a sliver of wood.

Holland stepped closer, ready to set the hare free, but the animal pulled its head back, wiggling out of the net before bounding off in the direction it had first come.

Holland was left all alone. The strange fence and an overgrown field beyond it stretched before her. But even from this distance, she could make out the telltale signs of a town a little way off.

Was it more of Andaimon? She'd never been this far north before. If she explored it, maybe she'd have better chances at finding a purple ribbon!

Holland hiked up her dusty hem and climbed over the fence, the wood scraping against her bare ankles. In the tall grass, she dropped her skirts and clutched the basket tighter to her side before she took off running.

A few more hares, a white-tailed fawn, and a red fox darted past her in the tall grass, but otherwise the land remained undisturbed.

Town approached quickly, and pretty soon her feet were on cobblestones and her nose smelled something rather pleasant. Like warm bread and herbed spices. Like farmland and fresh earth.

Holland walked forward, surveying the town before her. Though the houses were older, they weren't falling apart, and the road gleamed of polished stone rather than dust. Most people wore shoes, and the children looked to be dressed in hand-me-downs rather than threadbare frocks.

If this place was part of Andaimon, it was definitely different from the Andaimon she knew back home. Why couldn't Mr. Kershaw have chosen to live here instead? Maybe he'd died before he knew this place existed.

She ran a hand down the front of her dress, smoothing out the wrinkles and attempting to shake off some of the dirt from her travels. The people here weren't dressed in fineries, but at least they appeared better off than what she was used to. Their confused looks made her nervous, like she didn't belong.

Holland walked deeper into town and felt her stomach growl. Had she forgotten to eat breakfast this morning? The hunger pains overtook her senses, and pretty soon, she found herself at a vegetable stand, her mouth watering over the earthy-smelling produce.

Andaimon didn't have fresh vegetables like this. At best, the produce was usually a few days old by the time it got there.

Maybe she'd have enough to buy something. Maybe Mrs. Kershaw wouldn't notice.

"How much?" she asked, eyeing the creamy parsnips sitting in a neat little clump next to some cabbage. Her hand moved to the pouch hanging from her neck; she turned it over and counted the remaining darics that fell into her palm. Five gold pieces smiled back at her, their smooth, uneven edges reflecting in the sun.

Holland had learned at an early age what darics were and how to use them. Earlier than most. It was the currency in Griskol, and it had been since the very beginning of time. Two darics could buy a half foot of fabric or a loaf of bread. Surely one parsnip wouldn't cost as much.

A tall man looked at her with kind eyes and responded to her question. "That would be three darics, miss. Would you like one?"

Three darics? Even the man could tell that was a rip-off, she was sure of it! That many darics could feed a family for a week back in the old Andaimon.

Holland picked up a parsnip and turned it around in her hand.

Though the price was outrageous, she felt the temptation to purchase it nonetheless. Her stomach was churning now; she really should have eaten breakfast before running errands. She could afford the parsnip, but where did that leave the purple ribbon? If the vegetable cost three darics, surely a ribbon would cost even more. Not to mention, Mrs. Kershaw would find out. She always did.

Holland contemplated the tough decision when a jarring noise behind her made her turn around. The parsnip fell to the ground by her feet, rolling out of sight.

"You come back here and pay for that, boy! Don't think you

can get away with it this time!" an aggravated voice shouted from somewhere up the street.

A boy of about eleven years stumbled through a crowd of people and into Holland's view. In his hand was a goose egg.

The man at the vegetable stand swore under his breath before running out to the street. He grabbed hold of the boy's collar before he could run off again.

"Markus! What have I told you about stealing from other people's carts?" The man was clearly upset.

"Oh, thank heavens, Jaimus! You've got him." An angry and out of breath woman pushed her way through the gathering crowd of people and pointed an accusatory finger at the young boy. "I could have you reported to the authorities for this."

The man named Jaimus turned to face her, a concerned look on his brow. "I'm sorry, Hildaus, but that won't be necessary. I've told my son numerous times to behave himself, but I think now he won't forget it." He leveled Markus with a look that could skin the hide off a suckling pig. "Tell Mrs. Carole you're sorry and give her back the egg unless you wish to purchase it like a respectable man."

Holland watched the drama unfold. She could tell Markus was reluctant to hand over the egg by the way he cradled it. Almost like how she was reluctant to let the parsnip go. Speaking of which, where had it gone? She was still very hungry...

Holland spotted the vegetable behind one of the stand's wooden legs. Maybe the man would understand. He had his unruly son to take care of after all, and stealing a parsnip couldn't be nearly as bad as stealing a goose's egg. Her argument sounded *convincing in her head. She picked up the vegetable and chanced a glance in the boy's direction as she placed it in her basket. She stilled instantly.*

The boy stared right at her. Surely, he'd seen what she'd done and would give her away. She'd be caught like him! What would Mrs. Kershaw say? Holland hoped the woman would never have to find out. Fear wove its way down her legs and rooted her in place.

The boy continued to look at her, first eyeing her basket and then meeting her gaze. His hair was brown and wavy, his skin tanned from the sun, and his hands caked in grime as if he'd been playing in the dirt all day. A corner of his mouth quirked up in a smirk as he watched her, and then he had the audacity to wink.

What's this boy doing now? Heat rose up Holland's neck, sprouting into red blossoms on her face. He was going to rat her out, she knew it!

"My father's right. I'm sorry, Mrs. Carole. It won't happen again," Markus said. He held the egg out for the woman to take but not before Holland caught his gaze once more.

What was he doing with his head? He seemed to be motioning somewhere to his left. What was on his left? She glanced in that direction and saw the crowd slowly dispersing. There was nothing there, just a path that led out of town.

A thought struck her. Did he want her to take it? Was he helping her after all?

Holland didn't question it further. Mrs. Kershaw's wrath scared her more than anything, and her feet finally found their ability to move again. She dashed down the side path that led away from the main road.

"Well, I'd best be going now!" She heard Markus call behind her.

"Why, I never..." Mrs. Carole said, but Holland didn't hear the rest. She was already too far away.

She ran as fast as she could, relief flooding through her at the sight of some thick trees. If she could just hide behind one...

"Hey, wait up!"

Was that Markus behind her?

Holland didn't stop to find out. She kept running until she disappeared behind a tree, her pulse pounding in her head.

"Where did you go?" Markus called to her. "I'm not going to hurt you."

Holland hesitated before peering out from her hiding spot. She breathed a sigh of relief when she saw he was alone. But why had he come at all?

Finding courage, she stepped out from behind the elm and smiled timidly. "Hello." She dipped into a quick curtsy the way Mrs. Kershaw had always taught her.

"Hello." Markus bowed more slowly. There was a genuine smile on his face and two dimples to match when he straightened. "My name is Markus Fenn. What's yours?"

"Holland, just Holland."

"I like that. It suits you."

"Thank you." She found her timid smile now grew to match his confident one. For some reason, she knew this boy could be trusted.

Guilt pricked her conscience; she shouldn't have taken that parsnip. She reached into her basket and withdrew the vegetable, holding it out to Markus. "Th-this belongs to you. I shouldn't have taken it. I needed the darics for purple ribbon"

"No, you keep it. I admire a girl with guts! And besides, it technically belongs to me anyways, so think of it as a gift." Markus smirked.

Holland appreciated that thought, and she liked him even more.

The two of them exchanged giggles as they sat down to share the stolen parsnip under the shade of the nearby elms. The songs of twittering starlings sang above them from the boughs of the trees, and the clouds floated by, creating a patchwork design against the blue of the sky.

Between their chewing, Holland noticed Markus studying her with a gentleness she'd never seen from anyone before; his gaze was kind, almost perceptive, as if it housed a lifetime of unspoken promises.

If only she understood what his look meant.

Regardless, it was the beginnings of a special friendship, and one she knew she'd treasure for a lifetime.

Holland smiled to herself as she remembered such a fond memory. Of course, she wouldn't dream of stealing anything now, but she couldn't help laughing at the thought of it.

Ever since that day, Markus had been one of her closest friends. Her confidant. They told each other everything—well, most things anyway. And he was the only one she knew of who willingly left Kirkus to travel to the "filth" of Andaimon.

Holland had been concerned that Markus' mother would scold him for coming down so often, but it was quite the opposite. He said she would come down, too, if it wasn't for her weak limbs and younger children.

The thought warmed Holland's middle. Markus had a good family. If only others could see the injustice of how the poor were treated in Griskol. They didn't need the palace of Famar in order to live happily, but some fresh produce and the ability to earn an honest wage could go a long way. Too bad it would take talking to the king and queen in order for that change to happen...

Holland lifted the gloves she'd been working on so the light shone through them. They were soft and as weightless as feathers, the fabric dainty yet sturdy enough to endure countless uses. Hopefully, they would do.

She packaged them up and wrapped the boxes with some ribbon. It'd been twelve years, and she'd still yet to find the kind of purple Mrs. Kershaw demanded. Holland promised herself one day she would; she hated leaving any task unfinished. Until then, blue would have to do.

She pushed back on her stool and stood to leave the shop. The sooner she got this delivery out of the way, the sooner she could begin dreaming of traveling Griskol.

If only there was a way.

CHAPTER NINE
Holland

Dreaming of traveling seemed as promising as Griskol's love of magic. And currently, her job. There was no hope for it.

Holland sat at her table, fixing the stitching on a pair of gloves. One of the ladies at the Abermann's Tea House hadn't been pleased with Holland's work. It was rather ridiculous; the details were nearly perfect! At least the other woman, Mrs. Rook, had the decency to apologize on her friend's behalf, saying the gloves were exceptionally made. Holland had silently thanked the woman.

But as for the other one? At this rate, it seemed she might move into the Row in no time; she wouldn't have to walk as far to require Holland's business over such trivial matters.

Holland sighed, casting her work aside. She leaned forward in her chair and arched her stiff back. It was hard on her muscles to sit for so long every day.

Mrs. Kershaw spent most of her days lounging and hosting, complaining Holland didn't work hard enough to get good business or that there weren't enough darics to go around.

Holland had a *brilliant* idea.

If Mrs. Kershaw humbled herself enough to seek employment, both of those "issues" would be solved by now.

She sighed again. Sometimes the easiest solutions were often the ones most overlooked.

The shop bell jingled, and Holland lifted her head to see a young boy enter. His clothes were too small on his growing body, and in his arms was a bundle of bunched up duds.

"Hello, what can I do for you?" Holland asked, smiling.

"Hello, ma'am, I'm here to get these taken out." The boy handed the clothing to Holland.

"Sure! Anything in particular I should know about the garments before I begin?" She lifted from the bundle a pair of worn, brown pants not much bigger than her own slight frame.

"They're for Cadmon, my older brother. He's a Runner, so he told me to make sure the green armband stays."

"Green arm band?" She sifted through the pile and first untangled a worn cap before pulling out a faded blue jacket. Sure enough, a green armband was wrapped around the left sleeve. The number *17* shone on the fabric in clear, black ink.

"Cadmon said he could get killed without one if he got caught. He told me it's for his identification as much as it's for his safety."

Holland nodded, mulling over the new information. King Randor and Queen Rosin were now making Runners mark themselves... Since when?

"And who should Cadmon be thanking for doing all his bidding?" Holland quirked a brow.

The boy grinned. "Benjamon, ma'am," he said, bowing.

"Benjamon's a fine name. And you can call me Holland." She smiled. "I'm sure Cadmon realizes how wise he was in enlisting you to help him."

"I'm not so sure about that. He's too busy 'schmoozing the ladies,' whatever that means." Benjamon shrugged. "That's why he sent me."

Schmoozing the ladies? *Oh dear.*

It was clear Benjamon loved his brother, looked up to him even. Holland was glad he didn't know what 'schmoozing' entailed, and she hoped for his sake, he wouldn't for a few more years.

The thought pulled at her heart. Too many boys in this town were growing up as rakish flirts. She'd witnessed it firsthand. Sure, some of it was innocent, but that wasn't always the case. She only hoped Cadmon wasn't a cad like his name suggested and that Benjamon wouldn't follow in his footsteps if he was.

"Well then, maybe he could learn how to properly talk to a lady like his *younger* brother." Holland emphasized the word, pulling another smile from Benjamon. "When does Cadmon need these ready?"

Benjamon scrunched up his nose and scratched his head.

"How about I get them to you by the end of this week?" Holland saved Benjamon the struggle. She'd altered enough clothes to know the time-frame usually suited fine.

"That sounds good. He has another armband he can wear in the meantime."

Holland couldn't help her curiosity. "Do you know when these armbands started? Or why?"

"Two weeks ago, maybe less. I heard my father say it might have something to do with Famar. He guesses that with the birth of the king and queen's new baby, they've gotten stricter about who enters when and where in Griskol. Something about minimizing threats…"

Did Famar's fear know no bounds? Andaimon was hardly a threat.

So, the rumors were true. Did Markus know? He was closer to the gaggling tongues of the villagers than she was.

Queen Rosin was pregnant. But no longer, it seemed. It couldn't be a mere coincidence that the green armbands would be demanded right after the birth of their child. No, she was sure Benjamon's father was right. This was just further evidence of their control.

A sudden thought struck her.

"Does that mean any Runner with an armband can come and go as they please?"

"I guess. Two weeks ago, a sentry from Pembroke Fally came to our home and gave Cadmon two of them. Apparently Famar keeps a list of all Andaimon's Runners; they go by numbers instead of names now."

Holland looked at the green armband again, the black ink now a sign of bondage.

She needed to know more.

"And if someone were to say, pose as one of these Runners… Do you think Famar would check?" Holland wasn't sure why she was asking a twelve-year-old such strange questions, but Benjamon was proving most helpful.

Benjamon quirked a brow and crossed his arms. He seemed to hesitate before speaking, but proceeded anyway. "I don't know. I heard soldiers are now patrolling the upper regions and the border of Pembroke Fally like hawks. It sounds dangerous." The boy's eyes narrowed. "Why?"

Holland shifted in her seat. She cleared her throat. "No reason. Only curious."

Benjamon shrugged and didn't press further. "I'm curious, too, you know. My brother told me he's seen the executions... He was in Tiri getting salt when he heard a trumpet blare behind him. He said when he turned around, a soldier was reading a death summons for a man and his wife—something to do with magic or a mistaken identity. I can't remember which.

"They were hanged that day. Cadmon tried telling me what it looked like, the agony...but I stopped my ears. I have enough bad dreams already." Benjamon shook his head to prove his point. "That's what I get for being too curious."

Holland didn't miss the warning, nor could she blame him. She had nightmares of her own. Nothing like the details of a gruesome execution to make them worse. She smiled at Benjamon and took in the state of his clothing, noticing again how they didn't fit him correctly.

"You know, I think your clothes are in need of being taken out, too. Why don't you come by tomorrow and I can get working on yours as well as Cadmon's?"

Benjamon's smile grew wide and then it faltered, replaced by a knit in his brow. He shook his head. "I can't."

"Oh. Is something wrong?" Holland didn't like seeing this

helpful boy so sad.

"I-it's only…" He reached into his pocket and fished out something shiny. He laid his hand flat and two darics rested in his palm. "I only have enough for Cadmon's."

In truth, he didn't even have enough for that. Andaimon was poor, but the going rate for a seamstress' work was at least three darics a project. Most villagers knew that when they came here. Benjamon's family must have forgotten.

Or…

She had a sneaking suspicion that he was paying for this with his own money.

Holland reached over and rolled his fingers into a fist. She wouldn't take his darics. Not for Cadmon's clothes or for his.

"Keep them." She smiled.

The boy's eyes widened. "Truly?"

"Yes, truly. I want to do this for you." Holland couldn't help laughing at the surprised look on his face.

"But I need to pay you back somehow. If you won't take my darics, what can I give you?" Benjamon seemed bewildered, like he had never been given an ounce of grace in his life.

"How about when you come by tomorrow, I can let you know then?" Holland hoped the boy wouldn't remember, but maybe it would appease him for the time being.

"Okay!" Benjamon nearly knocked a small stool over in his excitement. He steadied the wooden piece of furniture and pocketed his money once more.

Holland stifled a laugh. She could tell he needed the darics more than she did. Mrs. Kershaw never had to know.

Benjamon headed toward the door, but before leaving, he looked over his shoulder, his grin reaching his ears. "Thank you, Miss Holland. Now I can get my mom a birthday present."

Holland's heart swelled. Benjamon was a wonder. She hoped he'd always stay this sweet.

"I'm sure she will love that."

Benjamon left the shop, whistling. The shop bell mimicked his joy, and Holland was left feeling deeply satisfied.

She wouldn't be getting paid, but it was for the best. Besides, Benjamon had given her priceless information about Griskol.

Now that she knew green armbands were required for Runners, and one just so happened to be sitting right in front of her, she had an idea. An idea that didn't seem so impossible anymore.

She got up and walked to the trunk set against the back wall. She lifted the lid and rummaged through the layers of fabric, pushing aside fraying bonnets and torn skirts. Finally, she pulled out a pair of pants, a jacket, and a cap, all of which were stained, frayed, and sported holes.

She gathered the clothes, biting her lip. She would fix them up. She'd fit the role.

But if she wasn't careful, this new idea could very well get her killed.

CHAPTER TEN
From "The Tale of Endlewood"

*T*he past few weeks were tedious and tiresome. The activity near the border was nothing to report. No one showed up, and there was no bloodshed. My stomach is only too thankful, though my body is itching for action...

My palace is almost finished, but answering the countless questions about which wood to use for the furniture and what herbs to grow in the greenhouse were not what I had in mind. My patience is stretched thin; I can only sit still for so long. The nonstop inquiries have pushed me to retreat yet again.

I pace the oaks near the ocean, letting the salty breeze sweep the hair across my forehead. I hesitate to walk on the sand, to step foot into the light.

This place is the only spot of sunshine in my new home, the place where the sun meets the earth.

The forest is dense all around me, the canopy an endless sky of deep green. It's cool and humid at the same time.

Just one step forward, and the harsh sun could change it all.

I don't often need the sunlight, but on rare occasions, I can't *stay away. All those weeks traveling at sea have somehow branded the sun's memory into my skin. I come for a recharge. For a way to feel myself again. To try to remember.*

But not often.

At one time, Lamia had been beautiful. I still hope it can be.

Images flit through my mind. Of wood lilies and zinnias dotting the grove near Harfooth's Mill, the bubbling brook twining through the maple trees, the ravens fluttering about the guild where I often retreated, and the women and children dancing among the sheep and heather… All to be replaced by screams and smoldering ash.

A bitter feeling twists in my gut, and I can only account for it as nostalgia gone awry…or guilt—a form of weakness.

I slap my cheek, sending a jolt of pain through my bones.

Such thoughts are dangerous—forbidden. Even from me.

Rule number three in the written scroll says as much. No one is to speak about what once was. To pine after it as some unrequited lover is the lowest of lows.

The new kingdom is here, and I am its king—a role I have spurned my entire life but have slowly grown to accept. I was a carefree prince before the dragons, often shirking my duty. I had never wanted to become like my father, angered that I had little choice in the matter.

But alas. Here I am. A leader—my destiny was chosen for me.

I stretch my hand beyond the shade of the oaks, letting the warm rays of light kiss my skin. The touch sends heatwaves up my arm and into my veins, recharging me.

The sun has learned the gentle art of caressing rather than the scalding of the Dyvrat. I am only too thankful.

I breathe deeply, soaking in the ocean, sun, and shade. Three worlds in one. It's only a little, but it has to be enough.

My hope is that it sustains me on my visit to the opposite border. A border often faced with intrusion, and where the Overseer makes sport of death.

I spin around, expecting to retreat back into the shadows, but pause when I come face to snout with the stag. His breath wafts against my skin and relaxes the plight of my hurried steps.

"Ah, moth ghràthidh, Elethün—earth dancer." I stroke his side and his presence eases something within me. "I'm glad you're here."

Elethün leans in closer and nudges me with his nose, his touch knowing. "You are weary. So I came."

The words weave their way into my chest. I am *weary. It's good to have someone who knows.*

The first day I met Elethün was the first day I came to this forest. It was his copper coat and deep-searching eyes which struck me the sharpest. For the first few months, I never saw much of him, but slowly, as I grew more accustomed to the wood and the wood to me, he came.

He flitted through the shadowing trees like a coppery beam of light, the crescent on his face like a beacon in the night. He looked to be dancing, and that's when I learned his name.

That day, the stag—for that is what he is, though now he is more friend than creature—claimed me as his own. He is the king beneath these trees, and so am I. He rules the beasts, and I the fae. And it's his leadership which spurs mine.

"Thank you, Elethün." I step away from the stag and head deeper into the woods, letting the shadows enfold me like a cloak.

He follows.

We don't speak, but his silent presence, in addition to my visit with the sun, are enough to embolden my steps. It's about time I make another trip to the perimeter.

* * *

Voices reach my ears as I stand at the edge of the forest. They are drawing nearer.

Ever since Nindrol took me to the Overseer weeks ago, I've made a habit of visiting the perimeter at least thrice a week on my own. Partly to escape Nindrol's questions and the prying eyes of Almar and kin, but mostly to strengthen my resolve. If I watch the killings, will that not make me a stronger leader? Knowing my people are safe?

Nindrol has said as much.

What's left of the Dyvrat's scourge seems to be dwindling. The last newcomer to my kingdom came over four months ago, and she was barely skin and bones. Lamia's living find themselves here in hopes of respite; I don't mind, as long as they remain peaceful.

According to Nindrol, that's what the Swamp Wispsnare is for—a pit of justice and reckoning. He created it, and though I don't think there's any need, he insists on its purpose. With the Overseer protecting us from the outside, he assures me of the need to protect us from within.

If the Dyvrats ever find this place, though, we'll be ruined regardless. In all my years of sneaking off to Lamia's guild, learning spells and defense charms, I've only read of one type of material that can pierce through their hellish hides. This material not only pierces their hides, but acts like a repellent and staves off the magic they feed on, rendering their blood cold. Two in one, it is their demise.

But we're fae. We don't possess the material. We are wielders of magic. Our weapons are words that come from within, and on occasion, a sharpened pike. In most cases, that's enough. The Overseer will give us aid, but against a Dyvrat, it might still prove weak.

Let us hope we never have to test the extent of its capabilities.

I scan the perimeter of the forest and wait nervously, my stomach flipping in circles.

Elethün stands by my side, but if anyone approaches, I know he'll disappear. He doesn't care for the Overseer, nor does he care to be seen. As far as I know, I'm the only one who has seen him. Perhaps the scent of my blood keeps him close, as if it runs through his veins alongside his own.

Speaking of which, blood outlines these woods. I have to remind myself it's for a good cause. For the protection of my kingdom. Those who wander too closely receive the penalty due their actions.

Elethün feels differently.

The voices are closer now. Elethün's ears twitch as he analyzes the approaching tones. Without a moment's hesitation, he bounds away and vanishes into the forest.

I stare after his retreat, already wishing he were still beside me. I suddenly feel weak. How am I to do this on my own? At any moment, these intruders will meet their fate, and I'll force myself to watch.

In truth, the watching has grown easier the more I've done it, the cries a death knell, signifying the safety of my kingdom.

Still, I wish it didn't have to be this way. And right now, the idea of bloodshed sends nausea up my throat. I'm only trying to do what I feel is right. To attack first before anything can attack us. No mercy. My gut twists again, souring my breakfast. Something like guilt stabs at my chest with a sudden thought.

Am I not much different than a Dyvrat?

I hastily push the worry aside. No. This is purposeful. I am no killer without reason.

I continue to wait. I can hear their words now. The voices are female, I can tell that much, and they are nearing the Overseer.

"I've never gone this deep before, Josi."

A laugh like twinkling bells follows. "We're hardly deep at all, Mirrand. Come on, only a few more steps. I want to see what's beyond that tree just over there." The voice moves like honey down a stream.

I am entranced.

I peer cautiously from my hiding spot, and my breath catches in my throat. I can hardly swallow.

Two women are bent near a tree, picking up morels and sticking wildflowers in their hair. One maiden is fair, the other...

I can hardly keep my mouth from going slack.

Hair like rivulets of night sky frame a porcelain face whose skin is as radiant as the moon. Eyes as green as emeralds peer from behind thick lashes, full lips revealing a cunning smile filled with curiosity.

I've never seen such beauty before in my life. And I know beauty.

My people are known for their looks. Our ways are filled with all forms of enchantments from poetry, to dwellings, to attire. We speak and breathe beauty in all things.

But this...

This woman is unlike anything I've ever seen, putting all the beauty I've ever known to shame.

Something like butterflies stirs in my chest, circling around my heart. I am unsteady, only my strong determination willing my knees to keep from buckling.

I watch as the two women draw nearer, and my pulse quickens. So much beauty, and to be destroyed at so young an age.

My heart tears in two, breaking. I can't stand to see this. I can't stand by and watch this lovely vision get mutilated before my eyes.

Without hesitating, I pick up a tree branch and hurl it in the direction some pace behind them. The log hits the boughs of a tree, crashing and splintering wood as it cascades to the forest floor.

The women turn their heads toward the sound, frowning.

"What was that?" Mirrand bites her lip, her eyes darting back and forth.

"Probably just an animal or a rotting tree limb." Josi shrugs.

Mirrand looks out to the clearing of the woods and scans the sky. "Either way, it's nearing lunchtime. Don't you think it's time to go home?" she asks, wringing her hands.

"You can go home if you'd like. I still want to explore." Josi smiles.

Blast. The one woman I really want to save isn't letting me.

"You sure you'll be okay on your own?" Mirrand asks.

"More than okay." Josi nods, assuring her.

Mirrand, seeming to believe her, turns to leave. She starts out slow and bolts the last stretch of woods as if the very forest itself were on fire.

Why can't this Josi girl do the same?

I can't shake my gaze; I watch her every move. An uncontrollable urge to protect her surges through my chest. If she comes any closer to the Overseer, I know what I'll have to do.

It looks like rescuing beautiful women is now on my list of duties next to spell-caster and king.

A spark of light pierces my soul. Maybe I've found my destiny after all.

CHAPTER ELEVEN
Holland

It was the same old routine day in and day out. Holland woke up, got dressed, and slid down the banister. The only plus side about this particular morning was there had been no Mrs. Kershaw at the bottom of the stairs to break her fall.

Oh, how she preferred the wall.

Holland worked on Cadmon's clothes, undoing the stitching around the cuffs and hems, hoping to stretch out the garments more than they already were. She wasn't sure how much longer he'd be able to wear them if he kept growing.

Her eyes lingered on the green band around the jacket's sleeve.

She'd gone to bed dreaming about all the possibilities that little band promised. At first, she'd thought about making her own, using it to traverse across Griskol. All she'd need was some green fabric and black paint.

But after this morning, she knew that wasn't possible. She'd spent hours searching the local fabric shops for the specific shade of green material, but it seemed Farmar had confiscated that too.

And she couldn't very well use another color.

That only left Cadmon's... But could she take it in good conscience? She'd already stolen once before, and Markus never let her forget it. But that was different.

This was different. This could mean her life or Cadmon's, depending on who got caught first.

Holland shook her head.

No. Not Cadmon's. Chances are, they would spare the boy— he was a Runner after all. This was his job. He had another armband. He was *supposed* to leave Andaimon.

She on the other hand... Was her life worth the risk?

Holland stilled, the material puckering in her grasp. She closed her eyes, conjuring up memories from her past.

This was something she couldn't shake. Ever since reading *The Tale of Endlewood*, things had seemed different. She'd felt different. Finding the story had been the sprouting of a seed she hadn't known was planted even years before then...during some point in her childhood. Maybe even when her parents had been alive.

Somewhere deep down, she'd always had a restless spirit that dreamed of something more. Dreamed that she didn't have to be confined to four walls for the rest of her life.

And that scared her.

If she didn't leave the Row soon, she never would. She'd waste away; old age and worn limbs would overcome her, and she would resent anything that held her back. Including herself.

No. As much as it pained her, she *had* to do this. Unlike *Endlewood*, she didn't want to end up alone and aimless. She needed to know where she belonged. She, too, had a story to tell, and she felt it wouldn't begin until she left home to find it.

Holland sighed deeply, her pulse pounding against her temples. The idea of finally leaving Andaimon was nauseating as much as it was thrilling.

She now knew what to ask Benjamon in return for the free alterations. She only hoped he wouldn't hate her for it.

The thought made her stomach twist. She liked having the boy's trust. It made her feel important. How would she go about bringing it up to him?

As if on cue, the shop bell rang, and the very boy stepped into the workspace, a bundle of clothes in his hands.

"Hi ma'—Miss Holland." He smiled sheepishly. "I brought the clothes like you asked."

"Good morning, Benjamon. It's nice to see you again." Holland motioned him closer.

He placed the bundle down and stepped back, looking as if he didn't know what to say.

His clothes fit him better today, but they were almost too big now, like he was trying to grow into the outgrown garments of his older brother.

"Thank you again for doing this." He wouldn't meet her gaze, scuffing his toe on the wooden floor.

"Is something wrong?" Holland leaned forward, trying to catch his line of sight.

He looked up, shrugging. "I spent last night rummaging through my stuff, looking for something to give you in exchange for the free work. I'm afraid if you ask me, I have nothing valuable to give you." He reached into his pockets and drew out a thimble, some very crinkled drawings of flowers, and what looked like a fish hook. "I had really hoped to find something better."

Holland's stomach twisted. Benjamon really was too thoughtful. In truth, she'd gladly take any of those things he offered, but she already had her sights set on something most precious.

This was it. The time to ask.

"You know, I already had something else in mind. Something that's already in this room." Holland eyed the green armband in front of her, sudden butterflies stirring in her chest.

"Really? Where is it? What is it?" Benjamon's gaze was everywhere, scanning the shelves and any surface of Holland's workspace.

"Right here." Holland held up the sleeve of the jacket.

Benjamon lifted a single eyebrow and cocked his head. "You want Cadmon's clothes? But I thought you were gonna fix them."

She shook her head, chuckling. "No, I only want this, the armband. I'll still fix his clothes, though. Don't worry."

Benjamon's face twisted from disbelief to confusion. "But why?" He crossed his arms over his chest, frowning. "Why do you want it?"

How else was she to explain this to him without coming right out and stating her true aim?

Here goes nothing.

"I want to be a Runner." There, she'd said it. And her heart was pounding like a hammer to an anvil.

"A Runner? But why?" Benjamon's brows puckered together.

Holland didn't want to bore the boy with her laundry list of reasons why. Mercy, she was growing tired of them herself.

"Have you ever wanted a chance to leave Andaimon, Benjamon?"

He shifted from one foot to the next, his gaze traveling from Holland's face, to the window, and then back to her. He nodded. "Ever since Cadmon got the chance."

"So, you understand, then. Sometimes there isn't so much a reason as there is a desire to go," Holland said. Oh, she *had* her reasons, but they felt too personal to share with the boy.

"Like you're afraid to miss out on an adventure. Afraid to be left behind and...forgotten." Benjamon filled in the gaps, his eyes wide. His words were heavier than he knew.

"Yes. And Cadmon's armband will help me with that."

"But you're a girl. All Runners are boys. What if you get caught?" Benjamon asked rapidly.

"Let's hope I don't." Holland bit her lip. "I haven't worked out all the details yet, but I have some old clothes and if I wear this on my arm, I might not need to." She held up the sleeve once more, the green armband a sign of her freedom.

"When will you leave?" he asked.

Holland looked outside, watching the sun flit through the clouds and the dappled light dance along the dusty street. How she longed to walk the cobblestone roads of Kirkus again. To smell the warm bread. To explore more than just the town. What would Tiri be like? And Pembroke Fally?

"Soon." She turned to him and smiled. "But all your clothes will be finished before I go." She assured him.

Soon. It felt too good to be true. But it was true, nonetheless. That is, if Benjamon said she could have the armband. She'd already pegged her hopes on taking it and going; she hadn't thought of what might happen if he said no.

"If you don't want—" Holland began.

"You can have it." Benjamon interrupted her, diffusing aloud her fears. "I want you to."

Holland released a relieved breath. She was taken aback by his willingness. "Thank you, Benjamon. I was hoping you'd say so."

He shrugged, playing with the hem of his shirt. "You're nicer to me than Cadmon. Plus, I don't think he'll miss it. He already has one, anyway." He paused his fidgeting and looked up. "Will you tell me what it's like?"

Holland nodded. "Every detail. Minus any gruesome parts. I'm sure it will be a grand adventure!" Her middle tingled in little dips, her pulse quickening at the thought. She would be free to find her purpose! But only if she wasn't stopped. She looked Benjamon in the eyes. "You mustn't tell anyone where I've gone. Will you promise me?"

It was a scary thing for a young boy to promise, but Benjamon looked trustworthy with his large, brown eyes. Plus, she figured he might like keeping a secret.

A mischievous smirk lifted the corner of his mouth. "I wouldn't tell a soul, Miss Holland. Your secret is safe with me."

Holland nodded. This was shaping up to be quite the plan.

She only hoped Benjamon would keep his end of the bargain.

CHAPTER TWELVE
Markus

Dirt coated Markus' skin the deeper he dug into the earth, his untouched shovel and spade resting behind him. He preferred working with his hands rather than his tools, though his mother often shook her head in amusement whenever he did.

"So much like your father, Markus. And you don't even realize it."

She said those words often.

And she had repeated them when he returned home from the river yesterday morning. He'd been drenched from head to toe as if he himself had been the fish rather than the one doing the fishing.

It wasn't too far from the truth.

Apparently, his father had had a penchant for similar antics, but Markus had only known him as a serious man. One who had instilled family values and a hard work ethic rather than fun and mischief.

It made sense his mother would know otherwise, though Markus wished he could say the same. If he had known his father would die so young, he would have asked more questions, spent more time with him… It was too late now, and his grief didn't let him forget that.

He continued to dig at the earth, only stopping when he realized he had reached the end of his row. He stood and arched his back, rotating at his hips. His spine crackled and popped, a sign that he'd been bending down for too long yet again.

He surveyed his work.

Three long rows of twenty holes stretched before him. Only two more rows to go and then he'd begin planting the beetroot and snow peas. If the crop yielded well like it did last year, he'd be feeding a hundred or so families for the winter months to come.

He only hoped the blight wouldn't hit this season…

The wagging tongues of his neighbors were never far. They were taking strides against their superstitions: only planting in broad daylight; watering the crop three times a day, but never before noon; locking up leftover seeds at the onset of a full moon… The list ran on.

"These are the best ways to protect against the enchantments of the Forbidden Wood," or so they said.

How the forest could affect Griskol's crop yield, Markus didn't know. People would rather blame something else for their problems than take ownership themselves.

He didn't usually pay much heed to their extreme protocols, though. Or at least, he hadn't before this morning.

The river had changed everything.

Now that Markus knew mermaids existed, he couldn't deny that magic did, too. Hadn't Adra enabled him to breathe underwater, if only for a moment?

If the rest of Griskol found out the truth, he was pretty sure King Randor would hire assassins to kill off the rest of the Kelbis. And then put a ban on sea-travel due to magic polluting the waters… It sounded crazy, but Markus had heard enough stories to know that the fear in Famar stretched far and wide.

Magic was—and would always be—forbidden.

But perhaps it shouldn't be. He had to remind himself that the world wasn't suddenly going off course because of it.

The thought shocked him as much as it worried him.

Maybe there was a place in Markus' realist world for the make-believe to dwell.

Maybe.

He shook his head. He was sounding more and more like Holland. The thought pulled another smile from his mouth.

What was he going to do with that woman?

It was that ridiculous *Tale of Endlewood* that was getting to him. She wouldn't stop reading it, and he couldn't stop thinking about it, especially now that it was rumored to be real.

Especially now that its touch had awoken icicles along his spine for the second time.

She should have left that book behind where they'd found it years ago…

It was a cool, spring morning. Markus had just turned eighteen and decided to sneak across the border of Andaimon to visit Holland. It was usually easier for him to visit her rather than the other way around.

He opened the door to Benneforth Row's Seamstress, flowers in his hand and a tentative grin on his face.

He'd seen his father bring his mother flowers often enough to know it made her happy. He hoped it'd do the same for Holland.

She turned to see him enter, her face lighting up like a star. "Markus! I hoped you'd stop by today. Happy birthday!" Holland smiled, her eyes traveling from him to the flowers in his hand. Her expression changed to wonder. "Oh, those are beautiful!"

"They're for you. I got them from that place you like to visit. Near the hedgerow past the trader's post." He walked over to her, placing the flowers on her work table. He wasn't sure how to go about arranging them, so he just left them there.

"Thank you! But aren't you the one who's supposed to get a gift today?" She smiled knowingly and stood up from her chair. She went to the bookshelf at the side of the room and pulled down a parcel wrapped in blue ribbon. She returned to Markus and held it out for him. "This is for you."

"Thanks." He smiled.

He loosened the ribbon before folding back the wrapping which revealed some sort of tan fabric within. Lifting it up, Markus noted the fabric was sewn into a circle. He had no idea what it was.

"Um, thank you, for...this!" He held up the material, trying to sound confident like he knew its purpose.

"Oh, Markus." Holland started laughing; she'd called his bluff. "It's to hold back your hair. You've told me how much it bothers you when you work. And since you won't cut it..."

"To hold back my hair?" Markus had said how annoying it

was to have what felt like a dog's rear end tickling his forehead while he farmed...and she had remembered that. But with this? He'd look ridiculous.

"You don't have to wear it," Holland said, trying to take it back.

"No." Markus raised his arm higher. "I want it." And I'll find something to do with it. *"Thank you for the thoughtful gift."*

Holland nodded. She returned to her flowers, brushing her hands along the soft petals and green stems, smiling to herself. "I've never been given flowers before. Is this why you came? To bring me flowers?"

"Well, I was hoping you'd want to go somewhere with me." Markus shrugged. He shifted from one foot to the other. He didn't realize giving flowers to a girl could feel so awkward.

"Oh, I'd love to! But Mrs. Kershaw..."

"It would only be for half an hour. That's all I've got anyways." Markus smirked. "My father doesn't know I'm gone."

"I don't know. I'd get in huge trouble if she found out." Holland bit her lip.

"I promise to make sure she doesn't!" Markus wasn't sure how he'd do that, but he'd gladly take the fall if it ever came to it. He was a man of his word, or at least trying to be. He'd stopped stealing things a long time ago.

"I guess if it's just for a short while..." Holland stood, grabbing her shawl and placing it around her shoulders before walking to the door. Each step forward seemed to bring her more confidence.

"You won't be disappointed!" Markus ran down the steps and

waited for her at the bottom while she locked up shop.

Holland followed after him, and once her feet hit the road, he grabbed her hand, leading her further into town.

They ran like that for a few minutes. Laughter seemed to bubble up from someplace deep in them both as it poured from their lips without hesitation.

Freedom had never tasted so good!

Markus led her around various wagons full of molding produce and through a narrow alleyway that opened up into a rundown courtyard. What looked like torn pieces of paper were scattered all about the mangled stone, and in the middle was a pit filled with ashes.

They finally slowed enough to catch their breaths.

"Why did we come here?" Holland asked, looking around the disheveled area. She used her toe to pry up something that looked like a book's spine.

"On my way to come see you, I saw this place. I figured you'd be as curious to explore it as me." Markus could tell he was right by the way Holland nodded, her eyes growing wider with each discovery.

"What do you think happened?" Holland bent down and picked up a match.

Markus stepped closer and neared the pit. He grabbed a stick off the ground and poked inside it, pushing the ashes around. Charred logs moved and revealed blackened paper beneath.

"It looks like a book burning."

"A book burning? But why would anyone…?" Holland paused, picking up a half-charred book from off the ground. She

stood and read the title. "An Apothecary's Magical Guide
To...*the rest is cut off." She pursed her lips and walked to another
section of the courtyard, yanking two half-burned books from
beneath a pile of leaves. "This one says,* From Herbs to Fairy
Gardens, *and this is a book about mermaids." She looked at
Markus. "All these books have to do with magic!"*

*"It seems Griskol isn't taking lightly to a little daydreaming,"
Markus joked.*

*He'd grown up knowing Griskol's wariness toward the make-
believe—toward anything magical. Most people were
uncomfortable with it and preferred it stayed in stories where it
belonged. And with the passing of the old king, his son Prince
Randor, along with his wife Rosin, had come to power a few
months ago, claiming the throne as king and queen. Since then,
things had only gotten worse.*

*Magic was banned. Any and all forms of it. Even the kind that
promoted imagination.*

*"You don't think this is the new king and queen's doing, do
you?" Holland asked.*

*"Maybe not them directly, but I'd wager it's some of their
men. This is only the beginning, Holland. I fear it may get worse."*

*Holland continued to poke and prod the debris along the
ground as if she was searching for something. She paused when
she reached a certain stone beneath her foot, bending to peer at it
closer.*

*Markus watched her as she traced the stone with her fingers.
She creased her brow, as if very focused, and began to pry the
rock loose. It came up with little difficulty, as if it had been*

waiting to be lifted.

"Markus, look!" Holland waved him over.

He didn't know what she was showing him. Some pill bugs or ant hills, maybe? When he reached her side, he was just as shocked as she was.

How in Griskol...

"It's a book!" Holland reached into the hole and pulled out the worn looking novel, its leather face scratched and discolored. "And it's completely whole! Someone must have hidden it here on purpose..." She turned the book over in her hands. "The Tale of Endlewood. *I've never heard of this one. Have you?"*

Holland gave the book to Markus who gently took it in his hands. He turned the novel over and felt a stinging creep along his spine. It started low and traveled toward his ear.

He twitched his shoulder, shrugging it off. He must have pulled a muscle or done something to provoke his back while working the day before.

He tried ignoring it, opening the novel and leafing through the pages. Suddenly, the pain was a fiery stabbing like a million arrows had lodged themselves in his skin. Sparks of red colored his vision, and he swore under his breath as he lost all will to stand.

He released the book; a gasp caught in his throat.

"Markus? Are you okay?" Holland dropped to his level, her hands on his arms. "Markus?"

He blinked, the red dissipating from his vision. He could see. He could breathe. He was okay. His back killed him, but it was more bearable now.

What had just happened?

Markus hadn't experienced that amount of pain since... He reached back and touched the space where the scar met his neck. How long had it been?

"Markus? Answer me!" Holland's voice shook him from his thoughts.

"I'm okay. I just...tripped." Markus lied. He didn't want to worry her further.

"Tripped? I watched you fall!" Holland crossed her arms over her chest.

She wasn't stupid. She could see right through him.

"I promise I'm okay. I just lost my balance." He wasn't lying there. He'd lost his balance from too much pain.

"I don't know if I can trust you, Markus Fenn. But since it is your birthday, I will." She stood, and after making sure he was well, picked up the book lying on the ground. "I'm taking this home with me."

Markus didn't think that was such a good idea. But how could he explain that to her? He didn't know for certain if it was the book's fault his spine had been demobilized. That couldn't be right.

Chances were, it was a coincidence. All this talk about magic: magic books, banning magic books, burning magic books... It was getting to his head.

"Are you ready to go back?" Holland extended her hand to Markus. In her other she held the book.

Feeling like a fool, he heaved a sigh before placing his hand in hers.

He had a feeling he'd remember this day for the rest of his life, no matter how much he tried to forget certain parts of it.

It had been five years since Holland had first discovered *The Tale of Endlewood*, and in truth, Markus hadn't remembered the intensity of the stinging pain since, the way it clouded his vision and weakened his knees. It wasn't until he'd held the book for the second time a few nights ago that the memories came rushing back.

He reached a hand toward his neck and massaged the tender skin beneath his shirt. The stinging had stopped, but he could still feel the lingering bite deep in his bones.

At the base of his neck, his hand brushed against Holland's hair band which reached behind his ears and stretched across his forehead. He'd worn it almost daily since she gave it to him; it didn't take long for Markus to realize it was useful as much as it was special.

Holland had been right; he'd never cut his hair. He'd made that vow a long time ago—since the day he got the scar. He didn't want anyone to see it. To worry or think of him as strange…marked, especially in a land such as Griskol.

The less people knew, the better. That way he could live his life the way it was always supposed to be. A farmer's son. Tilling the land. Taking care of his family.

Markus had just finished digging his fourth row of holes and was onto the last one when something hit him square in the back.

His jaw ticked to the side. Dru needed to learn Markus wasn't target practice.

He turned and shielded his face from the sun, ready to give his brother a lesson on throwing. But it wasn't Dru who was walking toward him.

"Well, look who it is." Markus couldn't keep the smile from his voice. "Is taking out my spine your way of a greeting now?"

"Ah, pity. And here I was thinking I'd aimed for your head." Calsius Brenner walked closer, his short, blonde hair a direct contrast to Markus' longer and darker strands. A burlap bag with the Fenn Farm insignia was strung over his right shoulder.

"Stealing from me, again, I shouldn't wonder." Markus laughed. "And broccoli?" He picked up the offending weapon and faced his friend. "Good thing you've always been a poor shot."

Calsius laughed, and the two men embraced, slapping each other on the back. Calsius had always been slightly shorter, but he was equally as broad and strong. They'd had countless arm wrestles to prove it. "Watch it, Fenn. I was being nice." He stepped back. "Besides, I figured you could use a snack."

"A snack? Are you my mother?" Markus guffawed.

Calsius shrugged. "You work more than you eat, you know." He pulled out another head of broccoli and took a huge bite out of it like the vegetable was an apple.

"Some people have to work to make a living around here." Markus resumed digging.

"Yeah, but not for the entire village. You work too hard, mate."

"I don't work nearly enough." Not at the rate his thoughts kept racing, anyway.

"I think we're saying the word 'work' too much. Which brings me to my next point. Why not take a break? Hit something at the smithy like old times." Calsius tossed his half-eaten broccoli in the air and caught it in his hand. "A few hours won't make the field go fallow. Besides, my mum made pottage stew. You know how much you love Hanaus Brenner's cooking."

He had a point. Markus was growing tired, and he *did* love her food. Besides, hadn't he wanted to talk to Calsius earlier? Maybe this was perfect timing.

Then he'd finish the field.

And then maybe visit Holland. Surely their conversation was just a passing fancy. She wouldn't actually do something as rash as *leave*, would she?

Blast. He really couldn't stop thinking about her.

He needed Calsius more than he realized.

"Let me wash up first."

"Since when have you ever washed up for me?" Calsius smirked. "Am I your sweetheart now, too?"

Throttle him. Markus would have if he wasn't provoked to laughing. Calsius was a nuisance. "Fine. Let's go."

Markus left his tools behind and headed toward the main road, his best mate, Calsius, by his side.

He was starting to feel better already.

CHAPTER THIRTEEN
Markus

The sound of a hammer clanging against metal reverberated in the small forge, consistent like church bells, though much less appealing to most.

Markus thought it was wonderful. It brought back fond memories, filling him with ease alongside the already-devoured pottage stew in his stomach.

"See, didn't I tell you this would do the trick?" Calsius walked over to him, iron tongs in his hand.

Markus shifted his position and held the hammer above the old pauldron he'd been beating the life out of. It was, in fact, just what he'd needed.

"It's been too long since I've hit anything." Markus released a long breath. "Too long since we've done this sort of thing."

Markus and Calsius had grown up a neighborhood apart. Markus' farm plot was in the southwest part of Kirkus, and Calsius' family forge was in the west right off the main road. They'd gone to the local school as kids and had been inseparable since then.

But it'd been years since Markus inhaled the scent of burning metal. Heard the hissing iron as it cooled in water. Felt his shirt stick to his body from the heat of the flaming tongues of the furnace.

He'd missed this.

"Figured we both needed it." Calsius clapped a hand on Markus' shoulder before walking away. He reached a table laden with horseshoes and picked up an iron rod before stuffing it in the fire.

"How are things with Damirus?" Markus asked, tracing his fingers over the jagged carvings along the hammer's handle. He'd engraved his initials in the wood when he was ten. Had so many years passed already?

He looked around the room and noted tall, bronze spears leaning in the far corner against some wooden shelves. *Still? Some things never change.* They'd been there for as long as he'd remembered. Markus had always wanted to play with the weapons as a child, but Mr. Brenner wouldn't let his son or Markus anywhere near them.

"One touch, and they'll take your skin clean off."

That had only served to fuel Markus' curiosity all the more. How could spears be more dangerous than a sword? Mr. Brenner compromised, though, and trained the boys with iron replicas, and that had appeased them for a time.

But much like the pain of his scar, he'd soon forgotten about the spears entirely.

"Oh, you know. Same old. She wants me to propose soon..." Calsius brought Markus' attention back to him. He took the rod out of the fire, scrutinized it, and thrust it back in again.

"And?" Markus lifted a brow.

"And I told her I will. Just not yet." Calsius shrugged, smirking.

"What are you waiting for exactly? You've found your woman—why prolong it? It's not like you're getting any younger."

Calsius was only older than Markus by nine months, but he'd never let him forget it.

"Trust me, I have it all figured out." Calsius reached a finger to his head and pointed at his temple. "Right in here."

"Well, that's not a scary place, so I'm sure it will all work out great." Markus snorted and lifted his hammer. He was about to strike the pauldron again when Calsius' words stopped him.

"What about you? How are things with Holland?"

His stomach dropped. *Great question.*

Markus tightened his grip on the hammer and smacked the pauldron instead of answering.

"That bad, huh?" Calsius laughed, retrieving the rod from the fire and started hammering it into the shape of a horseshoe.

"I can't figure her out." Markus sighed, running a hand through his hair. "She drives me wild."

"Ah, yes. Love can do that."

"Love?" Markus stilled.

"You've loved her for years, Fenn. Why can everyone admit it but you?" Calsius shook his head, thrusting the finished shoe back in the fire. He turned it and prodded it with his tongs.

Everyone? Markus swallowed. Was that true?

He watched as Calsius took the horseshoe out and laid it on his anvil. But this time, he took a chisel out of his back pocket and hammered its tip into the hot metal. Then it went back into the fire again.

"I don't want to ruin our friendship." The excuse sounded poor even to *his* ears.

"I think you have a better chance of ruining it if you do nothing."

Markus shook his head. "She wants to leave Andaimon—to travel Griskol. But it's a fool's errand; does she not see the risk in it? In her mind, she has no reason to stay."

"No reason to? You sell yourself short, mate." Calsius retrieved the orange-tinged metal and stuck it into a bin of cold water. A hissing sound followed, tauntingly resounding in the small smithy.

Markus wanted to believe Calsius. He wished he could. What was stopping him from figuring it all out? He'd never told Holland how he'd felt.

Was it love?

Deep down he knew it was; but he'd hardened his heart at the possibility, not wanting to get his hopes up. He'd known her for years—twelve, to be exact. If she hadn't shown signs of interest before, why would she now? Especially when she wanted nothing to do with Andaimon anymore.

Markus ran a hand through his long waves and groaned inwardly. No matter where he went, Holland was always on his mind. His hand reached the base of his neck and touched the tip of his scar.

The subtlest pinprick of cold reached his fingertips even in the stuffy room.

Endlewood.

The name churned his stomach.

In the calming familiarity of the smithy, he'd almost forgotten about the fin-maiden, Adra, and her goading words. He'd almost forgotten that Holland's book was supposedly real. That mystical beings allegedly lived in Griskol.

He'd almost forgotten.

Almost.

He needed to tell someone. He needed to know he wasn't crazy.

He cleared his throat. "Have you ever heard of *The Tale of Endlewood*?"

Calsius tilted his head and cocked an eyebrow. "No, can't say I have."

"Figures."

"What about it?" Calsius asked.

"It's a banned book. It was meant to be burned years ago." Markus said.

"Ah, *magic*. The greatest fear in Griskol. Speaking of which, there are new rumors in Famar." Calsius rolled his eyes. For years, his family had outfitted Famar's soldiers. The Brenners were privy to insider information sooner than most. "Randor and Rosin are cracking down on Andaimon's Runners since the birth of their baby. Always worried about something, those two."

A baby? So, the rumors were true, then?

Calsius explained to Markus about green armbands

with numbers on them being used as identifiers.

"They're to be earmarked like cattle?" Markus gripped the hammer again. "To what lengths will this madness reach?" He asked the second part more to himself.

Calsius sighed. "It's only a matter of time before they start requiring us 'common folk' to identify ourselves, too. Who's to say I'm not some interloper from Andaimon trying to earn an extra daric? Or some arrogant Snoot from Tiri trying to upend our rural life? Pretty soon, all our liberties will be stripped and laid bare, prostrated at the feet of Famar. I say, let people be and do as they wish; there'd be more peace in these lands because of it." He shook his head. "I fear it'll only get worse from here."

It'll only get worse. Markus could speculate what that meant. He had said similar words to Holland years ago. He hadn't realized just how right he'd turn out to be.

Markus massaged his temples and closed his eyes, thinking. If these armbands were required for travel, and if Griskol confiscated all green fabric in the regions to avoid falsifications...

That meant Holland couldn't leave. Not safely, anyway.

He hadn't wanted her to be a Runner, but in his mind, it was no longer him who was holding her back. It was Griskol.

Relief flooded him.

Holland wasn't his. He couldn't force her to stay no matter the circumstance. But Famar could.

What if she didn't listen? Markus' throat went dry at the thought.

He knew she was stubborn at times; when her mind was set on something, she usually followed through. Being a Runner was dangerous to begin with—now even more so. If it came to it, Markus cared too much for her safety to encourage something so foolish. And to travel alone as a woman... He'd have to say something.

He glanced out the window of the smithy and saw dark clouds rolling in. It was getting late, and by the looks of it, a storm was approaching fast.

He would visit her in the morning and tell her the news he'd just learned. There was even less of a chance she'd heard of it. He only hoped she would make the sound decision herself and drop this foolhardy dream on her own.

If he was lucky.

CHAPTER FOURTEEN
From "The Tale of Endlewood"

*T*he woman named Josi draws nearer, her emerald eyes darkening beneath the shades of the oaks as she scans the canopy above her.

Her beauty draws me like a midge to a flare. Some things can't be avoided—the attraction, instinctual. Like we were made for one another.

I push forward my hair to hide my ears and take a steadying breath before stepping out from behind the trees. A nest of moths flutters in my stomach to accompany the butterflies already there, and when Josi notices me, they tear through my skin and push up my throat.

Enthralled doesn't even begin to describe it.

Poets have it all wrong. Any muse to ever inspire a sultry word has never met Josi. In fact, there are no words in my native tongue that render this beauty justice.

I can hardly breathe.

"Hello." Her eyes smile as much as her mouth, joy written in the laugh lines creasing delicately in the corners.

I can hardly speak.

"These are beautiful woods, are they not?" She inclines her head to the side, studying me with a curiosity I find only increases her appeal.

She must think me daft.

I clear my throat, my tongue sticking to the roof of my mouth. "They are, indeed." I manage a weak smile, but I fear it comes across as a grimace.

"Do you live nearby? I've never seen you before—in town, I mean." She twirls a morel between her fingers, belaying only a hint of nervousness.

"I..." I can't fathom telling her the truth. Telling her where I prevail is inviting death to her doorstep. She can never enter these woods and live, not while the Overseer is at work. She can never know who I am. "I live close by. Just beyond those hills, near the hedgerow past the trader's post." I point in the direction of the clearing where the town resides a little way behind.

I know enough of the neighboring village to identify countless landmarks. Enough to know which buildings are vacant and which ones are let. Enough to know I'd never want to dwell in such a place.

"How strange! I live near there, too. You would think we would have run into one another."

"You would think." Studying the beautiful woman before me, I am resolved that to imagine a world with Josi would make even the dingiest and grimiest of places appear like a palace fit for a king.

Even such a place as a town.

"Do you explore these woods often?" she asks.

Again, with the woods. I need to bring her attention elsewhere. I rub a hand down my arm to steady my nerves. As poets, we are often deceivers. But something about Josi compels me to tell her the truth, that somehow, she holds the key to all of life's elusive secrets.

I lie to her instead.

"I have once or twice. But they are filled with thistles and overgrown thickets. The morels you love end here, I'm afraid."

She can't know the depth of that lie. The heart of the woods holds a treasure trove of morels and all things edible and beautiful. In fact, my palace is being built near a patch of them with a ravine that pools into a lush basking trough and ethereal lights strung from the trees above. Magical doesn't even begin to describe what it will become.

Then again, it doesn't compare to Josi.

"'Tis a pity. I had so wished to venture further. Won't you explore with me anyway?" Hope rises with the inflection of her voice.

My heart beats unrhythmic pulses against my ribs. She has invited me to go with her. Can happiness exist so close to a wall of death? If circumstances were different. If I was only human. I hate to disappoint her.

"I-I can't, I'm afraid. I am needed back...home. Won't you come with me? I can walk you to your cottage."

The question assumes too much. In fact, I am stunned by my boldness. But maybe she will say yes. Maybe I won't have to pry her from the Overseer's claws with force.

She studies me again, and for a beat I think she'll say no. Then her grin spreads wide, revealing perfectly white teeth as glistening as the stars. She nods. "I'd like that."

My shoulders relax.

"But first...what's your name?" Her question startles me.

I run my tongue across my teeth, my title on its tip from months of use. But just as quickly, I cast it off as carrion for the birds. "Vesstamon." Her presence strips me bare. I am merely a fae willing to take the role of a man. I'd willingly change my name a thousand times for her.

"Josilland." She nods, dipping into a small curtsy, her dark hair falling away from her shoulders.

Josilland. The name tastes sweet on my tongue, like sugar on a wood lily. And what I'd give to run my hands through her dark tresses.

I take another steadying breath. One thing at a time. To simply bask in her presence is enough. To know that Josi will be safe for another day.

I extend my arm toward her, gesturing into the clearing ahead of us. "Shall we?"

She looks at my arm and wraps her hand around it, drawing nearer. She smiles boldly. "We shall."

My pulse quickens at her touch, and I wonder if she feels the attraction, too. My head spins, fuzzy and yet clearer than it's ever been before. I'm walking on a cloud, the sun guiding my steps.

With her side pressed against mine, I forget I am the ruler of the kingdom I'm leaving behind—a ruler alongside Elethün—of a kingdom I was steadily growing accustomed to.

But it seems I was wrong. Perhaps I am the author of my own destiny after all.

For a moment with Josi is worth forsaking all else.

CHAPTER FIFTEEN
Holland

It was well past sunset, and the night's darkness was nearly black—the kind of blackness that happened when the stars shielded themselves behind a skein of storm clouds. Even the moon seemed to be missing. Within the hour, rain would fall. And Holland would welcome it.

The dim candle on her bed side table was the only source of light, illuminating her bedchamber in soft waves of dancing warmth. She worked diligently, her fingers moving faster than she'd ever needed them to before in her life. She was finishing up Benjamon's alterations; Cadmon's alterations were already done and sat beside the clothes from the trunk, stretched out on her bed.

She couldn't risk working in the shop downstairs. Too many prying eyes would see the flickering rushlight and wonder why she was up so late, burning away precious daric. Candles were sparse in Andaimon and few families had them. Holland and Mrs. Kershaw were fortunate to own two, but they were only to be used in emergencies.

This was an emergency.

Once Holland finished the alterations, she would be sneaking out of Benneforth Row well before dawn. Timing was everything, and she only had so much.

A door slammed somewhere nearby, and Holland dropped her needle, her hand jumping to her chest. The reverberating noise settled somewhere deep in her middle, goading her to keep going with her task.

It was probably just a stable hand letting in the horses, or perhaps a loose hinge gone awry in the wind. Either way, it was over.

The stillness left in the wake of the noise seemed to sprout eyes and watch Holland, the hair on the nape of her neck standing on edge.

Why was everything more terrifying in the dark?

She picked up the sewing and did two more stitches before cutting the remaining thread clean. It would have to do. She folded the clothes and placed them beside Cadmon's. Hastily, she scribbled a note and tucked it underneath the folds of Benjamon's shirt.

He'd find it and read it, keeping her secret. He had given her a chance at freedom, and he knew only a portion of what it meant to her. It was the least she could do to say 'thank you.'

Holland pushed off from the bed and grabbed a worn coin pouch in the back of her dressing cabinet. She peered inside and counted the darics within: twelve gold coins; they would have to be enough. It was more than what Mrs. Kershaw would ever let her keep—hence why Holland had had the foresight to hide some of her earnings.

She took two of them and slipped the darics inside the front pocket of Benjamon's shirt. A gift. If she was lucky, he'd think they were his to begin with.

She stood and undid the lacings of her dress, the fabric pooling at her ankles as she stepped out of the skirt. She grabbed the sprawled clothes off her bed, sliding on a brown pair of pants. Next came the jacket. She looked down at her chest and bit back a groan. Thankfully, she was a petite woman, but anyone looking at her would realize she had more curves in places than any man should.

Holland grabbed a roll of extra fabric and wrapped it under her arms, binding her chest closer to her ribs. She took a deep breath, the action more constricting than she realized. But she'd get used to it.

She fitted her arms through the sleeves of the jacket, buttoning the front from the top down. She turned and faced the cracked mirror hanging behind her door.

She gasped. What stared back through the looking glass wasn't someone Holland expected to see. She didn't recognize the rugged woman standing there in baggy clothes. The garments fit her, but they were made for someone broader and taller. They left just enough extra fabric in all the right places to hide her obvious curves.

Relief surged through her. She might be able to pull this off.

Her gaze traveled to her face and then her hair. A sinking feeling replaced that brief spark of hope.

Holland trailed her fingers through her long, thick strands and gathered all her hair over her shoulder. There were no boys in

Andaimon with hair like this, let alone hair that landed well below their waist. Only Markus' seemed to rival her length, but even still, his had the decency to stop near his shoulders.

She eyed the scissors laying on the bed next to Benjamon's and Cadmon's clothes. She'd never cut her hair before—distant memories of Mrs. Annbert combing her fingers through it as a child came to mind. It wasn't the same as having her mother's, but she imagined it would have been similar—lovelier, perhaps. She held onto those memories.

Like Markus, Holland would never cut her hair. But she figured it was for a much different reason.

Instead, she eyed the cap that had fallen on the ground. The blue fabric matched that of the jacket she was already wearing. She divided her hair into three strands and braided them as tightly as she could, winding the braid up and around her head before pinning it in place. Last, she tugged the cap over it all.

She stood and found a few wisps of dark hair framing her face. Holland tucked them in. The cap bulged slightly in places, but she hoped it would pass all the same.

She studied herself once more in the mirror. Aside from the small lift at the end of her nose, Holland could easily pass as a young boy. Her green eyes were veiled in thick lashes, but thankfully most boys in Andaimon had fuller eyelashes than the girls. A fact that was hardly fair.

A flash of lighting suddenly illuminated her room; it was later followed by a crack of thunder which sounded far away. The pitter-patter of rain began, the droplets now hitting her window. It was only a matter of time before it worsened.

She should leave now.

For all her eagerness to go, Holland's feet remained rooted in place. She continued to stare at herself in the mirror, all twenty years of her life feeling like accumulated dust just swept clean. What if Griskol wasn't what she expected? What if she didn't find what she was looking for and ended up even more lost than before? The thought of unmet expectations was like a fist squeezing her heart.

At least in Andaimon, Holland had her dreams. But if she were to leave, what then? Would she get to live them, or would she wander aimlessly until she went mad? Was it worth the risk of leaving all she knew behind?

Markus. The thought of him made her stomach dip.

Could she leave *him*? In all her dreams of traveling Griskol, she hadn't confronted that question. He was the closest thing to family she had; they would always be friends. That hadn't changed over the years, so why would it now that she was leaving? She'd see him again—one day.

Lightning flashed beyond her window, illuminating the room in electric light before casting it in flickering shadows once more. Holland glanced outside, but it was pointless. She couldn't see anything.

She fidgeted with her shirt, running her fingers along the buttons and heaved a sigh. It was now or never.

She fitted her pouch of darics around her neck, stuffing it beneath the folds of her garments. Then she grabbed *The Tale of Endlewood* and put it in one of the deep pockets on the side of her pants. She would travel light. Like most Runners who purchased their goods from other regions, she'd leave with nothing. But in her case, she wouldn't come back home.

Home. The word soured on Holland's tongue.

If her trip was successful, she wouldn't need to go back to Andaimon for a long time. There was nothing for her here, anyway.

She scanned her drafty room and took in the surroundings one last time before grabbing Benjamon's and Cadmon's clothes and leaving her bedroom.

If she left now, she'd make progress well before the first signs of dawn.

CHAPTER SIXTEEN
Markus

Cold water splashed across Markus' face, the sting numbing the potency of his bad dream. He was at the river again; the sun had only just begun to soften the darkness that came before dawn. He'd awoken early—too early—and walked down to the water, hoping for a chance to clear his head.

And as always, Hamish was by his side.

Ever since Holland had shown him *The Tale of Endlewood* again, his back seemed to be giving him more problems than ever—taunting him through familiar nightmares. He couldn't remember how he got his scar, but last night's horror felt like the story he couldn't recall.

In his dream, he was a young boy—not yet thirteen. He was in the woods by the very same river he was at now, only he was fashioning a bow and quiver. Something rustled in the brush behind him, startling him and causing his hand to slip on his father's pen knife, the cool blade nicking his thumb.

He sucked on the wound, trying to staunch the bleeding, only to have his vision go red and a cry wrenched from his lips. First came the searing pain and then what felt like an icicle's tip carving a ravine along his spine. Fire. Burning. Blurring. His stomach heaved, and blood pooled around his ankles.

That's when Markus had awoken, his brow creased with sweat and his spine on fire as if the dream had been real. He hadn't had a nightmare like that in years. Not since he'd first received the scar. But each time the dream had been a little different: he was either making a bow, carving a tool, or building a fort in the trees. The only consistent parts of the dream were his father's knife and the blood on his thumb before the aching pain, followed by an earthy taste in his mouth when he awoke, as if he'd eaten dirt. And the scenery—it was always here in the woods by the river.

That's partly why Markus went to it. Instead of running from the memories, he tried to recall them. But no amount of racking his memory was proving helpful.

He also hoped that Adra might show herself again. There were still questions he needed answered, and he was getting sick of overworking his body in order to calm his thoughts. His mother was growing tired of it, too.

Twenty minutes had gone by, and Adra still hadn't appeared. Perhaps it was just wishful thinking that she would.

Markus stood to leave, Hamish's tail wagging against his legs. He'd visit Holland this morning, instead. Something pressed in the back of his mind that he should have showed up last night, but he pushed the thought away. Last night Calsius had needed him— rather, he had needed Calsius.

Something orange flashed in his peripheral vision, and Markus turned to face the river. A mermaid darted through the water, her glistening scales dancing in the current. It was Adra—she'd come back!

Markus couldn't believe his luck. He took two steps in the direction of the stream and faltered. A man cloaked in gray rowed a wooden boat through the water, the bow slicing the river in half.

Thallon? Was this the guy Adra had pined for?

Instinctively, Markus sidestepped and disappeared behind a cluster of trees, his heart picking up speed. Hamish still lingered on the path, his head cocked to the side in confusion.

"Hamish, come here," Markus whisper-shouted.

The dog didn't listen; he merely started sniffing the ground.

Markus heaved a sigh and poked his head from behind the trees. The man and Adra still hadn't seen him. Yet. Thanking the fact that Hamish hadn't let out one of his monstrous barks, Markus grabbed him by the scruff and hauled him behind the trees. Just in time, too, because Markus was sure they had just looked in his direction.

He took a few seconds to steady his breathing. There was nothing to worry about. Adra liked him, in her strange sort of way; she hadn't *actually* drowned him. She'd even mentioned how she'd like for Markus to meet Thallon. Why, then, did he feel the need to hide?

He wasn't even sure if the man *was* Thallon. Regardless, Markus didn't want to meet him just yet. He was still grappling with the idea of mermaids...and now the fae? One thing at a time.

He pressed closer to the bark, adjusting his head so he could peer between the crack of two trees. Adra and the mysterious man were nearer now, docked on the side of the island closest to him.

Their voices carried, as if they weren't even trying to hide what they were saying.

"Oh, Thallon, I'm so glad you came today," Adra said in a sing-song voice, her tail splashing in the water as she leaned against the island.

So, Markus *had* guessed correctly.

"You know I can't stay away for long." Thallon winked, his long, blonde hair falling to his waist. He leaned on his side; his legs stretched before him with one knee propped up in a carefree manner. In his hand, he twirled some clover.

"Then what kept you the other night? I was stuck in some fishing line and someone else had to rescue me." Adra sighed dramatically.

"Someone else?" Thallon's head snapped up, his brow narrowed in what looked like jealousy...or fear. Maybe both.

Markus was only too glad he wasn't on the receiving end of that glare.

"Oh, just some farm boy. He didn't say where he was from." Adra shrugged. "It doesn't matter."

Just some farm boy? Markus couldn't help feeling slightly offended. Though he was, in fact, just as she said.

"Doesn't matter? Sweet Adra, for years, this river has just been *ours*—a place away from the watchful eyes of my people. If someone from Griskol saw you, touched you..." Thallon fisted his hands and brought one to his mouth, shaking his head. "Do you know how dangerous this is? For us? You could have been killed and maybe still will be."

The gravity of the words descended upon the water, but Adra

just brushed her hand in the air as if to shoo them away. "Oh Thallon, how you worry so. He was harmless, I assure you. He hardly believed I was real to begin with. Besides, he needn't have rescued me if you had kept our rendezvous."

Thallon ran a hand down his face and sighed. "You know I wouldn't have placed my attention elsewhere had it not been for something exceedingly important."

"Oh, I know that, so your explanation better be a good one." Adra leaned her head to the side, studying him.

Thallon nodded, running his tongue over his teeth before beginning. He swallowed hard. "It's time."

Adra gasped. "Already? Are you sure?"

"How can I not be? I've heard Endlewood's orders, seen to the preparations. Tonight, it will be done."

"And to think...after all these years." Adra stared at him in disbelief. "How must you feel?"

"I don't rightly know. I'm bound to fulfill my oath. I've trained for this moment my whole life—raised like *this.*" Thallon pointed to his chest. "At the apex of my crimes, I'm more monster than I am fae. But maybe they're one in the same." He dropped his gaze and shrugged, his face hiding traces of things unspoken.

"You're no monster, Thallon." Adra's voice held hints of understanding.

He didn't look at her. "Not all monsters have claws." Thallon's voice grew dark. "Words are just as sharp. And so are daggers."

Adra studied him further, her lips twisting up in a somber sort of smile. "We understand each other, remember? Cursed to be what we cannot avoid. Bound by our parents' transgressions. Forced into what we don't believe." She reached onto land and grabbed hold of Thallon's hand. His gaze locked onto hers. "I wonder, though, how much is in our power to control. Choice is a useful tool, is it not?"

"You speak in riddles more often than prose, Adra. If my spirit weren't this heavy, I might have a chance at solving one." Thallon adjusted his position and leaned forward, bringing his hand to her face. He pushed back a strand of her auburn hair and tucked the sprig of clover behind her ear.

Markus' chest clenched. He wished for Holland by his side, her face looking up into his the way Adra was Thallon's. Watching this scene unfold felt invasive, too intimate a moment to be eaves-dropping. Yet, he couldn't look away.

"It's time I leave. The first vessel dispatches at noon," Thallon said, his thumb trailing a line across Adra's jaw. "I don't know when I'll see you here next, *thaem gavth*—my love." He bent his head and gently brushed his lips against hers before pulling away. *"Thae gaveth thu."*

"I love you, too." Adra sighed, her eyes betraying only hints of sorrow. "I'll see you to the end of the river before I go back. I'll remain hidden—don't worry."

Markus' heart twisted at their exchange. He watched as Thallon stood and boarded the boat on which he first came. Adra was beside him, turning the vessel in the direction of the Crendian Sea. Before leaving, Thallon grabbed the oars and scanned the distant shore, passing over Markus' hiding spot.

For a moment, Thallon's piercing blue gaze met his, and

instantly his back was on fire again. This time, the icicles were lodged somewhere deep in his spine, sending ripples of nausea up his throat.

He fell to his knees, his hand on the bark before him and his brain pounding against his skull.

Hamish's warm snout brushed up against his ear.

What's going on with me? First *Endlewood* and the dreams, and now Thallon? Markus shook his head. When would it end? And why now?

He forced his glance once more to the river. Relief flooded him; they were both gone. Markus silently cursed the couple for their elusiveness. Apparently, they hadn't minded talking loudly because they *both* spoke in riddles.

Thallon had mentioned *Endlewood.* But it was curious. Markus knew it to be a book, but the way Thallon had spoken the word... It sounded like a name. A name that belonged to a living and breathing person. Maybe there were two different Endlewoods after all... But what were the chances?

Markus determined anything mentioning that name must be trouble. Something was going on, but what?

There was no help for it. He would visit Holland—now. And he would talk to her about Griskol's new laws, the river, and Adra and Thallon.

He'd even tell her how he felt, too. Perhaps Calsius was right; Markus' declaration could have the power to change things. To make her stay...

His legs couldn't move fast enough.

CHAPTER SEVENTEEN
Holland

It had taken Holland longer to get through Andaimon than she'd thought it would. The storm had made travel difficult and cold, blocking out the moon with thick, menacing clouds. Her only source of light was the sporadic lightning splitting open the heavens in jarring and unpredictable bursts.

She'd gotten stuck, too; her boots had submerged themselves in the muddy potholes along the street. After the third instance, she'd had enough. Veering off the main road, Holland crept between alleyways and behind people's homes instead.

Walls of trees and stone were better camouflage than the open road anyway. Not to mention, a blanket of grass was a far better footpath than one solely made of mud.

Holland paused at a familiar courtyard, shocked to see it looking very much the same after the passing of five years. Absentmindedly, she reached toward her pocket and traced the outline of her book, her fingers tingling in memory.

This was where she'd found *The Tale of Endlewood*. Markus had taken her on an adventure here for his eighteenth birthday…

Why hadn't she been back since?

Holland left the courtyard with mixed feelings, stopping once more when she reached the forest at the outskirts of town. A familiar, brown fence that stretched for miles greeted her like an old friend at the edge of the clearing.

Under the shade of the thick, leafy trees, she hunkered down for the remainder of the night, preparing for her long-overdue entrance into Kirkus before sleep claimed her.

Dawn now approached, and the hazy sky gave way to light. Holland sat at the base of a birch, her back sore from lying on the ground during the night. She tucked stray hairs into her cap and mulled over last night's adventures.

Something about the day she found *The Tale of Endlewood* still puzzled her. What had happened to Markus when he'd touched the book? It was a similar reaction to when he'd held it again on the hill behind the Row a few nights ago.

Holland didn't understand it, but she felt that maybe there was something Markus wasn't telling her. The thought stung. They were best friends; they told each other everything.

Or, at least, she'd thought they did.

But how could Holland be mad at him? She was the one who had just left *him* behind—or was about to once she got through Kirkus. An action that would sting worse than anything Markus was withholding.

She glanced to her right, biting her lip. Across the field stood a cluster of trees, and behind them, a large farm. She supposed Markus was probably just waking up, the soil of a new day calling his name. That was the only thing that ever kept him away from

Andaimon, from Holland; he was always tending to his crops. Though he never stayed away for long; he often braved the thirty-minute walk across the border to see her.

Holland shook her head. It couldn't be helped. She'd made her choice, and she wasn't turning around. And she wasn't stopping by Markus' farm either. In fact, she hoped to avoid it at all costs, no matter how much she wished to see the weathered farmhouse and silo, the livestock, or Markus' family again.

She'd only been there a few times when she was younger, all before Markus' father had passed. She remembered fondly the way Jaimus and Jannus Fenn had both welcomed her as one of their own, even despite Griskol's growing fears.

Time sure has a way of changing things—sometimes for the worse, others for the better.

If not for *Endlewood* all those years ago, she wouldn't have dared to leave home in the first place.

She held the book in her hands, leafing through its pages. Rereading the story was like becoming acquainted with an old friend, and she was picking up on details she had missed prior.

So many parts of the story called to her, and for reasons she couldn't explain, she felt it mirrored parts of her life here in Griskol. Even though it was a fictional story, the little similarities here and there made Holland's need for freedom that much more poignant.

The thought gave her courage. Soon she'd be stepping into Kirkus, exploring the western and northernmost borders before crossing the line into Tiri for the first time in her life. And from there, maybe even Pembroke Fally. Though she knew chances of getting through those iron gates were slim.

Holland caught herself; her clammy fingers were breaking *Endlewood*'s spine. At this rate, it'd be lucky if the fragile novel survived another day.

She closed the book and shoved it back in her pocket before standing. Her whole body tingled. Here she was, on the verge of something new. It almost didn't feel real.

She took a cautious step forward, then another, before her stride grew in confidence. At the fence, she hoisted herself up and over before landing lightly on the ground below.

A few more steps, and the tall plants brushed against her pants like they had once done to her skirts. She walked onward, looking in the direction of where she knew town would be, and that's when she felt it—the familiar smells assaulting her nostrils.

Warm bread, mixed herbs, clean air.

It still smelled the same after all those years. Funny how certain scents could transport someone back to a certain place, no matter the span in time. It was as if Holland had never left, like she was on Mrs. Kershaw's mission to find the purple ribbon all over again.

Holland picked up speed, eager to explore more of Kirkus. And, if she were honest with herself, to sample some of its goods. She'd left Benneforth Row well before breakfast.

Fresh bread seemed like just the thing.

By the time Holland reached town, her stomach was growling, and her daric pouch felt strangely heavy. She approached a nearby street vendor, her boots thumping along the familiar cobblestone streets.

"What will it be today, lad?" An old woman leaned forward, her glasses barely staying on the bridge of her nose.

Holland blanched slightly. She'd nearly forgotten she was supposed to act like a boy. If this was any indication of how her travels would go, she was doomed before she'd even begun.

Holland swallowed back her fear and deepened her voice. "One loaf, if you will."

"Just one? Won't your family back in Andaimon have your toes for that? By Tokal! Runners never just buy one!"

Tokal. Holland had almost forgotten about him. He was a bronze fox, a statue thought to be the protector of Griskol. A manmade spirit, created years ago by people who believed he kept the magic at bay. It was nonsensical at best. Holland was shocked there were still people who actually believed in him. But Markus had told her King Randor and Queen Rosin kept the fox themselves, and for all intents and purposes, Tokal resided happily in Famar.

She tried staunching the nerves bubbling up her throat. How was she to answer this troublesome woman? "Uh...one will be enough for now. I want to see what else is being sold today." Holland croaked, feeling the blood rush to her face.

"Taking your business elsewhere to some money-grubber, are you? Well, I'll be. Some of us have to make a living 'round here." She crossed her arms, and Holland swore she could see fumes coming from the woman's nostrils.

Since when were those in Kirkus so greedy? Did they need darics as much as those in Andaimon?

"I'm sure I'll be back," Holland said, slipping a daric into the woman's now upturned palm and grabbing a loaf from the table. The key was to back away slowly.

"That's what they all say. You're all the same." The woman threw her hands up in the air and watched Holland closely.

Holland tried to ignore the woman's gaze boring holes through the back of her head as she moved away from the stand. She needed to be more elusive, not draw so much attention.

And she needed to walk like a man. How did Markus do it? She remembered his carefree gait, his relaxed shoulders, and his confident stride. She could do that...

It felt awkward and foreign to silence the normal sway of her hips, but she reminded herself it was necessary. A few more hours and she was sure she could master it.

Kirkus resembled a lot of what Holland had remembered from her childhood, and yet, it didn't seem as lustrous as she recalled. Whenever he could get away from his farm, Markus mostly came to her, not the other way around; Griskol had grown stricter about visitation over the years. Sure, the smells were similar, but what had once looked new and well-maintained now looked to be covered in dirt or merely concealed behind chipped paint or hammered clapboards.

Kirkus was better than Andaimon, but only just. It seemed the middle-class weren't too much better off than she thought. Maybe that's why Markus never seemed to care about Holland's station.

Overhead were strung empty clotheslines, and to her left and right were buildings, shops, and places of trade built close together, their stone walls creating narrow alleyways that looked to harbor front doors to people's houses.

Stray dogs darted across the streets, lapping up the puddles from last night's storm and begging for food scraps at every corner. Some children followed, doing the same. It was a quaint town, if a little untidy.

Holland walked forward, ignoring the gestures of other street vendors begging for her business. She would do well to hold her darics closely.

She scoured the street, looking for a place to hide and recognized a path to her left. Biting her lip, she slunk down it, leaving the chaos of the main road behind.

The path opened up into a wide meadow. Starlings greeted her and twittered overhead, their familiar songs a comfort. She sighed in relief, sitting down to eat her bread in peace, if only for a moment. She knew she shouldn't sit still for long, but she enjoyed the feel of her back pressed against the bark of an elm.

If only Markus was here.

The thought stilled her chewing. She'd been gone less than a day and already she'd thought of him a handful of times. It felt wrong to enter Kirkus after all these years and not see his home.

She knew how much he loved his farmland. She knew he missed his father, loved his family. That he would do anything for the people he cared about most. There was so much she knew about him, and yet, his eyes still held secrets.

She felt that she could learn all there was to know about Markus Fenn and still be left wanting more. He was that kind of person—when he entered someone's life, he found his way under their skin and into their hearts, never leaving.

It was a kind of friendship which made saying goodbye hard.

Which is why she hadn't.

Holland ate her bread and studied the landscape around her. If she was correct, she could follow a path north through the woods and come up to Kirkus' northwestern border from there. The Fenn farmland was to the southeast, so there would be no way Markus would find her.

Why would he? He'd never left his land or family behind for long. He wouldn't now.

Holland's chest knotted. She swallowed the last bite of bread and brushed off the familiar weight of confusion. She reached for her pocket once more and pressed her palm against the outline of the book.

This is what she wanted. And she would chart her course to Pembroke Fally before the week was up, seeking an audience with the king and queen. She was taking control of her life, and if she was lucky, she'd find the freedom she was looking for. For both her and Andaimon.

She only hoped she wouldn't be stopped before then.

CHAPTER EIGHTEEN
From "The Tale of Endlewood"

*I*t's been a year. And the same words stare up at me from the page on which they're written.

'When will you return, your Majesty?'

I fight the urge to tear the letter to shreds. I've received endless correspondence from Nindrol these past few months, all of them shoved into a corner and ignored.

This isn't his worst offense. Upon leaving the woods, he'd sent one of my men to look for me. I intervened before he'd gotten too close. I'd pointedly said never to bother me again, never to think of coming within a yard of my house. What if Josilland were to find out my true nature?

It's hard enough pretending to be a mortal. I don't age. My ears are pointed. I can see deep into the night. I'll never die unless I'm killed.

But Josilland doesn't know these things. And she doesn't need to. All we need is each other and our love.

I pick up my quill, begrudgingly penning a response.

'Chath eithl mi a 'planthadh eirth—I don't plan to.'

The words sweep across the page without hesitation. I know Nindrol and the others are secure. They have the Overseer, they are safe. And besides, Elethün is ever-present. They have their 'king.'

But here? Josilland needs my protection, especially now that she's pregnant. She's due any day now. I can hardly believe my fortune.

It didn't take us long to realize our love, though in truth, I'd known mine from the beginning—ever since that fateful day we met at the edge of the woods. It wasn't even a question if I loved her then; my heart did, as if it was already hers to begin with. But Josilland needed time, and I vowed to wait for her for an eternity.

Thankfully, she spared me the waiting and declared her love to me on the night of midsummer's eve. It had been a beautiful night, the kind filled with stars and the smell of jasmine in the air. I recount it with a deep joy, only brought deeper on the day of our wedding.

Which followed only two days thereafter.

And now? We plan to raise our family here, to grow and settle our roots. I can just picture our little ones running about the yard, pulling at their mother's apron strings, and sucking blackberry preserves from their fingers.

Ah, the joys of parenthood. At last, I am content.

But is my wife? Fear crouches in the back of my mind; it's been there for some time. Josilland hasn't mentioned the forest since the day we met, but I can tell she thinks about it often. When she looks out the window, it's always in the direction of the woods; there's a daydream behind her eyes. What is she imagining? The wondering drives me mad.

I take every pain to bring her attention elsewhere.

Hence our garden—have I mentioned its loveliness?

Any time I see Josi growing restless, in need of an adventure that I fear only the woods can quell, I take her to the flower nursery to pick out a new shrub. A new plant. A new flower.

Our garden is a bright array of colors because of it—bursting with every edible and deciduous sapling one can imagine. Bachelor's Buttons? We have them. Mountain Laurel? In spades. Morels? They line our stomachs most every night. Zinnias? Snapdragons? Peonies? We have a flower for every occasion.

For now, it does its job. The garden brings delight to my wife's eyes. Though, I can't help but feel it won't be enough.

I must think of other things to distract her.

Despite it all, I'm impossibly happy, living in our small bungalow near the hedgerow just past the trader's post. It feels more like home than any palace ever could. I miss nothing of my old life. Nothing aside from Elethün, that is.

But here, Josilland makes me feel like a king. What are gilded thrones and golden crowns to a life of bliss with the one you hold most dear?

In truth, even the very breath in my lungs can't compare to my love for Josi. My need for her. She is my everything. My eternal starlight.

"Vesstamon? Dear? Come quick!" Josi calls for me, interrupting my thoughts. There's a strange urgency in her voice.

"Where are you?" I drop the pen in my hand and stand.

"By the lilacs! Hurry—please!"

I run for the door, my chest in knots. "I'm coming!"

I round the foxglove and forsythia, ducking beneath the tendrils of a flowering wisteria. A few more steps bring me to the lilacs with Josi sitting beside them on the ground.

"Josi-love?

"It's the baby... I think it's time!" Josi reaches a hand toward me, and I crouch beside her, running my thumb across her knuckles.

I push the stray, damp hairs from off her forehead before pressing a kiss there. "Let's get you inside, then." I'm about to become a father. The thought sends flutters to my middle.

"No. I don't think I can manage... Let me stay...here." Josi gasps, her grip tightening on my hand.

"Of course, anything for you, my love." I ease her on her back, making sure she's comfortable.

"Don't go—don't leave me," she pleads. Clenching her teeth, a groan of pain escapes her lips.

Her words break my heart. I wouldn't leave her for the world. "I won't, Josi-love. I'm right here. I'm not going anywhere."

CHAPTER NINETEEN
Markus

By the time Markus' feet hit the dusty streets of Andaimon, his pace slowed only long enough to avoid implanting loose gravel into them. Yes, he hadn't even bothered to don a pair of shoes; he was that adamant.

He knew Holland, probably even better than she knew herself. After twelve years of being her friend and studying her mannerisms, he could tell when an idea was just a passing thought, not amounting to much. There were other times, though, where he'd seen a passing thought turn into something more—something solid—and take hold of her to her very core.

It was like that with her parents. She'd always wanted to know where she came from. To know the truth. Her identity meant more to her than anything she possessed, so naturally, she'd sacrifice anything to find it—even her life, Markus feared.

He'd recognized that same look in Holland's eyes when she'd held *The Tale of Endlewood*. That look of determination—that if she didn't leave home now, then perhaps she never would. He knew she feared being trapped, of being stuck in Andaimon without any truth of her past... It was enough to make her do something foolish.

Markus groaned as he ran, dust clouds kicking up behind him. Why had he stayed away longer than a day? He'd been exhausted and too focused on working away his fears rather than doing *something* useful instead.

He chastised his work ethic. If he was too late, he'd never forgive himself.

Benneforth Row finally stumbled into view. Markus ran to the stairs and relief flooded through him at seeing the door opened. *Holland is here; she is still in Andaimon!*

He calmed enough to take the steps one at a time, pausing when a young boy came out of the shop, a bundle under his arm and a worried look on his face as he closed the door behind him.

Markus stepped forward, but the boy didn't move aside; his hand still rested on the doorknob.

"Are you all right?" Markus asked, his legs itching to keep moving.

"Ye-yes, sir." The boy nodded, his gaze cast on the steps.

"Are you sure? I think the doorknob you're suffocating might say otherwise." Markus jested, hoping to bring a smile to the boy's face.

"Oh." The boy reddened, snatched his hand down, and hid it in the folds of his clothes.

"Did Holland fix those up for you?" Markus motioned to the garments in the boy's arms.

"Yes, sir."

"Well, you're a lucky lad. Holland is the best in town. I'm

actually here to talk to her myself." Markus couldn't wait any longer. He took a few steps closer, and still, the boy didn't budge.

What gives?

"Uh, she-she's busy," the boy stammered, pressing his back against the door.

"Probably not too busy to see me. We're friends, she and I. Have been for a long time. She won't mind a little distraction." Markus craned his neck to catch a glimpse of her through the window, but there was a glare. It didn't help that the boy seemed to intercept Markus' attempts at getting closer to the door.

The fear was back; Markus' stomach twisted and dipped again. He needed to see Holland.

Now.

"I wouldn't go in there if I were you," the boy warned, his face now panicked.

"Why not? You just did," Markus challenged, growing more irritated by the second. "Please. Just step aside so I can see her—"

"She's not here!"

The words tore through Markus' shirt and stabbed him in the heart. *She's not here.*

"What did you say?" Markus narrowed his eyes at the boy.

The boy swallowed, pulling his collar away from his neck. "I-I said she-she's not here, sir."

Suddenly, Markus' hand was on the doorknob, and he was inside Holland's shop. The sight confirmed his fears. It was empty, save for a few bunches of cloth bundled here and there. No needle, no thread, no Holland; by the looks of it, it seemed there were no traces that she had been there at all that morning.

Markus glanced at the boy still standing near the door. When their gazes met, the boy seemed to remember he had legs and turned to flee, but Markus grabbed his shirt before he could get far.

"Not so fast there." Markus tried to hide the aggravation in his tone. This was only a kid; he most likely was innocent and didn't deserve Markus' guile. The boy struggled to get free, his eyes wide. "I'm not going to hurt you, lad. I promise. I just have a few questions." Markus dropped to his knees and kept a firm hold on the boy's arms.

The boy seemed to realize his fighting was useless; he wasn't going to leave that easily. He stopped squirming and readied himself, standing straighter as if to take whatever questioning like a man.

"For starters, what's your name?" Markus asked.

"Benjamon, sir." The boy met his gaze, albeit nervously.

"What brought you here this morning?"

"I-I came to see if my clothes were finished. Miss Holland said she would have them done before she…" He snapped his lips closed as if realizing he had said too much.

"Before she what?"

Benjamon shook his head, his gaze not meeting Markus'.

Markus ground his molars together, his hands unintentionally tightening their hold on Benjamon's sleeves. He reminded himself to draw in air, to relax a fraction. "I know you don't trust me, Benjamon. But I need you to. I care about Holland. Very much. And if something were to happen to her, she'd probably want me to be the first to know." *At least I'd hope.* "I fear she may have done something incredibly—" Markus couldn't finish the words. He choked on another instead. "Please." He let go of Benjamon and ran a hand over his face, his shoulders sagging forward.

He already knew it in his heart. Holland had left Andaimon.

She'd left him without saying goodbye.

Benjamon stepped back, but he didn't run away. Instead, he studied Markus closely. "What's your name?"

Markus glanced up, probably looking even more weary than he felt. "Markus." Had he forgotten to mention that? It seemed like a paltry thing considering the circumstances.

"Well, sir, maybe I should trust you after all." Benjamon shifted and pulled something out of his pocket. He handed it to Markus.

"What's this?" He snatched the crumpled paper and unfolded it. *A letter.* His eyes roved over the handwriting. It was Holland's. He didn't have to see her signature to know it to be true.

He couldn't contain his urgency as he read, soaking in every word for hidden clues, as if reading them would somehow make Holland reappear.

Dear Benjamon,

I'm leaving, but don't worry—all the clothes are fixed. They should last both of you a few months, maybe more, be it that you do not grow too aggressively.

I want to thank you again for agreeing to our exchange and for keeping my departure a secret. You know as well as I do the danger of my decision, but let's not focus on that. Your brother's armband is my confidence.

When I return (which won't be soon, if I can help it), I'll

151

tell you all the wondrous adventures of Griskol. It shall be as if you came along and enjoyed them with me.

In the meantime, build forts, contrive schemes, and don't forget to live as boys your age do.

Though you may fear it, you won't be forgotten.
Your seamstress and friend,
Holland

P.S. If a man by the name of Markus comes knocking, tell him I am all right. He's a dear friend, and I hope he'll understand. My only regret is that I didn't get to say goodbye.

Markus swallowed, tasting bile in his throat. He put all the pieces together. Benjamon's brother must be a Runner; that's how Holland had gotten the armband. Markus clenched his fists and fought the urge to slam them against his thighs. At least she knew about Famar's new laws; that alone could keep her alive for a little while. That is, until she was questioned.

What then?

Markus bit back a groan and stood as the weight of it all sank in. He couldn't be mad at Benjamon; he was only a boy. He *should* be mad at Holland. Instead, all he felt was emptiness, a sense of loss as vast as a starless sky. It stung. It burned. It ached.

And there was nothing he could do for it.

She had left him. Andaimon wasn't enough for Holland. And Markus wasn't either.

"Thank you, Benjamon. Knowing Holland, I can only imagine she put you up to this. Made you promise to keep her secret." His voice sounded hollow even to his own ears.

Benjamon nodded, his arm tightening on his bundle of clothes. "Do you think it was a mistake, sir? Her leaving?"

Markus didn't answer. Was it a mistake? In his mind it was lunacy. The very act could get her killed! He had every intention of finding her and bringing her back home, but what then?

She'd leave him again. But the second time would only hurt worse. He'd be forced to watch her walk away, knowing full well the dangers that awaited her.

Holland had left to seek her destiny, compelled by that confounded book. If Markus left to bring her back, she'd resent him forever.

Why is she so stubborn?

He ran a hand along his neck, pacing the room and familiarizing himself with every detail of Holland's workspace. It didn't take long. He'd practically grown up in Andaimon alongside her, splitting his time between home and Benneforth Row.

Holland had become his home. And she'd taken a piece of his heart with her when she'd gone. But he could surrender his wants and feelings, easily. He'd been doing it for years, according to Calsius.

It was her safety which left him in turmoil.

He feared she'd made the gravest mistake of her life.

He faced Benjamon once again, sighing. "Yes, I'm afraid so. A big mistake." Markus still held her letter in his hand. He couldn't part with it. Not for the world. "Mind if I keep this?"

"Sure." Benjamon shrugged, shifting the clothes into his other arm, causing something to fall out of one of the pockets.

The sound of metal hitting the wooden floor drew both their gazes downward. Benjamon bent to study what had fallen. "That's strange."

"What?" Markus needed a distraction. His thoughts were too full of Holland.

"It's two darics. But I didn't put these here." Benjamon stood, studying the coins. "Why would... Do you think Miss Holland did it?" He asked, pressing the darics between his fingers, his eyes belaying hints of disbelief.

Markus nodded. "I'd wager she did." His chest tightened of its own accord.

That was another thing. Holland regarded others' needs above her own. She was selfless to a fault. She didn't have much as it was, though Markus tried to remedy that as much as she allowed. Holland would give every spare daric if it meant helping someone else.

This act of leaving Andaimon—yes, Markus thought it was lunacy, but in truth, it was the only self-serving act Holland had ever taken. It wasn't even selfish, only dangerous.

How could he wish that away from her?

If circumstances were different... If magic wasn't scorned and feared. If they had lived in another time where Griskol hadn't lost its mind. If danger didn't lurk around every corner... He would encourage her dreams.

But maybe he still could.

Markus knew his plot of farmland and all the livestock like the back of his hand. He was a farmer's son, after all. It was his birthright. He'd never left Kirkus aside from his visits to Holland.

If he had his way, he'd remain just as he was, but with Holland by his side.

How could he do that, though, when she didn't even know how he felt? Was he willing to give up his familiar comforts in order to pursue her across Griskol?

He knew the answer before he even had to ask. When it came to Holland, she was always worth it. Always.

He just needed something first.

Markus walked toward the shop door, but instead of leaving, he spotted a strip of white fabric on the floor, torn and cut with frayed edges. He bent and pocketed the material before he stood and faced the boy again. "It was nice meeting you, Benjamon, but it's about time I head home. Time is precious."

Benjamon scrunched his brow. He followed Markus out of the shop and down the steps. "What do you mean?"

"I mean I'm going to find Holland." It had taken Markus only a moment to decide. He knew his course of action, and he was going to take it without hesitation.

He'd go after her, and sticking to the shadows, he'd be her shield. Then he'd tell her how he felt. He'd bare his heart raw, the way he should have years ago. And if she rejected him... He didn't know what he'd do from there.

But finding her came first. His heart could wait. He'd vowed to always protect her...and it was even more pressing now than before. He'd protect her from the law, from *Endlewood*, and if everything went against him, perhaps even from his own feelings.

He shook his head, pushing away the unwelcome thought.

He hoped it didn't come to that.

CHAPTER TWENTY
Markus

Markus stopped at home long enough to grab the essentials: his father's pen knife, a pair of shoes, and a sack of parsnips. He had planned to travel on his own, but Hamish insisted on tagging along.

Markus only complied to save his mother the trouble. Hamish's whimpering had the tendency to wake the whole village if he didn't get his way.

The spoiled mongrel.

But with Hamish's track record of sniffing out damsels in distress, he might prove helpful after all.

The two of them set off west in the direction of town, Hamish's tongue hanging out of his mouth in what looked like a roguish smile.

Markus bit back a laugh, mulling over his thoughts.

He'd told his mother he'd be gone for a few days, but if those days turned into weeks… He didn't want to worry her. There was enough produce already harvested, not to mention all that was still growing in the fields, that could hold their family over for a few months. It all depended on if Dru remembered to water the crop…

He shouldn't feel guilty for leaving, but he did. His mother was too weak to manage things on her own, and Dru too young to be depended on for very long.

But there was no use for it. Part of Markus' heart had left Andaimon last night, and he was bent on restoring it to his chest, to hold it safely in his arms once more. He couldn't rest until he did.

"All right, Hamish. We need a game plan here." This was what Markus' life had come to: strategizing with his dog. "If Holland left last night, she couldn't have gotten very far. Which means she's probably still in Kirkus."

He fished in his pocket and drew out the soft material he was looking for. He paused and knelt before Hamish, letting him sniff the white strip of fabric he'd taken from Holland's workspace. "It isn't much, but I bet Holland touched this at one point."

Hamish sniffed every inch of the material and before Markus knew it, the dog was off in the direction of town, but at a much faster pace than before.

They crossed the last stretch of his farmland, entered a copse near Andaimon's border, and ended up at a field where a long, wooden fence stretched for miles to their left. Markus walked a little further and noted trampled lady's mantle and bugbanes, and what looked like fresh footprints, now fossilized in the drying mud from last night's storm.

His stomach dipped. Holland had been through here; either that, or another Runner. But he had a feeling it was the first. He was getting closer; this search party would be over before it even had a chance to begin.

He could hope.

"Do you know where she is, Ham?" Markus ran to keep up with his over-eager bloodhound.

Hamish barked, his long ears and jowls flapping behind him with every step. He looked excited, like he was about to dig up some big secret.

"I'll take that as a *yes*. Lead the way, champ."

Markus followed Hamish through the remainder of the overgrown field and then through a narrow alleyway which opened up onto a familiar bustling street. They were now in town.

Markus had grown up on this street as much as he had his farm. All those years of selling their family produce with his father, of running the cobblestones, stealing from the local vendors. It had been a blissful, if not highly immature, stage of his life.

One he often recounted with nostalgia. That's how he'd met Holland, after all.

This road was the beginning and end of all things. It didn't stretch south into Andaimon, which was the gripe of all the lower-class. How difficult would it be to extend the cobblestone a few extra yards? It did continue into Tiri, however. Markus had never been that far north, but Calsius had told him this road wound all the way to Pembroke Fally, right up to the gates of Famar.

It was just last night that Markus had walked this same road to the Brenner's family forge. The smithy was set in the western part of town, a decent walk from his farm, and the main road was the easiest route to get there.

Markus continued to follow Hamish and nearly stumbled into him when the dog suddenly stopped, his muzzle raised and rigorously sniffing the air. His nose brought him to a woman's booth, her table laden with bread and spices. There he jumped and placed his front paws on the table, rattling the structure. He barked, signifying he had completed what he'd been required to do.

Leave it to Hamish to find food instead of Holland.

Markus groaned and ran a hand down his face. He should have known. "You'll have to excuse my dog, Dame Olgaus. He doesn't mind his manners." Markus addressed the aged woman behind the table and dragged Hamish by his collar, bringing the dog to sit beside him.

"Wouldn't be the first customer today who didn't mind his manners. Fancy a Runner stopping by and only buying one loaf. *One!* By Tokal, practically starving his family for the sake of his darics. The nerve!" The woman tsked and shook her head, her heavy-set shoulders heaving.

Markus was tempted to ignore Dame Olgaus, seeing as he was used to her constant ramblings, but his ears perked up instead. "Excuse me, did you say a Runner?" His hands twitched of their own volition on the strip of fabric he still held.

She hmphed and nodded. "A mite scrawny lad, too! One would think he'd need more than just the one loaf for himself." She threw up her hands in defeat. "I'll never understand teenagers. Always doing one thing when you expect them to do the other. I'm only too aggrieved on behalf of their mothers' hearts. I, for one, have never had any children and I, for sure, never will—"

"Dame Olgaus, which way did this Runner go?" Markus cut her off, his grip tightening its hold on the fabric.

"Where they all go! Further into town to feast on the goods of my competitors. It's cutthroat here in Kirkus, Mr. Fenn, and that won't be changing anytime soon, I'm afraid." She hmphed again and ripped a loaf in half, stuffing a large chunk of it in her mouth.

Surely business couldn't be that bad. It hadn't been competitive back when he sold crops with his father. But in truth, it'd been years since Markus had set up a booth in town; nowadays, most villagers came directly to him for food, or he made the trek to their houses.

He didn't have time to contemplate that further.

"A daric for your troubles." Markus flipped a coin onto the table and snagged a fresh loaf before turning and heading deeper into the bustle of town.

"My livelihood thanks you—or at least, what's left of it!" Dame Olgaus shouted to his back.

Markus raised a hand and kept walking, feeding part of the loaf to Hamish while putting a chunk of warm dough in his mouth. It tasted of sweet herbs, reminiscent of his childhood ventures in the village. He hadn't had bread in what felt like years.

Holland had to be nearby. From Dame Olgaus' descriptions, it seemed likely. Markus had seen Runners before, and all of them knew the etiquette of buying more than one of anything at a vendor's stand. To do otherwise was like a slap in the face.

Holland had just given herself away in spades.

Markus scanned the sides of the street as he walked, taking in the size and build of anyone in passing.

There! Up ahead was a Runner. They were small in stature enough to pass as Holland. If Calsius had been in earnest, the green armband was now a dead giveaway, and sure enough, there it was on the person's left upper arm.

Markus increased his pace, holding his breath. A few more feet, and he'd be able to see if this young boy wasn't a young boy after all.

He reached out his hand and grabbed the Runner by the shoulder, bracing himself for what was to come.

The Runner turned around, his face scrunched up in sudden fear. "I have a right to be here, I swear!"

Markus flinched, finally letting out the breath he'd been holding. "My apologies. I thought you were someone I knew." He removed his hand and placed it atop Hamish's head, his stomach sinking. How could he have confused this young man for Holland?

Markus must be desperate indeed.

The Runner's eyes seemed to lose their wide-eyed shock and were replaced with sudden aggravation. "Sorry to disappoint," he said dryly, starting to walk away.

"Wait!" Markus didn't know what possessed him, but he needed a lead. "Can you spare a moment?"

"I'm pressed for time as it is; I don't need random people questioning me in the streets. It looks bad." The Runner crossed his arms, the sack over his shoulders already bulging with vegetables.

Markus could have sold him some of his own for a good price. But now was not the time for that.

"I…" Markus didn't know how to respond. He should have known why Runners were as scared as they were, with King Randor and Queen Rosin's new laws in place. Nowhere was safe. The thought soured the bread he'd recently swallowed.

All he could think about was Holland.

"Have you heard of any Runners getting questioned? Detained?" Markus' throat went dry.

The Runner seemed taken aback by such a question, hesitant even. Then something shifted; a wave of determination shadowed his eyes—a look too serious for one just reaching manhood. He stepped forward and swallowed hard. "Three. It's only been two weeks since these blasted armbands, but already they're proving to be more like walking targets than anything. Even though we're 'protected' with them, Famar's soldiers think they have the right to question anyone they see wearing one. I'd as soon burn mine or throw it in the Crendian if it was only me I had to feed."

Markus nodded. This man was powerless against Famar. They all were. "Where are they now?" he barely managed.

"Taken. Along with some others. The gates of Famar are strong—iron. Able to keep things in as much as they are able to keep things out. They question Runners if they're found in the outskirts of Kirkus and Tiri's main streets. Apparently, we're solely confined to this road." The young man gestured to the street he was standing on, his scowl deepening.

"When were they taken?" Markus felt something grip his throat, his heartbeat sending pain to his chest. Had Holland…?

"Sometime last week. Been trying to figure out how to break 'em out since." The young man drew closer, lowering his voice.

"A group of us want to storm the castle, but…we're too few. But if we keep biding our time in the shadows, growing in number, maybe we'll be ready to stage a coup."

Stage a coup? Over three men?

No. It was more than that. It was over everything, the countless years of wrongdoing. But at what cost? A group of young men's lives? It might not be worth it. But how long until Famar took complete control over everything? Was it worth the risk to sit back and do nothing?

Something settled in Markus' chest. A resolve? A determination? No…it was lighter than that. A hope? Maybe.

But more importantly, there was relief. For now, Holland was safe. If she stuck to the main road, she should be fine.

But just in case…

"I wish you luck, then. Stay safe, and if you ever find yourself in the southeast of Kirkus, my farm is just over the border. I can give you some produce for a far better price than you'd find in town."

The Runner nodded, reaching a hand out to shake Markus' before turning and disappearing into the throng of busy villagers.

Markus touched Hamish's head, looking down into his mournful, coppery eyes. "You ready for a change of plans, Ham?"

The dog tilted his head, trying to lick Markus' face. His tail wagged in tune to his eager panting.

Markus chuckled. "All right then. Follow me." He headed up the road a few paces before turning left onto a narrow path—one that he'd taken long ago—with Hamish trailing behind him.

He hoped Holland had stuck to the main road, but just in case, he'd do some back-roading. This path was the most likely of places.

Maybe he was worrying for nothing. Maybe he was overprotective. But he'd promised to keep her safe, and if not for her sake, at least for his own peace of mind.

Holland would be okay.

She had to be.

CHAPTER TWENTY~ONE
From "The Tale of Endlewood"

I *wake to the sound of crying. It's the same every morning, and after three months, I've gotten used to it. But I had hoped for a few extra hours of sleep, at least. One can never be too hopeful.*

I roll off the small cot and sidle up next to the crib. Last night was Josi's turn to take the bed in our room. We alternate, but in most cases, I volunteer to sleep in the kitchen beside the bassinet. I'd rather she get her rest.

Peering into the crib, I see two sets of eyes staring back at me, cries mingling together like they're in some sort of conspiracy. I reach in and take a child in each of my arms, gently rocking them.

In all my dreams as a father, I had never envisioned twins. They are only three months old, but already I can tell our daughter is the spitting image of Josi and our son is the spitting image of myself.

They are the light of my life, though nothing can compare with my love for Josi. She will always be my ethereal light.

The children still cry in my arms, and I assume they're hungry. They eat more than I do on most days. I walk toward the bedroom, ready to wake Josi up, but I falter in my steps.

The bed is empty.

Unease winds its way to my middle. It's too early. She should still be sleeping.

Where is she?

"Josi-love? Are you here?" I walk outside, poking my head around the garden wall. "Josilland?"

No answer.

I try again, but this time near the lilacs—that hallowed ground where she birthed our son and daughter. Anticipation fuels my steps, my heart clanging around my ribs like a ball in a jar.

She's not there, either.

I call again for Josi, and all the while, our babies are crying alongside me, the noise a chaotic frenzy. It sounds mangled, like an uneven waltz. Our neighbors must think someone has died.

Where is my wife?

A thought nags at the back of my mind, and my head snaps in the direction of the forest. I now know desperation like a friend.

"No."

Anything but that.

I run inside, placing my weeping children in their crib, their sobs echoing against the small timber frames of the house. It's only gotten louder.

"I'll be back. Daddy will be back," I assure them, committing each of their faces to memory—a daughter and son so similar in looks to both their parents.

They will be fine. Josi will be fine.

I sprint out of the house like a Dyvrat is on my heels, a fierce determination causing my lithe steps to turn brazen. I am determined, unwilling to let my fear take hold.

Stride accompanies stride. Adrenaline fuels my gait. And it's hope that trails on courage's heels. I will find my wife.

I dart across the dusty road, sprint through a field of grass, bolt up a hill, and finally make it to the edge of the forest. I only pause long enough to catch my breath before plunging under the shade of the trees.

"Josi?" Something like a shiver creeps up my back the deeper I go. It's been so long since I've stepped foot in these woods. "Josi-love?" I call again.

Still no answer. My stomach drops.

I press on, scouring the ground for footprints or any sign that my wife has passed through here. But it's been dry as of late, with no rain in weeks. The undergrowth won't be aiding in my search today. Confound the dreaded drought!

I pass under a low bough, ducking my head to avoid contact and feel a shiver crawl up my spine once again.

I see the Overseer now. Just a few more paces. It's a beautiful and terrible sight—stretching, arching, writhing in golden shimmers of light, like a wall of perpetual defense, invisible to the human eye. Nothing enters or exits it at will. Except the fae. Except those with magic.

I swallow hard. Where's Josi?

My heart thrums in my chest, and I remind myself of the need to breathe. Josi isn't beside me—usually she is my oxygen.

I round a thick oak and blanche, my knees suddenly weak.

"Josi!" I scream, the sound a bloodcurdling cry. My chest

feels stabbed by a million invisible knives.

I am torn in two.

I'm by her side in an instant, cradling her head in my hands, my tears splattering like flower blossoms across her cheeks and raven hair.

Blood. So much blood. She's cut in too many places to count, her eyes wide and empty. Gone.

"Josi. My dearest, Josi," I cry, barely containing my agony. I bring her body onto my lap, rocking her mutilated form in my arms. "Thaem gavth—my love. My everything." Tears cascade down my face; there's enough to fill the ocean twice over. Blood and water surround us.

For every beauty found in this world, there is now double the anguish. The flowers no longer hold their colors. The laughter of babies now a funeral dirge's melody. The sun a sweltering hand, filled with hellfire.

What of love? It doesn't exist if Josi isn't here to receive it.

And hope? It's a fool's dream.

My soul burns. My hands ball into fists, tangling in Josi's hair. Fury mingles with my broken heart.

"Your Majesty?"

I snap my head around, taken completely by surprise to see my advisor, Nindrol, standing nearby, a look of intense bewilderment screwing up his features.

I hadn't heard his approach. Elethün's presence would have been preferable.

"I heard your cry... Is she...? Is this your wife?" Nindrol has the nerve to ask.

"Was." My words are ice. I can't bring myself to say she's dead. The word alone sends bile up my throat.

Our bungalow might as well be a tomb. For without Josi in it, there is no life. Her death is mine as well. All this world is death.

The Overseer sings above my head, its golden lights slashing like a million blades. I had once considered it beautiful; I scoff at the notion.

"Your Majesty, what can I do?" Nindrol asks, wringing his hands on the hem of his shirt. He looks uncomfortable, like he's used to giving orders, not taking them.

I want to grip his throat. Make him feel the pain in my chest.

"I want the Overseer destroyed. Now. I'll never see the likes of it again, as long as I am king." Resuming my neglected title seems the only thing for me now. There is nothing else.

"But, your Maj—"

"Did I stutter, Nindrol?" I sneer, baring my teeth. Why couldn't the Overseer have taken him and spared my Josi instead?

I'll come up with other ways to protect my people. Other ways to keep us safe. But this magical shield has just stripped me clean of my life's greatest joy.

The Overseer shall burn. Along with anything else that gets in my way.

"No." He dips his head, lifting it once more to meet my gaze. "Is there anything else, your Majesty?"

I know he asks out of obligation. A king never has just one request.

I look down into Josi's face, my heart wrenching as I close her eyes. Eyes so green and once full of life. Eyes so much like my

171

daughter's. The realization stops my heart. Haunts me. Destroys me all over again.

To look upon my daughter every day would be like reliving this horror, a reminder of all that I'd lost. I'll have Josi or nothing else.

I look up at Nindrol, my eyes hard and set and most assuredly bloodshot. "Go to my house in the village. Bring me my son." I pause for a moment. "Leave the girl."

CHAPTER TWENTY-TWO
Holland

D ust clouds swirled in the air, the particles of dirt lodging
themselves in Holland's throat. The past few hours
consisted of walking through endless fields of corn, kale, broccoli,
and some plants she couldn't place. She'd known Kirkus was
famous for its farmland, but she didn't realize just how true that
was.

There wasn't much for shade in this part of the region, but she
was nearing a cluster of trees. Though sparse, they'd provide some
relief from the heat of the day. It would have to do.

Her limbs were tight and on fire, eager for some respite, but
something caught her attention first.

A little way in the distance, a white-bricked shed stood on a
small plot of grass, peering out from behind a towering maple as if
it couldn't decide if it wanted to remain hidden or not. There
wasn't much to it save for wisteria climbing up its side, the purple
flowers a welcome sight amidst the stretches of grass and dirt.

Holland approached it slowly, her heart thudding with each
footfall. *What a curious little place.*

The shed was even more rundown up close. Its one window had a crack in the corner like the veins of a spiderweb. Its white walls were smattered with dirt, and the door hung open at an angle on rusted hinges.

Holland cautiously poked her head inside. It was dark, but she didn't see any movement. It seemed the place was abandoned on the inside as much as it was neglected on the out.

The shed was weary and forgotten, and Holland had a sudden affinity for it. It was an outcast to the rest of the world; it didn't belong anywhere—much like herself.

Wasn't all humanity like that, though? Empty houses, waiting for the right people to come along and fill the spaces—enough to make them feel like home.

Had anyone filled *her* home?

Holland shook the thought away and stepped over the threshold. To the left of the small space was a circular table, a singular upturned chair, and a spilled mug of some sort of beverage. Wispy draperies hung haphazardly over the window, and a water spigot in the corner reflected off its brassy surface what little light the sun offered.

Holland turned and took in the other half of the room, stopping short. A pair of boots peered out of the deep shadows. She stepped closer. A scream caught in her throat, her heart dropping to her stomach. The shoes were attached to a body!

It was a young boy lying on his back—unmoving...perhaps sleeping? Holland could only hope. Her hands clammed up the closer she approached, and she knelt before checking his pulse.

Holland bit back another cry, her chest constricting as sudden tears ran unbidden down her cheeks. The boy wasn't breathing. "No...he's so young!" *Was.*

A quick examination of the body revealed rope burns around his neck and a knife wound near his side, the cut deep and clearly already bled clean. Murder? Execution?

Holland couldn't understand it. Why this boy? Why someone so young and innocent? She brushed the lank hairs off his forehead and adjusted the collar of his shirt, a mournful prayer on her lips.

She didn't trust herself to stand, her spirit filled with an unspeakable sorrow. A hollow space carved out a place in her chest. Though she wasn't unfamiliar with it, grief often came at the strangest of times. And even stranger still to be mourning the death of someone she never knew.

"What do you think you're doing here?"

An unknown voice snapped Holland's head to attention, the sudden appearance of someone in the doorway sending her emotions into a somersault-type dance. She hastily wiped the tears from her eyes, but she couldn't keep the sorrow from her voice.

"This boy...he-he's dead." Holland squeaked, her hands shaking. The words felt final, like she couldn't take them back,

"I know." The newcomer crossed his arms, the light from outside casting half of his face in rigid shadows. His scowl was a language in itself.

He knows? Is he the killer? Holland stiffened.

"What are you doing here?" the man asked again. His tone held a sternness Holland couldn't place. Fear? Malice? Anguish?

"I..." What was she to say?

"You're a Runner, aren't you? You should be near town, not some backroad country hideout." The man stepped closer, his gaze roving over Holland's form—scrutinizing. "You're not a man."

It wasn't a question.

Holland couldn't help her gasp. Was it that obvious? If this man could tell her identity in the darkness of the shed, what did that say about the rest of society in the light?

Suddenly, she feared for her life. If this man had killed this boy, what was stopping him from doing the same to her? Oh, why had she stepped into the shed?

"What is a woman doing dressed as a Runner? And out here, of all places?" The man stopped two feet in front of her, his chest at the same height as her head. "Are you going to answer me or not?"

Holland swallowed the lump in her throat. She had a feeling that the truth was all she could muster at this point. Maybe it would keep her from getting killed. "I'm not a man." She didn't bother disguising her voice anymore. "I am seeking my destiny elsewhere, and I'm taking pains to avoid getting caught because of it."

"Pity, then, that you'd end up here after all your efforts. Maybe it's fortunate, though. For I may spare you further pain." The man's tone rang bitter now.

"I don't understand—"

"You stand over my brother; he died late last night in Tiri. I can only assume you're from Andaimon, the lesser region. You want to move up in the world, hence your costume." The man gestured to Holland's clothes.

"This isn't a cos—"

"My point is, our regions are in upheaval. My brother had strayed too close to Tiri's border, and a soldier from Famar found him and questioned him. Jaerus didn't have the required papers; he tried to run away. That's when I found him. They tore his shirt, they saw something they didn't like, and they dragged him to Tiri to…to get executed." The man's voice choked at the end, belying only a hint of the emotion he must be keeping inside.

"What do you mean by telling me all this?" Holland suddenly wanted to reach out a hand to comfort the man, but she held herself back. What was it about pain that drew strangers together?

"I mean that the king and queen are searching. All of Famar is. For anything and everything that looks suspicious. My brother died needlessly. He died trying to uphold his last ounce of honor before it was stripped clean off his back." The bitterness returned, his eyes hard and his jaw set. "And you—you scream suspicion in all the right places. I suggest you head back home if you value standing while you still can."

Holland knew what she was doing was risky, but she didn't understand what a young boy's death had to do with her decision to leave Andaimon. Though she wished more than anything that she could have saved his life.

How was she to respond to this grieving man? "I-I appreciate your concern. The loss of a loved one is…" *What?* Anything she had to say would sound inconsequential in light of his loss, her words meaningless. "My heart breaks—"

"Your heart breaks? *Yours?*" The man scrunched up his face as if he were in pain. "Was it you who watched my brother get taken away, severed from your life forever with a wretched blade? Was it you who saw them stab his side and drag his wounded body to Tiri? Was it you who tried to intervene by clawing your way through their metal hides, only to be bound and gagged instead?" He paused, his voice cracking. "Was it you they forced to watch him take his last breath—hung for the sake of a ruthless crowd's enjoyment? And for what, their own fear appeased?"

The man turned and ran a hand down his face, clearly trying to steady his nerves. When he spoke again, this time his voice was barely above a whisper. "Is it you who dreads telling your folks the news? Putting off the burial just to keep him above ground a little longer?"

A knot formed in Holland's throat. To know this kind of pain, the loss of a sibling after so many years together... She'd only ever read about it in stories. But this was real life, not some sort of twisted tale...not her *Endlewood*.

In real life, she'd also been dealt her lot. But hers was of a different kind; she'd lost something before she'd even had the chance to find it.

"I'm so sorry," Holland said, emotion lacing each word. "My heart breaks *with* yours—not in its stead. I don't know your pain, but I know loss keenly, like a sixth sense. My parents died at my birth, and I've lived twenty years of my life with this hollow pit in my chest, just wondering when it will ever get filled again."

The man didn't turn around, but the tension in his shoulders eased a fraction. "I guess grief makes friends of us all," he said bitterly.

Does it? Holland didn't speak, the silence between them filled with the weight of their sorrows. It was too heavy for just the two of them alone, but maybe she should go. This man was still a stranger; she didn't even know his name.

Holland whispered another silent prayer, but this time for the older brother. She turned to leave when a hand suddenly grabbed her upper arm.

"Wait." The man stayed her, remnants of tears glistening in the corners of his eyes. "I'm not in my right mind and fear I won't be for a while yet. But I can't have you walk out of here knowing what I know without telling you. I couldn't save my brother, but maybe I can help you. One death is enough for Griskol."

Holland's heart pounded against her ribs. What else was this broken man going to say to her? He was in agony, the grief still raw and deep within, and yet, he was taking pains to be selfless.

"Last night, I carried Jaerus' body home." The man ground his teeth. "Famar's soldiers said I should be thankful—that it wasn't every day a man from Kirkus could cross the border freely.

"As I was walking, I heard some Snoots cackling to themselves. They didn't think I could hear, but their intoxicated words pierced through my anguish. *'Serves 'em right! No one's safe with the likes of 'im around. Witcher! All the marked shall hang!'"*

The man's grip tightened on Holland's arm as if reliving the memory renewed his anger.

"I wanted to throttle them all tenfold, but I kept walking. It was then that I learned why they killed my brother. Learned what Famar is now searching for—signs of witchcraft."

Witchcraft? Holland swallowed the sudden bile rising in her throat. Now Griskol was worried about witches?

"When Jaerus was two, he got an unusual cut along his arm. It never healed properly, and the scar showed signs of...enchantment. My parents never breathed a word of it, vowing me to do the same. Jaerus knew better than to show it off. We all knew Griskol wouldn't take lightly to it. Seems we were right.

"Famar killed my brother because of his scar. And now the king and queen are spewing lies about witches walking among us, filling any willing ear with falsehoods. Famar is on the hunt for anything out of the ordinary, and a Runner away from the main road fits their criteria." The man fixed Holland with a pointed glare.

She wanted to vomit. Famar was the pinnacle of evil; did their ruthlessness know no bounds? She had so many questions, but she only landed on one. "But why are they doing this?"

The man grimaced, shaking his head. "I fear I've left out the most crucial detail. This new unrest in Famar... Well, I've only heard the rumors as of yesterday, but the current blame is placed on the emergence of witches. It seems the king and queen's baby is missing."

* * *

The sun was still warm, but sometime after noon had come and gone, the heat relented. Holland had been walking for miles, the thought of the white-bricked cottage never far behind. She didn't stay long enough to see the boy buried, wanting to give Jaerus' family that time to grieve alone. But it had left its mark, regardless. She could visualize images of dirt coating the boy's face, of the sun saying goodbye as it kissed his skin for the last time, of his parents, most assuredly weeping.

It was too much. Too close—like a mirror into her own grief.

Holland shook away the images and pressed on, her boots thumping over cobblestone.

After learning the latest news, she didn't know what to think anymore. What did it mean for Griskol now that King Randor and Queen Rosin's baby was stolen? Who had the gall to undermine their power like this? It seemed the palace of Famar was getting stricter now because of it, but she feared she didn't even know the half of it.

Going back to Benneforth Row was tempting, but she knew what awaited her there. Mrs. Kershaw was probably fuming in her hosiery, anticipating Holland's return so she could knock some sense into her.

Holland wished she could knock some sense into her employer instead. She shook her head at the thought, instantly feeling remorse. Mrs. Kershaw treated Holland the only way she knew how, and in some way, it was as loving as she could muster. After all, it was nigh impossible to keep a porcupine from its quills.

Holland couldn't go back to Andaimon. Not yet, anyway.

She'd thought about it long and hard. Her resolve to travel to Pembroke Fally seemed absurd. There was no point in seeking an audience with the king and queen on Andaimon's behalf, especially not now. They'd hang her on the spot. She wasn't naïve. She knew people were dying for things they'd never done, for reasons that weren't justified; Jaerus was the perfect example of that. She also knew how dangerous it was for her to pretend to be a Runner.

But if she turned around, she'd be right back where she first started. Nothing could shake this feeling that she had to keep going. She'd never know unless she tried. Maybe her answer lay in Tiri. If she could just catch a boat and row to Onklo… That way she might feel a little closer to her parents.

Somewhat confident in her new course, she stuck to the main road.

A few miles back, she'd passed the Brenner family forge. She'd only met Calsius a handful of times, but she could point him out anywhere with his blonde hair and green eyes.

He was outside with a bag of weapons slung over his shoulder, bidding an older woman goodbye—perhaps his mother? And he glanced at Holland, nodding his head in greeting.

Does he recognize me? Her heart sped.

"Hope the pickings are good today, mate!" he called.

Holland sighed in relief. So he didn't recognize her.

She nodded and increased her pace, leaving the forge behind in the dust.

If only he knew. What then? Would he tell Markus? They were the closest of friends. According to Markus, Calsius was a stalwart companion, as dependable as the weapons he fashioned. Markus never failed to mention him at least once in any given conversation…save for that night on the hill.

She thought back to that starry sky and Markus' hand brushing against her own. The way the breeze tousled the bottom of his hair as if asking him to dance. She didn't miss the way he had looked at her, had made her feel known and cherished in that singular moment. Of their almost kiss…

A warmth nestled its way into the emptiness inside her chest, the place where grief had sprouted roots anew. There was ample space to fill; it's only she was a sieve, all too familiar with the fleeting glimpse of hope.

It hadn't meant anything. And if it had, what then? Markus was her friend, the same way he was to Calsius. There was nothing there, and there never would be.

The idea didn't sit right with her. But there was nothing for it.

It was rather ridiculous how much she thought of him. He was practically her neighbor back in Andaimon, only a thirty-minute walk standing between them, but she'd hardly gone a day without wondering when she'd next see him. Hoping to.

"Confound it." Holland hmphed and pressed on. If she was supposed to look like a man, she might as well talk like one, too.

"Hey, Runner!"

It took a minute for Holland to realize someone was talking to her. It was a middle-aged man, his mustache as oversized as the shirt on his back.

"I've got the finest mutton on the block! Come, see for yourself," the man shouted again, but this time clearly showing his aim. He gestured to the many slabs of lamb hanging from the awning of his booth.

"No, thanks." Holland dropped her voice an octave. "I've my eyes set on something farther into town." She kept walking, trying not to show her fear.

"There's nowhere better! Besides, I need the business."

If anyone needed the business around here, it wasn't him. His girth alone was an indicator he was well off enough to afford the loss.

"You'll be disappointed!" he called again.

"I'll take my chances." Holland sped up, not looking back. But no sooner had another vendor called for her attention.

"Runner, over here!"

"No, over here!"

"I saw him first!"

They came all at once and from all directions. Holland's heart raced, her eyes darting from one person to the next. She didn't know what to do. Could she ignore them? Surely, they'd leave her alone. They weren't that desperate, were they?

She didn't wait to find out.

CHAPTER TWENTY-THREE
Markus

He'd been traveling for hours, Hamish lumbering loyally by his side. Miles back, they'd walked past an unhappy nesting grouse, made even more territorial by Hamish's curiosity, and then a stretch of corn that rivaled Markus' field back home. He'd also observed a grieving family, crying over a mound of dirt with purple wisteria blooms gently placed on top.

He bowed his head in condolences, the sight wrenching his heart. He didn't know who had died, but he recognized the tears. He had experienced his own when his father had been buried the same way.

Markus had seen all these things, but there was still no sign of Holland. Maybe she hadn't come this way after all.

He surveyed the land before him. This was as far north as he'd ever dared go, and the land was already starting to look different than the rest of Kirkus. In the west, the farmland became rockier, stretching into hills and then mountains. Markus knew from studying geography as a child that those mountains served as a border into Eskal and Irthlen. He didn't know much about those countries, but he knew passage into them wasn't easy. Their borders were patrolled even more than Griskol's regions.

He licked his lips, his mouth dry. He needed water, and Hamish probably did, too.

Blessedly, Markus spotted a little creek up ahead, babbling through a cluster of cattails. He pushed aside the reeds and knelt down, scooping handfuls of cold water to his mouth. It trickled down his chin and landed in little droplets on his clothes.

Hamish plowed right past him, standing in the creek with the water up to his stomach. He lapped up the liquid like he'd never tasted water before, and Markus couldn't help but chuckle.

Something rustled in the bushes. Markus peered over the edge of the creek to see a duck family, the little babies following behind their parents. There were seven of them, all clustered together and kicking their webbed feet to keep pace.

Hamish's ears perked up, watching the ducks with marked curiosity, though he stayed right where he was. He seemed content to just observe.

The gentle stream, the quacking ducks—it was an image that felt like hope, reminding Markus that there was still some good in the world. That if only he took a moment to slow down, he'd find it right under his nose. Not everything was tainted by Famar... Not everything could be touched. Where there was light and goodness, the shadows could only abide so long.

Markus pushed himself to stand; renewed vigor had filled his weary spirit. He didn't know where Holland was, but he would keep trying. And he wouldn't let Famar win.

It was only a few hours more to Tiri's border. And by then, it would be well into the night. But if he picked up his pace, maybe he'd cut his time in half.

Hamish might give him grief for it, though. The bloodhound could run, but he was getting older. It was a lot of ground to cover in a short period of time, especially for a dog with signs of rheumatism.

On second thought.

"All right, Ham. Let's go. We'll find a place to hunker down for the night once we get a little closer."

Hamish barked as if in gratitude, following after him.

* * *

Nightfall encased Markus like a cloak, the stars and moon revealing only traces of their light from behind stretches of cloud. It was getting late, and there would be no use in searching for Holland in the dark.

Markus squinted into the shadows, spotting what looked like cylindrical silhouettes in the distance—something he hoped could provide a decent shelter. He edged closer to one, reaching out to find the coarse fibers of straw beneath his fingers. Hay bales. He'd seen some earlier before the sun had set, but he didn't expect to see more this far north. He didn't need much for coverage, just something to shield Hamish and him from the world.

A hay bale would have to do.

He pulled at the straw, forming a small tent just big enough for him to sleep inside. Openings were on both sides, in case he needed a hasty retreat, and Hamish lay at his feet—a guard dog.

Markus rested on his back, staring at the sky while chewing a parsnip. The clouds had parted just enough for some stars to poke through, their twinkling filled with secrets. It was quiet like it was back home. Similar to the barn loft. But here, it felt different. Lonely even.

His heart ached for Holland. The truth stung, a sensation strangely hollow. How he wished she were marveling at the sky beside him, pointing out constellations with her dainty finger, a smile on her lips.

Would she whisper their stories? Talk of Orion and Castor like they were her friends? Or laugh at the shooting stars, claiming they were actually runaway children, hell-bent on finding their destinies, too?

The thought sobered him. Maybe he was searching in the wrong spot. He knew Holland wanted to blend in, but she'd be smart about it; perhaps she had actually chosen to walk the main road after all.

Tomorrow he'd double back and check. Just in case. But tonight... He was suddenly growing tired. His eyes were already halfway closed when a hand landed on his shoulder.

Markus stilled, all traces of slumber gone. His mind was alert and spun to keep up with his pounding heart. Whose hand was on his shoulder? Why didn't Hamish bark?

He was dragged to his feet, an orange spark erupting before his vision only to peter to a steady flame. The light revealed a decorated soldier, the lantern casting his face in unearthly shadows.

"Name?" the man questioned.

Markus' stomach dropped; he was sure this man was one of Famar's generals. He should have been more careful being this close to the border. And where was Hamish?

"What for?" Markus crossed his arms.

"What's your name?" the general demanded yet again, his grip tightening on Markus' shoulder.

It was degrading to be held as such, like cattle tethered to a barn post. His jaw ticked to the side, and he swallowed his pride. Some of it, anyway. He spoke through clenched teeth. "Markus Fenn." Maybe he should have given a false name, but he was still in Kirkus. He should be safe.

"Papers?" The man put the lantern down and held out his other hand, waiting.

Papers? Markus blanched, his pulse in his throat. What papers? *"It's only a matter of time before they start requiring us to identify ourselves too."* Calsius' words rang in his ears. His friend had been right.

Markus' brow beaded with sweat, and his hands suddenly felt clammy. "I, uh…let me get them." Markus slowly pretended to search his pockets, wondering if he had anything that would suffice. He would make the blasted general wait all night, for all he cared.

Famar requiring paper identification was hardly fair if the whole of Griskol hadn't yet learned of it. Since when was this a thing? Was he to bring his birthing papers with him wherever he went? Or were these papers of a different sort? The thought was madness.

"Hurry up," the soldier demanded.

Markus felt his pockets once more, pausing when he remembered his father's knife. *My boot.* "Ah, I almost forgot... I usually keep these sorts of things in my shoe." He bent toward his boot, his fingers finding the weapon tucked near his sock. Its presence alone bolstered his resolve; he'd do well to use it. He stealthily slipped the knife into his palm and pocketed it before standing. "I seem to have left my papers at home, I fear," he said with as much confidence as he could muster. "But I can assure you my family owns the plot of farmland in the south."

"I wonder then, why you're at the edge of Tiri's border, hiding away like some country rat. Who's to say you're not some southern *filth*?" The general sneered. "Tell me, do you value your neck while it still holds?" he asked the question nonchalantly, as if he had just inquired about what Markus preferred for breakfast.

"I—" He could tell the man was baiting him, waiting for him to crack. Markus swallowed past the sudden lump in his throat. He wouldn't give the man the satisfaction. "I find it holds better the farther north I go."

His words achieved their desired effect.

The general seemed taken by surprise, his nonchalance dropping into another sneer. "That's enough outta you. You'll pay for your crimes." As quick as lightning, he whipped out a blade and tore through the fabric of Markus' shirt, ripping it clean off his body.

Thunderation.

A thin trail of blood dripped down his abdomen from where the blade nicked his skin. It stung something awful. Fear clawed at his throat; he felt naked. Exposed. He never took his shirt off in public, as long as he could help it. And now, this man was making sport of him for who-knew-what reason.

"Turn," the soldier commanded.

Markus' back went rigid. All he could think about was his scar. No living eyes had seen it, and he'd like to keep it that way. He needed to fight back. He reached into his pocket and grabbed the knife...but was spilling blood worth it? And what if he failed? He'd lose his father's last parting gift.

His gaze was drawn to the lantern on the ground, its flame licking the panes of glass. He had an idea—one that might get him killed. He feigned compliance, making the motion of turning around, but before exposing his back to his captor, he twisted from beneath his grip and kicked the lantern, diffusing the light.

He sprinted into the dark.

"After him!" the soldier barked.

Markus' pulse skyrocketed. But why would one man yell unless... *No.*

For too brief a moment, the shadows kept him, but then the dying embers must have found the hay, using it as fodder to bloom. Before he knew it, his entire hay bale was in flames, illuminating the host of men surrounding him.

Markus didn't stop. He ran hard, ducking around hay bales and sprinting as quickly as he could. Exhaustion was a thing of the past, a foreign notion to his pounding adrenaline. The firelight shrunk the farther away he ran from it, but that didn't matter. He kept running, the towering trees before him a promising shelter.

He squinted into the hazy night, running at the silhouettes with marked determination. If he could but reach one and climb into its boughs, he'd be able to disappear.

Thunder reverberated all around him, but it didn't belong to the sky. Hoofbeats pounded behind him, telling him he wouldn't get out of this without a fight. Markus ran on, but his attempts were futile when pitted up against horses. He was soon overtaken, surrounded by three men on white chargers and three soldiers on foot—two of whom were holding lanterns. The general was the last to join the group, sitting atop a horse of his own. It was a total of seven against one.

Markus was outnumbered. He'd only just realized his dog was still missing, that he wasn't by his side even now. Then Markus remembered the fire, the hay bale going up in flames. His stomach dropped. *Where's Hamish?*

"Want to try running away now, witcher?" The general spat at Markus' feet, his dagger pointed toward his heart.

Witcher? "Where's my dog?" Markus fixed his stare at the man, unwavering.

"A drugged dog is a good dog. Thanks to your fire, a dead one is even better." The general had the audacity to laugh.

The hope Markus had felt earlier was all but snuffed out. Part of his soul collapsed, the reality a devastating shock. But he couldn't show weakness now, not when his very life depended on his strength.

He needed to believe this wasn't the end. He'd vowed to protect Holland, but he couldn't even protect his own dog. The thought crushed him, a despairing blow to his pride.

Suddenly, his legs were kicked out from beneath him, and a sharp stab of pain plunged into his side. Agony, burning, searing agony. He choked, gasping for air. His vision blurred, and all was becoming night. He was sprawled on his back with a bloody broadsword pointed at his throat.

"Bind him. In Tiri, he hangs."

Holland

A barn owl's call sounded into the night, a welcome noise as much as it was alarming. Nature was Holland's friend, and trees and animals of any variety always had a way of soothing that unsettled ache inside her chest. A reminder that she wasn't alone, and that she too could find her wings and call into the night. If only she knew how.

That's why she was here, wasn't it? To find her purpose? She'd find a boat and go to Onklo. Just to be on the ocean would be enough, to know she was touching the same water that held the corpses of her parents. She was told they'd been buried at sea. If she could but listen to the tune of the waves, would she hear their voices?

Perhaps it was a fool's dream, a merry fancy or too much to hope for, but here at night, in a cast-off hollow tree, it felt strangely comforting.

Holland had walked in haste most of the day, exhausting herself beyond measure. And she hadn't even crossed into Tiri yet, though she must be close. It was strange to her how large Kirkus was compared to Andaimon. Holland could walk the full stretch of her village back home in the matter of a few hours, but Kirkus' was proving rather difficult.

193

So, she left the safety of the main road and retreated to the deep recesses of a nearby park. An abandoned hollow had called out to her like a beacon in the night, its trunk providing a barrier between her and the outside world.

She pressed her back up against the decaying bark, peering out of the crack and into the darkness. The stars danced between the clouds, winking and unmoving as if they were pushpins to a black cloth. Holland suddenly found herself missing her needle and thread, the satisfaction of finishing a project and seeing the happiness of her customers.

She had plenty of stories to tell Benjamon already. Her escape through town had been anything but relaxing, not to mention seeing Calsius. It was as if she'd been a match and every vendor had been a midge, drawn to her presence simply because of her uniform.

Holland leaned her head back and sighed. At least for now, she could catch her breath and rest her body. She wondered what Markus was doing. Had he even realized she'd gone? Had he visited the hill in the back of the Row, missing her company?

What of the stars? To think, the same expanse of sky connected them no matter the distance between. It was still the same moon and stars which smiled upon Griskol. The same moon and stars upon which they both looked. Was he looking even now?

Again with her thoughts about Markus. It surprised her. He wasn't here with her, and yet, thinking of him was like a warm breeze in the midst of winter. Like coming back home after a long day away. Heat rose to her cheeks.

Home? Nothing had ever felt like home. That's what she was trying to find after all—a place to belong. Wasn't it?

She shifted her position and laid on her side with her legs cozied up to her chest. The gentle call of the barn owl came again, but this time farther away. Holland closed her eyes a moment, the need for sleep fighting with her desire to keep them open. But try as she might to avoid it, she soon drifted into dreams in the arms of the tree, the hoot of the owl and the kiss of the starry sky her lullaby.

CHAPTER TWENTY-FOUR
Holland

A sudden chill nipped the back of Holland's neck, rousing her awake. The morning felt different than yesterday's heat, but the change in temperature was to be expected. One could only keep Griskol's frosts away for so long, a season that struck with a vengeance once it arrived. It was a wonder that the land thawed enough for the spring and summer at all.

Holland stretched, a yawn escaping her lips. My, she was hungry. She'd been so concerned with avoiding yesterday's vendors that she'd only eaten a loaf of bread all day. She'd have to summon all her courage if she didn't want to travel on an empty stomach.

She pushed to stand and poked her head out of the hollow, the empty park a sign that she was alone. She left her hideout only to face the tree one last time. She'd miss this timber, its protection against the night, and its companionship during her contemplative hours. It had felt like a friend, like it had been rotting away all these years just to give her respite for a night.

The thought warmed. She didn't know what the rest of her

journey would bring, but here, at least, she felt safe. Felt a moment's reprieve and a sense of assurance. She placed a hand on the tree's bark, smiling up into its lifeless boughs. "I know you can't hear a word I'm saying. But I thank you anyway. For keeping my thoughts safe and for making me feel less alone... I wish you'd stand here forever."

Tears stung the corners of her eyes. Why was she crying? And over a dead tree? But it was more than that. She hadn't said goodbye to anyone back in Andaimon. She hadn't waved to her neighbors or warned Mrs. Kershaw. She hadn't even hugged Markus, and here she was, saying goodbye to something that would never even remember her.

She wasn't built for this. Years of loneliness had left her heart shrunken and empty. It wasn't used to harboring so much emotion, to holding it and letting it be felt. But after finding Jaerus' body, seeing the grief on his brother's face, and realizing all she'd left behind, her heart cracked anew, as if breaking apart the empty space that was already there.

And all this from a hollow tree? Perhaps she was more like this tree than she realized. Like the white-bricked cottage, too. Was everything to remind her of the state of her brokenness?

Holland shoved away from the bark, running her sleeve across her face. She was supposed to act like a boy—a man. And men didn't cry. She needed to get away from this place; it made her vulnerable—a thing she needed to avoid.

Her goal was to make it to Tiri's fishing ports, and she couldn't do that by crying over a dead tree. She left the park without looking back, her boots soon hitting the familiar cobblestones of the main road. The sooner she got out of Kirkus, the better.

Markus

A cool breeze stirred the air, the kind that got under one's skin and reminded the bones of winter's inevitable approach. But not for Markus. His bones were on fire. So was his side. He was fatigued, wearied from the struggle in trying to loosen his bonds. He'd made little progress.

The only comfort he had was the feel of cool metal between his palms. He'd been able to conceal his father's knife when the soldiers bound his hands; he blamed their negligence on thinking him a lowly farmer. Their underestimation would work to his advantage.

It was just after sunrise, the heat of yesterday all but a distant memory. They were back on the main road, hoofbeats clomping along the cobblestone street. The foot soldiers had stayed back to patrol the border; it was only Markus with the four horses and their riders in front of him.

They had rested most of the night at some outpost, only to begin the march into Tiri at first light. His captors had stopped to relieve themselves in the homes of willing villagers and let their mounts drink their fill at the local watering trough. Markus hadn't been given such an opportunity, and he was feeling it.

They bandaged his side with pointless rags, lashed his wrists with a rope, and attached him to the saddle of the general's charger. The horse, though it had a mind of its own, bent to its master's will, cantering at too grueling a pace for Markus, limping behind on foot.

And he'd been walking for what felt like ages. He considered himself in good health, strong, capable, and able to weather many storms—much like his crops—but those things didn't make this any more endurable. The horse lurched forward, and he ground his teeth as the rope bit into his wrists and the wound on his side stung afresh.

His throat was dry, the gag over his mouth rubbing against his skin. Apparently, the soldiers thought he was some sort of witcher, one who could utter incantations at will. They'd inhibited his ability to speak, and therefore his ability to swallow.

What he'd give for a fresh drought. Or some brandy to make his insides feel more alive. To burn his throat. Anything to cure the blasted pain.

He wanted to fight back. His fingers itched to wield the knife in his hands to its fullest capacity. But that would come. First, he was thinking of a plan. If there was one thing Markus was good at, it was strategizing. A farmer never planted in the wrong season, and he knew how to combat the harsh frosts should it take him unawares. He'd learned his whole life how to get out of a fix, to make good out of lousy situations.

And now was no different. Slowly, but surely, he was sawing away at his bonds. It was painstaking progress, but it was progress.

For now, he'd let Famar's soldiers have their fun, but sooner or later, he'd fight back. They wouldn't know what hit them.

Holland

Holland walked through town, her gait more like a hasty stroll rather than yesterday's sprint as she wove through villagers. Thankfully, the vendors' stands were more spread out the farther north she went, but she still feared their unwanted attention from the day before. She couldn't avoid them forever, though. Her hunger from this morning was only growing, and sooner or later, she'd have to buy something to eat. Hopefully, the whole ordeal wouldn't start all over again.

Something green drew her gaze forward. A little farther up the road stood a Runner, a faded *27* on his armband. He talked to a man who was trying to sell him jars filled with something earthy. "I promise you, they're fresh! Just made them myself this morning!" the man said.

Holland squinted at the jars. Relish? Sauerkraut? Spinach? It was hard to tell. She edged closer, shielding herself behind a group of villagers walking in the same direction. She was curious to watch the Runner in action; for all her travels, she had yet to see the type of person she was epitomizing. This one, however, looked older than she'd imagined a Runner to be.

"I'll take your word for it." He drew out his coin pouch and placed six darics on the table, collecting three jars in turn. He seemed pleased with the transaction.

Suddenly, someone stepped out from the shadows, grabbing his shoulder.

"'Ey, watch it!" The Runner swerved on his heel as he turned to face his accoster, his face pale.

Holland stifled a gasp. She hadn't seen the man lurking in the alleyway, as if he had been sitting and waiting. But now that he was in the broad daylight, she understood why. The man wore livery as dark as the night sky and looked like some sort of soldier. Was he from Famar? Holland could only guess. His sword was sheathed at his side, the hilt glinting in the morning sun.

"Name? Papers?" he addressed the Runner. His grip appeared firm, his words like iron.

The Runner hastily rummaged through his pockets and pulled out what looked like parchment. The soldier snatched the papers, leafing through them, and nodded as the Runner spoke, glancing up at the man every now and again.

Holland's palms twitched, her stomach swooping like a million birds. She needed to disappear before the man-in-arms demanded the same from her. Suddenly, the main road didn't feel safe anymore.

She swallowed hard and followed the throng of villagers further north, keeping her head down low. To look back would show her fear; to look forward would ensure her confidence. She kept walking, only picking up her pace when she rounded a bend. Blood pounded against her temples with each thump of her feet. She was running now, missing the safety of the hollow oak.

In Andaimon, Holland may have had a roof over her head, but even so, she was never truly secure. For how could freedom exist in a land that determined everything for her? Where endless laws were put in place to strip people of their dignity, peace could only reside so long. It was masked behind a message of 'progress,' but the truth was like a steady stream, leaking from the fissures of Famar's heavily fortified walls. Nowhere was safe.

Before Holland knew it, her hands flew out in front of her, breaking her fall. She landed hard, bruising her wrists from the ground's impact, her heart skipping wildly. Had the soldier caught her after all? A look behind her revealed no one in black livery. Instead, she looked toward her feet, a rush of relief flooding her wearied mind. A black shoelace, untied and lank like a noodle, was wedged under the sole of one of her boots. Holland amended the problem, missing the ease of her slippers; they at least didn't make her trip. But she'd taken pains to look like a man. Her boots wouldn't be coming off any time soon.

She moved to stand but not before realizing the road looked different. It was laden with brick rather than cobblestone. She glanced behind her and then looked ahead once again, the brick stretching in both directions. Was this Tiri? When had she crossed the border? In all her haste, she hadn't been paying much attention to her surroundings.

Holland scanned the buildings on her left and right, seeing them more fully now that she wasn't moving; they were yet another giveaway that she wasn't in Andaimon anymore. The walls of the houses and shops were pristinely clean, and various women with mops were outside on their stoops, washing away the day's grime. Their clotheslines sported garments of superior make; Holland could tell their quality even from afar. There were also men pulling trash carts, ridding the street of anything and everything that didn't belong.

Holland guessed that included pinecones, for she just saw a man put several in his cart, casting them off as useless goods. In Andaimon, they were a novelty and had many uses: mulch, stew enhancers, or even pincushions, just to name a few. But maybe that was only fitting. Wasn't Andaimon the *filth* of Griskol? Pinecones weren't good enough for the Snoots.

She rolled her eyes. She disliked Tiri already, though her nose seemed to think otherwise. Spices like nothing Holland had ever smelled before danced beneath her nostrils, taunting her. A growl followed, erupting from her stomach, and her mouth salivated at the thought of food.

"I guess now's the time." Holland bit her lip and surveyed the line of houses. Vendors' booths were only a little further ahead.

She groaned inwardly at the prospect of having to purchase something to eat again, especially after running for her life because of it. But the pangs in her stomach had her feet moving forward of their own volition; she couldn't help herself.

She stopped at a booth where the smell had come from, her eyes widening at the sight of a large brew, practically bubbling over. Was it soup? It smelled even more glorious up close, enough to almost make Holland forget her fear of being caught by a soldier. Almost. She finally noticed the person standing behind the table.

It was a petite girl who appeared a few years Holland's junior. Her hair was auburn and she had countless freckles splayed across her cheeks. She looked friendly, though the smile on her face didn't seem the authentic kind. Was she nervous? "H-how may I help you, sir?" the girl asked.

Yes, she was definitely nervous. Why?

"What are you cooking?" Holland made sure to smile, hoping to ease the girl's discomfort. She leaned over the pot and noticed something green and feathery. She inhaled deeply. "Whatever it is, it smells like heaven."

The girl's countenance brightened. "It's lamb olio—a thick stew with potatoes and fennel. I made it this morning, and it's mighty tasty, if I dare be so bold." Red dotted her cheeks as if she'd suddenly said too much. She looked downward but not before glancing at Holland's arm. She froze, her gaze fixed with marked horror. "That—Your number...!"

Holland followed her gaze, looking at the upside down *17* on her arm. "What about it?" she asked, cautiously. She knew exactly what was wrong with it, but she wouldn't offer the truth out here for all of Tiri to hear. She had a feeling this wasn't going to turn out well.

"It-it belongs to Cadmon. Cadmon Glock. Is he...? Did he...?" The girl raised a shaky hand to her lips, her eyes glossing over.

This girl knew Cadmon? Holland recalled the conversation she'd had with his brother Benjamon. Was this girl just one of the many on the receiving end of Cadmon's 'schmoozing'?

Oh no.

Holland had to stop herself from reaching across the table to comfort the woeful girl. It wouldn't do well, dressed as she was. "No, as far as I know, Cadmon is very much alive." She tried to sound confident in her assurance. For all of Cadmon's supposed faults, she truly wished him well.

"Oh. Thank the stars!" The girl sighed, sagging against the table. She swiped the moisture from her eyes. "I don't know what I would've done if I learned he-learned he..." She couldn't finish the sentence.

And Holland couldn't help it. She reached over and placed a steadying hand on the girl's forearm. "Please—don't go there. He is alive. You don't need to fear."

The girl nodded, seeming to appreciate the assurance. She resumed stirring the pot of olio, biting her lip in the process. Looking up once again, she seemed to study Holland with an air of curiosity. "Why do you have his number then? I thought all Runners only had one."

Holland's stomach churned inside. How could she avoid this conversation? She couldn't. She'd have to lie, and she only prayed that it wouldn't crash and burn at her feet. "You're right. But, uh…they changed our numbers…"

The girl's eyes widened. "But Cadmon would have told me! He usually tells me things!" She stopped stirring the stew and gripped the spoon tightly. "Maybe he forgot…"

Gads. Holland had to steer the conversation in a different direction. It was dangerous and people were beginning to stare. "Why are you so worried about Cadmon's safety? How do you know him?"

The girl slowly lost her frantic look and resumed her stirring. A blush climbed her cheeks, but this time, there was a sincerity behind it—a secret smile. "Well, in truth, he's one of the few men I trust. He's my friend, my truest friend, and he's loyal. He keeps the other men away…"

Holland couldn't believe what she was hearing. Cadmon Glock, the schmoozing boy from Andaimon, wasn't actually a schmoozer? "Why does he need to keep other men away?" She was skeptical.

"Because some are scoundrels. Well, the few I've encountered anyway. Thankfully, you seem the exception. But Cadmon's come to my rescue on many occasions. He even knocked someone out once." The girl blushed again, her voice suddenly going quiet. "But you want to know a real secret?" She paused, waiting for Holland to nod. "He's promised himself to me. Can you believe it? He said he'd wanted to leave Andaimon, but that becoming a Runner was the best thing that's ever happened to him because it led him to me. Me! Of all people." The girl sighed happily.

Promised himself? Were they engaged, then?

"He said once he has enough darics, he'll buy me a ring and ask me properly. In the meantime, I count down the days, serving my olio and avoiding disrespectful men like Griskol does magic." The girl's nerves had all but disappeared. It was as if talking about Cadmon bolstered her spirits and gave her courage.

How was their relationship possible? Regions weren't allowed to mix through marriage. It was illegal!

As if reading her thoughts, the girl leaned in closer. "I don't worry much over the details. I know Griskol has its rules, but we'll find a way to be together. I know we will." She smiled, the corners of her mouth edged in contented lines.

Holland nodded. She was happy for the girl, but her confidence spoke of her naivety. Theirs was a relationship doomed from the start.

The girl's words weighed heavily of a resounding truth: no one wanted a girl from Andaimon. That's why Cadmon had sought one elsewhere.

Holland gripped her chest, rubbing at the subtle ache. No one paid much attention to Andaimon in general, and especially not to someone as broken as *her*. No one except Markus, that is. But he didn't have any romantic interest in a girl like Holland. She had nothing to offer him except an uncertain past and her poverty. He deserved better. Besides, he was from Kirkus. Different regions didn't mix.

Why do I keep thinking of him like this? They were only friends! She heaved an exasperated breath, blaming it on her limited interaction with men. She knew the risk of giving one's heart without restraint. That's why she kept hers so close; it was too mangled to do otherwise. She'd do well to remember that.

And she'd also do well not to pity herself because of it.

Regardless, Holland's opinion of Cadmon was improving by the minute. Apparently, he hadn't cared about his reputation or else he wouldn't have told Benjamon such misleading information. Cadmon was actually a gentleman.

Holland looked at the girl and smiled, genuinely. "Congratulations are in order then." *No matter how impossible they appear.*

"They are, indeed!" The girl beamed, her smile like a half moon.

Holland's stomach growled loudly, drawing both of their attention to the present moment. All this talk had only prolonged the inevitable. She needed to eat. "I think it's about time I tried some of that olio of yours."

"Oh, right!" The girl looked flustered at forgetting to offer Holland food. "One bowl coming right up!" She set to work scooping the stew into a porcelain dish, the brown gravy dripping over the sides and splattering on the table. "Here you are, sir."

Holland received the food, gratefully. She tossed a few darics on the table and nodded. "Thank you, I'm sure this will be just what I need." It was true. Her stomach was practically wailing now. "It was nice talking to you," she offered before turning around. She lifted the wooden spoon to her lips, the broth promising nourishment as she walked into the throng of villagers.

Their conversation was as enlightening as it was unsettling. She'd learned Cadmon had become a Runner because he'd wanted to leave Andaimon. Was it so wrong for him to want something more? Holland had just done the same thing; it's what she had wanted, too. But why did Cadmon's actions seem to affect that already bruised place in her chest? Perhaps it was because Andaimon was all she'd ever known. It was the only claim she had to her identity, and if someone wanted to leave it, it was as if they were willingly leaving her... Cadmon was just one example out of many.

Holland shook the depressing thoughts away, vowing not to dwell on them any longer. She really shouldn't allow herself to think on an empty stomach.

She moved farther into town, all the while heaping her spoon, and noticed what looked like a town square. On its outskirts, people sat on benches, chatting away the noon hour. Brick and green grass stretched beneath their feet like a patchwork quilt, and sculpted bushes were arranged around the whole area in a symmetrical design. In the center of the square stood a fountain, its stone structure depicting King Randor and Queen Rosin in all their royal raiments. It shot out water in five different directions, the gentle breeze teasing the streams and sending a refreshing mist into the air.

Everything looked perfect. Too perfect.

A ram's horn suddenly blared, disrupting the tranquil peace of Tiri—a sound Holland had only heard once before. She knew it was used at the onset of a hunting party and then again at its end— a way to bookend the excursion. But there weren't many hunting parties in Griskol, at least not in Andaimon.

Why was the horn sounding now...and in the street of all places? There was nothing to be hunted that wasn't under the shade of trees.

The horn sounded again, this time louder than before. It echoed in the square, and the Snoots stopped what they were doing, looking expectantly toward the road. Holland turned and saw four white chargers stalking through town, a soldier on each of their backs. The man in the lead held the horn to his lips, his other hand tight on the reins. They trotted forward, heading in the direction of the fountain with a weary-looking man bound, gagged, and tethered to the horse in the rear.

She followed the horses with her gaze and studied the captured man closely. Her heart suddenly stopped. She let go of her bowl of lamb olio, shattering the pottery on the brick. Her stomach clenched, restricting her breathing.

Markus?

CHAPTER TWENTY~FIVE
From "The Tale of Endlewood"

*M*y elbows are propped up on a table, my hands snaking through my hair as I stare at the plan before me.

"Your Majesty?" Nindrol calls from somewhere down the corridor. "Are you in your study?"

Tomorrow marks ten years of being back in these woods. My palace is finished, and the wooden desk I sit at feels more like a weighted chain about my ankles. Such is the duty of a king. But there's nothing else for me.

"Your Majesty?" Nindrol's voice sounds again.

I don't answer him. He'll find me soon enough. I continue studying the map before me, a crude rendition of my kingdom. Red x's mark the places where watchers are stationed along the perimeter, and I wonder if I can afford reinforcements should my system fail. With the Overseer gone, I've had to get creative.

For the past ten years, this wood has had its fair share of activity. Once my beloved wife passed, her father came looking for her. There was no Overseer to keep him away, and my fear was great. To think he might blame me for her death... He couldn't know the truth. It would be too much. The watchers had been told to get rid of anyone should they enter these woods. Thus, I let them do their job. They followed through.

I swallow hard. It was never meant to be like that. First my love and then her father. But others came as well. Over the years, it was old men with swords, curious teens with bows and arrows, and even what looked to be foot soldiers from who-knows-where.

They all died. Every last one of them. But not before a few of my watchers were taken in turn. I'd lost some stalwart men, and though my kingdom has grown in number, there aren't many of us left to fill the holes. But I've another plan up my sleeve. One I've been working on for years. With my son now ten, it's finally time for the first phase to begin.

Death used to stir my stomach, but now it only fuels me. I once hated the sight of blood, especially when Josi had spilled an abundance for us all. But now I find the world can't give me enough. No amount can bring Josi back, and for that, the world should be colored red. The world can burn.

Something like guilt niggles the back of my mind. I push it aside. To have a conscience is to have a weakness. I've grown numb, but occasionally I still feel. To feel is also a weakness, and something I stamp down before it even begins.

Elethün thinks otherwise. He believes that a feeling heart is successful in all the ways that a hardened heart fails. To feel is to heal; that is a balm in and of itself.

Someone clears their throat behind me, the sound breaking the silence. "Your Majesty?"

I glance up. Nindrol has found me at last. He's in the

doorway, standing rigid with his hand held fast to the collar of my son's shirt in an attempt to keep him still. The boy keeps trying to break free from Nindrol's grasp, and I don't blame him.

"You have need of me?" I ask, not bothering to hold his gaze. I don't have time for his machinations which involve endless lectures and discipline regimes.

"Not I. Your son. He's been out at the swamp again. If it wasn't for my intervention, I fear the Wispsnare would have finished him at last." Nindrol tsks, shaking his head.

I shift in my seat, ignoring the thread of fear snaking its way through my chest. The Swamp Wispsnare is lethal. Everyone knows enough to stay away from it. That is, everyone but my son. "Well, I see he's safely in your care. Why give me cause to think otherwise?"

Nindrol frowns, pushing my son forward and leveling his gaze with mine. "Your Majesty, he was not merely by the swamp, he was inside it! Floating around like a rogue log. If he continues in this way, his lungs will soon fill with water and a siren's song will be his funeral dirge."

"That's not true!" my son argues.

"No need to be so pessimistic, Nindrol. I know my son, and he's no fool. But I'll take him off your hands now, for I have something important to tell him."

My son's eyes light up like a will-o'-the-wisp; a broad smile stretches across his face. Nindrol releases him rather reluctantly and turns on his heel, expelling some sort of exasperation as he leaves the room. I ignore him and face the child before me.

"What are you gonna tell me, Father?"

"I've a secret." I open the bottom drawer of my desk, push aside some papers, and lift a loose board of wood. If I must be king, I'll do it in my own way, even if it means hidden compartments for things that don't belong here—that aren't fae-kind. I pull the object from its secret location and hold it up in the light.

My son's eyes widen, his mouth forming a perfect circle. "Where did you get that?" He stretches his hand forward and tries to touch it.

I pull back. "Not yet, son. In due time. Do you know what this is?"

"It looks like a blade! But how did you find one? I didn't think weapons were made here."

"You're right on both accounts. That's why it's a human blade, though I've infused it with magic. And I have my ways. I am king, am I not?" What I don't tell him is that the knife belonged to Josi's father; a weapon I filched off his limp body. For years, it remained hidden in the castle's strong-room, locked away with the countless other weapons discarded by the Overseer.

"But why do you have it?" My son reaches for the weapon again, but I still him with a hand on his shoulder.

"Before I became king, I worked at a guild. I studied means of war, of defense, of weaponry—all in the name of magic. Our greatest weapons are our words which can create and destroy as much as any sword. But you're young and have yet to master the art."

"What does that mean?"

"I'm getting there, son. Let me finish." I twist the knife again, *letting the lantern-light reflect off its silver edge. "Many years ago, something terrible happened to our kingdom. It made our greatest defenses weak, and it caused many of us to flee in fear. Your grandfather was killed in the scourge, naming me as king after him. I fled here to these woods, the only place that you've ever called home." I don't have the heart to tell him of his birth in the village. He won't ever learn of the bungalow by the hedgerow as long as I can help it. "I vowed to protect this land against the failures that destroyed Lamia. For a while, it seemed to work, but then disaster struck again.*

"Our defenses were compromised and then your mother…" My voice cracks. Speaking of Josi hasn't gotten easier after all these years, the missing all the more potent. I swallow hard and continue. "Your mother died. She was taken from me—from us— before you could even walk. I then vowed to protect our land anew, but I had to come up with a new plan."

"A new plan, Father?"

"Yes. One that I knew you'd play a role in. You see, after living here for the past decade, I've learned a lot about my enemies: what they like, what they love, what they fear. And it's their fear from which this plan has derived. The lands beyond the trees fear magic—the very thing which gives us life. And in their minds, this wood—our home—has been the cause of all their strife. But it's their fault that your mother has died." I blame Josi's death on those in the village. If it wasn't for them, the Overseer never would have existed in the first place.

"What am I to do?" my son asks, nervously.

"I need your help. For you see, I will make my prediction now.

ALISSA J. ZAVALIANOS

The current king is old, and it's only a matter of time until he passes his reign onto his son. And when he does, I know they will want an heir. And it is that heir we will take."

"A baby, Father? You want me to steal a baby?" My son looks mortified, and his hands are shaking like a leaf in the wind.

"Not now, son. But that will come in time. I want you to do something a little more discreet. You see, when the child is stolen, people will naturally look to our home as the cause. They will come here, looking for a fight. But our legion is few, and I fear we won't stand a chance against their forces." Like how Lamia didn't stand a chance against the Dyvrats. "To avoid this, we will create a diversion."

"What does 'discreet' mean? What's a diversion?"

My speech wavers, my heart twisting. In light of everything, my son is so innocent. To make him do this next thing could ruin him. Break him, even. I can't think about that right now. "It means something that isn't showy and will cause a distraction. Instead of blaming the woods for their stolen child, I want them to blame each other—the 'witches.' The lands beyond our trees are terrified of magic, and what better way to stoke the fire than to make them believe witches walk among them? A marked person is a bad person in their eyes."

"I don't understand. What do you mean by 'marked'?" My son creases his brow, his eyes now on the knife.

"Now is the moment where I tell you the first part of your task." I inhale deeply and try to steady my voice. I need the words to come out even and strong, enforcing the importance of the deed while not inciting fear. "You will sneak through every village and

216

find at least forty people. Age doesn't matter, but they are to be found alone; that, you must be sure of. Then, you will take this knife and mark them as the witches and witchers they are."

My son takes a step back, his eyes rounding like saucers. "You want me to hurt people?"

My vision blurs slightly, and it takes everything in my power to keep my hands from shaking. This is my plan, and it must be carried out. I am too old, too assuming for the job, and my son is only half-fae. His humanness will aid him in the task, my fae-blood will only inhibit me. I swallow back the guilt and nod, resolved. He must do this, not me.

"It's but a mere flesh wound. You won't be hurting them as much as saving lives. To protect our kingdom is the greatest service you could ever perform, son."

"But what if...what if I don't want to do it?" He takes another step back. "There must be another way..."

"It is your duty to do as you're told. Your duty as the prince. My heir. My son." I sit up a little straighter, my grip tightening on the weapon.

"I-I can't." He steps back further. "I won't!"

"You will, and that is final!" I yell, stabbing the blade into the wooden grains of my desk, the hilt gripped viciously in my palm.

My son winces, his face scrunching up into something like fear mixed with incredulity. His feet are glued in place, and he looks at me like I'm a monster. Like I've just betrayed him. Are those tears in his eyes?

I sigh heavily and yank the blade from the table. I stand and walk over to my son who seems to cower with every step I take toward him. I hold the dagger out, and he flinches, all curiosity for the weapon gone.

My mouth suddenly feels too dry. "It's time. When you touch this blade, you are bound by an oath. To mark people now and then steal the child later. If you do these two things, you will hold your oath fulfilled." I pause, running my tongue over my teeth. "You will leave at dawn. And if all goes as planned, you'll only be required to do the first part once. Do I make myself clear?"

He nods with hesitancy, not bothering to meet my gaze as he reluctantly takes the knife. He holds it like it will hurt him. And then he turns, the tears streaming down his face as he flees from the room.

In his wake, guilt pricks my heart all the more.

What have I just done?

CHAPTER TWENTY-SIX
Holland

Holland edged nearer, her curiosity bettering her senses. The man whom the soldiers were leading looked familiar; it had to be him. "Markus?" she shouted before she could stop herself. She had to be sure.

He turned at the sound of his name, his brows pushed together. He looked lost, and then his eyes lit up as if in memory. He scanned the gathering crowd of people, his gaze not quite finding hers.

What are they doing to him? Why was he here? Holland ceased all movement, suddenly realizing Markus wasn't wearing a shirt. She'd never seen his bare chest before, nor the muscles ridging along his shoulders and arms. She knew he was strong from all his hours tending to his field, but she never expected *this*. Heat blossomed in her stomach and climbed her cheeks. A more sculpted man didn't exist, of this she was certain. It was hard to look away.

But why was his side wrapped with bloody cloth? Was he bleeding? Holland fisted her hands together. What had they done to him?

One of the men-in-arms dismounted and cut the rope that tethered Markus to the horse. He then dragged him to the far corner of the square toward a section that Holland hadn't paid much attention to.

Her heart leapt to her throat. *No.*

The telltale wooden posts now stood out to her like harrowing wraiths; how could she ever have missed them before? The looped ropes at the end looked like ravenous maws, waiting to devour the life out of anyone who dared get too close.

Bile rose to her throat, and she fought the urge to wretch on a Snoot's shoes. They were going to hang him! Images of Jaerus' limp body flooded her vision. *Not Markus. Not him, too.*

The perfection of Tiri's public square was overshadowed by the presence of death at its doorstep. She watched with bated breath as the soldier brought Markus closer. The flurry of warmth in her gut was now replaced with a fiery knot. She clenched her teeth, her vision starting to blur. She needed to do something—anything to stop this.

Why on Griskol was he being punished for being perfect?

Holland had known Markus for most of her life. Never once had he ever done anything against the law—well, aside from continually going into Andaimon. That, and stealing food from the market as a kid... So, she guessed his record wasn't exactly clean. But those things hardly counted. He was as loyal and trustworthy as a dog, always there when he was needed most. He took care of his people; she knew that first hand.

The soldier shoved Markus forward, pushing him to his knees.

He fell, exposing his back to everyone.

A collective gasp resounded in the square. All was silent. Chills ran up along Holland's spine. She admired Markus' strength, but now what she saw was horrifying. She couldn't look away for a different reason.

A vicious scar tore itself across his flesh, snaking up toward his ear. Each end dissolved into offshoots near his lower back and neck, as if a snowflake had frozen itself to his skin. And like a snowflake, the scar was white, unearthly in all its hideous glory.

Holland's pulse beat against her temples, her hand inadvertently reaching out as if she were tracing the marks along his spine. Tears ran unbidden down her cheeks. How come he had never told her about this? Had he purposefully kept it a secret? Did he think she'd judge him for it?

Hurt warred against the fear clawing at her chest. She wanted to touch him, to make sure he was okay. Who had given him this scar? Was this why he was being hanged?

She didn't have to wait to find out.

Another soldier dismounted from his horse and pulled out a scroll before clearing his throat. "Gather 'round. Gather 'round." He signaled for the crowd to be quiet.

Everyone scooted closer, the murmurings of the onlookers suddenly silent. It was so still, Holland could hear her own heartbeat.

"I hereby announce, in accordance with the decree of King Randor II and Queen Rosin of Famar, that this man shall hang for his crimes now and hereafter." He pointed at Markus.

Holland wanted to faint. Instead, she wove through the crowd and edged closer, a giant knot in her throat. She needed Markus to see her.

"For it is written: all shall pay who bear the mark of magic. All shall die who undermine the throne. For it is either the witches or the Forbidden Wood who stole Prince Ranor."

Markus' captor pushed him forward again, but this time to his feet. He motioned for Markus to step up on a wooden block and face the crowd.

Witches or the Forbidden Wood? Stole the prince? This was madness!

Holland reached the edge of the platform, her gaze boring holes into the top of Markus' skull, willing him to respond. As if he sensed her presence, he lifted his head, his gaze locking onto hers.

"Holland?" Her name was written in his expression as much as the mumbled word he spoke through his gag. His eyes were filled with anguish, and yet, he looked at her with longing, as if it were just the two of them standing there, and one not about to meet his death.

Holland's breath hitched in her throat, her stomach flipping.

"This man bears the mark of a beast. His witchery shall die with him along with the witches in the Forbidden Wood. The first search party dispatches tonight!"

The crowd cheered, clapping their hands. Some were even crying, relief clearly displayed on their faces. This made them happy?

Holland bit her lip so hard that she drew blood. Tiri was filled with heartless leeches.

"You all are witnesses. May Tokal help us all." The soldier bowed, a showy act of irreverence for the situation. He then raised his hand in the air—waiting.

The other man-in-arms fixed the noose around Markus' neck and pressed his foot against the wooden block.

Holland's heart stopped, her mind racing. She had to do something, but what? She couldn't let Markus die!

"Hey, Runner!"

Holland ignored the call. For all she knew, they could be talking to someone else. Instead, she kept her gaze on Markus, searching his expression for something, anything that might help her. Perhaps if she stormed the platform?

She couldn't lose her best friend. She couldn't lose him—not after having lost everything else. She would do anything, anything...

A firm grip came down hard on her shoulder, and Holland screamed. A large hand covered her mouth and she was yanked away from the platform through the leering crowd. She wrenched herself free of the man's grasp, only to be restrained once again. She clawed at people or anything she might use to sustain her, but it was of little use.

She was forced to watch Markus grow smaller, her eyes not leaving his; his brow was creased in a harsh line. He looked afraid. Or was it anger? Her throat constricted the farther away she was dragged from him.

She tried screaming again, but the man's fist was in her mouth. Tears poured from her eyes, and her limbs shook uncontrollably. Her detainer's grip was strong. When he finally released her, she was at the outskirts of the square and tucked into some sort of alleyway. When she met the gaze of her captor, she met the gaze of one of Famar's soldiers.

She tried running back to Markus, but the man pinned her against the wall. She swallowed hard.

"You should know by now that to try that is useless. If my records are correct, *Cadmon Glock*, you seem to have a death wish upon your head." The man smirked, knowingly. He yanked Holland's cap off, sending her raven braid tumbling down to her waist.

Holland gasped, her heart in her throat.

"You see, the real *17* crossed Tiri's border shortly after you did. He seemed ignorant to the fact that there were two of him. And one of them being a girl, no less." The soldier moved a fraction closer, raking her figure with his leering gaze. "As I'm sure you are somewhere underneath these rags." He laughed, pulling the fabric at her shoulder, and she vehemently shrugged him off. He only laughed more.

Holland's insides burned. She was mortified by his audacity. She wanted to kick him where it hurt most, but what then? She'd be on the receiving end of something far worse than his churlish gaze. Her hands twitched at her sides, her feet eager to trace the path back to Markus. But she was rooted in place by the man's iron grip.

"You should be hanged for your crimes, but I've been instructed to do otherwise. Instead, you'll be joining the first search party for Prince Ranor in the Forbidden Wood."

A shiver ran down her back, her tongue sticking to the roof of her mouth. She was what?

"And it is there you shall die all the same. Though it will be easier for us. You see, we won't have to discard your body." The soldier sneered, gripping Holland's shoulder even tighter. "Come. You'll leave at dusk."

Holland was pushed deeper into the dark recesses of the alleyway. Where was he taking her? She wriggled beneath his grasp, struggling to see the square a little way behind her. She could still glimpse Markus, his gaze drawn to where she'd disappeared, but beyond that, the details eluded her.

When would they pull the block out from beneath his feet? Would he live through it? Her heart ached to go back to him. To feel his skin against hers, just to know he was alive. Breathing.

Tears stained her cheeks as the soldier yanked her farther along the narrow path. A cry escaped her lips, but the man clamped his hand over her mouth once more. So she bit him.

"Bloody wench." He shook the offending wound and looked about to hit her, but thought better of it. Instead, he increased his iron grasp ten-fold.

It seemed of little use to keep fighting. Markus would be dead by morning, if he wasn't already. He wasn't weak. He was built to protect others; he wasn't meant to be protected. Yet, she knew his fate was sealed.

She wished more than anything that it could be otherwise.

Her heart was shattered beyond repair.

Markus

Markus watched as that blasted soldier hauled Holland away from the crowd. He wanted nothing more than to slug the man and whisk her away to safety. Markus jostled forward, nearly meeting his doom had he managed to step off the block. But he didn't care. The rope couldn't kill his love for Holland nor his need to rescue her.

The general by his side steadied Markus, holding him back all the same. Urgency flared inside his chest. Where was she being taken?

He'd known relief like it was his friend when he finally spotted her in the crowd. He'd know those green eyes anywhere no matter the state of dress that came with them. Sure, it had jarred him to see her in men's clothes, but nothing could dim her beauty. In fact, it only seemed to enhance it, making him wonder what Holland would look like in one of his own shirts.

Blast. Now was not the time for this.

Markus was near death, and at any moment, the signal would be given and the wooden block kicked out from beneath his feet. But not until then. Which meant he only had so much time to unfetter his hands.

He curved his wrists and felt along the rope's fibers. Anticipation twitched in his fingers. He was nearly free! If he simply pulled with all his might, he could snap the rest of the rope clean through. It was worth a shot.

The soldier's hand suddenly lowered—the signal! The block was kicked out from beneath Markus, and he fell a couple of inches, his feet tasted nothing but air. Rope burned his neck, and a gasp lodged itself in his throat.

The crowd screamed, and Markus detected the faint sounds of metal scraping against scabbards, of a tousle just below the platform. Were they going to stab him again, too?

The general beside him drew his sword and jumped to join the fray. What was going on?

A million stars danced in his vision; he couldn't breathe. But that didn't mean he couldn't think.

He yanked his hands apart with all his might, snapping the remaining fibers. His bonds fell to the ground, and his hands immediately went to the rope suspending him in midair. Markus sawed fiendishly, every second devoid of respiration zapping away at his remaining strength. He was beginning to forget the taste of oxygen, the feel of it in his lungs.

Suddenly, his feet hit the ground before he fell to his knees; a hoarse cough racked his chest as he sucked in air. He was alive. Just barely. Why had the soldiers let him escape?

"Make yourself useful, will you?" A sword hurdled toward him on the platform, skidding to a halt just before his knees.

Markus knew that voice. But it didn't belong to anyone in Tiri. He looked up into a familiar face. "Cal?"

"Fight now. Questions later." Calsius turned, bringing his arm across his body, slicing at the soldier that snuck up behind him.

Markus replaced his knife, grabbed the sword, and jumped into the fray. Combat was as familiar to him as planting his crops; he'd grown up knowing how to wield a blade, or any weapon for that matter, and utilize his strength, thanks to Mr. Brenner. The man had trained both his son and Markus, saying it was a necessity to learn how to defend oneself. *"You never know when it'll be needed."*

He was right.

Markus arched his arm and wheeled around, his blade clanging against that of the general's, only seconds from stabbing through his back.

"Trying to finish what you started?" Markus goaded, not keeping the snark out of his voice. "There's no honor in attacking a man from behind." He transferred his weight forward and advanced, forcing the soldier back a few strides. All his training returned to him as he slashed with his sword, testing the weight of the metal in his hands. It was heavy, well-balanced. Perfection. The kind that only came from the Brenner's forge.

The general scoffed. "You're not a man worthy of honor." He shifted his stance and advanced, arching his sword high and cutting from above.

Markus feinted left and rolled right, kicking the general's legs out from beneath him. He fell to his knees as Markus brought the hilt of his weapon down hard upon his head.

The general groaned, and Markus punched him in the face for good measure.

The man reeled and ran a hand over his bloodied lip. "Want to try that again?" He seethed, reclaiming his stance and jabbing his sword before him, pulling blood from Markus's already wounded side.

It burned, but he clenched his teeth and swallowed back the pain. Markus' body was a battlefield of its own; he had more than enough marks to prove it. He barreled forward, taking the general by surprise. With his sword raised, he twisted it beneath his opponent's, dislodging his weapon before tackling him to the ground. Dust clouds danced around the scuffle, and a few solid punches rendered the general unconscious.

Markus stood, clutching his side and surveying the town square. The crowd had dispersed, leaving only a handful of onlookers on the outskirts, their interests piqued by the fight. He saw Calsius fending off two soldiers and an older man fending off another. Mr. Brenner was here, too?

Markus stumbled forward, eager to put an end to the brawl. They needed to leave—to find Holland. It was only a matter of time before Famar sent more soldiers their way.

Before long, the three of them had managed to knock two of the soldiers unconscious, but the third had given up, retreating to what Markus guessed was the safe confines of Pembroke Fally. It was about a day's journey north from Tiri's square, and by then, his wounds might bleed him dry.

"That's the most action this body has seen in years." Mr. Brenner wiped his sword on his shirt, the fabric coloring red.

"And let's hope it stays that way, Pops." Calsius shook his head, sheathing his sword before tossing an empty baldric to Markus. "Here, take this. You've definitely earned it."

"Thanks." Markus knotted the material in place and sheathed his sword in turn. The leather felt strange on his bare skin. Foreign. "How did you both find me here?" He was thankful but very confused. If not for his friend, he probably wouldn't be alive.

"I've been in Famar for about a week," Mr. Brenner said. "Queen Rosin is in hysterics over her son; naturally, King Randor wants better weapons. Cal was supposed to meet me last night to help. But he was delayed."

"And for good reason," Calsius butted in.

"Well, I dare say your lateness may have spared your friend's life, so I won't hold it against you. You see, Markus." Mr. Brenner turned to face him. "I was worried about my son. He's usually always on time. So, I left Famar yesterday and arrived in Tiri just this morning. The Fates may have smiled upon you, for that's when I found Cal coming the opposite way. When we saw a man being dragged through the streets, we realized it was you. We devised this plan to set you free." Mr. Brenner nodded.

"I'm only too glad for it."

"Though you look worse for the wear." Mr. Brenner's gaze landed on Markus' side.

"It's nothing." That was a lie, but there were more pressing matters at hand. It was late, and the sun had begun its descent, which made his next task all the more difficult. "I need to find Holland. I don't know where they've taken her." Markus was surprised at how steady his voice sounded. He was all but writhing inside. He moved in the direction of the alleyway he had seen her last.

"Holland?" Calsius' eyes narrowed. "Are you mad? She actually left you?"

The words stung Markus more than he let on. "I spotted her at the noose dressed as a Runner. One of Famar's soldiers hauled her away before I could free myself. I fear for her life."

"And right you should. This doesn't bode well, I'm afraid." Mr. Brenner shook his head.

"What do you mean?" Markus gave up on the alleyway and

stepped closer to the two men, his stomach churning. Whatever was about to be said, Markus feared it wasn't good. He swallowed hard, running his hand along the rope burns around his neck. "What have you learned?"

"Before I left Famar, I heard word of search parties going to the Forbidden Wood. King's orders."

"Yes, I heard that too. While I was nearly hung to death."

"Well, do you know who makes up these parties, Markus?" Mr. Brenner's eyes were somber, grief stricken in the features of his face.

Markus' stomach twisted. He didn't like where this was headed.

"It's not any of Famar's soldiers, I can tell you that. Their cowardice runs deep." He paused, running a hand over his mouth as if the words that came next pained him. "It's the Runners."

The truth hit Markus in full force. He clenched his jaw. There was no debating it; he didn't have to know Famar personally to see this was just the kind of injustice they would serve. He hated them with every fiber of his being.

"If your Holland was caught here in Tiri dressed as one, son, I fear she's on her way to meet her end."

CHAPTER TWENTY-SEVEN
Holland

The first signs of dawn approached. If it wasn't for the sword pointed at her back, Holland would make a run for it and retreat into the hazy blue that came with the early morning. But as it was, she didn't have a death wish.

After getting caught and dragged through some sort of woods by one of Famar's soldiers, she found herself in a locked shed with a host of other Runners. There were ten of them in total.

"Where are we?" she had whispered to number *15*, the lantern's faint light illuminating the markings on his armband.

"Not sure. Somewhere in Kirkus, I'd guess," he whispered in return, shrugging.

"Already?"

She soon learned the man was right. It hadn't taken long for them to be ushered onto the cobblestone street, this time going south. They had walked all night, the endless hours a testament to just how long one could go without sleep.

Holland had hoped to escape the soldiers by now, but she was not so fortunate. Apparently, they worried the Runners would do what their name implied: run off and return home rather than fulfill the duty foisted upon them.

They weren't wrong. But instead of running to Andaimon, Holland wanted to run back to Tiri's public square. She didn't know what Famar did with the cold bodies upon their deaths, but she hoped for a proper burial. It was the least they could do.

The thought twisted her stomach. How must Markus have felt when he took his last breath? Had he been afraid? It was too much to think about, and yet, she couldn't stop herself. A new batch of tears stung her eyes, threatening to run rivulets down her cheeks. She inhaled deeply. She was so…lost. His death hollowed out the emptiness in her chest even more, rounding out the jagged edges and haunting her with this truth: she was now completely and utterly alone.

The realization was suffocating. Holland tripped on a loose stone and nearly fell to the ground. She would have had someone not steadied her.

"Thank you." She gulped, glancing up. Her helper was number *27*, the Runner she passed earlier on her way into Tiri.

"Don't mention it." He nodded, a sincere smile on his face. "If you walk on my right side, I can catch you better should you fall again."

Though she still wore her cap, it hadn't taken the Runners long to wrap their minds around Holland being a girl. In fact, all of them had responded kindly to her—all except the real Cadmon Glock, that is. The *17* on his arm revealed who he was before Holland even had to guess, and the scowl on his face clearly showed he didn't appreciate her wearing his number. She'd talk to him and explain everything soon, just not yet.

"Why are you being nice to me?" Holland asked. "You don't even know who I am."

Number *27* seemed to consider her words before answering. "Don't take this the wrong way, but you're a girl. When a man is all but stripped of his power, it feels good to be able to protect someone again. To be useful."

She hadn't thought about that, but now looking at the rest of the Runners, she noticed the deflated shoulders and the defeat written across all their features. To be flanked by a dozen soldiers must be emasculating beyond measure.

It was something she was well used to. She'd never had any power to begin with and grew up fending for herself most days. The fact that a Runner wanted to protect her sent a flood of gratitude to her middle. It reminded her of Markus. Her stomach reeled once again.

"On most days, being a Runner isn't bad; I work enough on the weekends to earn my darics. It goes for a lot of these men— some of them just boys." He nodded to the rest of the group. "But I've a wife back home, a babe on the way. With this new *mission* we've been given, I don't know if..." His voice shook; he pursed his lips as if avoiding the words would somehow hurt less.

Holland placed a steadying hand on his arm, a small comfort as tears stung the corners of her eyes.

The man continued. "I guess you're a symbol of hope. To all of us." He nodded, strengthening his resolve once more.

Me? The tears threatened anew, but this time they were bittersweet. How could she symbolize what she did not feel? How could something so encouraging be found in the darkest hour? She swallowed back the emotion and wiped at her eyes. She needed to distract herself from the tumult inside her chest.

"What's your name?" These men were more than numbers. She would make an effort to honor that.

"Grismon Rook. But you can call me Gris." He nodded.

"Rook? Is your wife Margithand?"

He smiled fully now, as if just hearing his wife's name brought him joy. "Yes. She goes by Margi. How do you know her?"

"She tried saving my fingers from the extra work at Abermann's Tea House, and I will never forget that. Her friend, Mrs. Scuttle, didn't take too kindly to my handiwork, I'm afraid." Holland shook her head.

"Ah, yes, that place is Margi's favorite. Why she hangs out with that woman, though, I'll never understand. I think she hopes some of her good nature will rub off on her." Grismon smiled, his gaze wandering to the brightening sky as if in thought. "Do you remember the bakery on Cliff's Corner? It was always *my* favorite. My father owned the place when I was just a lad. He passed ten years ago, but my memory still tastes of lemon tarts and peach cobblers."

Holland nodded. "When I was little, my guardian, Mrs. Annbert, brought me there a handful of times. I remember the chocolate eclairs were my favorite. But I haven't been in years. Whatever happened to it?"

"Lack of business. The poorer Andaimon gets, the less people have to spend on sweets or non-necessities. I had to shut the bakery down, but while it still stood, those were happier days." Grismon shook his head, his smile turning somber. "Do you have a favorite place back home?"

Home. There it was again, but this time, Holland only slightly bristled at the thought. "The flower garden by the hedgerow, just past the trader's post. It's so colorful, and the scent is heavenly; it's as if an other-worldly presence had a hand in making it come to life. To me, it's always been a form of *magic* that Griskol can't touch. I used to visit with Mrs. Annbert, but since getting older, I don't get out much—"

"Except when you decide to become a Runner and come up here." Grismon laughed.

"Yes, that, too." Holland joined him. It was freeing to laugh in spite of all she was feeling. It was odd, really, to be feeling so much in such a small span of time. Her heart was broken, and yet, speaking of Andaimon felt like springtime in the midst of a harsh winter; for the longest time, it had only been a cage. Familiarity was a thing of comfort, she supposed. If only Markus was here beside her, too.

Her heart twisted again, but she stamped the feeling down. She needed to stay alert, and grieving on the open road would render her senses useless; she'd already tripped once because of it. She would allow herself to feel it all later.

Grismon cleared his throat beside her. "If you don't mind me asking, why *did* you become a Runner? It's not a glorious role by any means."

True. She'd learned that the hard way. She looked up at him and shrugged. "It promised freedom and a chance for a new life."

"And why would you want that?"

"Because I don't have one." She sighed. "I finally reached the point where I was willing to risk it all for the sake of finding who I am. To find the truth about my parents. In Andaimon, I'm a nobody. Out here, I could be anybody. At least, that's what I had thought."

"And what do you think now?" Grismon tilted his head, curiosity in his gaze.

Holland faltered, taken aback by such a question. The answer was as clear as a murky pond. "I don't even know." In leaving Andaimon, she'd lost more than what she'd first set out to find. She was no closer to discovering her identity; a boat to Onklo was now out of the question. And her best and only friend was dead. Her chest constricted. "This world is full of pain, an unforgiving darkness that stretches its grip wherever I go. There doesn't seem to be any good left in it. Anything worth fighting for."

Grismon looked at her in a way that said he understood, but his eyes held a curious gleam. "And yet, the crocuses still bloom in early spring. The crops still push forth from the earth, taking its nutrients and transforming them into something good. I have to believe that a world that grows beauty can't be all bad, can it? There is still some light left in Griskol, though it be just a spark. But maybe it's enough."

Grismon's words weaseled their way into Holland's heart, twisting both despair and hope into a bittersweet knot. How could he say such things when he himself was as near to death as she? When he might never see his wife and unborn child? How could he see goodness in a world that only ever brought cruelty? A tear slipped unbidden down her cheek, trailing a singular river to her chin. She didn't bother wiping it.

Her heart was broken, but this time, light was attempting to shine through its cracks. It hurt, felt exposing, and yet, Holland welcomed it. Maybe Grismon was right. Maybe some good still existed, and it could be preserved. Salvaged amongst the ruins of their broken world.

She could acknowledge some positives about her journey so far; if nothing else, it had at least opened her eyes. She now knew Tiri was unfit for good company, Pembroke Fally likely even more so. Kirkus was only a step above, and though Andaimon was poor, at least it wasn't lacking in honor. It seemed the hierarchy had flipped on its head when it came to morality. She still didn't know who she was, but her perspective had shifted.

And now she was heading back the way she'd come.

Never had she thought she'd be returning to Andaimon so soon, and this time to the Forbidden Wood. As a young girl, she'd always wondered what was inside it, and on countless occasions, had even been close to stepping foot within its borders when Mrs. Kershaw wasn't looking.

She couldn't help her curiosity. If the stories were true, then the Forbidden Wood really was as bad as they all feared. But what if they were wrong? What if the stories were all lies, brought about by Famar's incessant need to control Griskol? What if the forest had nothing to do with the king and queen's son after all? What if she and all the Runners made it out alive?

And what if she could have saved Markus?

Holland's head spun with her unmet questions, her chest tight.

The answers felt a thousand miles away. Could anything good really come out of all this? Even from the past?

It might be too much to hope for.

And if there was anything Holland had learned in all her twenty years of living, it was that hope was a dangerously fragile thing to hold on to.

CHAPTER TWENTY-EIGHT
Markus

Markus glanced over his shoulder. Mr. Brenner was walking as fast as he could to keep up with the younger men, but his gait couldn't hide his obvious limp. The unevenness of the cobblestones probably wasn't helping either.

Markus was in pain, too, but he didn't slow his pace. He couldn't afford to.

Calsius had suggested they each shoulder one of Mr. Brenner's arms, but the old man refused, saying, *"It's a mere nuisance, nothing more. A little motion is good."* But this was more than just a little motion. Mr. Brenner was as stubborn as the steel he forged. He kept walking, waving Markus and Calsius on ahead as if not to worry about him.

Just as well. It was pertinent they all kept moving. Even though the Brenner family had free passage across the borders, there was little hope of that after their display in the public square. They were probably all being hunted now, a hefty bounty upon each of their heads. A moment spent lingering was a moment in favor of Famar.

Markus had been walking—no, more like staggering, in the direction of Andaimon for what felt like an entire day. The sun was already beginning to set. His limbs were weary, though not as weary as his faith. Was Holland safe? Where had that blasted soldier taken her? Markus swore to himself that if she was harmed, he'd make sure that blackguard had a taste of his own medicine.

He wasn't a violent man, but he would do anything to keep those he loved safe. Vengeance was a whole other beast that he'd have to tackle later.

"You have a look that could bend steel," Calsius said, his pace matching Markus'.

"I have a lot on my mind."

"Is it about that scar on your back? You never told me how you got it."

"I never told you about it, period. And I don't know. The memory eludes me." Markus thought back to his dream, of the searing pain, the icicles snaking up his spine. He shivered, rolling his shoulders to assuage the tension.

"You're worried about Holland, then?"

"How can I not be? So much of my life is hers, Cal."

"How so?"

Markus shrugged. "We've grown up together. Our stories are intertwined like tangled fishing lines—nearly impossible to decipher whose is whose." His memories were filled with her—of their childhood, their teenage years, their *now*. Of days spent in the sun and chewing parsnips. Of stolen glances and endless laughter. Of whispering stories and gazing at the stars. When she'd entered his life, it had suddenly filled with vibrant color. He despaired of his world going black and white should he ever lose her. Like he worried he was losing her now.

Where is she?

"And to think you didn't call that love." Calsius clapped him on the back, his tone suddenly more serious. "We'll find her, Fenn. Don't lose hope."

Markus swallowed the lump that settled like a knot in his chest. He didn't want to get sentimental by too much nostalgia; he'd been down that road before. His determination fueled him. Kept him vigilant. Calsius was right; they'd find her. They had to.

And he needed to change the subject.

"So, what made you late enough to end up saving my life back there anyway?" He motioned with his head to Tiri.

Calsius' wry grin spoke for itself. "Oh, I didn't tell you? I finally proposed!"

"You what?" Markus widened his eyes.

"I told you I had it all planned out, didn't I? And believe me, it went even better than I'd expected." Calsius had the audacity to waggle his eyebrows.

"What did you do to the poor woman?" This was proving a good distraction, indeed.

"You offend me. I'm a gentleman, through and through." Calsius bowed.

"I'll believe it when I see it. Your word is rather suspect." Markus laughed, shifting the baldric rubbing against his skin. What he'd give to find a clean shirt. "When's the wedding?"

"Woah. One thing at a time, mate. I just got engaged!"

"So in ten years, then?" Markus provoked.

"Try this spring. I can't keep the woman off me long enough to even plan it." Calsius smirked.

"Something tells me it's the other way around. Damirus does know *who* she agreed to marry, correct?" Markus' implication was as clear as water.

"Oh, she knows, and she loves every second of it."

Markus had no doubt. Women seemed to fawn over Calsius' antics. Damirus was just lucky enough to have caught his eye; she was something special indeed to willingly put up with him.

"I'm happy for you, Cal. Just don't mess it up."

"When have I ever messed things up?" he joked, and then his tone turned serious. "No, you're right, but I always come through in the end. And speaking of the end, it's getting late. Should we stop soon?" he asked, looking back toward his father.

Markus wanted to keep going. If they stopped now, that only prolonged the distance between him and Holland. He didn't have time to spare, nor the restraint to. But one glance at Mr. Brenner told Markus that they'd pushed the old man far enough.

"For a few hours at most," Markus said. "But we'll need to find a place to stay."

"I've already got one. It's not far." Calsius closed the distance to his father and told him of the plans.

Markus watched as the hard-set line of Mr. Brenner's jaw relaxed a fraction. He nodded, his eyes bright. "It'll be good to see Beck again. Lead the way, son."

Markus followed them. He should be grateful for a chance at rest. His side was on fire.

* * *

Markus twisted his hands behind his back, controlling his urge to pace. He wanted to keep going, not stop for the night in some courtyard. It was a small enclosure connected to the narrow alleyway they'd all recently exited. Somewhere past the many twists and turns, the main road lingered beyond, but he couldn't make heads or tails of their location. They were still in Kirkus, he knew that much.

He studied the walls in front of him; doors stretched across their rough, stucco surfaces, but in a corner stood a gap between the buildings where a single iron gate barred entrance to whatever lay beyond it.

"How did you know about this place?" Markus whispered.

"When you travel Griskol as much as we do, it's necessary to find people you can trust. We've known Beck for years, ever since my father started in his trade," Calsius said.

"That's right." Mr. Brenner nodded. "Beck used to work with me before he started a business of his own. Though it's been many moons since I last saw him. Our forge is about half a day's walk from here."

Calsius approached one of the doors and studied it closely; it was as if he was trying to remember something. After a moment, he raised his hand and knocked quietly in a strange, rhythmic pattern. It sounded like some sort of code.

All was silent, the minutes creeping by. An eerie stillness filled the courtyard, making the hair on Markus' neck rise as if someone was watching him. Was no one going to answer the door?

He itched to move, to shake off the uneasy feeling that traced the scar up his back, but Calsius looked at him, a finger raised in the air as if commanding him to wait. Calsius knocked again in the same way, and before he even finished, a door opened in response. But it wasn't the one he had expected; the gate on their left swung open instead. Calsius frowned, his hand frozen in midair.

"Calsius? Finagus?" A bearded man who looked to be in his mid-thirties stood in the entrance, staring at them and blinking in the twilight. He seemed surprised. "Come! Come in quickly!" He motioned for them to step through the gate. He nodded when he saw Markus and fastened the latch behind them. "Let's talk inside, and not a word before."

The man, who Markus assumed to be Beck, led the way over a narrow cobblestone path and through the tall, thick trees that stretched before them. When they reached a pond and a small sitting area, the path suddenly stopped.

Markus paused. Calsius and Mr. Brenner did the same. Were they meeting here?

As if reading his thoughts, Beck shook his head and motioned everyone onward.

After skirting the edge of the pond, Markus plunged into a thicket, the cobblestone pavers all but forgotten. This path was made of dirt and partially hidden by dense undergrowth. Tall trees flanked the sides like formidable soldiers.

Where is he taking us?

Markus followed in the rear, his hand above his head to take the brunt of the low-hanging branches. He squinted ahead of him, trying to make out something in the distance. Pinpricks of light cut through the darkness, and it wasn't until drawing closer that he realized the light belonged to some sort of house.

Was this Beck's home? Out here, in the middle of the woods?

The man opened the door, and ushered them all inside, locking the bolt soundly. "Viv dear, can you get these folks some refreshment? I need to fix the shades; the light is creeping through again." Beck addressed the woman sitting by the stove, knitting what looked to be a pair of mittens. He went to the windows and pulled the curtains taut.

Viv set aside her yarn and went into the kitchen.

Markus observed the small house. It had three rooms: a living room with a bed in the corner, a kitchen, and a sliver of a washroom. A wood stove stood in the center of it all, the flickering fire just another sign of the colder months to come. It was snug and cozy, warming Markus' skin and reminding him yet again that he needed a proper shirt.

Finally, he noticed an old dog lying down on a rug, curled up by the fire and seemingly unaware of its visitors. Markus' heart constricted. If he were Hamish, he'd be greeting everyone, tail wagging and tongue hanging out of his mouth. Markus swallowed hard.

Hamish was dead, and Markus hadn't had the time to go back and give his dog the proper burial he deserved. The realization bruised his heart anew, but he'd made the sacrifice in hopes that he wouldn't lose Holland, too. Though it didn't lessen the fact that he missed the dog something fierce.

The woman named Viv emerged with a tray of raspberry

cordials, the glasses clinking together with her movements. Her dirty-blonde hair framed her kind features as she smiled warmly to the newcomers. "Welcome to our home. Had I known Anton would bring me visitors, I would have tidied up a bit. But I hope you'll enjoy your visit all the same."

Anton? Who was Anton? Markus nodded at the woman despite his confusion. He liked her instantly, appreciating her hospitality on such short notice.

"*Our* home? Antonius Beck, it's good to see you finally settled down. Marriage looks good on you, my boy." Mr. Brenner's eyes gleamed with pride as he patted his younger friend on the back.

Ah. That explains the name. Beck was his surname.

"Aye, we got married five years ago. Viviand's made me a better man ever since." Antonius smiled at his wife.

Markus didn't miss the way the mood in the room shifted. Had he heard Antonius correctly? Did he just say…? Was his wife…?

"Excuse me…but did you say Vivi—*and*?" Mr. Brenner nearly choked on his drink, vocalizing the question that had been on the tip of Markus' tongue. The man looked from Antonius to his wife, as if eager for an explanation.

Antonius nodded solemnly. "We have a lot to catch up on. Take a seat over here, and I'll explain it all."

He led them to a cozy section of the living room where everyone helped themselves to a floor cushion. Viviand sat beside her husband, and after a few minutes, Antonius cleared his throat before speaking. "As you can well guess, Viviand is from Andaimon. We had met as kids on a whim many years ago when

Griskol wasn't as stringent, and I was more reckless. I crossed the border often, unbeknownst to my parents. It didn't last long, though. I was caught and forbidden to enter Andaimon ever again. To make matters worse, they'd forced me to get a job, and that's how I ended up at your smithy." He looked at Mr. Brenner. "No offense."

"None taken." Mr. Brenner nodded.

"By the time my parent's authority lessened on account of my increasing years, Griskol's fist clenched even tighter. I wanted to become more than a blacksmith's apprentice. I wanted to make a name for myself and find the woman I'd fallen in love with over correspondence." He grabbed Viviand's hand.

"You see, Viv and I had snuck letters across the border through passing Runners. Back then, they had more freedom than they do now, and no one seemed to question them. But I wanted more than that. I wanted to deliver the letters to her myself. But first, I needed money. In Griskol, darics can buy one power—at least, they used to.

"So I moved out and created my own business. I became a cobbler. After working with you, Finagus, I realized I was rather hopeless at the anvil." He shook his head, chuckling to himself. "I find I'm much better with leather."

"You at least had heart, which is what I value most." Mr. Brenner said. "Kirkus needed a cobbler anyway."

"That being said, I worked for years. I slaved away in my trade, but for what? Darics couldn't buy me love, no matter how hard I bent my back and bruised my fingers. I still didn't have what I longed for most. So, I did something crazy." Antonius turned to look at his wife. "Viv, I think you should take this part."

"If I must." She smiled knowingly, looking at Markus and everyone else in turn. "Anton wrote me another letter. But this one was daring. After fifteen years, he wanted to see me; there was something he needed to say. He suggested Errol's Weir—a waterfall in the northwesternmost part of Andaimon, right on Eskal's border. I'd grown up near it, and we'd often visited the place as children, so it wasn't new to me. In my mind, there was only one answer to his question..." Viviand paused for dramatic effect.

"You decided to go," Calsius provided.

"Aye, that I did. Anton brought with him a priest and got down on one knee, asking for my hand. We were married right then and there, at the base of the waterfall with mist like spring rain kissing our cheeks. It was nothing short of magical." Viviand sighed. "But it didn't last long, I'm afraid.

"When we told my parents, they wanted nothing more to do with me. They thought I was discontent with my 'poverty,' a money-grubber, marrying up for the sake of a few extra darics. They couldn't see that I had married for love. Money had nothing to do with it." Viviand shook her head. "I would have married Anton if he were a peasant without a home."

"That's kind of what happened anyway." Antonius laughed. "I took Viv back to Kirkus, but my home wasn't safe. I had to get creative." Antonius leaned in closer. "I made this makeshift hut for us, built right into the side of a hillock. Come the morning, you'll have to see it for yourself; it's almost imperceptible to the eye should anyone stumble across it. The door you tried in town is our second home. We still keep the space furnished to appear like we use it; Famar's soldiers have the propensity to come knocking at all hours of the day. One can never be too prepared."

"How did you hear me knocking, then? If you live all the way up here," Calsius interrupted.

"I happened to be out for a stroll, stargazing near the pond. It's a particularly clear night, and I couldn't seem to pass up a good opportunity to view the stars." Antonius smiled.

Markus nodded to himself. He agreed with this man more than he knew. The stars were what seemed to connect him and Holland no matter the distance, what made her feel closer and less far away. Surely there was nowhere Famar could take her that the stars couldn't reach.

"We were in luck, then," Calsius said.

"That you were. Viv and I live exclusively up here. I don't get out much aside from work. You couldn't have picked a better time to come, though, for it's twilight now and the world is abed. In other words, you are safe.

"Our hope is that our home continues to be a safe haven away from the corruption of the Crown. For visitors, for friends, for fugitives...even if it's always just the two of us here to host."

"Have you no plans for wee ones, then?" Mr. Brenner asked.

Antonius looked at Viviand whose smile turned pained, her shoulders dropping. He reached for his wife's hand and stroked the back of it in small circles. A string of silence stretched between them before he cleared his throat to speak. "I'm afraid we can't. Our livelihood depends on our silence. Babies cry. To bring a child into this world just to have him or her taken from us... It's almost too much to bear."

Viviand leaned into her husband, and Antonius held her close; the truth of their situation hit Markus like a host of throwing knives. They sacrificed so much just to be together. They were risking it all for the sake of love.

The half-alive dog on the carpet suddenly made sense. It was about as much life this house could hold without bursting at the seams.

Markus stilled. Is this what a future with Holland would look like? Markus wanted a family. He wanted to work the land—the birthright his father left him. Was it worth giving up his ideal vision of a content life on the farm? Of a wife and kids and the future he'd hoped to create? He didn't know if he could go into hiding like Antonius and his wife, to abandon everything he'd worked hard for just to see it all fade to dust. To leave it all behind and never look back...

His head spun and nausea assaulted his stomach. His legs itched to move and his hands to work. He clenched his fists, his poor attempt at calming the racing thoughts berating his mind. He needed to run.

Holland's face suddenly flashed before him in a vision of the soldier pulling her struggling body away from Tiri's public square. In that moment, he had wanted nothing more than to break his bonds and hold her in his arms. To keep her safe and tell her no one else could harm her. He'd wanted to smooth back the crease in her brow and kiss the worry lines away. He had wanted to do all these things, but would she have let him?

A strange feeling fluttered in Markus' chest; it was

anticipation mingled with despair, of optimism pitted against desperation. If hope were a bird, it was a bird with a broken wing. Would it ever learn to fly?

The prospect of Holland's rejection... It would be like losing her all over again. It was a punch to his middle, and he felt it keenly, though there was nothing he could do about it. Not now, anyway. His mind was as muddled as a thicket of fog.

He unclenched his fists, his stomach still churning like a gristmill. Despair seemed his only friend tonight.

He looked at Antonius and Viviand again, but this time he thought he detected something new. What was it? He studied them closer, and the revelation stunned him. Behind their sad smiles, there seemed a glimmer of hope. They were grieving the loss of a child they could never have, and yet, they seemed content. Happy, even.

He marveled at them with a token of envy, their devotion pouring forth like a loosed dam, albeit, a quiet one. For their love was genuine and unlike turbulent waters, but it was observed in their gazes and their gentle regard for one another.

To be this content when they had nothing, when Famar had stripped them of their freedoms... Markus wished—no, hoped—that maybe he could experience that, too. But the despair rang louder.

He rubbed his eyes, exhaustion getting to him. His body and soul needed rest.

"Enough about us. I'm curious. I want to hear your story now, about what brought you all to our home," Antonius addressed the room, his voice growing distant.

Markus slumped against the wall, his head lolling to the side. Almost two nights without sleep were beginning to take their toll. His eyes were heavy, and his energy all but depleted. Tonight, he'd allow himself this one kindness, and come the morrow, he'd be himself again.

All he remembered was the sound of Calsius clearing his throat. Markus was checked out, his eyes blessedly closed before he'd even heard a word.

Tomorrow, if he was lucky, he'd connect the dots that led his stars to Holland's and bridge the gap between them.

CHAPTER TWENTY-NINE
From "The Tale of Endlewood"

*M*y son hasn't talked to me in years. Ever since the *assignment I gave him, things have felt different between us. Off. It's as if his very existence loathes mine. Like we're ships drifting apart at sea. Almost like he's the one that came away scarred and I the one who marked him.*

It had taken him a fortnight to complete the task. During that time, my mind was a wreck. Was I afraid that I'd sent my ten-year-old son out by himself? Not as afraid as I was of the failure of my kingdom; if the worst should happen, then it would be more than just my son's safety at risk.

While he was gone, though, I couldn't keep the guilt from roiling in my gut. Should I have consulted Nindrol? His prudence would have either bolstered my resolve or led me down another path entirely. And Elethün? He would have cautioned me against such deeds at all.

Consulting either of them would have been too risky. It was best to leave things to the dark. Harboring secrets produces fear, and fear makes people cautious. *My son would follow through.*

And he did.

When he returned from his mission, he walked by my study and paused in the doorway. It took me a moment to notice the blade in his hand. He sent it skidding across the stone floor, the weapon only stopping when it reached my feet. When I looked up to meet his gaze, his expression was one of steel, and if it were possible, he looked years older than when he'd first left. Weary. Haunted. Aged.

"Son?"

He only nodded; a glint of the emotion he harbored breaking through with a quiver of his bottom lip. And then he fled.

When I bent down to retrieve the knife, I noticed it was still bloodied, the red not wiped clean. Either it was to prove that the deed was done, or my son's constitution was too weak to handle a little blood.

Even now, I sit in the same study, twirling the same blade between my fingers. The stale, metallic scent lingering behind reminds me of what I've done. No amount of washing it away can remove the stain of what I've asked my son to do.

Safety comes at a cost. I know that all too well. My chest tightens as visions of Josi's face flash before my eyes. She was perfection itself, an artifact of beauty untouchable by humankind. And yet, humankind had taken her.

The Overseer needn't have been constructed if not for the threat of assault in the first place. Because of the Dyvrats and the people beyond the trees, my sweet Josi is now dead.

I swat away the remaining guilt. Circumstances have forced me to this point. The decisions I make are for her. To honor her existence. To exact revenge because of what was taken from me.

Reinstating the Overseer is the last resort. If all else fails, I'll have no choice but to see it whirl to life once again. Nindrol warned me as such, which is why he specifically can never know of my plans. I will succeed, and his interference won't be necessary. Where he would rather the Overseer protect my kingdom, I'd rather utilize every inch of power I have. He can stick to the keeping of the castle; I'll do my job. One that includes parenting my child. Alone.

I stand up, almost knocking the chair over in my haste. I've had enough sitting to last me another hundred years. I gather my courage and decide to face my son. The chasm between us has stretched far enough. But it's nothing compared to the chasm that separates me from my daughter.

I flinch, gripping the edge of my desk, my knuckles turning white against its dark wood. Since when have I thought of my daughter? I left her all those years ago to be forgotten, a memory buried beside Josi's tombstone.

For all intents and purposes, I no longer have a daughter.

I make for the hallway, for any beam of light to illuminate the darkness of my thoughts. I can't escape the shadows of my study fast enough; it's as if the chamber houses all my shortcomings and parades them around like beads to a string, dancing before my eyes.

I need to breathe. I need to find my son.

My hasty amble turns into running as I race down the corridor, my cloak billowing out behind me like a storm cloud. The stone floors are cold beneath my bare feet, but I heed them not. My pursuit is hot, and my heart is pumping with adrenaline.

Where's my son?

I stalk to his bedchamber and thrust the door open. I must speak with him, to still the inklings of conscience attempting to invade my ease of mind. I stare into the empty room, his four-poster bed unmade and the curtains pulled back to reveal one of the few spots in the forest that allows more than a little dappled sunlight to filter through the canopy.

My son has the best view, and he's not here to enjoy it. For the third time this week, he isn't in his room when I try looking for him. He evades me like humans avoid magic.

Where is Nindrol? He's usually watching my son. If anyone knows where he is, it's my advisor. Though the thought of asking him grates on my nerves. Haven't I just resolved to do things on my own?

I turn on my heel and head for the back entrance of the castle, two arched, wooden doors barring my exit to the outdoors. Once outside, my feet touch thistles and pinecones before my eyes adjust to the change in brightness of the morning. If I know my son like I think I do, then maybe he's out here—somewhere. Nindrol has mentioned his infatuation with the Wispsnare. Could he...?

I swallow the lump in my throat as my legs pick up speed. I'm suddenly sprinting. Over streams. Under fallen trees. Around towering oaks. The idea settles like a rock in my stomach, and I find it difficult to breathe. I'm getting closer. I finally reach the edge of the swamp, my hands trembling as I stare at the still water. He's so young. He couldn't possibly...

"Father?"

I start at the sound of my name, my heart leaping to my throat as I turn to my right.

"What are you doing?" Confusion is written on the crease of my son's brow.

These are the first words he's said to me in so long. It's a sprig of hope. But he's not looking at me; he's looking at my hands. I gaze down and see in their grip a stick that I hadn't known I'd picked up. I cast it to the ground. "I-I came to find you."

"Find me? What for?" His brow hikes up even higher, his arms crossed over his chest.

He's fourteen now, practically an adult. So much has shifted between us I almost forget what he was like as a child. I study him further; he appears hardened and distant, but there's something else in his appearance. He looks resolved, content even. How can this be when I know he resents me? What is he not telling me?

Harboring secrets produces fear, and fear makes people cautious. *Yes, that's what it is. He's acting cautious. But what for?*

"Yes, I...uh..." Why am I suddenly so nervous to talk to my son? "I haven't talked to you for some time."

"What's there to talk about?" At fourteen, he has already mastered the art of indifference.

I want to know where he's been, but the sprig of hope I'd felt earlier all but wilts under his gaze. I am resigned to his disregard. He's already bound to fulfill my oath. How can I expect more?

"Maybe you're right. What is there to talk about?" I ask the question, hoping that maybe he'll take the bait and meet me halfway. Instead, he hardens his gaze even more, his shoulders

pushed back in a determined sort of way I've only ever seen in a grown man.

Where has the youth of my son gone?

"If that's all, then." He brushes past me and retraces my path through the forest. It's slight, but I catch his retreating words as he mumbles them beneath his breath. "You've made me a weapon of war. I'll never forgive you for it."

I freeze, his admission rooting my feet to the ground. Guilt pools in my middle, and my hands twitch by my sides. What more can I do but watch him walk away?

I assume he's heading for the castle. But all I can think of when I watch his retreating figure is where he's just come from and what would have happened if I had never given him that secret blade in the first place.

CHAPTER THIRTY
Markus

Markus awoke to a shirt being thrown against his chest. When he opened his eyes, Calsius stood over him, a wry smile screwing his features. "Rise and shine, sleepyhead. I think it's 'bout time we got a move on."

Groaning, Markus moved to a standing position. His limbs were as stiff as a garden hoe. He felt along his neck, rope burn evidenced from the touch of his fingertips. The skin was still tender, and his side still sore, but someone had dressed it with new bandages. He was fortunate enough to have made it out alive.

"You snore like a mule, by the way." Calsius interrupted his thoughts.

Markus cracked a smile. "Shut up."

"Fine. Like a house cat, then."

Markus ignored him and looked out the window, the sunshine a clear indicator that he had slept much longer than he'd intended to. Panic shot through his veins. "Blast. We're late."

"We? *You're* late. By the looks of it, you needed the sleep more than I did. You look terrible."

Markus rolled his eyes and donned the cotton shirt before strapping on the baldric. "Where'd you get this?" It felt good to finally have something covering his chest again, let alone his back.

"For that, you can thank Beck. Now the villagers won't cross themselves on the road for fear of your 'witchery,'" Calsius jested. He walked toward the door. "Come on. Everyone's waiting outside."

Markus followed after his friend and stepped outside. He was stunned. Trees towered around him, and shrubbery rose high, brushing against his legs. There was no path in sight; they were unmistakably somewhere deep in the woods.

When he turned around, the house all but disappeared. Well, house might be too generous a word, for this looked like some sort of hole carved into the base of a large mound of rocky earth, covered up by bark, sticks, and leaves. Markus had to tilt his head in order to locate the door but found he couldn't discern its location. Antonius had been right; any passerby wouldn't think to look twice here.

"I can't tell you how good it was seeing you both again." Antonius' voice snapped Markus back to the present. The man clapped his hands on Calsius' and Mr. Brenner's shoulders. "My only regret is that you must leave so soon. But your hearts are bound elsewhere, and that is something I'm all too familiar with." He looked at Markus now, his gaze one of understanding. "I wish you well."

"And I thank you." Markus nodded, wondering just how much of his story Calsius had revealed last night.

"Please, take these." Viviand walked toward him. "I baked

you some apple scones for the journey. You'll need all the fortitude one can afford in order to step foot in the Forbidden Wood." She extended her wrapped bundle, a kind smile on her face.

Apparently, Calsius hadn't spared any details.

"You're too courteous. Thank you." Markus accepted the gift, the sweet smell of warmed apples wafting just beneath his nose. If Viviand was as proficient at baking as she was at knitting, he was sure these would taste delicious.

He made to follow after Calsius and his father, who were heading back through the woods, when Viviand stilled him with a hand to his arm. "Just one moment. If you don't mind."

Markus nodded.

She searched his eyes with her knowing gaze. "You're worried," she said.

He was taken aback. Yes, his circumstances weren't ideal, and he wished more than anything for Holland's safety. But was it that obvious? "Excuse me?"

"You're worried about this girl—Holland, Calsius said. She's someone special to you."

Markus could only nod, his tongue sticking to the roof of his mouth. What was this woman getting at?

"But it's more than that. You're worried she might not share your same feelings. Beyond her safety, you fear she might reject you." Viviand tilted her head to the side as if that somehow helped her see things differently.

Markus stared at her—stunned. "How—?"

"Errol's Weir." She laughed. "The waterfall was rumored to

be enchanted, a pool of ethereal light, but no one speaks of it anymore, especially during times like these. The day Anton and I married, we drank of its waters as a binding of our troth. Two weeks later, I was given the gift of sight only to find out Famar had dammed the river and drained the weir dry."

"What do you mean?"

"I can't predict the future, Markus. But because of Errol's light, I can sense things that others cannot. You are hurting. You carry much despair."

The words struck him like a sharp chord. She was right. He was at war with himself, not knowing whether it was wiser to hold onto hope or to abandon it altogether. What would hurt less? To hold onto faith, only to have it dashed along the dusty streets of Andaimon, or to cling to despair as a sort of defense, protecting him from further heartache?

Coward. I'm a coward. He was running away yet again, though this time, in circles. He was acting like a fool. An indecisive, hopeless fool.

"Chin up, Markus. There is light yet on the horizon. It does not do well to let despair keep you from living nor dreams to keep you from facing reality. But hope. It is the greatest of friends. Don't be afraid to cling to it, for by it you will find solace in the midst of the darkest nights. Without hope, what else do you have?"

Markus sensed the knot in his stomach loosening its grip. His internal struggles from the night before didn't seem as harrowing in the daylight. Did Errol's Weir give magic to Viviand's words, too? He suddenly felt much lighter than he'd felt in days. Weeks, even.

Holland may not feel the same way about him, but he wouldn't know unless he told her the truth. And he wouldn't be able to say anything unless he found her.

If they were meant to be together, they would figure it out. No amount of hopelessness or fear could take that away from them— their right to *choose* love in the face of evil. And come what may, he wouldn't let Famar win again.

Viviand's words struck him anew. *Without hope, what else do you have?* He'd have nothing. Just his endless routine of assuaging his problems by overworking his body. He needed to cling to hope like it was his lifeline.

"There is *magic* in Griskol, whether Famar likes it or not. And where there is magic, there is also hope. Follow the signs, and don't fear it." She reached into her pocket and drew out a leather strap. On its end was a vial, filled with what looked to be a clear, shimmering liquid. "These are the last lights of Errol's Weir. I took some of its waters before coming to Kirkus. And I'd like you to have them." She handed the talisman to Markus, closing his reluctant fingers around it.

"I can't take this." He pushed it back toward her.

"I insist." She closed his fingers again. "Visiting Errol brought me great comfort all those years when Anton and I couldn't see each other. It gave me hope that things would be well in the end. It's as the saying goes: *'May the waters serve as a light amidst the darkest of night.'* And though the falls are no more, you hold its last parting gift to our world. You'll need it more than I will. And something tells me your Holland will, too."

Markus didn't know what to say. He was a stranger to this family, and yet, he felt as welcomed as their child. Maybe Antonius and Viviand parented any of those they could, and it would be courteous to let them. "Thank you." After the third time, the words felt paltry in light of all he'd received.

"Take heart, despairing one. And don't fear to hope."

Holland

The night passed quickly, making way for the coming of the dawn. And with that, Famar's soldiers still flanked them like unfeeling shadows. Holland's feet ached, and she wished more than anything for the comfort of her hollow tree a few nights ago.

They were almost out of Kirkus, but the landmarks were still unrecognizable in their newness; it was hard to keep track of how much progress they'd made. Had they already passed the path that led to the elms and twittering starlings? What she wouldn't give for a parsnip and to retreat once more into the safety of those trees with Markus by her side.

Holland turned her attention to the present and didn't miss the way villagers had all but disappeared off the main road, pressing their backs against their houses or darting inside just to poke their heads out the windows. Curiosity kept them nearby, but they didn't dare get in the way of Famar's soldiers. In that regard, they were wise.

She was now in the middle of the group of men but was somewhere near the back, struggling to maintain the pace of those with longer legs. This put her beside Runner number *17*. The teen she was supposed to be impersonating. The sweet-talker no-longer. Cadmon Glock. He was about her height and appeared to only be a few years her junior. His shoulders sagged forward a touch, making him look just as exhausted as she was, if not more so. But above all, he looked angry.

She couldn't avoid talking to him any longer. She needed to come clean; her conscience was begging her to. She took a steadying breath before jumping right in. "I'm sorry I took your armband."

Might as well be direct.

Cadmon didn't look at her, his furrowed brow only dipping farther. His scowl was proof enough that he was not happy. "It doesn't matter."

It doesn't matter? Oh, yes, he was angry indeed.

They walked side-by-side, but unlike Grismon's encouraging chatter from the day before, the tension from this one reminded her of the direness of their mission. They were heading to the Forbidden Wood; there, she very well could die—that is, if Cadmon didn't spear her with his gaze first.

Though he'd be dying alongside her, too.

The thought almost knocked the wind out of her lungs. *Oh no.* The sweet girl she'd met in Tiri would be crushed—devastated. They were planning on getting engaged, but Cadmon was walking the road leading to his death. There wouldn't be a wedding after all, no matter how impossible it seemed.

What had Holland done?

It was a sober reality knowing that all these Runners were heading to their doom, but it was Cadmon's life for which Holland felt responsible. If she hadn't borrowed his armband, if she hadn't chosen to impersonate him... Maybe he could have avoided Famar's notice. Anger flared up alongside her guilt. No one should have to sneak around in their own country in the first place—no one should have to evade the notice of those who were supposed to protect them.

Holland sighed. There were no possible words to make up for her actions, but she had to try. To say *something*. She swallowed past the lump in her throat before speaking. "I'm afraid it *does* matter. If it wasn't for my selfishness, you wouldn't be here. I, too, wanted to leave Andaimon, but mine was a heedless cause, whereas yours was born of necessity." The knot in her stomach twisted tighter. Wasn't confessing all of this supposed to make her feel better? "I'm really, truly sorry. I wish I could take back what I've done."

Cadmon's face shifted slightly, the lines between his brows smoothing into something less perturbed. He seemed to turn over her words. At long last, he finally glanced at her and nodded. "Thanks."

Thanks? That was it? For all of Cadmon's 'talk with the ladies,' he sure was doing a good job of doing the opposite. Holland pressed her lips together. She hated tension, and the void into which Cadmon had cast his few words seemed to swallow her whole. She didn't need to be forgiven, but she at least needed to know she could be.

"It wasn't Benjamon's idea, by the way." If she was going to ruin the life of one Glock boy, she needn't ruin them both. She had to clear his name.

"Benjamon? You know my brother?" Cadmon frowned, all silence between them gone as he turned to look at her fully.

"Yes. He came to my seamstress shop last week. He'd brought your clothes and asked if I could mend them for you. He was going to pay for them with his own money, too. But that's when I had my *brilliant* idea." She tugged on her sleeve and felt her cheeks heating from embarrassment.

"Let me guess, you took my number instead of his money?" Cadmon quirked a brow.

"Guilty."

"Well, for that, I can at least thank you—genuinely. Benjamon is too good for this world. He deserves more kindness than most." Cadmon glanced at his feet, something unreadable in his expression. He looked deep in thought, as if trying to recall memories, or perhaps forget them. Was that a look of regret?

"He loves you more than you realize." Holland didn't know what compelled her to say that, but she felt it was the right course to take. "He respects you greatly. As do many others, I'd assume."

"That's what I'm afraid of." Cadmon stared straight ahead now. When he glanced at Holland, he must have read the confused expression on her face, for he continued, "I always seem to disappoint those I care for most. So, I tried to stop caring and became a Runner to avoid that. More time away from home meant less opportunities for failure. But then I met a girl…" He sighed, running a hand across the back of his neck.

"In Tiri, right?" Holland asked.

Cadmon snapped his head up and leveled her with his gaze. "You know Ani?"

"More like just met her. She served me some of her olio and may have told me about you two."

"You seem to know everyone I do." This time Cadmon chuckled. "She drives me wild. She completely threw off my goal of independence and the whole 'I need to avoid disappointment' thing. I blame it on her hair."

Holland nearly tripped at that, adjusting the cap on her head. "Her hair?"

"I've a weakness for redheads." Cadmon smirked, shrugging like it was normal.

"She told me you're going to propose soon."

"And let the inevitable disappointment sink in..." Cadmon's jaw ticked to the side. "Griskol would never allow it anyway. She'll be heartbroken when I don't return. I don't think I can bear it."

His words punctured her heart like a needle. She knew their chances of survival were slim. If the Forbidden Wood lived up to its name, they were all going to die. Still, Cadmon's belief in his death rattled her nerves. How was he so sure he wouldn't make it out alive?

Was Holland any better, though? She was worried about the same thing. If there was no hope to hold onto, what else did she have? She would be a reed growing by a river, and when the waters rose, the current would sweep her away with no safe place to land. At least hope would give her some roots.

But were they too dangerous to grow?

Holland looked at Cadmon and placed a steadying hand on his arm. The two of them stilled in the street, the rest of their party moving away from them. They only had a moment.

"We might have a chance. A chance to make it out alive," Holland said, with more hope than she felt.

"What makes you so sure?"

"I'm not, but if we don't have something to hold onto, we'll both go mad. Ani hasn't lost you yet, and you'd do well to remember that." *If not for your sake, at least for mine.* Holland didn't want Cadmon's death and the severing of his future relationship on her conscience. Then again, she'd probably be dead and wouldn't have one...

She'd already lost Markus, and for some reason, she felt that that was her fault, too. She could only handle so much heartache, but it seemed her life was just one big vat of it.

Stop it. Being negative was becoming far too easy these days. She had to fight against it, to believe some good could still happen. Grismon was right; the crocuses still bloomed in spite of Famar's evil. Maybe hope could, too.

"Hey, you two," a soldier finally noticed them a little way behind the group. "Get a move on if you don't want your necks wrung at the gallows!"

Holland and Cadmon exchanged a nod and pressed forward. They were nearing Kirkus' southern border, and in the matter of an hour, she'd be stepping foot once more on home soil.

And then, she'd be entering into the walls of an unknown forest.

CHAPTER THIRTY-ONE
Holland

Holland felt the telltale thump of *Endlewood* with each step she took. The book moved around in her pocket as if begging to be read. But the soldiers didn't know it existed, and she'd like to keep it that way. Her life was already perched on the edge of a knife.

But with every stride closer to the Forbidden Wood, she could feel the book growing heavier, its presence difficult to ignore. She wanted to crack open the pages and inhale the dried ink and papyrus, to read the words that spoke to her in ways she couldn't explain.

The Tale of Endlewood was written in such a way that it felt real; and oddly enough, the characters' struggles seemed to reflect the current pains of her life in Griskol. But wasn't that the power of stories? They had the ability to span realms and time, making one feel less alone through their relatable characters. In part, that's why Holland was so drawn to this particular story. And it was burdening her not to be able to open the book and read some of the words even now.

Holland accidentally overextended her leg, and she just managed to keep herself from falling forward before her knee buckled. When she looked down, the cobblestone street had ended and her foot was now two inches lower on solid dirt. She had finally crossed over into Andaimon.

For all her years, she had never entered her village by the main road—largely because she'd hardly ever left it to begin with, but also because Markus' home was set in the east. She'd usually cut through the forest and hopped the wooden fence. But seeing her region from this point of view was bittersweet; she had a strange sense of pride for it. Sure, it was poor and unkept, but it boasted some of the hardest-working people she knew.

Back in Tiri, Ani had mentioned that some men had given her a hard time, and Holland didn't find that hard to believe. But that didn't mean *all* men were scoundrels. The Runners in her group were nothing but gentlemen. Griskol sported many kinds of people, and the good existed alongside the bad; it didn't matter if they were men or women or even where they lived. Though, she had a hard time extending that grace to Famar.

It was their power which spilled from the seams of Pembroke Fally and poisoned any who got in their way. They were the upholders of the ultimate evil—debasing human life to the point of death—and they were abusing that power even now, sending Holland and company to their dooms.

Stride accompanies stride. Adrenaline fuels my gait. And it's hope that trails on courage's heels. Holland gulped, the novel in her pocket haunting her with the memory of its words. *The Tale of Endlewood* suddenly felt more real now that she was approaching a strange forest like Vesstan had in the book. What awaited her inside? She prayed she had the courage to face it, and the strength to hold onto the hope of better things should the darkness threaten to overcome them.

Holland glanced at the two men beside her. Cadmon was on her right, and Grismon was on her left; they walked with their shoulders back and heads held high. Maybe they had felt the pride of returning home as well.

All of them were ushered along the narrow, dusty street of Andaimon. But unlike Kirkus, the villagers here stood their ground and simply stared. A woman dressed in rags crossed her arms and scowled. If Holland could guess her expression, it might have said, *I'm not afraid of you. What more can you take from me that you haven't already?* Holland only hoped the woman would keep her mouth shut. Famar would find a way.

A few more steps and Holland heard Grismon catch his breath beside her. He leaned down and pointed to an abandoned corner storefront. A wooden sign hung on rusted hinges with the faded words *Rook's Confectionary* splayed across it.

"That's the place I was talking about." There was somber pride in his voice.

Holland followed his gaze and noticed the boarded-up windows and snapped weathervane on the roof. The flower boxes were overrun with weeds and the chipped paint looked as if the building were intentionally trying to rid itself of the filth.

It was a pitiful picture. Holland tried to remember the bakery of her youth, but try as she might, the image evaded her. One look at Grismon told her the opposite. He seemed to behold it as the token of his childhood, memorializing it as it once was—a birthright passed down.

Like Markus and his father's farm.

Holland's stomach dropped, her chest constricting yet again whenever she thought of him. Would it always be this way? It was as if a part of her heart had died along with him. Would it ever recover?

They headed deeper into town, and Holland had the sudden desire to veer left. If she could but follow the side road, it would lead her to Benneforth Row. She only needed a glimpse of it. To make sure it still stood. To see Henrietta and her plucky brood.

"Straight on." A soldier pushed her forward and snapped her focus back to the present. The dusty road stretched onward as the side road all but disappeared. They were heading to the heart of the Forbidden Wood and entering it straight down Andaimon's middle.

But something else caught her attention. Another quick glance to her left revealed a rundown bungalow with a hedgerow growing at its back, the one she'd grown to love but rarely visited. Beyond its shrubbery, she glimpsed the tickseed and goldenrod popping their yellow heads above the hedge—a last tribute to early autumn before the chilling winds of winter took hold. She longed to fill her senses with their sweet perfume, to lay in the grass and watch the changing clouds beneath their colorful petals...

But there would be no time for such frivolities. Those were amblings of her childhood—the past—or what was left of it. She suddenly felt much older than twenty.

They walked for a few more miles until she could see the

foreboding timbers coming into focus. The forest was so dense it almost looked black; the deep green of the trees was cast in endless shadows, and as Holland was pushed forward, the gravity of what she was about to do spun her mind in circles.

The last time she was near the Forbidden Wood, she had been stargazing with Markus. He had held her hand, had leaned in close and stared at her in a way that made her skin prickle with gooseflesh. She hadn't been afraid then; the forest had almost felt friendly. But there was something else...

She'd almost forgotten the *voice*. That same night, she could have sworn she'd heard her name whispered in the darkness. Markus had denied it, and she wanted to believe him. It's not like the forest had eyes and a mouth. But where else could the sound have come from?

Still, with every stride forward, *Endlewood* felt heavier, and her misgivings grew in proportion. Just what lay ahead in the Forbidden Wood, and what were they all getting themselves into?

The soldiers pressed in closer, as if approaching the forest meant Holland and the others would try to run away. There was no hope for that, though; not unless one wanted to die *before* stepping foot beyond the wall of trees.

Would the men-in-arms linger behind, then? Only time would tell just how far they were willing to go.

They approached the forest, the timbers looming precariously tall like giants. A tingling sensation ran up Holland's arms and down her legs. She'd never been this close before, but here she was, not only getting close, but being forced to step foot inside.

She glanced at Grismon and Cadmon, their faces set like

chiseled stone. If they were afraid, they didn't show any signs of it. The other Runners proved to look the same, and Holland was left feeling more alone than before.

The soldiers now gave the Runners a wide berth, still flanking them from the sides and from behind, but they didn't dare step closer to the woods.

That answered Holland's question, then. They weren't coming. Famar's soldiers were cowards.

"Get on. Go in, the lot of you," one soldier goaded, his arm pointed in the direction of the wood as if he were speaking to a dog. "There's no backing away now. Not for all of Griskol."

Holland swallowed hard, her hands twitching by her sides as she took a step closer. She wanted to appear confident—strong— but she felt far from it. Where was her courage?

"Look for the prince; you won't be coming out unless you find him. Not like you'll be given the chance otherwise..." Another soldier snickered. "Three more search parties will be here within a few hours' time to pick up your broken pieces."

Holland's blood ran cold. It was what the man implied that wrecked her nerves; she and everyone else were going to die no matter what. That even if they *were* to make it out alive, there wouldn't be a chance for them to actually do so.

One by one, Runner after Runner stepped into the shadows of the trees, resigned to their fate. Soon it was just Grismon, Cadmon, and Holland left; then the two men nodded before following after the others.

Holland watched them go and glanced up at the sky, taking in the sight of sunshine for what she felt may be her last time. And it struck her as ironic that the very region she had been born into was now the same place she was sent to die. Andaimon, once her birthplace, and now her tomb.

She again felt like Vesstan from *The Tale of Endlewood*, but this time in another way. Vesstan fled destruction only to find himself amidst even more. Holland had come to the conclusion that sometimes there was no escaping monotony and pain, no matter how much one wished to.

"You're taking too long." A soldier pushed her forward, causing her to stumble under the shade of the trees. "And don't think about turning around. You're a wild one—let the forest claim you as its own."

Wild one? Holland didn't dare turn around. Instead, she thrust her shoulders back and walked farther into the trees. She wouldn't let them see her shaking limbs.

She wasn't nearly as wild as she was scared. It was one thing to travel Griskol under the guise of a Runner. It was another thing entirely to get caught and forced to pay for her actions, entering an unknown land rumored to be the demise of Griskol in the first place.

Famar's fear knew no bounds. Soldiers forced people to their knees because they were too cowardly to treat them with dignity. Holland was convinced that Famar's fear blinded them from seeing anything other than how they wanted things to be seen. There was no swaying an immovable fortress fortified by iron and an iron will, no matter the hypocrisy that screamed louder than their lies.

Holland walked forward under the cover of oaks and ashes.

And pretty soon, the sunlight she had seen only a moment ago dimmed in the encroaching darkness.

She was going to meet Griskol's bane.

CHAPTER THIRTY~TWO
Holland

The forest was still. The only sounds that it boasted were the ones Holland and the others brought in with them: their feet shuffling along the undergrowth and their near-silent breaths taking up space beneath the boughs.

As she trod the forest path, she followed the other Runners, their steps even more hesitant than her own. They avoided any tree or shrub, walking in the middle of any path they could find. It's as if they thought the trees would suddenly sprout arms and mouths, consuming them whole. But Holland knew that was false. Somewhere deep in her gut, she understood these woods wouldn't harm her. At least, it wasn't the trees they should be afraid of.

She glanced in Grismon and Cadmon's direction. They broke away from the group and headed left as if on a mission of their own. Holland glimpsed the other Runners before tracking after the two men, hoping they knew what they were doing.

She treaded carefully, her eyes scanning her surroundings, drinking it all in. She squinted into the dim lighting, the dense canopies blocking out most of the sun. It was a strange kind of beauty; here, the sun was merely a distant neighbor, and yet she felt that the trees knew it well. Even the soil. For reasons she couldn't explain, she knew the woods were more alive than they appeared.

Despite being careful, her boot kicked something into the leaves. She bent to study the object; spreading the foliage aside revealed a cracked acorn shell, the remnants of which were about half her palm width. It was the largest acorn she'd ever seen. Squirrels and other creatures must live here, too, and they definitely weren't starving.

As Holland knelt, a tingling sensation crept up her legs and spread into her arms. It was almost as if she could feel the pulse of the earth. *Yes. This place is alive, indeed.* She suddenly felt eyes watching her.

She lifted her head and parted her lips, her gaze latching onto the creature before her. It was a large stag, its antlers a shimmery gold, and its coat a cinnamon hue mixed with honeyed-copper. But it was the small, silver crescent just above its eyes that gave her pause. *"Elethün,"* she whispered, the name weaving its way around her heart before escaping her lips of its own volition.

"What was that?" "Huh?" Grismon and Cadmon asked at the same time.

At the sound of their voices, the magnificent creature startled and bolted before they had a chance to see it. She watched its retreat, the movements of its body strangely like an ethereal dance.

Holland snapped out of her trance-like gaze and looked to her friends whose confused expressions said it all. She felt a blush climb her cheeks as she thought about her next words. "I've been here before."

Both men frowned, but it was Grismon who spoke. "Truly?" He had the decency to ask, though Holland could tell he didn't believe her.

She pictured the stag in her mind. Something about it had seemed so familiar. She'd given it a name...but *Elethün* was a beast of fiction. Surely it didn't mean anything. It had to be coincidental. "I don't really know. At least, I feel as if I've been here before." The stag had sparked a memory, and she felt that if she followed it, she'd find the answers to the forest's familiarity.

Grismon studied her before sharing a shrug with Cadmon. Though the event had happened so suddenly, it was just as soon forgotten.

They all walked for another five minutes, Holland's mind now swimming with images in lieu of the forest's returned stillness. There was nothing to distract her from her nerves except her racing thoughts. She wondered about the stag and what was happening to the other Runners; she hoped they'd all make it out alive.

As if in response to her thoughts, cries split through the hush of the woods, causing Holland's heart to beat wildly against her ribs. Birds flew free from their perches, and squirrels skittered across the forest floor. The wood was waking up.

Grismon and Cadmon looked at Holland, and the three of them nodded before running back in the direction of the other Runners. Surely the noise had come from one of them. But they didn't get very far.

"Chanth eilth chol luath." Strange words resounded in the

darkness before turning to common speech. "Not so fast."

Holland understood both tongues, the foreign and the familiar. *How? What language is this?* Suddenly, her limbs froze, her feet immobilized before she had taken her next steps. One glance at her friends proved they were in the same predicament.

Within minutes, the familiar faces of the other Runners came into focus, but it seemed two were missing. Where were they? Her stomach plummeted. Holland had so many questions, but the captors who led the group rendered Holland utterly speechless.

Tall men, lithe and yet somehow very strong, approached. They were cloaked in black, had pointed ears, their hair ranged from various shades of blondes to blacks, and all of their eyes were a piercing green. Strapped to their backs looked to be some sort of weapon, but upon closer examination, Holland noticed they were merely sticks, hacked away to a point. They looked more decorative than anything.

They were the strangest, most fierce-looking men she had ever seen. Even without armor and iron weaponry, they seemed more formidable than Famar's soldiers. Perhaps that's why they were more alarming; they didn't need those things in order to boast of their strength. Were these men even human at all?

When they shifted and moved aside, one of the tallest strangers held an ankle in each of his hands; the rest of the bodies trailed on the ground behind him.

Holland gasped when she recognized the limp figures; they were both Runners lying dead like fish out of water, the numbers *36* and *08* on their arms the only indicators that they belonged to Andaimon and not the woods themselves. *They died here in the forest, and no one will even know. No one will remember their names.* Her chest tightened, but she couldn't move her hands to massage the affected area. Her arms were glued to her sides.

"General Fariah, what am I to do with the bodies?" one of the men asked.

"Toss them. Those who can't resist a simple spell aren't a threat. Those still standing... Well, they're another matter." The man named Fariah focused on the Runners with his chilling gaze, and his eyes lingered a little too long when they passed over Holland.

The hairs on her neck stood straight as a trickle of unease wormed its way up her spine. *Why is he studying me? Is he going to kill me, too?* Holland tried avoiding his gaze and instead returned hers to the bodies lying on the ground. Her chest ached anew. Why them? Not even twenty minutes into the forest, and there were already casualties.

Maybe the Forbidden Wood was as Griskol feared. Maybe there was some truth to Famar's suspicion. Holland's head spun, and her stomach was in her throat. It couldn't be that. Anything but that.

She needed to sit down.

"What are we to do now, General?" the man asked again.

"We bring them to the Center. You know Endlewood. He's advised to take care of these things with *her*. Can't say I don't prefer it that way."

Endlewood? The name snapped Holland from her nausea, though now she had a pounding headache. Had she heard the man correctly? Had he just said *Endlewood*? Impossible!

The vagueness of the mysterious men's words set Holland's mind to sprinting. If she was going to die, she would rather be told upfront—to her face preferably. That way, at least she could prepare. She had never imagined she'd have to prepare for death itself; rather, that it would...sort of just happen on its own.

And what did they mean by saying *Endlewood*? Perhaps it was just coincidence that whoever they were going to see had the same name as her book. And the same thing with the stag.

Holland's knees buckled as the spell which held her captive gave way. But by this time, her wrists were already bound, and she was being led deeper into the heart of the forest.

She wished she could tug down on her cap and cover her face from the prying glares of Fariah and his men. Their eyes were too searching. She didn't want them to know she was a girl, that she didn't belong.

The strange men pressed in closer and each grabbed hold of their bonds. It was almost comical, really, that within minutes these strangers had replaced Famar's soldiers.

It felt like weeks since Holland last tasted freedom. By becoming a Runner, she had sought liberation, but in the end, she only lost what little she had. Benneforth Row seemed like a glistening spark on the horizon compared to the depths this forest held.

And there was nothing she could do about it. Each step forward was a step into deeper uncertainty. But there was one thing for certain: she would be meeting *Endlewood*.

* * *

Their parade through the woods was anything but celebratory. The rope was already beginning to chafe around Holland's wrists, and she wondered for the umpteenth time how Markus' neck must have felt back in Tiri. She swallowed back the bile. She couldn't think about that right now.

She had hoped that during their trek through the trees she'd be able to glimpse more of the stag, but it never came. Holland was beginning to wonder if she had seen the animal at all.

An especially dark shadow swallowed up the light on their path as Holland was shoved through a dense archway of trees. In front of her, she could see the other Runners weren't enjoying being manhandled, and she silently prayed they wouldn't act out and get killed because of it.

She wasn't sure how many more deaths she could take. Already, the toll was incredibly high—enough to last a lifetime. Loss wasn't a foreign concept to her, nor was the loneliness that often followed in its wake. It wasn't fair, to say the least. And it made holding on to any thread of hope nearly impossible.

Holland followed the rest of the group, General Fariah leading the way. She was grateful, at least, that he hadn't been the one to hold her wrists.

She surveyed the forest around her and realized they were now entering some sort of clearing. The deep shadows pushed aside to make way for dappled light. It shone in little pockets here and there along the forest floor, creating a patchwork design like Tiri's public square.

Holland was pushed forward a few paces before she was

forced to a halt. She gasped inwardly; there was nothing left for her to do than to cast her gaze skyward. She was suddenly in a world of twinkling, dancing lights—as if they were stars themselves and the heavens weren't just a forest canopy. Houses were in the boughs of nearly every tree, and spiral staircases wound around the trunks to meet them. Bridges strung between the branches, their wooden planks swaying ever so gently with the vibrations of the earth.

If the strange men that flanked their group hadn't just killed two of their Runners, Holland would have thought this place was beautiful. However, the beauty was tainted. But there was something else—something deeper than mere observation.

Another string of pulses trickled up her ankles, as if the earth had a heartbeat. Something like a feathery kiss brushed against her cheek, sending gooseflesh along her skin before it disappeared. A warmth spread in her middle and then traveled to her leg. The book in her pocket thrummed against her thigh, and she wanted more than anything to take it out and open its pages.

An eeriness crept into Holland's senses; she knew these woods. Or rather, somehow, she belonged to them as much as the stag did. She wasn't so much a stranger as she was late, it seemed. That's it. She was merely late in arriving here, as if the woods had been waiting for her all these years.

The thought unsettled her. She wanted nothing to do with these woods; not after what its inhabitants had just done to her friends. She was struck again with the horrid thought that Famar might be right after all.

But she couldn't reconcile that with everything she knew

about them. Was it possible that not *all* of Famar was at fault? That not *all* of them wished to ruin the lives of the lower-class? Bound by duty, perhaps they had little choice other than to comply.

That thought didn't sit right either. If something was wrong, Holland knew she'd fight back, no matter the repercussions. Wasn't she proving that even now?

Something else caught her attention, snatching Holland's focus. She was in the back of the group, but she could still see a man stalk forward; his blonde hair rivaled the fairness of his skin. His eyes were deep and piercing, and in his gaze, he held secrets, the depths of which Holland wished to never understand. He was intimidating; he was anything and everything that she couldn't place, and yet, he was familiar like the stag.

An older man who looked graying, wise, and somehow youthful all the same, followed closely behind.

"*Moth ghràthidh*, trespassers," the blonde man addressed their group. His voice slid over Holland's skin in its cool tones. His speech sounded tempered, as if he was stilling some raging beast inside him. He turned to the men who held the Runners captive, his gaze like ice. "Too weak to finish the job yourselves, are we?"

Fariah stepped forward, his pike in his right hand. "We could have, your Majesty, but we know you prefer when *she* finishes them off instead. Less of a mess that way. *"*

Your Majesty? This strange man was some type of king? But why here, in the woods of all places? Holland's brain pounded against her skull. This was yet another thing that felt too familiar.

Suddenly, her pocket was on fire, so much so that Holland felt her skin start to burn. She was certain she'd combust in a matter of seconds. Her head spun amidst the pain, the warmth burning her flesh.

"I see," the king said, his jaw ticking to the side.

"Vesstan," one of their captors said. "Err, I mean, your Majesty. I meant to tell you, I—"

Wait. Vesstan? Holland's mind reeled, her hands tugging against her bonds as she tried reaching for her still-burning pocket.

"You are to address His Majesty as such the first time, Almar. We've been over this." The older man beside the king stepped forward, his scowl made of stone. "But seeing as you continuously forget, I'll have no problem sending you to the swamp along with the others!" He gritted his teeth before he grabbed the man roughly by the arm.

The king's expression twisted in irritation and something deeper like anger, his cool façade cracking. But he remained silent, not pleading on behalf of the frightened man.

Almar looked mortified, his limbs trembling. "No, please! I beg of you." He slid to his knees, pleading. "It—it was a slip of the tongue. I'll remember next time."

"I'm afraid there won't be one." The older man tugged him to his feet. "Your Majesty, Almar will line the swamp as bait. Bring the rest when you're ready." And with that, he left.

Holland's heart raced. What had just happened? Poor Almar was one of their own men; he had only said the name Vesstan. Why was he being punished like he had just thrust a knife in the king's throat?

The pieces were coming together rapidly. Could it be? Suddenly, it clicked into place, only a few vacant holes left to fill. How could she have been so blind? Everything from the Forbidden Wood to the garden by the hedgerow, from the stag to Vesstan, and to all the allusions of Griskol—the signs had been there the whole time.

The Tale of Endlewood; it's real. She was now in the midst of it, though, what part was she to play?

Realization burned like the book in her pocket, the truth weaseling its way to the pit of her stomach. She grew unsettled, her pulse beating uncontrollably beneath her fingertips.

There were so many questions, but there was one that stuck out to her the most: *Who's the daughter he left behind?*

The king cleared his throat before returning his gaze to the Runners. When his eyes finally met Holland's, something shifted inside them. Even from beneath her boyish clothes and cap, she felt fully and completely vulnerable under the king's gaze. It was as if he knew everything all at once, just by looking at her.

It was now the two of them: Holland and the king. Everything else seemed to disappear around them, the world holding its breath in anticipation.

His face grew pale, his eyes wide. He reached out a tentative hand, but pulled back as if he thought better of it. *"Jos-Josilland?"* he whispered, hope filling his aggrieved eyes.

Holland's heart stopped, twisting in its shell of bone.

This was another piece to the puzzle that had just claimed its place alongside the others. There was only one other person who could be mistaken for Vesstan's wife. Only one other person who could produce so much hope and anguish in the same look.

It was then that Holland knew; she had the answer to her question. Deep in her heart, she may have known it all along.

I am. I'm the daughter he left behind.

CHAPTER THIRTY-THREE
Holland

As soon as the king locked eyes with Holland, he'd shaken his head and pretended she hadn't affected him otherwise. He'd averted his gaze and uttered only two words, "Follow me."

If he hadn't said the name Josilland, Holland would have believed his attempt at ignoring her. But as it was, she knew he sensed what she did. He was her father, and she was his daughter returned home.

Home. Suddenly, the word tasted even more bitter than before. Home was not to be had where there lived a man she hardly knew.

Everything was becoming a little clearer. The strange men who stopped them at the border must be fae-kind like her father; that explained their odd appearances. What else lurked beneath the shadows of these trees?

She was led forward beneath the twinkling lights, trying as hard as she might not to marvel at their splendor. The glistening silver of the staircase rails made her think of starlight and wondered how it might feel to climb them and touch the makeshift heavens.

It was a passing fancy, for she was led around a tall and mysterious-looking castle of stone, and pushed deeper into the heart of the forest, the illuminating host winking goodbye behind her. It was better off this way. Trees and brambles stretched ever onward and morels as far as the eye could see littered her path.

But there was something else—a curious sight Holland had never before seen. Tiny wisps of brilliant blue light flitted beneath the boughs, dancing between the trees only to disappear and then reappear farther down the path once again.

Holland thought she could hear them speaking, their voices strangely a cross between starlings and whale song. But to that end, she could only guess; she'd never actually heard a real whale before. Still, their voices mingled together and were carried by the wind, twisting about Holland's ears as she walked on.

There were a few words she couldn't make out, but their tune smote her heart, drawing her nearer.

Cabhagth, cabhagth—hasten
Weary traveler
Rest your head
And wander no longer

The road is winding
The journey long
But awaits, thee, a pool
With its calming song

Slathod, slathod—turn back
Weary traveler
Rest your head and
In eternity slumber

The road is winding
The journey long
Take heed of the pool
And its siren song

As quickly as the song came, it dissipated altogether and the blue lights with it, though Holland's gooseflesh remained. A moment later, she was brought to an abrupt halt, Cadmon and Grismon by her sides, their expressions drawn like taut bowstrings.

"Did you hear them singing?" she whispered to Grismon.

"Hear what singing?"

"Did you?" she whispered to Cadmon.

"Have you gone mad?"

Holland's shoulders slumped forward. Maybe she had. And that's when she knew she'd been the only one to see the wisps. But why? They were terribly confusing to begin with. What did they mean to urge her forward and then warn her in the same breath? What was she to believe? And why come at all?

"Bring them closer," the king commanded.

Holland edged nearer against her will; the toes of her boots smooshed into the Runner in front of her. She was curious about this elusive king, but she was nervous all the same.

It was as if all the woes and tragedies of *Endlewood* paraded through her mind, reminding her of all her father's pains and shortcomings. If a man like that had no problem ending so many lives, what would he do to a daughter he never cared for?

Holland fought back the dizziness that threatened to swarm her head. She needed her wits about her, and that meant not allowing her emotions to take control. She wouldn't let him see her fear.

Eventually, all the Runners were forced into a line, overlooking a dark pool that stretched before them. It looked just as vast as it did bottomless, its murky depths a mystery Holland cared very little to solve. Some things were better left a secret.

The fae addressed as the king's advisor stepped forward and took his place next to his sovereign. If Holland remembered correctly, his name was Nindrol, and he had retreated here only moments before to usher Almar to his doom.

She swallowed hard. What lurked in the waters to cause such a brutal end?

"Good. Well, seeing as you all made it past the border-magic alive, this swamp will finish you off for good. Any last words?" the king questioned.

Holland was lightheaded. They were led to the swamp and now they were all going to die, just like that. The king had asked a question, but clearly it was a rhetorical one. He didn't care what they had to say, did he?

Suddenly, Grismon stepped forward and tugged his captor along with him. He cleared his throat before speaking. "Your Majesty, surely this is excessive. Can't we come to some sort of truce?"

"Excessive? Truce? Ha!" The king scoffed. "Speak to me of truce when you learn to mind what's yours."

"Are these your woods, then?" Grismon had the audacity to ask. "Did you plant every tree and give life to the animals?"

Holland's stomach recoiled, and her cheeks heated instantly. Even she knew not to question the fae-king. But maybe that's where she was wrong; if more people had learned to question those in power, to question Famar's authority like Grismon was questioning her father's, would Griskol be as corrupt as it was now?

Maybe it *did* matter what the "little people" thought. If they were all to band together, maybe there would be strength in numbers. Suddenly, Holland felt emboldened by Grismon's gall and stepped forward herself. "If you kill us, there will only be more search parties until the king and queen's son is found. Already, three others will be here in a matter of hours."

The king's glare turned harshly on Holland. "Search parties? For the king and queen's son? What makes you so sure that he's here?"

"I can vouch for her, your Majesty." Cadmon stepped forward, too, his face only hinting at the slightest blush. "For the search parties, that is."

Holland's resolve slowly dissipated beneath the king's gaze as it flitted between the three of them, but she held on. She knew the truth; *The Tale of Endlewood* spoke of her father's crimes. But she couldn't reveal that yet, could she?

Holland cleared her throat. "I know the prince is here. You've told me so yourself."

She felt Grismon and Cadmon look at her; she was sure they thought her completely mad now.

Nindrol scoffed. "Your Majesty, don't you think we've entertained these lunatics long enough?" Nindrol placed a hand on the king's arm, reclaiming his attention but for a moment.

"Perhaps, but I've grown curious." He returned his gaze to Holland, and a look of keen interest puckered along his brow.

Holland had his full attention now; it was as if father and daughter had unknowingly engaged in a battle of wits. She couldn't reach for her pocket, though the book had practically burned a hole through her flesh at this point. Was it even still intact? Was she?

The king studied her closer now, his gaze searching and knowing all at once. Did he see something the others couldn't? Why were her insides suddenly feeling all tingly, her mind a hazy fog?

What's going on? Holland shook her head and longed to rub away the sudden cloud over her thoughts. It's as if her body was suddenly filled with an electricity she couldn't explain, a tingling sensation spreading down to her fingertips and toes. But it didn't last long; as if in a blink, the electricity stopped and dissipated altogether.

"Ah, I see," the king said. He nodded and faced the rest of the group.

What does he mean?

"Nindrol, take care of the others. These three come with me." The king pointed directly at Holland, Grismon, and Cadmon.

298

The thrumming of her heart made it nearly impossible to hear the next words, her shock was so great. The three of them? Were they to receive some special torture?

"But, your Majesty—"

"Do as I command, Nindrol. Or else it'll be you who's claimed by the pool next!"

Nindrol gritted his teeth, and Holland was surprised to see it was anger rather than fear which prompted his actions. Did Nindrol not fear death? Suddenly, the man leaned closer to the king and dropped his voice to a whisper, but not so low that Holland couldn't hear his words. "You may threaten me all you like, but we both know your bark is worse than your bite. What of the other search parties? Will our borders hold? They hardly did today. It may be time—"

"No." The king cut him off. "They could be bluffing."

"Even still, why didn't your border patrol just kill them while they had the chance? I thought you didn't like the swamp—didn't agree with *her* ways."

"I don't. But you force my hand to no end. My guard already killed two men. Their magic is strong, but they'd rather not dirty their hands when another method works just the same—such is the way of the fae, if they can help it. *You* should be happy; the swamp will finish their job like it's intended."

"But *she* likes her meals spread out. Too many clog the pool."

"You don't think I know that? You've lectured me on its devices to no end." The king rolled his eyes.

"Your Majesty, need I remind you that safety was and is of the greatest importance for our—*your* kingdom. If three additional parties arrive, there's no way our borders will hold—or the pool. It might be time to—"

"No." The king ran a hand over his face. "Not yet. They will hold."

"You must hear me out, your Majesty—there is no other way. We've gone on like this for far too long. Our protection hangs on by a mere thread. At a moment's notice, it could break. Fragility isn't the way of kings! Do you trust me?" Nindrol's voice rose to just above a whisper, as if too impassioned by his speech.

The king seemed to ponder his words, an internal war of sorts dancing behind the depths of his eyes. Finally, the glint of steel softened into resignation, and he nodded. "Trusting you isn't what I'm afraid of."

"Good. We have our decision, then." It wasn't a question.

The king sighed, looking defeated. "I don't want any part in this. It's in your control now, not mine."

"Don't fear, your Majesty. At the onset of the moon, our walls will be fortified once again. Leave it to me; the Overseer shall be reborn." Nindrol backed away and grabbed hold of one of the nearest Runners. He raised his voice so all could hear him again. "Now about the pool. You'll go first." He pushed the man forward before he had a chance to fight back, landing him head first into the swamp.

There was a large splash accompanied by smaller ones as the man struggled to reach the surface. Then, the sweetest music filled the air. It came from somewhere deep, as if the belly of the earth had learned to sing. Everyone leaned closer to the glistening pool before a sudden flash of orange and a cry rent the air, slipping the man below the surface. Within seconds, all signs of struggle were gone.

Holland's stomach dropped. What just happened? The pool was as still as a sheen of glass. What was in the water?

A shiver snaked down her spine. She recalled Nindrol's words from a moment before. He was going to reinstate the Overseer! Did that mean...? *Oh no*. If that horrid shield from the novel was going to get resurrected, the chances of all of them getting out of the forest alive were slim to none.

The king turned and motioned for the three of them to follow, seemingly unbothered by what had just happened.

Holland, Grismon, and Cadmon were all pushed forward by their captors. They followed closely behind the king, whose trail left a path of impossibly light footsteps. Dread hovered about his persona, and for the second time, Holland wondered where he was leading them. A stroll about the forest seemed too demure to suit the harrowing occasion.

She knew this fae-man before her from the book that jostled inside her pocket. But there was still so much to tell. Who was he really? And how could a father abandon his child without a care in the world?

The mystery surrounding him grew and expanded all the more, and something told Holland that each step forward would lead her to the answers she sought.

Either that, or to her death.

CHAPTER THIRTY-FOUR
Markus

Markus fingered the glass vial dangling around his neck. The clear waters reflected the sun's rays, as if he were holding liquid sunshine. He still couldn't believe Viviand had gifted him such a talisman.

He walked beside Calsius, resuming the long trek along Kirkus' main road with Mr. Brenner lagging only a pace behind them. It was as if the new day had given vigor and strength to his weakened limbs.

They were nearing the Brenner forge, and at this point, they'd have to decide who was going to continue on with Markus to the Forbidden Wood and who would be staying behind.

Everyone stopped just outside the weathered smithy, steam drifting up from the chimney in small, coiled wafts.

"Looks like we're home." Mr. Brenner peeked in through a window. "And looks like the missus is stoking the fire for some afternoon brisket." He laughed, the sound a welcome noise amidst all the tensions of the task at hand. "Want to come in and rest a few?"

Markus shook his head. "Thank you, but I've lingered long enough. I can't afford to waste any more time."

"Son?" Mr. Brenner turned to Calsius and lifted a brow.

"I'll pass, too. Fenn needs me more than he realizes." Calsius clapped a hand over Markus' shoulder and chuckled. Laughter seemed to run in their family this morning.

"I thought that'd be the case." He nodded. "But before you go, I have some things I'd like each of you to take." Mr. Brenner opened the squeaky door of the forge and disappeared for a few minutes. There was some banging around of metal on iron, and then the shuffling sound of his footsteps returned to the door. Over each of his shoulders was a bow and a quiver, and in each of his hands were two bronze spears.

Markus stared at the armory, but it was the spears that surprised him. What was Mr. Brenner about?

Calsius didn't seem to have a problem with his tongue. "You want us to take *those*?" His brow was as high as the sky as he pointed to the pikes in his father's hands.

"I'm giving them to you, aren't I?" Mr. Brenner chuckled.

"Why now? We've never been allowed to touch them before. Right, Fenn?" Calsius elbowed Markus in the ribs.

He cleared his throat. "Yeah, you said they'd take our skin clean off." Markus looked at Mr. Brenner, curious about the sudden change.

"Parents tell young ones certain truths in order to avoid others. In this case, I hadn't lied when I said I didn't want you getting hurt. Though these spears are sharp, they're hardly more deadly than a sword." Mr. Brenner smiled sheepishly. "I must confess; I didn't want you youngin's messing with my handiwork. These were the first bronze pieces I ever crafted, and you can't blame an old man for wanting to protect them."

Markus couldn't help smiling. He was beginning to understand that all too well, wanting to protect his field of crops from his unruly siblings or the stubborn sheep who'd rather do otherwise. It was only natural to want to protect what mattered most. Which was why he was going after Holland.

"But, I've had a change of heart. You see, you're grown men now. I know these spears will be in good hands with you two, and I'll feel better knowing you have them. All those hours of training with iron ones will prove useful in the end. I don't know what dangers await you in the Forbidden Wood, but something tells me your swords won't be enough." Mr. Brenner moved both spears to one hand and shrugged off the bows from his shoulders.

"Here, each of you grab one and take a quiver. One can never be too prepared for these sorts of things." Mr. Brenner handed the pieces of expertly crafted equipment to each of them. The man wasn't only good with metal, he was good with all sorts of weapons, including the ones made with wood. His skill knew no bounds.

Markus fitted the quiver over his shirt before placing his arm through the bowstring and slinging it over his shoulder. He was beginning to feel like a walking armory.

And then came the bronze spear. It was cool to the touch and sent a thrill through his fingertips that spread down to the very soles of his feet. The metal was both sturdy and light, and yet, he felt it possessed more power than it boasted. Something about the bronze was strangely foreign—a metal he hadn't often used as most of his farm tools were of brass or steel.

Markus met Mr. Brenner's gaze, a surge of gratitude welling in his gut. "We can't take all of this. It's too costly."

Mr. Brenner waved his concern away. "Nonsense. It's only costly if it doesn't do its job, just sitting in the corner and collecting dust."

Calsius tossed his spear from one hand to the other as if testing its weight before leaning it against his chest. "You've outfitted us as if we were the infantry themselves, Pops."

"Ah, but I'd be doing you a disservice otherwise. Now, I shan't keep you any longer. Your mother is practically begging to—"

"Begging to what?" The very woman stepped from the doorway and paused when she saw who was with her husband, her smile broadening into the happiest grin Markus had ever seen. "Well, isn't this a pleasant surprise—everyone all together! Happy to see you again, Markus and—oh!" Her gaze traveled to the many weapons strapped about him and her son. "You two look as if you're ready for war!"

"Might as well be, Mum. We're headed to the Forbidden Wood." Calsius tugged his bow closer.

Mrs. Brenner's face paled, her smile dropping. "The Forbidden Wood? Mercy! Whatever for?"

"I'll tell you all about it inside, Hana, but right now, these two are on a mission. Markus is going after the one who stole his heart." Mr. Brenner placed a gentle hand on his wife's arm.

"The one who stole his heart?" She turned from her husband

to face Markus once more. "You mean, Holland?"

Markus nodded, not bothering to hide his true intentions. Did everybody know his feelings so plainly?

"How in Griskol...how'd she end up in such a place? What's going on?" She looked from Calsius to Markus, her brow scrunched up like a molehill. "Why are you both...? No, it's too dangerous!"

Calsius reached over and embraced her before placing a gentle kiss to her forehead. "It's all right, Mum. We'll be all right. Pops will tell you everything. Just trust us, okay?" He backed away, looking her in the eyes.

She nodded, but it clearly took everything inside her to keep her tongue from running.

Markus tried not to laugh, all the while his heart constricting inside his chest. Mrs. Brenner always evoked dual emotions; she was as hysterical as she was loving, and it just depended on the day as to which one carried on the greater.

Markus followed Calsius' actions, hugging both Mr. and Mrs. Brenner, and thanking them both in turn.

"Love you. I'll return soon. Don't wait up." Calsius blew his mother another kiss before turning around and motioning for Markus to follow. After a few paces, he leaned in closer to his friend, dropping his voice so no one around could hear. "It's best to leave quickly during these sorts of things. Mum's heart has been fiercely protective as of late; she'd fill our arsenal ten-fold if it meant assurance for our safety. If you catch my drift."

Markus did. He turned around and saw Mr. and Mrs. Brenner still standing outside the forge; the man's hands placed lovingly on his wife's shoulders as she brushed away the tears from her eyes.

If his own mother could see him now, he knew she would be feeling the same way. But there wasn't time, and Markus feared she would only impede his progress if he tried. Instead, he waved goodbye, hoping for the gesture to assuage that bitter twist in his gut. Hoping his mother would feel it, too, despite the distance between them.

Goodbye.

Something felt significant in this moment, as if finality had been etched into the very space between them and all they were leaving behind. Markus shook the foreboding feeling and tugged his weapons closer. The Forbidden Wood was already getting to him, and he'd do well to put things into perspective.

There were still many hours ahead of them before they faced whatever awaited beyond the trees; they'd tackle that supposed beast when the time arrived. If Markus let fear overtake his reasoning now, it would be like asking death if it'd like to attend his crops. A farmer knew better than that. *He* knew better than that. No one who sought to grow something good willingly invited blight.

But then again, hadn't villagers warned him that the Forbidden Wood was the cause of crop failure and disease in the first place?

Markus shook his head. The forest couldn't do such things, leastways, not from so great a distance; it was just a cluster of trees. Though, what lingered inside them…

This he knew for certain: the unknowing caused many people dread. All of Griskol, even. The palace of Famar knew this, and it served their purpose; fear was as bad a blight as any. *Spread fear, and nothing thrives.* Not naturally, anyway.

Markus suddenly missed his endless stretch of fields, the feeling of cool earth between his fingers, and the way Holland's headband kept the hair from his face while he worked. He missed the sights and sounds of the farm, and dare he say it, even the manure. It was earthy and yielded the best crops.

He missed tilling the ground, working his muscles until they burned, and dodging the antics of his siblings while he provided for them. Not to mention caring for the livestock. The Fenns had one of the few farms that boasted a most obstinate and headstrong cull cow, whose feisty spirit far surpassed her age. Though she was past rearing calves, she was too much a part of their family to part with.

It was bittersweet, these daydreams. Markus longed to go back, but he'd already made his choice. Holland was worth forsaking all else, even the comforts of home, for she was his greatest dream now. Still, it didn't cure the sting of all that he was potentially leaving behind for good. He only prayed there would be a bright future at the end of this unknown trek to an unknown wood.

Markus and Calsius continued down the cobblestone street, their weapons clanging against one another and their ragged breaths commingling in the afternoon air. Already, it was beginning to grow dark.

"Think we can make it to the forest before nightfall?" Markus asked.

"If we move uncommonly fast, I'd wager it's possible." Calsius chuckled.

"I'm always moving fast. It'd be uncommon for you to keep up." Markus smirked, tugging his bowstring closer.

"Is that a challenge, Fenn?"

Markus laughed. "Maybe. Though, the urgency I feel overshadows the fun in it. Still, might we try to hurry? I see clouds in the distance that don't bode well."

"Lead on, comrade."

The two friends journeyed through Kirkus, their steps sure and their endurance tested. Finally, as they crossed over the last stretch of their home village into Andaimon, a crack of thunder reverberated overhead, and in a matter of minutes, droplets of rain began to pelt against their skin.

Markus garnered his courage and pressed on. In the distance the trees of the Forbidden Wood came into view, and each step closer made their appearance grander in turn.

Calsius glanced his way, nodding to him reassuringly. They were in this together. They always were. No matter what troubles Griskol threw their way, they fought their battles as brothers.

This was no different. Theirs was a journey into the damp, dark unknown. But at least they weren't going it alone.

Holland

They were in a clearing now, a cluster of oak, ash, and birch surrounding them in a halfmoon.

"I'm taking this one." The king tugged Holland loose from her captor. "Tie the other two up." He instructed the three fae-guards to do his bidding.

They set to work, lashing Grismon and Cadmon's wrists to the base of long poles staked into the earth. "His Majesty will deal with you later." One of the fae spat on the ground beside Grismon's feet before standing.

Another fae slapped Cadmon on the cheek, leaving a red mark in its place; the contact looked like it stung, though Cadmon didn't show signs of it.

Then the three fae-guards left in the direction of the pool once more.

Holland's gut roiled. What would happen to her friends? What would happen to *her*? And where was her father taking her?

She watched in horror as Grismon and Cadmon grew smaller the farther away she was dragged through the remaining trees. Their faces were drawn, the creases between their brows fraught with concern. She couldn't blame them; in fact, she was sure her expression was doubly worse.

Her stomach churned as the pressure from her father's grip tightened about her wrists.

He led her through a cluster of trees and to a small hut tucked behind them. It was made of stone, its roof one of thatch, and from its little chimney smoke coiled into the air. A few more steps and he thrust the door open, pushing Holland firmly inside before stepping in behind her.

A sharp cry sounded upon their entry.

"Blessed stars! Your Majesty! I-I hadn't expected you so soon!" An old fae-woman, matronly and rounder in form than the men, startled at the sight of the king. She swept into a curtsy and knocked the kettle off the stove. She fumbled to retrieve it and stood rigidly in place, her fingers twitching on the handle. "So soon…"

"Ah, yes, well, something came to my attention." The king pushed Holland further inside and scanned the small cottage, frowning.

Holland did as well. As for the waning sunlight outside, this little hut boasted both warmth and comfort, and it was nothing at all like she had expected. It was one room; a small kitchen, table and chairs, and an empty cradle were the only things inside it, making the room appear larger than it actually was.

"Where is he?" The king snapped his attention back to the fae-woman.

Her face had gone even paler. "Your Majesty…I-I tried to stop him. I tried…"

"Stop him? He's not even two weeks old! Why would he need to be stopped?" The king stepped closer, his voice rising.

"I-I don't mean the young sire, your Majesty. I-I mean…your son. Prince Thallon."

"Thallon? What's he got to do with any of this?" The king fisted his hands together.

"He-I…I dare not say."

"Out with it, woman!" The king took the lady by her shoulders and nearly shook her to the point of confession. The kettle dropped to the floor once more.

She cried, "He took the little one! While I wasn't looking, he came and took him." Tears ran down her face. "Prince Ranor is no longer here. I've failed you, Your Majesty."

The king dropped the woman back onto her feet, his face

contorting into a simmering rage, as if he were kindling ready to stoke a fire. "I see."

"I'm so sorry..." The fae-woman's eyes were wide, as if she expected him to blow at a moment's notice. "Your Majesty?"

He held up his hand. "Don't. Leave me now before you utter another word. You can begin amending your ways by sending out scouts to do your job."

The woman's tears wore channels down her cheeks, but she still managed to curtsy before leaving. Her sobs could be heard even after the door swung shut behind her.

It was just the two of them now.

Holland and her father.

Alone.

He heaved a sigh. "Leave it to a witless nursemaid... I guess you've gotten your answer then. About the baby, that is." He slumped into a chair, his head in his hands.

Holland stepped back, finding comfort in feeling the door pressed against her backside, making sure to keep her father in her line of sight. Her bonds had fallen; she was free now. At any moment, she could run out the door and into the trees if she willed it...but something compelled her to stay. To challenge him. To hold her ground.

She cleared her dry throat. "I'd known for years this was your plan. I didn't need to come here to confirm it." Her bold words achieved their desired effect despite the trepidation coursing through her veins.

He looked up, staring, and then his expression steadied. "Ah, yes. How could I have forgotten?" His gaze traveled to her pocket and instantly the book heated again beneath the coarse fabric of her pants.

Holland couldn't handle it much longer. She reached into her pocket and drew out the novel, its frayed edges a sure sign of use and old age. But it was still intact; it hadn't burned after all.

"Where did you come by such a thing?" the king asked, his lips drawn in a tight line. It looked like he wanted to ask more questions, but it was as if he were holding himself back.

"I found it in Andaimon. You used to live there yourself..."

"Yes, but I never planted my book there! I never..." The king stilled, and then his face grew red as if struck by a sudden thought. "The blasted...*Thallon*..."

Holland didn't respond. As much as she was digesting the fact that her father was very-much-alive, she was barely swallowing the idea that she had a brother now, too. One who seemed to spite the man who raised him any chance he could. And from reading *The Tale of Endlewood*, she didn't wonder why. She was still trying to process much of it herself, knowing what she knew now. The novel practically served as a history for her own beginnings.

"Did you read it? All of it?" he asked.

Holland nodded. "Multiple times. I was drawn to it... But now I wish I hadn't been."

"And why is that?" The king shifted so he could face her better. He looked genuinely curious.

What was she to say to him? She dropped her gaze and fidgeted with the hem of her shirt. Was it worth risking a little vulnerability? "That was before I realized it wasn't a work of fiction. A horrid tale for the living—"

"And yet, you still read it—"

"Because it made me afraid! I didn't want to end up like the characters in this book, like…" *Like you.* "I wanted to find where I belonged, but now I'm not so sure it was a good idea. Perhaps some things are better left to the dark." She was shocked at her confession. After all her years of pining for her fate, she'd rather it had remained clad in shadow?

"Ah." The king nodded. "But it's near impossible to outrun who you are. It always comes back in the end. It's the hard truth, no matter how much you wish it to be otherwise. We are who we are."

We are who we are. Her heart constricted at the irony of his words. Was she still his daughter after he'd abandoned her all those years ago? And was she daft to have expected him to admit it? In truth, she hadn't expected anything at all, considering she thought *both* her parents had died at sea. Still. Things were different now. Weren't they?

"What do they call you—back in Andaimon, that is? Your name…?" He asked.

His question gave her pause. *He doesn't even know my name?* She swallowed hard. "Holland."

He nodded. "*Coilleth bheagth*—little woodland. A fitting name. For a time, I remembered you as Thayand—we called you Thaya…but Holland suits just as well."

He had no right to say what suited her. He'd lost that privilege twenty years ago. Was Thaya her name while her parents had loved her? Had their abandonment stripped her of that too? She fought against the urge to cry or ask too many questions. She didn't want to show how much she cared.

The king cleared his throat, shifting in his seat. "When did you..." He swallowed and pulled at his collar. "When did you know...?" His unfinished question spoke volumes.

When did I know you were my father?

"I didn't. That is, not until you mistook me for your wife." Holland's gut twisted, her need for the truth gnawing at the hollow places in her chest. She felt empty and desired to be filled, and yet she was terrified. How could she ever trust this man?

"Can you..." he cleared his throat once more. His expression looked pained. Was that a tear glistening in his eye? "Can you please remove your hat?"

The gentleness in his question startled Holland more than his outburst from earlier. It sent an unbidden pang to her heart. What wicked king—no—father, asked a question instead of demanding something to be done? And how could she say no?

Holland reached her hand up slowly and tugged the cap from her head. Rivulets of raven hair flew in front of her vision before settling about her shoulders and down her back.

The room went quiet.

Her father stared.

A silent war waged on between the tongue and the mind. Who would speak first?

Holland shifted uncomfortably beneath his gaze, her thrumming heart pounding loudly in her ears. She wished now that she'd never taken her hat off.

Her father stood, his eyes mournful and glossy as he approached her. He looked frail, haunted, and if possible, filled

316

with a flicker of hope. "So much like Josi...my dear, sweet Josi." He reached out a hand and tried to push back a strand of Holland's hair, but she evaded his touch.

Holland's jaw clenched, her expression hard. Her heart hurt too much to be treated solely as a lost memory instead of his daughter. Why couldn't her father apologize for what he'd done to her? How could he stand before her and think only of his wife?

He recoiled at her avoidance and took a step back. Was it shock, anger, or remorse that replaced the sorrow in his eyes? His expression returned to stone. He cleared his throat as if he were clearing away the cobwebs of his past. "Right, well. Now that we know where matters stand..." He smoothed down the front of his robes and nodded slightly. "Welcome home, Holland Endlewood."

He pushed past her and out into the cold of the night. He fled like an elk, or some wayward star in the heavens. And in his hand, he held her book.

How he'd taken it from her, she couldn't guess. It had been in her hand one moment and in his the next. It was as if it followed the call of its master.

She was left all alone, but at least she was free. She could go back to the Row if she wished it, couldn't she? A home that wasn't inhabited by a loveless and negligent father, only a loveless and negligent guardian. Mrs. Kershaw wasn't all bad, though.

And yet, she couldn't will herself to move.

Holland Endlewood? It suddenly struck her what her father had just said. She had a last name. After all these years, she now knew who she was...

CHAPTER THIRTY~FIVE
Markus

M arkus scanned the horizon. "We're getting closer." The foreboding feeling from earlier crept up his spine like an unwanted insect as he approached the trees. "Ominous, isn't it?"

"Aye, especially in the light of the moon." Calsius walked beside him, his gaze cast to the forest. "Looks like we didn't make it before dark, but we managed to make it before first light. That counts for something, doesn't it?"

"I don't know which is worse. Heading into this forest at night or waiting until the morning. But we can't wait until dawn. We have to go now; our choice is already made." Markus set his jaw.

The trees were only a few paces away. The moonlight did indeed paint them as the monoliths they were, and it made Markus wish he were stargazing with Holland in the back of the Row once more. There, at least, the trees didn't appear so sinister. Perhaps it had been Holland's presence which kept that idea of them at bay.

How is she faring inside them?

Sudden urgency inspired his gait to hasten, and he didn't stop until his toes were beneath the nearest oak's boughs.

"Can you believe it? We're actually going inside this beast." Calsius surveyed the trees from top to bottom as if sizing up his competition.

"You don't have to go inside, Cal. You've come with me this far. That's more than I've asked already." Markus said the words but didn't feel their truth. He could handle tough situations—he was a farmer after all—but that didn't mean he wanted to do them alone.

"You trying to get rid of me already? Come on, Fenn. I'm here, aren't I? This is like old times, remember?"

"Old times where I get your neck out of scrapes and you go home pretending your arm isn't broken or your nose dislocated? Oh yeah, I remember those quite well." Markus laughed.

"I've saved your sorry backside well enough, too. And if I come with you, I might just do so again." Calsius slapped him on the back as if to prove his point.

Markus winced. The contact sent a shock of pain along the scar on his spine.

"Sorry, mate. Still sore after all these years, huh?" Calsius chuckled.

You have no idea. Markus ignored the sting and looked at the trees. "You ready?" He studied the wall of bark before him and felt the hairs on the back of his neck rise as he took his first step. A few more strides and the air felt heavy with electricity, as if a whirring fog coiled around him.

Calsius followed behind, his spear poised and at the ready. "Better to be safe than sorry," he whispered.

Markus nodded, brandishing his own as if a wild creature were about to come out and devour them whole at any moment.

They proceeded onward in this cautious way, and all the while, the electricity seemed to thicken even more, and this time, Markus' spine grew cold. Icy fingers pricked at the tender scar, as if in memory, overcoming his senses.

It grew uncommonly dark beneath the trees, and Markus soon found himself wandering aimlessly. The vial around his neck began to glow subtly in the shadows, steadying his nerves. That, and the cool bronze in his hand were the only things keeping him grounded in reality, but even so, it did little to calm the buzzing in his head. He kept walking—around trees, over brush—and he stumbled a pace or two before he realized he was now alone. Apprehension filled his chest. And his back stung with a force he never knew existed.

Where is Cal?

Suddenly, a bloodcurdling cry echoed throughout the thick curtain of darkness. Markus' heart went cold at the harrowing sound, a shiver tracing down his spine.

Cal? Where was his friend?

Fear fueled Markus; he sprinted over ground cover and followed the cries. Anguish called into the blackened night like an owl's lullaby. But this melody echoed the tune of death. Sudden movement caught his eye.

There! In the brush only a few feet away, something moved in the shadows and writhed on the ground in pain beyond his glowing talisman. Was it an animal? He silently prayed that's all it was.

Markus ran to the creature, Errol's light illuminating the path before him in a soft halo of light. When the creature came into view, Markus' knees gave way. Grief smote his heart, and he swore under his breath.

The creature was no animal but his friend.

Calsius lay on the earth, blood covering his body in more places than skin. His sword, bow, and the bronze spear were cast aside like carrion beside him.

"Cal? Speak to me, brother. Cal!" *Blood. So much blood.* Markus' stomach curdled as he tried rousing his friend awake.

The soft light from the talisman wavered with his movements, sending the shadows to dancing.

Calsius' face contorted into something like unspeakable pain. He cried again, and Markus dragged his body backward, and rested him against the nearest tree.

"Cal, look at me. Don't close your eyes." Markus gripped his friends' shoulders, fighting to keep him conscious, but whatever had attacked him seemed to render him nearly useless.

"Fenn?" Calsius finally managed, the name slurred on his tongue.

"I'm here, brother. What happened?" His friend looked almost angelic in the purity of Errol's light.

"Do...do you remember...?" Calsius ground out through his teeth.

"Do I remember what?" Markus asked, urgency twisting his innards. What could he possibly try to remember at a moment like this? "We need to get you help. I'll carry you back to the village. I'll—"

"Fenn." Calsius' weak arm stilled Markus' haste. "It's

no...use..." His words slurred once again.

"Don't say that." Markus sucked back treacherous tears. "Don't ever say that—"

"Fenn..." Calsius groaned, cutting him off. "Just...listen. Please."

Markus swallowed back the bile in his throat. *Listen?* He wanted more than anything to get his friend the help he needed, but how could he when he was only supposed to *listen*? The pain ripped Markus' chest in two. How could this be happening? He'd get his friend the help he needed. He'd save Calsius even if it cost him his own life.

"Do you remember...the...stretch of meadowland in the west..." Calsius' words interrupted Markus' dark thoughts. "The way the hollyhocks and foxglove bloom in summer...and the golden arch of corn...when the sun strikes its leaves...?" Calsius struggled to get the words out, his breathing more rapid than before.

"What about them, Cal?" Markus hung onto his every word, waiting for the moment to usher him out of this forest and into safety. His friend was going delusional; a fever must be setting in rather quickly.

"That...that's the most beautiful place in all of Griskol... Where I planned to...to marry Damirus." Calsius groaned again and clenched his teeth before trying to speak once more. "Tell her that...that I love her...that I'm sorry...tell her..."

Markus couldn't keep the shaking from his limbs as he gripped his friend's shoulders harder. "Hold on, Cal. You can still marry her. We'll get you out of here so you can tell her yourself."

323

Despite Markus' best efforts, a drop of moisture trickled out of the corner of his eye, dripping down his nose and chin. It's as if his mind knew what his heart couldn't accept. "We'll get you out of here. I promise." He tried to move his friend, but his body suddenly felt cold.

"Tell her, Fenn…tell her." And with that, the light in Calsius' eyes went out, his body now limp and lifeless.

"Cal? Cal?" Markus shook his friend, trying to revive him. It was no use; his light dissipated into the darkness amidst the steady streams of Errol's waters. Markus' heart felt fit to burst. His tears came unbidden now, like a dam breaking at the onset of a storm. How had this happened?

Calsius would come back. He had to.

But the truth lacked that hope.

Markus never should have come to the Forbidden Wood. Holland never should have left home in the first place. If she stayed where she belonged, they wouldn't be in this mess. Cal would still be alive… He ran a hand down his face, releasing a shaky breath.

What's done is done. He couldn't blame Holland for this, no matter how foolish she was. Markus should have come after her alone, not allowing his friend to come along. His conscience would never be the same after this night. It would be a miracle if he ever felt again.

Something rough pressed against his neck, and when Markus turned, a wooden pike was only moments away from cutting into his throat. He stilled instantly, no will to fight left in his bones.

"Should we kill him?" a strange man spoke. He was holding

the crudely fashioned spear aimed at Markus. It wasn't sharp enough to do much damage, and yet, Markus had a feeling it could do more than it boasted.

"Nay. If the Overseer failed to do so, there's more to this one than meets the eye. Endlewood should deal with him first," another man responded.

Endlewood? Markus' mind was too muddled and his heart too full of pain to make much sense of anything. What was going on? His best friend had just died, and it was Markus' fault; there was no recovering from something like this. What point was there in fighting?

What about Holland? Unknowingly, he clutched the talisman around his neck. In the midst of this whirlwind tragedy, he'd nearly forgotten why he'd come to this horrid forest in the first place. *Holland.* His chest ached anew, but this time it felt like light was trying to infiltrate the cracks of his already broken heart. He had to keep going; he had to find her. Calsius wouldn't die for nothing.

"So be it. Bind him. I'll retrieve the weapons."

The strange man bound Markus and dragged his weary body away from Calsius' limp one.

Markus fought against his bonds as best he could, but there was no use. Calsius wasn't coming back; it was a crushing truth. But would they bury him? Give him the proper send off like he deserved?

He doubted it, which made his blood boil over. He'd find his way out of this desolation, and he'd rescue Holland and bury Calsius' body in the process.

Markus was dragged through the towering trees, all the while the calming light from Errol's Weir shone subtly against his chest. It was a small comfort in a place like this.

Small comfort, indeed, if comfort could be found at all.

After what felt like he'd been walking for miles, bright torchlight appeared in the distance. And it was steadily approaching.

Despite being able to see, Markus squinted into the night, his wrists burning by the impact of the rope. He hardly cared, though. What was a little discomfort in light of all that had just transpired?

"What is this?" questioned the stranger with the torch. He had met them halfway and appeared confused if his scrunched-up brow was an indicator.

"Nindrol, we brought you a curiosity. An infiltrator." Markus' guard shoved him forward.

"*Euith-comsacth!* This can't be. The Overseer is impenetrable. He must have already been inside our borders." Nindrol's gaze was one of stone.

"Nay, sir. He was with someone else on the outskirts. The other didn't make it."

Markus watched as Nindrol's expression changed from disbelief to horror. Fear was etched into every angle on his face.

"Then we must kill him. His Majesty can't know... His Majesty can't find out his system has failed. He would... His Majesty would—"

"I would what?" Another voice joined the fray, stepping out from the shadows and into the flickering torchlight. He was dressed in faded gray, and on his head rested a silver crown atop blonde hair and pointed ears. He looked like an older version of the man from the river...a *fae*. "What secrets do you hide from me, Nindrol? What do you fear?"

Markus glanced from one man to the next, his throat dry.

"Your Majesty." Nindrol dipped into a quick bow and paled. "I-I didn't see you there."

"Maybe you should start paying heed to your surroundings." The king grimaced. "What are you not telling me?"

Nindrol swallowed hard and adjusted the collar of his cloak. His gray hair showcased his age, though there was not a wrinkle on his skin. "I fear to say that the Overseer...it...well, it failed. But it's always worked...there must be a flaw in its design—"

"That's not possible. Its design is perfect. It will never fail unless it is broken."

"But this man... He walked through unharmed!" Nindrol pointed to Markus.

"A mere man doesn't possess that sort of strength." The king shifted his attention from Nindrol and fixed Markus with a piercing gaze. He seemed to search for something, his eyes narrowing in concentration. "Though there *is* something about you."

There is? Markus felt his tongue swell. What did the king see?

The king probed him with a searching stare, his gaze landing at the base of Markus' neck. "Remove his shirt," he commanded.

"My shirt?" Markus finally managed, his stomach dropping. His spine tingled anew, and it occurred to him that they were probably searching for the very thing he'd tried to conceal all his life. But the last couple of days had just proved that was no longer possible; why would he think now was any different?

Suddenly, one of the guards behind him took his pike and tore it through the fabric of Markus' shirt. Antonius' gift was no more as the torn remnants fell to the earth. The chill of the night crept into Markus' skin, and the scar on his back grew numb. Errol's talisman landed coolly against his chest.

"Stars above—" the guard behind Markus gasped.

"Turn him," the king barked.

Markus was abruptly spun around, and he could feel the moment the king's gaze latched onto his back; his scar stung with a force unlike anything he'd ever experienced. His knees felt weak, the pain almost unbearable.

The king approached; Markus could feel him stalk closer, and it was confirmed when his hand pressed against Markus' back. The king trailed a finger up the scar and stopped at the base of his neck, the pain even worse than before. Markus fought to keep his footing and not vomit, but the world was spinning and the ground seemed far too near.

Suddenly, he was falling, and the only thing he remembered were the rugged arms of the earth catching his speedy descent, and the whispered words of the king.

"Thallon's handiwork, I'd wager. The Overseer didn't fail. There is magic in his blood."

Holland

Holland walked briskly under the darkened canopy of the trees, not quite knowing where she was going, but nonetheless determined. She fled the small cottage as soon as her father abandoned her—*again*—and hoped the fresh air would clear her mind.

Her father was a fae; she knew that now, but how much of his blood mingled with hers? She also knew she had a brother named Thallon who was half-fae, and that could only mean one thing: she was half-fae, too—she had to be. This meant she could leave the forest... The Overseer would spare her, right?

The realization sent a jolt of electricity through her core. She didn't have to hear the answer to know the truth. Perhaps she'd known all along that magic lurked below her skin and flowed through her veins. It explained so much and yet, not much at all.

She thought back to the night she was stargazing with Markus; she had heard her name whispered in the wind. At first, she'd thought it was him, but after he'd denied it, she tried to forget the voice had happened at all.

But that's the thing about magic. It had worked its way into the memory, and try as she might, Holland couldn't forget it. The whispered voice was as much a part of her as her own heart, and the mystery behind it would always haunt her. But she was convinced this forest held its secret. She might not know how to wield magic like her father, but she felt she understood its ways.

"Holland."

She stilled instantly, the hairs on the back of her neck rising. Was her mind playing tricks on her? Had she just willed the forest to speak to her again?

"Holland," the voice whispered a second time.

Holland spun in a circle, her eyes wide and searching into the darkened night. It was so hard to see—so hard, and yet…was that a beam of light?

A thread of silver pierced through the darkness, and it steadily grew brighter. The closer it drew, the more prominent the shape became; it was a silver crescent, as familiar as the moon in the sky. Then the brilliance of the light dimmed enough to reveal the wielder of the crescent behind it.

Holland's heart stilled, her fingers tingling. "Elethün," she whispered the name, not trusting him to stay should she speak a fraction louder.

"I have come for you, Holland. I bring comfort in your distress." Elethün edged nearer, his silver crescent a beacon in the night.

"For me? You've come for me?" Holland couldn't believe it.

"Yes, as I did all those nights ago at the edge of the Wood. I've been watching you." Elethün pawed at the ground, his nostrils releasing puffs of hot air into the cold duskiness.

"That was *you*?" Holland couldn't believe she finally had her answer. It was the stag who had whispered her name that night under the stars. A bitterness twisted in her heart; the fact that her father hadn't been the one to call her, or even Thallon… It did strange things to her chest.

Elethün nodded. *"I've been calling you here for some time. The pull you feel is the magic in your blood. But you know that now."*

Holland didn't know what to think. "Why have you wanted to bring me here? There's nothing but pain in these woods"

"Ah, but that's where you're wrong, Holland. I admire your

father, but before he came, this forest was once one of peace. Generations of Famar's royalty have always cast blame here, and your father didn't help matters. But at the start of it all, these were good lands. Safe. Peaceable. Welcoming."

"You're right about him not helping things. I could have told you that, and I just met him." Holland rolled her tear-streaked eyes and crossed her arms, the space in her chest even more hollow than before. How could she still hurt when she was this empty inside?

"You are deeply burdened, Holland. I feel it like the antlers upon my head. Though much despair has fallen amongst these timbers and in your heart, there's good to be found in these fell woods. For there is still light. And where light resides, hope unfurls like the ferns. Not all is lost." Elethün stepped closer and nudged her with his soft nose.

Holland felt the emptiness in her chest expand and fill with a warmth she hadn't felt in a long time. It was a strange comfort amongst even stranger company. "How can you say these things, Elethün? How can there be light when there's none to be found?"

Holland thought back to Grismon's comment; he'd said that she was a symbol of hope for all the Runners. And now Elethün was speaking of light amidst a dark forest. How could hope exist amongst so much darkness?

"We often are afraid to accept what is the truth. Or rather, we don't always know how. But it's the times when your mind is at its darkest where you must rely on the word of a friend to remind you of what you yourself forget. You don't feel it, but there is hope, and hope is its own kind of magic. It exists alongside despair.

Much like the sun and the moon, you can't have one without the other." Elethün pawed the ground and shook his antlers, his crescent shimmering in the night. *"It may take you some time to see it."*

Holland swallowed back her tears, her chest constricting and expanding at once. She felt strangely light despite her burden, and yet, hope seemed as distant as the stars. Still, she fought to hold on. "I've lost so much, Elethün. So much. I don't know if I can afford faith... My friend, my Markus..." She couldn't seem to get the words out. His memory attacked her at full force, knocking the wind from her lungs. She missed him dearly.

"Ah, yes. That I am aware of." Elethün nodded.

The sound of twigs snapping nearby caught Holland's attention. She stilled beside the stag, her tears drying of their own accord.

"But I fear your doubts may be premature."

"What are you saying?" Holland frowned.

The rustling in the underbrush grew louder, and now she could hear voices accompany the noise. They sounded strangely hurried.

"Go. Follow the footsteps. But don't let yourself be seen. All will be made clear. And it's there you'll find the light you cannot yet see." Elethün nudged her with his nose.

"Elethün?" Holland looked over her shoulder, but the stag was suddenly gone.

"Go."

She could still hear his voice echo amongst the towering timbers despite his retreat.

She stood alone in the darkness. And she knew what she had

to do: heed Elethün's command and follow after the footsteps.

But what would she find when she did?

CHAPTER THIRTY-SIX
Holland

She followed the footsteps, cautiously tracking their path through the trees. They were distant, and Holland strained her ears to hear them. Step after step, she crept over sodden earth and leaves, but finally, the footsteps ceased. Silence filled the forest, and she was left spinning in circles, trying to find anything that might give her any indication as to the direction she should go.

Elethün must be mistaken.

She was caged in silence and utter darkness.

There's no light to be found here.

She hugged her arms to her chest and felt the ache. She wished she wasn't a forgotten princess, daughter to a reluctant father. She wished Markus was alive. She wished that things could be different—that everything could be different.

Go. Elethün nudged her memory. He wouldn't tell her to 'go' without a reason, would he?

What do you want me to find, Elethün? Holland closed her eyes. The air was wet, and so was she. She was shivering from head to toe. *Where is the light?*

Voices. She could discern them in the shadows.

Should I follow?

Yes. She could almost hear Elethün's reply.

Holland sighed and edged forward, hands splayed before her to feel her way through the trees once more. Elethün wanted her to find this source of light, and for reasons she couldn't explain, she did, too.

She just had to believe that it was there even though she couldn't see it.

Markus

Markus stirred, his eye-lids cracking open enough to see shifting shadows.

"You think it's wise to leave him here for the night?" one of the guards asked.

"It's Endlewood's orders. What the king wants, the king gets. Come the morrow, we'll bring him to *her*. Should take care of everything."

"Nasty scar."

"Rumor has it, it was all Thallon's doing."

"Leave it to the king's offspring. Messed up, he is. Rumor also has it that the baby's missing. Bet he has something to do with it, too."

"You sound so sure."

"I don't ask the questions. Nindrol asks enough for the lot of us."

The two men chuckled and disappeared in the darkness,

leaving Markus behind.

He shifted and the rope around his wrists dug into his skin, tethering him to some sort of stake in the ground. He was fettered like a blasted mule.

He squinted through the light rain, trying to see the details around him. There were a few other stakes surrounding his, and they were all vacant. The only signs that they, too, had once housed prisoners were the remnants of shredded rope around their bases.

He was alone.

The cool settled around him, and his chest ached. These fell woods harbored nothing but deceptive beauty. If only he wasn't bound so he could do something productive with what energy he had left. To find Holland and set her free from this living nightmare.

A twig snapped to his left, and his head turned to the sound. In the shadows, he could just make out someone, cloaked and lithe in form.

"Who's there?" Markus called out.

The man stepped into view, and though he was still veiled in shadow, Markus couldn't mistake his face. It was the man—no, fae—from the river back in Kirkus.

"Thallon?" The name came like a memory into Markus' mind. It burned a hole in his tongue.

He dipped his head. "Seems destiny wanted us to meet again. After all these years…" Thallon stepped forward, his blonde hair grayer now than in the daylight.

All these years? When Markus met his gaze, the scar along his back flaring up like a million arrows had pierced him anew. The agony was fresh, and this time, it felt like it was awakened by its maker. "You-you did this to me…"

Thallon cringed. His shoulders drooped forward. "I had little choice."

"Little choice? *Little choice?*" Markus gritted through his teeth. "Is that your excuse, then? Your rationale?" He thought back to the day he was marked; he'd healed in secret…too afraid to even show his mother for fear of her reaction. He'd taken pains to be reticent, to the point of growing out his hair. He'd lived many of those days in fear.

"You don't understand." Thallon's voice shook, the lines on his face highlighting his gaunt features. "When your father is the king, there's little room for negotiation. I learned that the hard way."

My back did, too. Markus clenched his fists. There was still so much he didn't understand. "How did you do it?"

"Excuse me?" Thallon frowned.

"How did you mark me?" The memory blurred; Markus couldn't recall the details.

Thallon was silent.

"The least you can do is tell me the blasted truth." Markus couldn't explain it, but he felt that if he knew what happened, his nightmares would stop. Maybe the truth would even play a part in the healing.

Thallon swallowed and fidgeted with his hands. He opened his mouth as if to speak, swallowed again, and averted his gaze. "You were thirteen. I was ten. You were by the river whittling a garden spade. You nicked your finger, I snuck up behind you, and..." he paused, the memory flashing hauntingly before his eyes. "You screamed...and I-I stuffed leaves in your mouth. Anything to make it stop. I couldn't bear to watch you, writhing on the ground. So, I dragged you to the river and washed away the blood. There was so much blood. Nothing could wipe away what I'd done." Thallon's face paled, a singular tear trailing down his cheek.

It all made sense now—all the little things he couldn't remember now snapped into place. He felt sick. And strangely relieved.

"Why have you come?" Markus demanded.

"To ease my conscience. I was too far away to see you properly when you crossed the border, but I had a sneaking suspicion you bore the mark of magic. Otherwise, you'd be dead." Thallon swallowed hard.

"Is this your apology, then?" Markus studied the man before him, parts of his resolve softening against his will.

"You must forgive me in my execution. My father's never been one to teach us about apologies." Thallon bowed.

"Not surprising. Power gets to people's heads." Markus grimaced. He hated the fae-king. He hated Famar. He hated everything. Was there no justice?

"That's something we agree on, then. Which is why I'm taking pains to spurn my father at every turn. I have Famar's baby in these woods, but with the Overseer, I can't take him beyond these prison walls." He gestured to the trees. "I had hoped to this afternoon."

"The Overseer?" Markus' stomach nearly emptied. "You

mean that dashed weapon that murdered my friend?" Recalling Calsius' limp and mottled form sent a wave of bile to the back of his throat.

"I've never agreed with it. My father's a man of messed up ways. I fear his own brokenness will lend itself to his own demise." Thallon sighed, and suddenly grew still. He leaned into the trees, as if listening. "Someone's coming." Before fleeing entirely, he turned once more and looked Markus in the eyes. "I have to go. Please. For-forgive me."

This time, the direct eye contact didn't send Markus' spine to burning. He watched Thallon retreat, his wrists tugging against his bonds. *If Thallon was really sorry, he would have set me free.* But such was not his luck; he'd have to work on that himself.

Stillness filled the space left in Thallon's wake. It was nearing dawn, the only noise the gentle whisper of the leaves rustling along the ground.

Suddenly, a gasp broke through the silence. Markus glanced into the shadows to see what had drawn his attention. Only, the shadows had mostly disappeared. He realized the vial on his neck was glowing once more, warming his chest and filling the small enclosure with light.

"Markus?" the voice came again. "Markus?" This time it spoke louder, and in a matter of seconds, a pair of arms were wrapped tightly about his neck, his back speckled with tears.

He'd know that voice anywhere. He knew this touch. "Holland?" He didn't trust himself to hope.

She pulled back, her eyes wide and shimmery. "You're alive! But how…? I thought—I thought…" She didn't finish her sentence and hugged him again.

Markus wished more than anything that he could wrap his arms around her, wipe away the tears from her eyes, assure her that he was well, but his aching heart was doing all that it could to remain intact. So much grief and joy mingled together—it was enough to set the mind spinning.

So, he just let Holland hug him, enjoying the feel of her clothes pressed against his skin. It'd been so long since he'd last seen her, touched her, been in her presence. She was as he'd always remembered, and yet somehow different. She was even more beautiful than he could fathom...

"Holland." He couldn't stand it any longer. He needed to tell her how he felt.

She pulled back, but this time, she left her arms around his neck, her green eyes searching his.

What was she thinking? Markus cleared his throat, his eyes watching her closely. "I escaped the gallows and tried coming after you. After that soldier dragged you away..." He shook his head as if to dispel the awful memory. "I'm so glad I finally found you—"

Holland's brow drew tight. "But it is *I* who found you." She glanced down at his chest and her fingers found the vial of light around his neck. She held it up and stared at it, tears glistening in the corners of her eyes. "Elethün was right after all!" She smiled, and met Markus' gaze, her expression suddenly turning serious. "But what about the Overseer? How did you...?"

Elethün? Markus had a million questions, but he didn't want to ask them or talk about the Overseer just now. His gaze traveled to her lips instead. He needed to speak about more pleasant things. "Listen, Holland... I—"

"Your scar!" Her fingers had found the lines along the top of his spine. "I-I nearly forgot."

Markus winced.

"What did they do to you?" She looked him in the eyes, practically begging him to confess.

"I've had this since I was young—just a boy." Markus answered, his recent knowledge of his scar still digesting.

"Can you show me?" Holland asked.

Markus hesitated briefly before nodding. She stood and allowed him room to shift his position.

He braced himself for her horror, for the shock that would drive her away. He was marked, ugly, broken, and it was now on display for the world.

But it never came. Instead, Markus felt a warmth unlike anything he'd ever felt as Holland's gentle hand traced the tender skin along his spine. She touched every part of his nasty scar, the contact strangely comforting...healing. Her touch was restorative, while the king's touch had only inflicted more pain.

"Why didn't you tell me?" she asked softly.

Gooseflesh prickled his skin as he felt Holland's lips brush the tender place near the nape of his neck. He felt known, seen, whole. For the first time, he didn't feel the need to hide the ugliness of the scar. "I guess I was afraid. I didn't want to be known by it."

Holland seemed to choke back tears. "Who did this to you?"

Markus didn't know what to say. He'd overheard the king's guard. Had talked to Thallon himself only moments ago. He knew who had attacked him, but was it right to admit that after the man had just come to apologize? What was an apology ten years late? It was better than nothing...

"Who, Markus?" Holland demanded.

"His name's Thallon—"

"Thallon?" Holland's hand stilled on his back, twitching just below the leather strap that held Errol's waters. Her voice suddenly turned cold. "He...he did this to you?" She moved around to face Markus head on.

"You know him?"

"Know him?" Her eyes were round like the moon. "He's my brother! I learned of him from *The Tale of Endlewood*. The book's real in more ways than I'd ever thought possible." Tears spilled from her eyes, traveling down her cheeks and dripping from her chin. "How could my father do something like this? Make Thallon do such horrid deeds? And to you of all people? It's like we're living in some twisted tale. It's unforgivable!"

Your father? Markus' jaw went slack. Was that the missing part in all of this? Holland was related to the wicked fae-king and cruel Thallon? His head spun even more, but he could hardly voice his questions in the face of Holland's anguish. She was crying as if she were a fountain.

He couldn't stand it any longer. He needed to touch her with his own hands. To comfort her. He remembered the pen knife inside his shoe, and his heart sped in anticipation. "Holland?"

She glanced at him, tears streaming down her face. The picture wounded his heart.

"I have a knife. It's in my boot. If you loosen my bonds, I can

343

comfort you properly. It's maddening watching you cry when I can do nothing."

Holland nodded before moving to his shoe.

Markus couldn't ignore the way her hand brushed against his leg as she pulled out the blade.

She moved to his back and filed at the bonds. The rope burned his wrists, but he hardly cared. What he cared about was holding Holland in his arms.

When the last of the blasted rope fell away, he replaced his knife and reached to brush the tears from Holland's eyes, his hands caressing the sides of her cheeks.

"I'm so sorry, Markus." Holland cried anew. "So very sorry. For everything."

"My love. Why are you sorry? You've done nothing wrong."

"I feel as if I'm responsible. For all of this. Even your scar."

"My scar? This blasted scar actually saved my life. Because of it, I have magic in my blood. It saved me from the Overseer." He recalled what the king had said at the border. The realization almost made him dizzy with gratitude, though part of him still burned with anger. But he couldn't think of Calsius right now. "Sometimes we don't understand why hard things happen to us, but we have to trust that it's for a greater reason. That good can still come out of it even when it hurts."

"Does it still hurt?" she asked, her eyes wide.

"Only a little." Markus held Holland tenderly, wanting to brush away any ounce of worry from her eyes. He wanted to kiss away the pain, but he knew better than that. A kiss wouldn't assuage the ache. A kiss wouldn't make this tragic tale any less grim. Though it might lighten their spirits.

"I should never have read that book. I never should have left the Row. I should have stayed home and been content with my lot. I should have—"

Markus placed a finger to her lips, stilling her speech. "Holland, you're going to drive yourself mad if you keep going. I love you too much to let that happen."

Holland's eyes widened. "What did you say?"

Markus dropped his hands, surprised at his confession. He hadn't meant for it to sound so...unromantic. "I said you'd drive yourself mad."

"No...the other part." Holland's cheeks reddened a tinge behind her lingering tears.

Blast. Markus couldn't help smiling despite all the turmoil in his chest. He was puddy in Holland's presence, and that spark of hope in her eyes was enough to make him lean in closer. "I said I love you. I don't know how I've waited to tell you—it's nearly killed me to keep it inside all these years."

"You love me?" Holland bit her lip. Her green eyes shone like glistening orbs in the night. She had never looked lovelier.

"Aye. Since the day we first met in Kirkus. That day you stole one of my father's parsnips, you also stole my heart." Markus leaned in even closer.

"Even then?" She looked like she didn't believe him. "I'm a nobody, Markus. I've only just learned who I am, and even then, it's nothing to be proud of."

He grabbed both her hands and studied her face. "You've always been someone to be proud of, Holland. Your perseverance despite your circumstances. Your selfless heart, your caring nature, your friendship—the list is endless. I've never once considered you a nobody." He wanted her to believe his words more than anything; they were practically tearing through his chest.

Holland looked at him as if she was seeing Markus for the first time. Truly and clearly. Her lips parted slightly, and her eyes danced in the remaining twilight. She tilted her head to the side and smiled nervously. "I-I think somewhere deep, beneath all the layers of loss, my heart has always been yours, Markus."

Her words pierced him with a spark of hope; he had never felt so light. It was odd, really, to feel this much joy at the edge of Calsius' death. In the midst of so much grief. It burned. It ached. But he knew his friend would be happy for him; he could at least enjoy this moment.

The light from Errol's Weir continued to glow brilliantly against his chest, the light drawing them together.

Markus gently scooted closer and placed his hand beneath her chin. "I've always wanted to kiss you, Holland. But not just kiss you for kissing's sake. I want it to be a promise, for things to come. For a future. I want to cherish you for the rest of my life, to love you the way you've always deserved."

Holland nodded, her tears slipping down her cheeks yet again. Her eyes strayed to the light on his neck, and the glow illuminated the tears dotting her cheeks.

"Why are you crying, love? Are you unhappy?" Markus brushed away the moisture.

She shook her head. "I've never been happier, Markus. I never thought this was possible. To be this full of hope." Holland smiled so large, she was the moon itself. Suddenly, she leaned in and met his lips with her own, the contact soft and hesitant at first before Markus deepened the kiss.

He pulled Holland into his lap and tangled his hands through her hair; it was as soft as he'd imagined. Markus had never felt so alive, and his heart felt like it would burst. He pulled away before he lost himself and leaned his forehead against hers, a contented sigh on his lips.

"I love you, Holland." The admission was as freeing as her kiss. He couldn't say it enough. And he'd say it for as long as he had life left in his lungs.

"I love you, too, Markus. I'm done running from my heart. I want it to be yours." Holland rested her head on his shoulder, her arms around his middle as Errol's light embraced them.

It was a glimpse of reprieve. Of peace. Of hope. And the retreating storm—even Calsius' death—dulled but a moment, enveloped by the light.

Markus kissed her forehead and pulled her in closer. "I'm done running, too. I'm not going anywhere. Once we're out of this forest, what do you say about planning a future together?" His heart constricted at remembering Calsius' dying wish. Oh, how he longed for his friend to have what was stolen from him. *Poor Damirus. Poor Mr. and Mrs. Brenner.*

"I'd like that." Holland smiled. "But where will we live? I'm from Andaimon; you're from Kirkus…"

Markus felt tempted to despair, but then he remembered Antonius and Viviand. They didn't have it easy, but they made it

347

work. And when he and Holland escaped these horrible woods, they'd make it work, too. Markus had already resolved himself to that fact. He'd do anything in order to have Holland by his side.

"We'll figure it out, there's still—"

"Time?" a familiar voice sliced through Markus' speech.

When he and Holland turned to see who approached them, Markus' heart turned cold.

"No, I'm afraid there isn't any. What is this? An early morning tryst?" The man named Nindrol stepped forward, his gaze venomous and pointed.

Markus got up and moved Holland to stand behind him. "What do you want?"

"What do *I* want? It's not my wishes but the king's. You're a threat here, but there's no time for such foolish talk. I won't consort with the enemy. The swamp awaits." Nindrol stepped nearer and eyed the discarded rope at the base of Markus' post. His eyes narrowed. "I see we're practiced in the art of escaping..."

Nindrol circled Markus and Holland, his gaze raking over them both. He took a curious step in Holland's direction. "You look strangely familiar. Are you—?"

"Don't go anywhere near her," Markus threatened.

"Or what? Have you a weapon?" Nindrol chuckled.

Markus remembered his father's pen knife still tucked inside his boot. His weapons may have been stripped from him at the border of these woods, but he still possessed the one he valued most.

Nindrol scoffed. "I didn't think so. You'll both be headed to the swamp, anyway. There, your love can die together."

He moved in closer, but not before Markus retrieved his father's knife. He whipped out the blade and held it out in front of him, keeping Nindrol at a distance.

"Ah. Still got some tricks up your sleeve, I see." Nindrol merely smiled and flicked his hand casually in the air. *"Chanth eilth chol luath."*

Suddenly, both Markus and Holland were frozen, their limbs immobilized. Markus' knife was still in his hand, but it felt strangely light and useless.

"Now, if you'll excuse me..." Nindrol stalked forward and plucked the pen knife from Markus' hand. "Enough of this nonsense. To the swamp—*she's* ready to feed."

CHAPTER THIRTY-SEVEN
Holland

Holland's blood boiled. Getting ushered, yet again, through this awful forest against her will grated on her nerves. At least this time, she was with Markus. Oh, how his presence changed things for the better.

She still couldn't believe his declaration—how much his love had altered that place inside her chest. It was as if she could breathe again; that fragile space that was hollowed out from years of neglect and loss was still raw, but it felt warm with the promise of healing.

All the same, parts of her chest ached. Did her father know what Nindrol was doing? That his own advisor was about to send his daughter to her grave?

Anger flared anew. Feeling so many emotions in such a short span of time surely meant she was losing her mind. But now was not the time to focus on that.

Nindrol shoved Markus and her forward, their numb legs barely finding purchase over the uneven terrain of the earth. After the storm had passed, the sun was beginning to poke its head from behind the clouds, rising enough to brighten the canopy above them. The earth was waking up, and with it, the horrors of the new day.

What awaited them at the swamp?

A few more paces, and they were nearly there. Holland had witnessed the mysteries of the elusive water only a few hours ago, but now that she was to be sent to the depths herself, the horror that had gripped her the day before was a thousand times worse.

Breathe. She wouldn't be facing this alone. She had Markus. But were they just to confess their love only to die shortly after?

"Here we are." Nindrol thrust them forward.

Holland would have fallen into the water had she not caught hold of Markus' steadying grip. He snaked his arm around her middle and drew her nearer.

"No time for an embrace. The swamp doesn't like to wait." Nindrol shoved their backs, sending them toppling into the middle of the pool.

Cold swallowed Holland. It gripped her throat and nearly choked her senseless. How could liquid fill the lungs so soon? She'd never learned to swim, and therefore, had never really been in water before. She didn't know how to make heads or tails of where she was when all she felt was water pressed against her every side.

A hand gripped her own and she rose upward. Slowly but surely, her head broke through the surface, and seeing Markus' face was relief itself.

"Are you okay?" he asked. How was he treading water with his legs and holding her in the process?

"I-I think so." Holland spat out the remaining water from her mouth. "I don't know how to swim."

"Just hold onto me. We'll try to make it to the bank." Markus motioned with his head to the land behind them.

Holland held onto his shoulders, counting the seconds it would take to make it back to the leaf-strewn earth. Nindrol lingered on the bank with a hungry look in his eyes; he clearly trusted the swamp to finish them off and was bent on its success.

Her insides squirmed at his confidence. This swamp was more than just a random pool in the middle of the woods. Whatever happened to the Runners from earlier... It didn't bode well for her and Markus.

She couldn't get out of the water fast enough.

"Can you move any quicker?" she asked. She hated to doubt Markus' skill, but something didn't feel right.

"I'm going as fast as I can."

Strange music filled her ears. It was like twinkling bells amid a steady rain—beautiful and incredibly hard to ignore. Where was it coming from? Holland looked down and thought she noticed something shimmering beneath the surface. Fear mingled with curiosity... She needed to get out of this pool and yet, something compelled her to stay.

Suddenly, she was wrenched from off Markus' neck and dragged under the water's surface for a second time. Deeper and deeper she went. Fear was louder than her curiosity, but her eyes opened of their own volition. The water stung and her vision clouded, but she could still make out something orange swimming before her.

What is it? Where's Markus? Panic seized her chest. She would surely die. She closed her eyes and tried to focus on conserving what remaining oxygen she had left.

Farther and farther down she was dragged, and it occurred to her that someone was now holding her hand. When she opened her eyes, it was to her astonishment to see Markus beside her again. And it was even more astonishing to see what looked to be a fin-maiden swimming before them.

A mermaid? Was she dreaming? Dead? Holland had always wanted to see one in real life, but her dreams had consisted of oxygen and her being on land...

"We meet again, farm boy." The mermaid flicked her tail and swam closer. "But this time, you've a friend with you. You're both afraid."

Farm boy? Holland could hardly think straight. She was so lightheaded, and her lungs were screaming; she was more than afraid.

"Lucky for you, someone like me never forgets a kind deed done, no matter what's expected of me. And you've the light of Errol's Weir, the sacred waters of my ancestors... You'll be spared." The mermaid touched two fingers to Holland's lips and then to Markus'.

Instantly, fresh oxygen wound its way down Holland's throat and into her lungs, filling her up with what she'd only ever tasted from the world above.

"But we can't have you emerge up there. *He* still lingers. No...you must come with me. Solace awaits after the deep."

The mermaid dragged Holland and Markus down an ominous

and dark tunnel, all the while touching their lips with her two fingers to replenish their oxygen along the way.

The only light illuminating their path was Markus' strange necklace. The light had a way of giving her peace in spite of the circumstances. It was enough to keep her sane. To give her hope.

Holland had so many questions. She was swimming with a mermaid while holding the hand of someone who loved her. And she was breathing underwater, no less! But she was slowly getting used to the strange events—magic ran through her blood after all.

Quickly, the mermaid pulled them through the tunnel, and after a sharp turn and countless twists, light suddenly filtered through the water from somewhere above. Holland then felt the pressure lessen as she was led toward its surface.

When her head broke through the liquid barrier, her lungs rejoiced; fresh oxygen had never tasted so sweet. She tightened her hold on Markus once more. His shoulders were her safe haven.

She looked at her surroundings, surveying where they ended up and was shocked to see a wide expanse of water stretching out around her in all directions.

The Crendian? She felt as though she'd just swallowed a bittersweet pill. She'd grown up thinking both her parents were buried at sea, that somehow, by touching the water, she'd be able to touch a part of them... She shook her head at how ridiculous that was now. Her mother was killed by her father's horrid contraption, and her father wasn't like a father at all. He might as well be dead, too.

When she turned around, a welcome sight met her eyes. A sandy shore lay a couple dozen yards away. Large trees stood a little way behind like a looming backdrop, stretching far and wide. She squinted and thought she saw what looked like strange shadows along the water's edge, but they were too small to be trees. *Are they people?*

Holland glanced back at the mermaid, finally able to vocalize all that was on her mind. "Thank you for saving us, but who are you? Where did you bring us?"

The mermaid smiled. "My name is Adra. Adra Oshiera Kelbi." She pointed in the direction of the wide expanse. "My home is Onklo, beyond the distant waters. And you are here, at the edge of the wood." She turned to look at Markus. "It's nice to see you again, farm boy."

"Farm boy?" Holland asked.

"Back at the farm, I'd rescued Adra from some fishing line in the river. She, in turn, rescued me after nearly drowning me first." Markus chuckled, and Holland felt the vibrations of his voice travel up her arms as she clung to his back. "I was going to tell you all about it, but when I went to the Row…"

"I had already left." Holland finished his sentence. "Sorry." The guilt tempted to sprout anew, but she knew better than that. She was forgiven.

Markus squeezed her arm reassuringly and tugged her closer as he treaded the water and swam in the direction of shore.

"How did that tunnel get us all the way out here?" Holland asked the mermaid.

Adra flicked her tail and swam beside them. "For years, my family has roamed these waters. My mother struck a bargain with the royal advisor, Nindrol, and volunteered my services. I 'haunt' the swamp and help keep these woods safe, and in return, my family gets more souls added to our clan." She sighed, growing somber.

"That sounds like a terrible bargain," Holland said. She was beginning to feel sorry for this fin-maiden.

"It is. Except, when many are fed into the pool in intervals, there are some I can usually spirit away to safety without getting caught." Adra smiled dreamily as if remembering something. "And I can't regret it completely. Because of the bargain, I met my Thallon."

My Thallon? Holland couldn't believe what she was hearing. "Are you and him...are he and you...?"

"Sweet on each other? Yes." Adra's cheeks reddened. "We often met at my pool. It was our rendezvous before the king became suspicious, but that was years ago. After that, we moved to Markus' river instead," Adra said matter-of-factly. "Oh, look, we're nearly there."

Holland followed her gaze. The closer they all swam, the more the strange trees slowly came into view. Holland could tell the figures were men, and they were dressed as Runners. Her heart sped up; she recognized them. "Grismon? Cadmon?" she couldn't keep from yelling.

They glanced up, shock written in their features. "Holland?" they both hollered at once.

"Who are they?" Markus asked, his arms cutting through the water like knives.

"Runners. Friends. Family." Holland felt the truth of the words deeply. She wouldn't have made it very far without them. "I met them on my journey through Griskol. Their friendship gave me courage when I had none."

They were almost to land, and Holland could hardly wait any longer. Once she felt the ocean floor beneath her feet, she detached herself from Markus' shoulders and crawled to land, the feeling of sand both foreign and welcoming.

Grismon and Cadmon ran over to her and helped her up, nodding to Adra in the water.

"This is a welcome relief. We were worried about you," Grismon said to Holland. He looked at Markus and extended his hand. "The name's Grismon. This here is Cadmon."

Markus shook both their hands and nodded, introducing himself. "Thank you for looking out for my girl."

"Markus and I have known each other since I was eight. I thought...I thought he was dead when Famar sent us on this fool's errand." Holland said, a lump forming in her throat. "I hardly dared to believe it—to hope—and now you both..." Speaking was suddenly bringing tears to her eyes. She was overjoyed to know that Markus and both her friends were still alive. After seeing their empty posts in the woods, she was certain they had met a cruel fate. She was overwhelmed with relief. Adra had spared them, too!

Grismon placed a steadying hand on her shoulder. "We understand. Love drives us mad and gives us wings. And friendship does no less." He smiled. "Now, let's all try to make it out of here alive so I can kiss my wife and wee one, and Cadmon here can get himself engaged." He clapped a hand on the young man's shoulder.

Holland smiled and grabbed Markus' hand, squeezing it

tightly. She couldn't agree more; she was looking forward to the same thing.

But all feelings of joy were soon replaced with a myriad of dreadful thoughts. How would they all get home? They'd have to go back through the woods, and they couldn't all pass through that magicked shield alive. Only she and Markus had that ability. Where would that put her friends? Could Adra swim them around the continent? But how long would that take?

Holland's head spun, and the truth was like swallowing a rock. There would be no escape. She was thankful for Adra's help, but they were no better off here than they were in the heart of the forest...aside from being alive, that is.

She leaned closer to Markus, her voice barely above a whisper. "What now? We can't all go back through the forest...not with the Overseer—"

All at once, the air grew stale, and a warm breeze seemed to blow in from off the ocean. The waves churned vehemently behind them, and what appeared to be some sort of dark vapor in the distance was moving in fast.

"Looks like another storm," Cadmon said.

"Some clouds those are." Grismon nodded.

Holland squinted hard and felt her insides churn. If those were clouds, they were the strangest she'd ever seen.

"Those aren't clouds." Markus had a knack for reading her mind. "They're moving too fast. I fear this doesn't bode well."

Suddenly, a piercing cry rent the air in two, and Holland's insides shivered. She'd never heard such a dreadful sound before—something that felt as if it preceded death.

The morning sun was high in the sky, but the mysterious shapes loomed closer and blotted it out, casting the world below in a skein of muted shadows. More ominous cries filled the air and suddenly, the sky turned orange. Fire split the heavens in half and rained upon the earth like some fatal spring shower.

Adra shrieked and dove below the water's surface. She wasn't seen again.

The strange shapes moved closer, and slowly their forms came into view.

Holland's heart nearly stopped. Markus was right; those certainly weren't clouds. And she had a dreadful feeling she knew exactly what they were.

Winged creatures circled high in the sky and approached the forest. Holland counted seven in total.

"What are they?" Cadmon yelled, his hand shielding his eyes as he glanced toward the sky.

"Some sort of dragon, I'd wager. Though I've only ever read about them in the old stories," Grismon said, his hand straying to his side as if looking for a weapon.

"They're not just any dragons." Holland stared at them as they hovered above the woods and spewed out fire on its canopy. She gripped Markus' hand tightly.

We all have our stories—every one of them marked by fire. And each either begins or ends with...

"'Take heed, beware the fell Dyvrat,'" Holland whispered, her knees shaking as she recalled Endlewood's words.

"Holland?" Markus drew her nearer and wrapped his arms around her. "What do you know?"

"They've found us. But why have they come?" Holland shuddered. "The Dyvrats will burn us all."

CHAPTER THIRTY-EIGHT
Markus

Markus squinted at the sky. "Dyvrats?" His hand flew to his head as a shower of sparks rained down upon the sand. He looked at the others. "Make for the edge of the wood. It's safer than standing out in the open," he shouted, pulling Holland forward and running for the shelter. The others followed behind. Out of habit, he bent to retrieve the knife from his boot only to remember Nindrol had taken it.

Blast. It would prove of little use anyway.

The Runners—Grismon and Cadmon—though tough in their exterior, looked like fish out of water without any weapon. Markus felt their pain. He was only too thankful they had helped Holland—no, was more than thankful. But he couldn't help wishing he could have been the one to help her instead.

But he was here now, and that's all that mattered. He wouldn't ever have to be separated from Holland again unless necessary. And he wouldn't let these blasted dragons claim any ounce of future hope that was theirs.

"What are we supposed to do now?" Holland gripped both of

Markus' shoulders from behind. "We'll die out here all the same, Overseer or not!"

They were stuck. They couldn't all escape through the woods and make it out alive, and if they stayed on the shore any longer, he was sure the Dyvrats would find them even still.

Markus stepped away from the trees and looked at the sky. He watched the dragons attack the canopy, fire pouring from their maws and cries reverberating louder than the waves hitting the shore. The forest was resisting the flames for now, but the trees along the edge of the woods were beginning to blister.

"You two go on ahead. Make for home while you still can." Grismon motioned them onward. "We heard about the Overseer. We know of its magic. We can't enter the trees and live. But we'll remain here and hold off for as long we're able."

"We've made it this far... We have to believe we'll make it farther still." Cadmon nodded.

"But we can't leave you! We have to stay together," Holland protested.

Markus felt that if he accepted Grismon's terms, it would only upset Holland more. But the man was right. Markus wanted—needed—to protect the woman he loved, the way he couldn't protect Calsius. When he got her safely through the woods, he would turn back and help the others, too. Much like an apple tree, people needed more than just themselves in order to thrive; there would always be strength in numbers.

"Holland, trust me. I'll come back for them—I'll figure out a way. But I won't rest until I know you're safe. These dragons will scorch us all if we don't move. Maybe there's even a way to bring the beasts down from the inside."

"But—" Holland tried speaking.

"We'll be all right. Go while you still can." Grismon waved them on.

"Please, love. All I ask is for you to trust me." Markus brushed a strand of hair behind her ear just as a smoldering bough snapped from the tree above them and crashed to the ground, burning at their feet. "And quickly. We don't have much time."

She nodded, a single tear trailing down her cheek.

Markus turned to Grismon and Cadmon. "We'll go. I'll see what I can do from the inside, and hopefully, we'll all make it out alive in the end." Markus clapped a hand on each of their shoulders. "Stay safe."

"Let's wish for happier tidings at the end of all this, brother." Grismon clapped him on the shoulder as well, and the three men shared a collective, silent resolve before separating.

Brother. Markus just met these two men, but trying times brought people together faster than leisurely ones. He suddenly missed Calsius and his father something fierce. He wished for a brotherhood that didn't have a timestamp, snuffed out too soon. Now he'd be entering through the very barrier that killed his friend, and for a second time, no less.

He looked at Holland, itching to move and get it over with. "You ready?"

She gave the two Runners hugs and wished them well before allowing Markus to lead her deeper through the trees. Her hand was small in his own, but it fit perfectly, feeling like home. It was a bittersweet comfort amidst the burning of the world.

They ran for a stretch of time and stopped for a moment to find their breath.

"Do you think it'll hold forever?" Holland asked, glancing at the sky.

Markus followed her gaze and startled to see red and orange peeping through gaps in the canopy, dark smoke billowing up from the flames. For now, the Overseer kept the dragons at bay. But for how long? "I don't know. Nothing lasts forever, not even the best-made swords." Mr. Brenner always used to say that to him and Calsius at the forge.

A pang twisted in his chest. How was he going to tell Mr. and Mrs. Brenner about their son's death?

Markus recalled when his own father had passed. When his mother had told him the news, grief struck him numb; he hadn't thought about how hard it must have been for her to relay the news, especially to her own children. No one should have to shoulder that responsibility alone.

A splintering sound echoed from somewhere above them, and the next thing he knew, a tree fell, crashing into another and sending sparks everywhere. The forest floor was engulfed in flame.

Markus' heart beat wildly. *Fire inside the forest… But that means…*

"The Overseer is broken!"

"Man your stations! Ready your magic!"

"Beware the filthy Dyvrat!"

From somewhere nearby, these cries could be heard echoing amongst the trees. Hurried footfalls padded closer, and suddenly,

Markus and Holland were surrounded by a host of fae who rushed past them as if they weren't even there. Strange chants and incantations escaped their lips and were cast toward the sky. And as soon as they came, they disappeared deeper into the forest.

Their spell-casting proved of little use; fire continued to rain down upon Markus and Holland, and this time with even greater force. A thick branch snapped overhead, falling in their direction at a great speed.

"Watch out!" Markus grabbed Holland by the waist and pressed her up against a tree, shielding her with his body as the branch landed only a pace behind him.

She poked her head around his shoulders and glanced at the burning log, gulping. "That was close."

Markus didn't like this. They had to leave this forest—fast. "I need to get you out of here. It's not safe." He moved aside and began walking, trusting that Holland would follow, but when he looked over his shoulder, she hadn't budged, the flames licking at her heels. "What are you doing?" Urgency coursed through his body. *Confound it. Why isn't she moving?*

"I don't like the idea of running, Markus—not from fear. I-I want to help. My brother...my father... I can't just leave them here to die." There was so much conviction in her voice, though her lip trembled ever so slightly.

Markus watched as her resolve hardened. She looked like she was in pain, trying to figure out her place in this misshapen tale. Guilt stung somewhere in his chest. How could he rightfully pull her away from the only family she had left? But her safety...

"Please, Markus." Her words cut through his thoughts. "You

asked me to trust you, and I have...all my life. But now I ask that you trust me in this. Let me stay and help my people. I can't explain it, but to leave now... It feels wrong."

He couldn't argue with her. He'd spent most of his life running from tough situations, overworking his body and his field in order to assuage the pain and make him forget. But here, seeing Holland choosing to stay after all she'd been through... Well, he felt downright cowardly. He'd be nothing better than a louse if he just cloistered her away.

But he'd die if something happened to her. His heart was next to breaking with the reminder of Calsius' death, and to potentially add another to the growing list of casualties?

He ran a hand through his hair, reminding himself to relax. The forest was burning. And the longer they stood there doing nothing, the greater the chances they'd *both* die. He turned to Holland and nodded. "All right, but stay close to me. I can't bear to lose you, too." He hated this.

She grabbed his hand. "I was hoping you'd say that." She picked up her pace and started running through the forest. "Come with me!"

"Where are we going?" Markus had a strange feeling that he wouldn't like where this was headed, but he could tell she was determined. Her frantic steps and vice-like grip said it all.

"I have an idea—a ridiculous one—but it's the only one I've got."

"Which is?" Markus caught Holland as she nearly tripped on a fallen tree.

"*The Tale of Endlewood* mentioned something about defeating

Dyvrats." She paused enough to look him in the eyes. "I believe my father knows the answer. We're going to find him."

Holland

The forest was ablaze, blistering the skin on Holland's arms and warming her face. She itched all over, and the acrid smoke burned her lungs. But she persisted. Markus was beside her, holding her hand. The contact kept her mind alert, and his movements beside her reminded her to keep going.

"Any idea where he might be?" Markus coughed into his arm, his face streaked with soot.

If possible, Holland thought the soot made him look even more handsome. His blue eyes were like clear pools amid the sweltering flames. But it was his willingness to support her decision which made her heart skip a beat. She knew he thought her foolhardy, but at least her conscience was clear.

However, now was not the time to dwell on such things. She needed to find her father. "I'd imagine he's near the castle."

They slowed their pace to pick over the fallen trees and burning timbers, all the while scanning the open sky for the Dyvrats. The forest was alight with color, and the heat was near intoxicating.

They passed countless fae; scorched or trapped beneath felled trees—all bloodied, lifeless, dead. Holland's gut twisted and she fought the urge to retch. She hoped Grismon and Cadmon wouldn't be counted amongst the fallen. Nor her brother—she'd yet to meet him.

The castle was approaching, and so were the ethereal lights and spiral staircases. But everything was warped and broken, signs that the Dyvrats had already left their mark. With so many fallen trees, the bridges and staircases were all but destroyed. Half of the castle wall was blown out, the stones scattered amongst the leaves like carrion.

And it was here where Holland saw who she was looking for.

Her father, standing alone, was in the ruined archway of the castle, his fingers trailing along the broken stones. He stood erect, and yet, she could tell there was sadness in his posture.

She stepped closer, her body shaking of its own accord. What possessed her to seek out the man who ruined her childhood? Surely there had to be another way.

"Endlewood," she said, for to call him 'Father' seemed like a lie.

He turned, his eyes wide and eyebrows raised. "Thaya—" he choked. "Holland, I-I had thought you'd be gone by now."

"Gone?" She stepped a fraction closer, Markus by her side.

"The woods aren't safe. Nothing is. Go home while you still can." There was a glimmer of sorrow in his eyes.

Home. He said the word as if home couldn't be found with him. As if it never had…and never would be.

Holland wanted to scream. "Home? What's to stop these beasts from attacking the rest of Griskol? Home won't be safe for long, no matter where it is."

Markus cleared his throat. "What we need is a way to defeat them. Holland thinks the answer lies with you. And I'm inclined to believe her."

She could kiss him for that. And then smack her father.

"What could I possibly share? All is lost amongst the rubble of broken dreams. There is no hope left in these woods." Her father traced the pattern in the cracked grout, his countenance heavy and dark.

"Your book says otherwise," Holland said, crossing her arms over her chest.

"My book? What does that have—"

"You mentioned there was something that could bring the Dyvrats down—a certain material that you don't possess here. What is it?"

"Holland, that was so long ago. You can hardly expect me to recall it now."

"You're lying. You know the material and are choosing to forget it." The truth was like a slap to her face. "You've given up…and you're taking everyone down with you."

Her father flinched, as if her words had speared him somewhere vital. Then his shoulders relaxed, as if remembering defeat once again. "What's the point in telling you? Speaking it aloud won't make it appear. Bronze isn't forged through words like spells."

Bronze? Holland felt a twinge of hope, but it soon dissipated. The only place that used bronze was a forge, and the closest one was about a day's journey into Kirkus. Maybe her father was right…

"This must be some sort of coincidence." Markus shook his head.

"What are you talking about?" she asked, facing him.

"Trust me." Markus placed a hand on her arm and turned to her father. "Your Majesty. Is bronze truly the means that will bring these beasts down?"

He nodded. "It's the only material that can pierce their hellish hides, rendering their blood cold. But it's not in our power to wield."

Markus took a step forward. "It might be. The spears. Where did you put them?"

Spears?

"Spears?" The king knitted his brow, asking the same question running through Holland's mind.

"Aye. When crossing into these lands, some of your men took them from us...from me." Markus shook his head as if remembering something painful. "Where did they go?"

"I don't remember seeing these spears you speak of. Perhaps Nindrol took them to the strong room." Holland's father waved a dismissive hand.

"Where is that?" Markus questioned.

"It's hardly worth going there. There's no use—"

"Where is the strong room, Father?" Holland cut him off, her patience growing thin.

His head snapped up. Was he as shocked as her by the use of such a familiar title? Her cheeks reddened, but she didn't care. She had his full attention now, his gaze suddenly alert.

"We're running out of time." As she spoke, another host of trees began burning overhead, and the cries of the Dyvrats were even closer. Were they going to alight upon the ground?

"Your Majesty, tell us where the room lies, and all our lives may yet be spared," Markus prodded.

Her father conceded, stepping aside as he pointed down the remains of the crumbling hallway. "Up the stairs. Second door on the left. It's usually locked, mind you."

They couldn't waste any more time. Holland followed Markus as he ran ahead. After following the flourishes of the castle, the strong room finally appeared.

A tree had smashed through the exterior wall of the castle, taking down most of the strongroom door with it. Markus burst through the opening and scoured the space for any sign of the spears.

Holland wasn't sure what they looked like, but how different were they from swords, really? She'd seen enough of those over the course of her journey through Griskol to know they were long and treacherous. She imagined a spear would look similarly. And how hard would it be to find bronze?

"Found my father's knife," Markus said, pocketing the weapon and continuing his search.

The castle shook as if an earthquake rampaged through the earth. Except, Holland felt that this disturbance came from somewhere above. Swiftly, a piercing screech sliced through the air and another wall of rocks exploded around them, sending Markus and Holland to the ground.

Everything went quiet, her vision white as a high-pitched ringing sounded in her ears. It was strangely peaceful, if not for the impending doom she felt thudding in her chest. Her sight slowly cleared; the sun mixed with the blaring heat of the beastly flames, stinging her eyes as they adjusted to the light.

When she saw what was before her, her heart leapt to her throat. One of the Dyvrats was perched at the top of the castle, its spiked tail swinging wildly like a battle axe and its mouth open, about to spew another round of fire through the opening it had just created. Its skin was a burnt red, and its talons were dagger-like, dripping with blood. It looked ready to devour her whole.

"Markus…" Holland barely squeaked; her throat was so parched. "Markus!"

The dragon lunged, but its head suddenly snapped to the side when a hunk of metal struck its face. The creature roared as pockets of blood opened on its skin.

"Get back, snake!" Markus yelled, throwing another breastplate at the dragon, followed by an axe.

The monster recoiled, the weapon embedded in its neck while it spewed a stream of fire in the sky. It roared again and leveled them once more with its gaze. It opened its mouth and snapped at Holland's ankles.

She screamed, kicking at the beast and desperately trying to scramble to her feet. "Markus!"

He jumped in front of her, wielding a spear that glinted bronze. He slammed the shaft against the dragon's skull, deflecting a blow from its talon and another from its tail. The monster blew a gust of fire, and Markus dodged, rolling to the side. When he came up, he thrust the weapon upward, stabbing through the fleshy jaw of the hideous monster and directly into its throat. Blood splattered on his face.

The beast roared, but the light soon dissipated from its eyes as it crumpled from the tower, its body hitting the ground below with a heavy thud. Dead.

Holland shuddered, her skin prickling with gooseflesh.

Markus dropped to her level and lifted her chin. "Are you hurt?" He searched her face, his brow pinched—a direct contrast to the dimpled grin she was used to.

She shook her head. She was alive, and that's more than what she expected.

He planted a kiss to her forehead, the contact sending tingles down her spine. "Let's go. Now that we know the bronze is effective... There's more of these dragons to fell before they make sport of us all." Markus stood and helped her up. He grabbed a second spear and handed her the other, and the two of them rushed out of what remained of the castle.

When they made it back outside, her father was gone, and in his place stood a younger version of him. It was someone she didn't know, and yet, by the way he stood, she felt she knew his name. And in his arms was a wrapped bundle.

"Thallon?" She took a hesitant step closer.

The man turned, his blonde hair almost orange in the light of the surrounding fire. He seemed to recognize Markus, but his brow puckered when he noticed Holland. He tugged the bundle closer to his chest. "Do I know you?"

She approached him, biting her lip. She looked nothing like her brother—didn't even know him—and yet, they had occupied the same space for their first nine months, growing alongside each other until they entered the world together.

"My name's Holland. I—" How was she supposed to say this? For all she knew, he didn't know he had a sibling. And introducing herself in the middle of a burning forest while being attacked by dragons? She continued anyway. "I'm your sister."

"My sister?" His brow scrunched even closer before understanding dawned. Suddenly, his eyes rounded, a new light in them. "My sister! You came after all!"

Holland released a shaky breath she didn't know she was holding. *So, he does know about me.* But what did his greeting mean? "You were expecting me?" For all that she knew, their father hadn't mentioned he'd abandoned his other child.

"I'd always hoped. After reading Endlewood's diary, I wanted to find you…"

Endlewood. Thallon wasn't used to calling him 'Father,' either.

"…but I had no clue where to start. I stole his book and hid it somewhere in Andaimon, hoping you'd find it. Magic seems to have a way of drawing things togeth—"

A splattering of trees fell around them, their heavy thuds vibrating against the earth. Six dragons flew overhead and released a line of fire atop nearby trees as sharp cries pierced the skies above. At any moment, the beasts would land and devour any remaining life.

Holland cringed, gripping tighter the spear in her hand. They couldn't keep standing here. They needed to bring down the rest of the dragons.

The bundle in Thallon's arms began to move and make noises. They sounded strangely like a baby's crying. *Can it be…?*

As if reading her mind, Thallon shifted, bringing the bundle closer into view. "Endlewood's nefarious scheme. The king and queen's son."

The baby was round in the face, with sparkling amber eyes. He looked so innocent, hardly royalty at all.

"Now that the Overseer is broken, he needs to get back home. To safety," Thallon began. "But to leave in the middle of all this..." He scanned the burning trees and the crumbling remains of the castle.

Holland wished it didn't have to be this way, that she could linger and make up for all the lost years between them. Thallon was like her, in a way; they both were hurt by their father. It was a wound that cut deep...deeper than the loss inflicted by their mother's death; she had left against her will, whereas their father had chosen otherwise.

But they couldn't linger. There was a battle to fight.

"I can't rightly let my people burn. They need me here," Thallon said, something like determination in his eyes.

"Leave the child with me," Holland suggested. "You two fight. I'll watch the little one." She exchanged her spear for Prince Ranor, tucking him securely against her chest. Thallon heaved a sigh, his expression relaxing.

Markus cleared his throat, nodding at the weapon in Thallon's hand. "Right. That is the only way to bring them down. Aim for their chests or their heads."

Thallon gripped the bronze. "Finally, a chance to wield a weapon for good."

The comment stirred something behind Markus' eyes—a memory, perhaps—and Holland watched as he nodded. She, too, felt the sting of his pain, of the scar he bore that would never go away.

The irony ran deep. Once-enemies would be fighting alongside each other as brothers, and this time with a common purpose.

Time has a curious way of mending things, even when the memory doesn't seem to forget.

Suddenly, one of the Dyvrats came hurtling through the sky and swooped low, only mere feet above them. Its breath reeked of decay and stale blood, but it was the heat its body gave which nearly singed the hairs on Holland's head.

She tucked the baby closer to her chest, praying they'd all make it out alive.

CHAPTER THIRTY~NINE
Markus

M arkus' gaze was locked on the sky. "Heads!" he yelled.
"They're coming!"

The remaining Dyvrats dove and would have split everyone in two, had they not ducked for cover. He and Holland ran for the ruined remains of the castle, Thallon following close at their heels.

Markus groaned. He knew Holland had needed the moment with her brother, and his heart had swelled with sympathy, but this was *not* the time to make introductions.

Six Dyvrats against two armed men… There had to be more fighters out there. Where were the rest of the fae? Surely, they hadn't all fallen.

The dragons swooped again, their spiked tails dragging along the earth and creating waterless channels. More fire burst from their maws.

When the dust finally settled, figures appeared behind the haze. Men with pointed ears stood alongside those with green armbands around their biceps. The fae had come, and the Runners with them! *Is that Grismon and Cadmon, too?* Their numbers would add much in their fight against the Dyvrats, though unless they wielded bronze, only Markus and Thallon would be bringing the monsters down. Still, their aid would benefit them all.

Relief surged through Markus. They weren't alone in this fight after all!

The reinforcements inched out of the forest and stood at the edge of the clearing, watching and waiting. The Runners weren't armed, and much like Grismon and Cadmon had been along the shore, they looked like fish out of water.

The strong room! There were plenty of weapons in there. He'd seen his own sword and bow amongst the lot of them.

The beasts regrouped and claimed the sky once more, their roars shaking the heavens. Markus needed to tell the Runners before the Dyvrats attacked again.

He pushed away from his shelter and sprinted across the burning field, dodging tree, root, and twig. Once there, he addressed the men. "Weapons!" he shouted, his spear pointed in the direction of the castle. "In the strong room. Go now!" He'd already killed one beast; he'd kill another soundly. For Calsius. For his father. For all who had died an untimely death. Fate wasn't kind, and neither was he.

The Runners sprinted in the opposite direction, heeding his advice. In a matter of minutes, all of them had either swords or bows brandished and knocked at the ready. Just in time, too.

The Dyvrats began their descent once more, this time spreading out their attack amongst the new fighters. One flew directly in Markus' direction, its wings held close to its side, making its body like an arrow head. Would it run him through?

At the last moment, the dragon unfurled its wings and released a stream of fire. Markus ducked and rolled, the scar on his back burning with the force of the heat. When he looked up, he saw Thallon raise his spear and plunge it into the side of the beast, just below its left leg.

It's not enough. This would only spark its ire. Thallon would be a meal in a few seconds.

Markus gripped his spear and ran toward the Dyvrat. He counted the seconds he had left. When the monster's head turned to feast on Thallon, Markus stabbed it in the chest, twisting the bronze deeper.

The cry it let out was deafening, and its last attempt at spewing fire was only cut off by its inability to breathe. The Dyvrat was dead.

Only five more to go.

Markus surveyed the small enclosure. The fae were attempting to hold back two of the dragons with their spells, but this only seemed to keep the beasts at arm's length. Sooner or later, they'd crash through, just like they had with the Overseer.

"Hold! Steady." Markus recognized the voice as Nindrol's. "Don't let them taste your fear!" The king's advisor paled, his hands shaking like leaves in the wind.

Fear has nothing to do with it. The dragons would eat them, fearful or not. They'd only hold out for so long without wielding bronze; the most they could do was weaken the beasts.

Markus should help them, but part of him thought otherwise. Nindrol was a scoundrel; he deserved to die.

"Steady, hold fa—!" One of the Dyvrats broke through the magic and knocked Nindrol off his feet, looming over him with its mouth open as if ready to strike.

Markus groaned, cursing to himself. He couldn't just let Nindrol die; he'd be no less of a scoundrel for it himself. Markus sprinted toward the action with his spear raised, but he was too slow. The Dyvrat lunged at Nindrol and sank its teeth into the fae, the crimson of his blood a stark contrast to the paleness of his skin. Nindrol cried, but it was muffled as soon as the Dyvrat finished him off.

Markus faltered, the bronze in his grip feeling like fire. Guilt settled in his gut. How many more men would have to die before all this was over? Suddenly, the beast turned to face him and roared, spittle flying in all directions. It clawed at the ground and charged.

Markus braced himself, a feint in the making, but he was suddenly sideswiped by another beast's tail and sent careening into a tree. The breath was knocked from his lungs, and his middle stung with fresh slashes. The spear went flying and Markus rolled to his stomach, groaning. The taste of blood clung to the back of his throat, and he looked up, his eyes wide.

Nindrol's killer charged at him anew.

Markus sucked in some air and gritted his teeth, pushing up from the ground. He saw his spear. It was only a few paces away. He ran for it. The beast lunged for Markus, but his hands found the burning metal just in time.

The beast lurched, its claws extended and mouth ready to take a deadly bite. Markus ducked and twisted, dodging the attack. He spun and arched his arms wide, sending the spear crashing against the beast's skull. It didn't do much, but it was enough to stun him.

It was the moment Markus needed. He thrust his arm back once more and speared the winged-demon clean between the eyes. The dragon wavered unsteadily before slumping to the ground.

Four more left.

Markus fixed his gaze on the Runners, Thallon alongside them, slashing and stabbing at the villainous hides of the Dyvrats. The two dragons had arrows notched in their flesh and a slew of gashes along their legs and sides. It seemed to slow them down a touch.

A sudden unease crept up the back of his neck. He turned toward the castle, needing to assure himself of Holland's safety. He scanned the crumbling stones with heart thumping anticipation.

She wasn't there.

His stomach heaved. *Where is she?* He scanned the battlefield once more. *And where is the fourth dragon?* Every muscle went rigid.

"Thallon!" he yelled.

The half-fae speared his kill, sending another foul beast to its death. That only left two more on the field. He turned to look at Markus, blood smeared across his face.

"Continue to fight on this front. I'm going to find Holland," Markus yelled, adrenaline pounding so hard in his ears that he could hardly hear.

"My sister?" His expression puckered. "Where is she?"

"I don't know. Where's the fourth dragon?" Markus gripped his spear and headed deeper in the woods. Something warned him that if he could only find the final Dyvrat, Holland wouldn't be far behind.

Holland

Holland ran as fast as her legs could carry her. When she'd seen the Dyvrats descending once more, she'd tried to sneak around the castle and find a better hiding spot. This had been a folly.

One of the beasts had spotted her and gave chase.

She was running for her life through the trees, little Prince Ranor firmly pressed to her chest. She was sure the baby could hear her pounding heart and only hoped it served as a comfort.

Holland neared a cottage and recognized it as the little house her father brought her to the night before. Maybe if she hid inside?

It was risky, though—the Dyvrats *and* the building's beams might crush her and the baby. Was it worth it?

The dragon spewed fire behind her before disappearing in the sky. She silently thanked the trees for serving as barriers. Holland dodged the flames and slowed her pace when she felt the beast's pursuit relent. She was closer to the cottage now; it would be so easy to hide within its four walls.

Maybe the beast had given up on her. Maybe it had found something else to draw its attention. Maybe—

All of a sudden, the monster crashed through the canopy before her, bringing down three oaks in the process. It landed heavily on the ground, its monstrous body heaving from what Holland felt was exhilaration. Its hide was a sickly green color with fish-like scales, and its size was at least ten times her height. Its eyes glowed with an eerie orange light, and its spiked tail swayed precariously close.

A scream died in her throat, and her heart plummeted; she had hoped too soon. The monster blocked her path to the shanty. There'd be no using it for shelter now.

Her body froze, and her legs felt as stiff as bone. She couldn't do anything save for stare into the hungry eyes of the Dyvrat before her.

"Fool," the beast roared. Its voice was deep and sounded like flint striking metal. With just a spark, she knew it would incinerate her. "It's time to meet your end."

Holland stilled, shock making her knees quiver uncontrollably. Why was this monster speaking to her? She wanted no part in its schemes.

And she didn't want to die alone...though now she wouldn't. She glanced down at the small prince and tried to hold back her growing terror.

"Prepare to roast." The dragon leered. "I like my kills crispy." It lunged at Holland, but didn't get very far. A roar escaped its snaggle-toothed maw, and it turned its head to snap at something behind it.

"You dare touch my daughter?" A familiar man with a gray cloak and silver crown came into view. A small dagger was clutched firmly in his grasp, the blade dripping with blood.

Holland's mouth hung open, and her heart sped. *Endlewood— my father. He's defending me?* The surprise rendered her nearly as immobile as her Dyvrat-induced fear.

The monster looked at him and sneered. "You!" Smoke puffed out of its nostrils. "I thought I destroyed you back in Lamia! The same way I destroyed your father. Your mother." The Dyvrat circled them both now, keeping a watchful eye as her father brandished his blade before him. "I won't make that same mistake again."

Something shifted in her father's expression as he inched nearer, but he didn't appear to let the dragon's taunts affect him. "Stay away from my daughter," he said again.

My daughter. Warmth spread in Holland's middle at hearing those words directed at her—especially from someone who had cast her off so willingly. It was surprising, seeming to quell her shakiness, even if only a fraction.

"Where's the fun in that? Making you watch her death would almost be better than killing you first. Almost—"

"How did you find us?" her father interrupted the beast.

He was stalling for time.

"Traces of magic. These woods are rife with it. Lamia's has been emptied. We've gone weeks without food, but no more!" The dragon cackled loudly and turned its gaze in Holland's direction. It stepped closer.

Soft cries came from Holland's chest. They soon turned into wails, the sound an added noise to the already chaotic forest. Holland tried to soothe the worried child, his tears echoing her silent fears.

The dragon narrowed its eyes. "A baby?" It licked its lips. The beast opened its mouth, readying its fire, when Holland's father ran in front of her, defending her yet again.

"I said, don't touch my daughter, you snake!" Her father spat, his dagger reflecting the surrounding fire. "Go back to the shadow from whence you came."

The Dyvrat laughed even harder, its tone deep.

Holland bristled. Laughter sounded formidable coming from the mouth of one bent on evil. Bone chilling.

"Nice sentiment." The dragon growled. "Now, step aside, peasant, and let me claim what's mine." The beast snaked its tail and rammed it into the king, sending him tumbling backward. It opened its mouth and stared Holland down.

She could see the fire igniting down its throat, like an ember amongst the ashes. In any moment she would burn to a crisp; she and the little prince.

But her father was quicker. He shot up and grabbed his dagger, plunging it into the very tail that hit him.

The beast groaned, slashing at him with his claws and carving a deep gash down her father's chest, nearly splitting him in two. "Now you *will* watch your daughter die."

Holland let out a shriek as her father slumped to the ground, motionless.

Dead? No—not yet. Holland fought the warring emotions raging in her chest. She was about to die; there was no time to act. If only she knew how to wield magic like the fae—but she'd never been taught the spells.

The Dyvrat released its fiery breath in her direction, this time unobstructed.

"Stath tiene. Sathail ilath," her father's weak voice carried to where she stood. *Stop the fire. Save them.*

The flames didn't reach her; they dissipated in the breeze and were followed by another blood-curdling screech. This time, a giant rod of bronze shot out from one side of the monster's head, and on the other side, there was Markus with the rest of the spear, pushing the weapon even deeper.

How had he snuck up on them? Relief pooled in her middle as the terrible beast took its last breath, tumbling to the earth with a heavy thud.

The ground shook, and her father groaned.

Holland ran to him, falling to her knees beside him with Prince Ranor nestled close to her chest. Tears stung her eyes. "Father?"

Markus was there, too, easing the king up on his back, revealing the Dyvrat's deathly blow. His cut was deep, and no amount of healing would make him whole again. He'd used every ounce of strength he had left to save her.

With a weak hand, he slowly motioned to his cloak, his fingers brushing against the folds of a hidden pocket. "Take it…please…"

Holland lifted the fabric and pulled out a familiar book, its title one she knew all too well.

"*Toirth maithenas domth*…forgive me." The last light in his eyes snuffed out, and his body went still.

The *Tale of Endlewood* had come to a close.

* * *

Grief burned in her chest. She felt empty all over again, and yet, there was a sense of peace lodged in her core. She couldn't make sense of it.

When she turned, Elethün was by her side. He nudged her gently with his nose. *"I'm sorry, Holland."*

She stroked his velvety fur, instantly comforted. "Where have you been this whole time?" Maybe, if he'd been here sooner, he could have saved her father.

"I don't fight. I heal. My defense is courage, not violence. This isn't my war, but I'll always be close by to help pick up the broken pieces in the end." Elethün was a king in his own right; he had rules of his own. He couldn't have saved her father, even if he had wanted to.

"Holland...the others!" Markus placed a hand on her back, the screams from the others still engaged in battle echoing in the distance. He looked to her father. "I'll come back for him. I promise."

"And I'll keep watch in the meantime," Elethün said.

She nodded and turned to Markus. "I'll come with you." What else was she to do? Her father's corpse felt foreign; she didn't want to stand guard over it. Besides, Elethün had already volunteered.

She needed to get the prince to safety. Maybe she should have fled the forest in the first place.

Markus gripped her hand and they were off, running in the direction of danger. When they got back to the battlefield, only one dragon remained, though countless fae and Runners had fallen. They paused once more at the discarded stones of the castle.

She heaved a sigh of relief at seeing Thallon with his spear, trying to hold his ground and defend his people. She wouldn't lose her entire family...not again.

"Hide here...or flee these woods. Just keep safe, Holland. I can't lose you." Markus pressed a kiss to her lips before joining the fray, his spear stained with blood.

Holland prayed they would live. That the final Dyvrat would die and all would be well. But she couldn't stay here and watch.

No—she'd head to Pembroke Fally and deliver Famar their prince...

The ground shook with thunder, the vibrations snaking up her legs and to her middle. *An earthquake? More Dyvrats?* Her heart leapt to her throat.

Close by, a dust cloud was approaching. With so many downed trees, the gap in the forest opened up to Andaimon's main road, allowing for whatever was coming to be in plain view.

The thundering grew louder, and when the dust abated, horses—at least a dozen of them—plowed through the edge of the forest. On their backs were men dressed in livery with weapons aplenty, carrying flags which sported Famar's crest and colors.

The royal guard? As if on cue, a man and woman with crowns on their heads pushed through the troops and came to the front of the line, their faces set. *The king and queen are here, too?*

"Where's my son?" King Randor bellowed. He was of average build with a thick beard, and his eyes were anything but kind. He looked from face to face, his mouth pressed into a thin line. His horse moved as if unsettled by such a crowd.

Then, the last standing dragon turned and roared in the king's direction, fury and malice etched into every contour of its hideous face.

The king's expression shifted from anger to fear, paling when his gaze found the dragon instead. "By Tokal..." He shuddered. "Wh-what sort of devilry is this?" His eyes widened, and his horse retreated a pace. "Get behind me, Rosin," the king said. He unsheathed the sword at his hip. "On my command, unleash your arrows!" he addressed his infantry, raising his hand in the air.

They knocked their bows and waited.

He lowered his hand. "Volley!"

His entire crew fired on the seething beast.

It roared again and twitched its head as if annoyed by the arrows. And then it charged. Directly for the king himself.

"Cover me! Cover me!" he shouted, but it was no use. The continuous arrows proved little more than an irritant when it came to taking the monster down.

The Dyvrat raced toward the king, its mouth open and fuming. The king drew back his sword and repositioned his horse, bracing himself for impact. The monster's sharp teeth cut across King Randor's chest and sent him careening off his steed, but not before the king had slit the beast across its snout.

"Randor!" Queen Rosin screamed. "Do something!" She looked from her guards, to Thallon, to Markus, to anyone willing to save her husband.

The king, protected by his armor, stood on shaky legs, his sword gripped firmly in his hand. "Go back to the abyss, you foul beast," he yelled, brandishing his bloody weapon.

Holland watched with rapt attention. Was the king determined to fight the monster himself?

The dragon charged again, but this time, hellfire burned in its eyes. The beast was nearly upon him, its claws spread and ready to end the king's tyrannical reign for good. The justice all Famar deserved.

But Thallon was quicker. Being part fae, speed and agility, along with the right spell, could make one move at great speeds. He dodged the demon's tail and jumped high in the air, letting the momentum of the spell carry him the rest of the way. He held the spear before him, point down, and landed soundly atop the dragon's neck. Before the monster could touch the king again, Thallon thrust his spear deep into its thick skull.

The dragon groaned and writhed before slumping to the ground directly in front of the king. Its body landed with a thud, and what followed was silence.

All the Dyvrats were dead.

Flames still licked the trees, the air smelled metallic and charred, and the sky was blackened with thick clouds of smoke, but something new shifted in the atmosphere.

"Randor!" the queen yelled. "My love."

The king, hands on his knees, exhaled a long breath. His limbs shook with muted fear. "Wh-where's my son?"

Holland inched forward, hesitant to meet the king face to face. What would he do to someone like her? "Right here, your Majesty." The prince was swaddled tightly, his round face beaming happily despite the direness of their circumstances. He was safe, and that was a relief.

The king snatched the wrapped bundle and studied him carefully. He hugged the baby to his chest before handing him to his wife. She'd dismounted sometime during her husband's duel and stood beside him, the little prince now tucked in the crook of her elbow. She cried tears of joy.

He surveyed the land before him, his gaze roving over everyone. "Who was it that took him? Was it you?" he asked a random fae, pointing his finger. The man shook his head. "You?" he asked another.

Thallon jumped off the Dyvrat's back and cleared his throat. "It was me... My father's—our father's orders." He looked at Holland. "I wish I could tell you otherwise."

"*His* orders? And where is your father now?" the king sneered.

"Dead." The word was hollow in Holland's throat. He was taken so soon.

"Dead? Is there no justice to be served, then? Are you to live, then, who carried out his bidding?" The king directed this toward Thallon.

"I think my people have been served enough justice these last few hours. As for me, I deserve death more than anyone," Thallon said, dipping his head.

"To that end, I agree. Who are—what *are* you people?" He studied them closely.

"Some of us are men. Others of us are fae. Or in our cases, half-fae." He gestured between himself and Holland. "Our lands are ones of magic, and our ways are peaceable...or at least, they should have been."

"Fae?" The king's eyes widened. "Magic?" He pulled at his collar. "But you...you saved my life."

"Are you insinuating that because I'm not fully human, I should have let that monster destroy you?" Thallon challenged, crossing his arms over his chest. Holland guessed that he was used to standing up to kings; he had their father to thank for that.

"Well...I—"

"I know of Griskol's fear. I've read about it as if it's a thing of legend. It's so deeply rooted that most of you don't even know why you fear it in the first place. It's simply become a byway for your people."

"Excuse me?" The king blanched. "You have no right to address royalty—"

"Magic isn't to be feared. It's only the few who misuse their power which paint everyone else in a bad light. I should never have followed through with my father's wicked schemes, though I had little choice. But are you going to let one man's actions determine your view of the whole? If so, saving you may have been a folly."

Collective gasps echoed in the crowd. The king grew red in the face and seemed about to burst, but cooled when his wife steadied him with a touch.

"Randor. He speaks wisely," she said, her voice a sweet contrast to his brazen one. "Maybe we should listen. He did save your life when he didn't have to. And we have our son, safe and alive."

"He *took* our son from us, Rosin!"

"Yes, but we have him back. He is alive."

"I had planned on bringing him back just this morning, but clearly, you can see how things got delayed," Thallon interjected, gesturing to the still-burning trees and dead dragons.

"Bah! A fae, holding my son! Ranor will be cursed along with the witches!"

Rosin held the baby close to her chest, her smile content despite her husband's tirade. "Randor, dear, you're missing the point. We have what's most important, and these woods you've feared all your life are now made desolate. I feel it may be time for a change: to go home and leave this all behind. No more death. No more fear." Queen Rosin shed more tears, likely because she was so happy to hold her son once again.

Either way, Holland searched her heart, looking for the inevitable hatred of Famar—of the king and queen—to well up, but found it wasn't there. Where had it gone? How could one go their whole life hating someone, only to meet them and feel pity instead? It was true; looking at the brokenness of Randor and Rosin, she felt nothing short of pity. A heart didn't need fortified walls made out of fear. No. It needed love, and love had the power to do what fear could not. Restore. Forgive. Mend.

And it seemed the queen was willing to move on. Would the king?

King Randor looked out to the horizon and his pensive expression betrayed deeper thoughts. He sighed deeply, his gaze unblinking.

"Randor?" the queen murmured.

He swallowed hard. "I saw a blackened morning and an orange sky illuminated from the highest pinnacle of Famar..." He paused. "I instantly thought of our son. I've never ridden so fast in all my life. The Forbidden Wood has been Griskol's bane for generations..." He ran his tongue over his lips and rubbed his eyes with his thumb and forefinger. "And to think...through its destruction, it may now be the means of Griskol's liberation...?" He shook his head.

Holland wasn't sure what was happening, but the change in the atmosphere was slowly beginning to veer toward hope. Thallon and Markus were by her sides, and she knew somewhere behind her, Grismon and Cadmon stood nearby. Relief and something like joy flooded her chest in spite of all the pain. They were still alive—they'd get to see their families once again.

Yes, many had fallen, but despite the odds, many still stood. The Forbidden Wood was broken and bruised, and it wasn't nearly as foreboding as at the onset of her journey. In fact, it had given her purpose and a family she hadn't known existed.

Queen Rosin cleared her throat, her tears all but dry. "Whether you like it or not, we're indebted to him. To all of them." Rosin stretched her arm to Thallon and company. She paused when her eyes latched onto something in the distance. She gasped.

The king did, too.

Holland turned and followed their gazes, spotting Elethün, his coppery coat and silver crescent a welcome sight. His presence was both a surprise and a balm among the swirling heat and rubble; he usually preferred not to be seen. He walked by the fires and breathed on them, the flames dwindling to nothing but ashes.

He turned and breathed in their direction, casting a gentle magic in the air, removing the metallic smell of blood and filling the senses with dewy grass and wisteria blooms. Holland felt peace settle in the broken spaces in her heart and watched as everyone's shoulders relaxed a fraction, even the king's. Then in a wink, Elethün retreated deeper inside the forest, disappearing.

"I think...I think it's time we should go." Rosin tugged on her husband's arm and hugged her baby closer. A look of wonder still lingered in her eyes, and Holland could only hope Elethün's magic had found its way into her heart and somehow, into the king's.

King Randor nodded, helped his wife remount her horse, and then mounted his. They turned in the direction of town, their guards leading the way back to Famar.

"...means of Griskol's liberation..." The king muttered the same words over and over again, as he retreated. He glanced once more over his shoulder and scanned the woods as if searching for something. Elethün, perhaps? He rubbed his eyes. Eyes that looked weary and tired. And yet, somehow changed.

He turned again and followed the others, disappearing from view.

At their departure, everyone let out a collective sigh of relief. Nothing was so formidable as an angry king. Or a confused one.

Holland observed the desolate landscape. Elethün had put out most of the fires, and the air had improved significantly. The rubble around them and dead dragons were the only signs that a scourge had occurred.

"What now?" She looked at Markus. So much had happened; so much was still unresolved, it seemed.

"We bury the dead. Honor them." He grabbed her hand. "And then, we go home."

Home.

It was funny how the word now brought comfort instead of

dread. Home was wherever Markus went. It was Andaimon and Kirkus. It was her brother, Thallon. It was the chickens behind the Row. Her mother's flower garden. Elethün. Home was so many things.

And yet, she'd spent her whole life looking for what was sitting right under her nose or lurking precariously close in the Forbidden Wood.

Home. Yes, she could get used to hearing that, indeed.

EPILOGUE
From "The Tale of Endlewood"

*I*t has taken me a long time to find the heart to pen these words, but at last, I think both I and they are ready. So here lies the epilogue, the closing of my father's tragic tale.

Five years ago, he was taken the same way as his father before him. And now, my brother is king. He's moved back to Lamia, the other fae with him. It's a journey which I have yet to take, but I plan to soon. When the spring comes and the seas are more willing.

As for him and Adra, well that's a story for another time.

It wasn't meant to be this way. This interweaving of two tales. Griskol never should have been led by fear, and my father never should have let his anger overrule his love. Death and pain deal out ghastly blows to the heart, but that does not mean hope and joy are obliterated in the midst of grief.

I've learned that through Grismon. Through Cadmon. Through Markus.

Though I'm still left with this emptiness in my chest, there are gaps that have begun to fill. It was hollow, a desert of neglect, an oasis for the losses I'd kept stored away. But no longer.

Parts of it feel the hope of final restoration. Other parts taste the bitterness of loss. My father—I'll never get to know him the way a daughter should. How can I ever reconcile what he's done with the final act of love he left me with before he died?

Am I to forgive him for his neglect? For the fear he's struck into the heart of Griskol? For the wicked task he gave my brother? How can I forgive such a man? A man who had marked the very man I love?

And yet.

And yet.

These words ring in my ears like a clanging gong. There are other parts of my broken heart that long to heal. And I've learned that's only possible through forgiveness.

I reach up and stroke Elethün's snout, my fingers tracing up to the base of his velvety horns. I can tell he agrees, and I can sense his sorrow even still.

He loved my father. He loves me.

I scan the trees surrounding the discarded stone I'm sitting on, the burnt trunks long ago sprung with new growth. The scent of charred wood and stale blood is a thing of the past, but if I squint hard enough, I can still see outlines of the scourge. Instead, I glance at the canopy.

The Dyvrats had felled many trees and left holes throughout, allowing in the sun. I prefer it this way; the shadows have fewer places to gather.

I've spent my entire life searching for this kind of freedom; the freedom found in walking the streets of Griskol or dancing under the boughs of a forbidden forest. I guess you could say I'm like my mother. She felt Endlewood call to her, and in many ways, I have too.

I had thought that if I could just connect the dots, find something to fill the empty places in my heart, perhaps even touch the sea that held my parent's bodies—that somehow, I'd be made whole again. But it was all for naught. I know that now.

All my pursuits left me wanting and just as directionless as before. And it only grew worse when I met my father. Before then, I had held onto the fraying strings of my parent's death, hoping they'd lead me to some closure; but sometimes the truth is painful enough to break down the walls you've built around your fragile heart. The truth clipped and gnawed at the places that had already scarred over, forcing me to bleed and heal anew.

I hadn't thought meeting my living father was possible. And it definitely wasn't what I had imagined. He couldn't take away the pain he had inflicted, and he couldn't give back the hope he had stolen. He couldn't fix me. No person—man or fae—can fix someone else. But somewhere down the road, I had always thought my parents could have. That it was their responsibility to make me whole again.

I was wrong.

Wholeness, while living in a world as broken as Griskol, is next to impossible. Where there is hatred and fear, darkness abides. But there's light enough to combat it, to keep it at bay for a while, much like the waters from Errol's Weir. I wear the vial around my neck now, a reminder of the hope I've welcomed. For I've found it is the light, the love, and the hope that I've come to

401

accept which have begun to mend the cracks in my own heart, pushing aside the shadows that have resided there for so long.

The shadows of anger, insecurity, fear, and now...resentment. I'll never know a happy childhood, but my children will.

My purpose is here. With them—my family. With Elethün.

Griskol has much healing to do. I have much healing to do. We all do. Fear isn't eradicated in a matter of weeks, months, or years—nor is hate.

But forgiveness is like a footstep toward hope. I may not have it in me, but I'm trying...

"Let's ask your mum what she thinks." Markus' voice carried over to Holland's log as he picked his way through some gooseberry and gorse. He held their son, Mikiah, on his shoulders and their daughter, Leiyla, pulled him forward, a ribbon of the perfect shade of purple in her hair.

Both of their names no longer adhered to the *Name-branding* law of old. For that, at least, Holland had the Dyvrats to thank. And her brother. Because of them, King Randor and Queen Rosin lifted some of the restrictions; it wasn't much, but it was a start.

Hamish sauntered after Markus, close on his heels. Though he was aged in body, his spirit was young. And his coat revealed only traces of the hay fire from all those years ago. It had been a miracle he survived that terrible night, but when it came to bloodhounds...they always followed their noses; because of Hamish's own, he'd found his way back home.

The dog brushed past Holland and rubbed against Elethün's side, his tongue lolling out of his mouth.

"Ask me what?" Holland closed her book and set down her pen, peering up into the eager blue eyes of her daughter—eyes so much like her father's.

She smiled wide, her dimpled grin revealing a missing front tooth. The gap warmed Holland's heart. "Can we sleep here tonight, Mumma? Under the trees! Like the faeries do in the stories! I don't want to go back to Kirkus."

Her excitement was contagious. At four, she didn't yet know that fae blood ran through her veins the way it ran through her mother's. She was made of magic as much as Elethün, and it was only a matter of time until she learned of it. Her brother, too.

Holland stroked back a lock of Leiyla's midnight tresses, hair just like her own. She glanced at the sunlit sky, traces of nightfall lingering only a few hours behind. *Bedding down under the stars is just what I need on a night such as this.*

She glanced at Markus who winked, as if reading her mind, sending a rush of heat up her cheeks. After all these years, he still knew how to make her blush. She turned and faced Leiyla once more, a mischievous smile curling up a corner of her mouth, and she nodded. "I'd like that very much. But what are we to do for shelter?" Holland asked this knowing full well her daughter would think of something. She always did.

"Well, we can gather some leaves and tie them together with…" Leiyla paused, scanning the ground.

Holland looked at Markus again. Mikiah squirmed on his shoulders and reached toward the bough of a nearby oak. At two, he was just as curious as his sister and as stunningly adorable as his father.

Markus knelt down and surrendered his wiggly bundle. Mikiah scurried off after his sister, searching for something with which to make shelter. Markus stood before joining Holland on the log, his side pressing up against hers.

It was just the two of them. They watched their children, smiles of contentment on their lips. Had Holland known such happiness could exist on the other side of suffering?

Markus took her hand in his and interlocked their fingers, tracing a path along the tender grooves of her knuckles. Their eyes were on their children, but their souls wove together like twisting vines. "I've always loved these hands of yours."

Holland smiled at him, raising a brow. "My hands? You've never told me that before. Why?"

"You don't see them the way I do." Markus chuckled and faced her more fully. He grabbed both of her hands in his, splaying them palms up. "This is what I see. These hands have served others during your hardest years, when everything was taken from you. You always give on behalf of others. And now they care daily for our children. These are the most selfless hands I've ever known, Holland. Hands I get to hold for the rest of my days. I count myself the luckiest man alive."

A lump formed in her throat, and she found it hard to speak. Moisture pricked the corners of her eyes, her heart swelling with warmth. After five years, she had learned how to receive this kind of love—but even still, she wasn't always good at it. When one's spirit was filled to overflowing, sometimes tears were the only answer.

Markus took Holland in his arms, a silent understanding as he brushed back her hair and planted a kiss along her hairline. Finally, she managed to squeak out the words she'd grown accustomed to saying to her husband. "I love you. So very much."

He squeezed her tighter. "And I love you. Always." He gently placed a kiss on her forehead before running a thumb beneath her eye.

Hamish trotted over and sniffed them both before nuzzling Markus with his nose. She couldn't help laughing. His warm eyes begged for attention, and Markus complied, stroking him under his chin. Suddenly Markus' sweet expression shifted, as if plagued by a memory.

It was subtle, but Holland had seen it often over the last few years. It was always the same look. She could see much in his blue-eyed gaze: his love for his wife, their children, their family, their farm. But beyond that, she couldn't just see his repressed sorrow—she could feel it.

Losing a father created a chasm not much could fill. She shared his grief. But it was in losing a best friend—one so much like a brother—that cut deeper than any sword.

Calsius' grave was on the border of their farm, his tombstone next to Markus' father's and Holland's father's—just beyond the last row of corn. The funeral had been a somber one; Calsius' parents had held each other even after everyone departed, his mother's tears a never-ending stream and his father's wet eyes and silence all signs of their devastation. Soon after, Holland had planted goldenrod and hyacinths there, the offshoots cultivated from her own mother's garden.

Markus visited the graves often, as did Mr. and Mrs. Brenner, and he took Hamish with him. The dog's presence helped to ease some of his burden, though Holland knew heartache pervaded every facet of his life. It took courage to choose hope when all the heart wanted to remember was despair.

They both knew this truth deeply, like a second skin.

Markus kissed her brow once more before standing. "I'm going to check on those wiley children of ours. Do you think they've found the 'magic' thread I hid?" He smiled, his infamous dimples making her heart do a little flip.

"You planned on us staying here all along, didn't you?" she asked, her tears all but dried and her smile matching his.

He shrugged. "I know how much you like it here. Plus, your birthday is tomorrow. Consider it an early present." He cast it aside like it was nothing, but she could tell he knew just how much it meant to her. Holland loved this forest—Endlewood. She'd renamed it after her father. Her mother. Her brother. Herself.

"Thank you." The words seemed paltry, but they were true.

"Anything for my Little Woodland." He winked again and went after their children.

Holland blushed at the moniker. He'd started calling her that once he realized the meaning of her name. It was rather fitting, was it not? Her father once thought so, too.

She watched from her seat, contentment once again finding its way into her heart alongside a blossom of warmth. Mikiah giggled as his father chased him, his little smile like a sliver of moonlight. And Leiyla, her eyes were as bright as the sun itself. And then there was Markus; her sun, her moon, and her stars.

She had so much to be thankful for. It was truly the little

things which held their own kind of magic.

Hastily, she picked up her father's book and flipped to the back pages. She took up her pen, aiming to finish what she had started.

And what about magic? The thing that all of Griskol fears?

Much like a sword, an arrow, or even a garden spade, magic should be gauged in accordance to how it's wielded. If used poorly, it has the ability to strike fear in the hearts of many; if used well, it has the potential to spread hope, life, and peace. It is a gift.

And what of the mundane things? I'm convinced they are made up of magical moments, too. Magic is just another conduit of hope, for with it, we see the world through a different lens. Dead leaves become ships sailing in the wind. Clouds become islands that bring weary travelers from one realm to the next. And the sea? It is but a pool of liquid silver, a mirror that reflects one's soul.

Yes, magic is a powerful tool, indeed.

And because of it, there is much change in Griskol. And much change yet to come. Where Famar had succeeded in stripping away our rights, the fight in Endlewood had succeeded in giving some of them back.

Isn't that true with these sorts of tales, then? The villain is vanquished; the hope is restored. The monster defeated and remembered no more?

But part of Griskol's restoration comes from the very man who had unknowingly destroyed so much of it. He'd saved my life, and in turn, the prince's.

My father—Vesstan Endlewood. I find I can't forget him, especially when his memory is so fresh in my own.

I write these few lines in remembrance of him. Imperfect and broken, but not forgotten. He was not so much the villain as he was some repentant hero; there was still some good left in him before he departed.

And it's that which I hold onto.

May he rest alongside my mother, his soul finally at peace.

That's it, then. The story is now told. And telling it has made me remember who I am now, too.

I am Holland Endlewood. Or rather, Holland Fenn. I never thought I'd have two last names, let alone one. But that's the way of it, I suppose. Many happy tidings are brought about when one is least searching for them.

And with that, here lies The Tale of Endlewood, *a tragic story that began without a trace of hope, but now abounds with hope aplenty.*

The End

GLOSSARY

Abermann's Tea House (abb-er-mans) – local tea house in Andaimon

Adra Oshiera Kelbi (ai-drah oh-sheer-ah kel-bee) – mermaid/fin-maiden from Onklo; sweet on Thallon. Name means *noble sea-woman*

Almar (ahl-mar) – fae-man under King Vesstan's reign in *The Tale of Endlewood*. Name means *famous fool*

Altus Fenn (ahl-tus fenn) – Markus' little brother; twin to Rizus. Name means *sun*

Andaimon (and-ai-mun) – poorest region in Griskol; home of Holland. Name means *visionary*

Ani (ah-nee) – red-headed girl from Tiri; loves Cadmon. Name means *beauty*

Antonius Beck (an-toe-nee-us beck) – lives the life of an outlaw in Kirkus; husband to Viviand. Name means *man of virtue*

Bathilda (bath-ihl-dah) – Markus' cull cow. Name means *bold*

Beatrand Kershaw (be-trund kur-shaw) – Holland's employer in

Andiamon. Name means *crow-like*

Benjamon Glock (ben-jah-mun glock) – young teen from Andaimon; brother to Cadmon. Name means *son of the south*

Benneforth Row (ben-neh-forth roe) – townhomes where Mrs. Kershaw and Holland live

Cadmon Glock (cad-mun glock) – older teen from Andaimon; Runner; brother to Benjamon; loves Ani. Name means *misunderstood warrior*

Calsius Brenner (cal-see-us brenn-er) – blacksmith from Kirkus; Markus' best friend; loves Damirus. Name means *artisan of humor and craft*

Crendian Sea (kren-dee-an sea) – ocean surrounding Griskol's southern and eastern borders. Name means *balmy coast*

Dame Olgaus (ole-gus) – crotchety bread merchant in Kirkus. Name means *unsuccessful*

Damirus (dah-meer-us) – lives in Kirkus; loves Calsius. Name means *gentleness*

Darics (dare-icks) – gold coins; Griskol's currency

Drusus Fenn (drew-sus fenn) – Markus' brother. Name means *determination*

Dyvrats (div-rats) – villainous dragons from *The Tale of Endlewood*. Name means *death-bringer*

Elethün (el-eth-yoon) – talking stag from *The Tale of Endlewood*. Name means *Earth-dancer*

Errol's Weir (eh-roles wir) – waterfall in Andaimon. Name means *lamp of light*

Eskal (es-kul) – country to the west of Griskol. Name means *land of mountains*

Famar (fah-mar) – the namesake and palace of King Randor and Queen Rosin in Pembroke Fally. Name means *formidable*

Fariah (fah-rye-ah) – fae-general in King Vesstan's army in *The Tale of Endlewood*. Name means *shady; slim*

Finagus Brenner (fin-ah-gus brenn-er) – father to Calsius; blacksmith from Kirkus; husband to Hanaus. Name means *courage*

Forbidden Wood – a large forest in the south of Andaimon, also known as Griskol's bane

Griskol (Gris-cole) – the country where *Endlewood* takes place. Name means *messenger*

Grismon Rook (gris-mun rook) – Runner from Andaimon; husband to Margithand. Name means *keeper of hope*

Hamish (ham-ish) – Markus' bloodhound. Name means *protected*

Hanaus Brenner (hann-us) – mother to Calsius; wife to Finagus. Name means *grace*

Henrietta – one of Holland's chickens. Name means *home ruler*

Hildaus Carole (hill-duss cai-role) – woman Markus steals from as a child. Name means *battle*

Holland (hall-ind) – main character; seamstress in Andaimon; best friends with Markus. Name means *little woodland*

Impa & Irma (ihm-pah, ur-mah) – Markus' sheep. Names mean *complete mischief*

Irthlen (earth-len) – country northwest of Griskol. Name means *smoking cauldron*

Jaerus (jay-rus) – boy from Kirkus. Name means *gift from above*

Jaimus Fenn (jay-mus fenn) – Markus' father; husband to Jannus; farmer. Name means *solid joy*

Jannus Fenn (jan-us fenn) – Markus' mother; wife to Jaimus. Name means *archway*

Josilland (joss-ih-lind) – flower-lover from *The Tale of Endlewood*. Name means *guardian of the flowers*

Kirkus (kur-kiss) – middle-class region of Griskol. Home of Markus. Name means *free-thinker*

Koriand Scuttle (core-ee-ihnd skut-ul) – Margithand's friend who frequents Abermann's Tea House. Name means *hollow*

Lamia (lamb-ee-ah) – fae-village in *The Tale of Endlewood*. Name means *prosperity*

Leiyla Fenn (lay-lah) – daughter to Markus & Holland. Name means *dark beauty; born at night*

Margithand Rook (mar-gih-thand rook) – wife to Grismon. Name means *star of the sea*

Markus Fenn (mar-kus fenn) – main character; farmer in Kirkus; best friends with Holland and Calsius. Name means *protector of things that grow*

Mikiah Fenn (Mih-kye-ah) – son to Markus & Holland. Name means *thoughtful truth*

Mirrand (mihr-and) – Josilland's friend. Name means *afraid to wander*

Name-branding – the method by which Griskol keeps people to their destined regions by 'branding' their names with different letter-endings

Nindrol (nin-drohl) – fae; advisor to King Vesstan in *The Tale of Endlewood.* Name means *deceptive kingdom*

Olio (oh-lee-o) – a type of stew/soup made in Tiri. Comes in many different varieties such as lamb, pork, and bison

Onklo (on-kloe) – island off the eastern coast of Griskol. Name means *island of scales*

Overseer – magic shield that protects King Vesstan's people in *The Tale of Endlewood*

Pembroke Fally (pem-broke fah-lee) – wealthiest region in Griskol; home to the palace of Famar where King Randor and Queen Rosin reside. Name means *land of heritage*

Randor Famar II (ran-door fah-mar) – king in the palace of Famar; lives in Pembroke Fally; husband to Rosin; father to Ranor. Name means *red shore*

Rankol (ran-cole) – country northeast of Griskol. Name means *land supreme*

Ranor Famar (ran-or fah-mar) – son to King Randor & Queen Rosin; prince of Famar. Name means *wise warrior*

Rizus Fenn (riz-us fenn) – Markus' little sister; twin to Altus. Name means *rain*

Rook's Confectionary – local bakery owned by the Rook family in Andaimon

Rossand Annbert (roze-and ann-burt) – Holland's first adoptive mother. Name means *blossom*

Rosin Famar (roze-in fah-mar) – queen in the palace of Famar;

lives in Pembroke Fally; wife to Randor; mother to Ranor. Name means *little rose*

Runners – those in Andaimon who travel on foot to the other regions in order to attain their wares and goods

Saimon Kershaw (sey-mahn kur-shaw) – known as Mr. Kershaw; married to Beatrand and was Holland's old employer. Name means *ambition*

Snoots – a crass nickname for those who live in Tiri

Swamp Wispsnare (whisp-snare) – a pool used for drowning intruders in *The Tale of Endlewood*. Name means *murky deep*

The Tale of Endlewood (end-uhl-wood) – the fictional book Holland carries around with her. Name means *magic*

Thallon (thal-un) – a fae-man with a dark past; sweet on Adra. Name means *reserved strength*

Thayand (thay-and) – Name means *forgotten gift*

Tiri (tear-ee) – the upper-class region of Griskol; home to the Snoots. Name means *conqueror*

Tokal (toe-kul) – a bronze statue of a fox; Griskol's made-up spirit to ward off the presence of magic. Name means *vixen*

Vesstan (ves-tan) – fae-king in *The Tale of Endlewood*. Name means *home*

Viviand Beck (viv-ee-and beck) – wife to Antonius; lives in Kirkus. Name means *lively; far-seeing*

Will-o'-the-wisps (will-oh-the-wihsps) – phosphorescent lights, typically blue, that are seen by weary travelers at day/night

FAE-TONGUE

Cabhagth (cah-bagth) - "Hasten"

Chanth eilth chol luath (chanth eel cole lue-ath) - "Not so fast"

Chath eithl mi a 'planthadh eirth (chath eeth-el me ah plan-thad eerth) - "I don't plan to"

Coilleth bheagth (coy-leth behgt) - "Little woodland"

Euith-comsacth (e-yooth comb-sath) - "Impossible!" an expression of shock

Moth ghràthidh (mothe grath-eed) - "Welcome" or "Greetings"

Sathail ilath (sath-ale ee-lath) - "Save them"

Slathod (slay-thod) - "Turn back"

Stath tiene (stath tee-en) - "Stop the fire"

Thae gaveth thu (thay gav-ith thue) - "I love you"

Thaem gavth (thay-em gav-ith) - "My love" as in addressing a lover

Toirth maithenas domth (tor-eth math-en-ahs dometh) - "Forgive me"

ACKNOWLEDGEMENTS

As always, writing a book requires a team of support, and *Endlewood* is no different. For reasons I can't explain, this story had me nervous from the get-go. When I finished it, I wrestled with self-doubt even though I had high hopes for its success. I guess you could say I was a lot like Holland.

That being said, I first want to thank my early readers Cheyenne van Langevelde, Tiffany Brockmann, Tara Koch, Kailey Jessop, Emma Dryden, Jamie Goudy, Kayla Jones, Morgan Hubbard, Natalie Contino, and Caitlin Anderson for taking the time to read *Endlewood* before it went through a first round of edits. Thank you all for your feedback and tremendous support.

A special thank you to my dear friend Renae Powers who not only served as an early reader but became my editor in the process. Thank you for your time and diligence in poring over my manuscript not once, not twice, but many times. Your friendship and support throughout this ongoing journey mean the world. I love that I'm the Diana to your Anne!

Thank you to Micaiah Keough for being an incredible

proofreader and giving *Endlewood* the extra polish it so desperately needed. I looked forward to our nightly Google Doc conversations and back-and-forth editing streak. I can't wait to work with you again in the future.

Thank you to my writer friends Erin Phillips, Victoria Lynn, Caitlin Miller, Tara Koch, and Jordan Nilan who helped keep me sane during this whole endeavor. Your sweet friendships and wisdom are things I cherish dearly. I love you all!

Thank you to my cartographer, Chaim Holtjer, who made a stellar map of Griskol. It was great working with you again!

Thank you to my cover designer, Germancreative, who was so gracious and patient with me throughout the drafting process. I tweaked the design so many times in order to get it *just right*. I love the result!

Thank you to my family, especially my parents. Without you, this book wouldn't have a dedication. Thank you both for always loving me and giving me a home. I love you.

Thank you to my husband, Zac, for being a constant rock and supporter of my dreams. You keep me grounded while encouraging my dreams to fly. I love you.

Thank you to my cat, Moo, for always being a good boy. You're the best. Elethün's character was written with you in mind.

Thank you, Jesus! Without you, these words would be empty and meaningless. With Jesus, true hope is possible, which is largely the message in this story.

And lastly, thank *you*, for picking up my book and taking a chance on *Endlewood*. I hope it was worth your while.

CPSIA information can be obtained
at www.ICGtesting.com
Printed in the USA
LVHW081748290322
714729LV00013BA/322

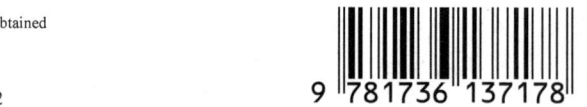